THE EYE OF GOD

THE EYE OF GOD

A Novel

Jonathan Bourgault

iUniverse, Inc.
New York Lincoln Shanghai

THE EYE OF GOD
A Novel

iUniverse books may be ordered through booksellers or by contacting:

iUniverse
2021 Pine Lake Road, Suite 100
Lincoln, NE 68512
www.iuniverse.com
1-800-Authors (1-800-288-4677)

This is a work of fiction. All of the characters, names, incidents, organizations, and dialogue in this novel are either the products of the author's imagination or are used fictitiously.

ISBN: 978-0-595-44339-0 (pbk)
ISBN: 978-0-595-68703-9 (cloth)
ISBN: 978-0-595-88669-2 (ebk)

Printed in the United States of America

P R O L O G U E

▼

Excerpt from: *A Brief History of the Church of the Adherent*
Written by Minister Gannon 2641

"The Great Unification Wars finally ended with the destruction of the Eastern Coalition in the early twenty fourth century. However, due to massive environmental damage and continuing security concerns, every Adherent Citizen had to be assigned to one of the surviving urban centers. Power in the cities remained split between the High Councils and local Church hierarchy, a balance that had proven quite effective in the Western cities prior to the war. The High Councilors handled daily secular matters, while the Ministers ensured that Church doctrine was followed and enforced throughout every level of society. Although the sizable Adherent military still reported directly to the High Councils, it was ultimately subject to the will of the Ministers, especially in times of crisis.

The challenges posed by Apostate terrorists during the latter portion of the century required the Church to institute new restrictive measures designed to ensure peace. This shift in policy also led to the Ministers assuming additional political responsibilities, including more direct control of the Adherent military. While an aggressive off-world colonization program helped to alleviate many social problems caused by overcrowding in the cities, the continued violence eventually forced the Adherent leadership to institute a final campaign to forcibly convert or eliminate those who still resisted the Church's teachings. It was only then that the true Golden Age could begin …"

PART I

CHAPTER 1

▼

EXODUS

"Why, God?" Brian Bishop whispered into the ghostly shroud blanketing the city. The stoic monoliths of Chicago's skyline peered back through the poisonous veil, deaf to his tortured question. He stepped closer to the massive window of his father's office, gazing 400 stories below. Today his home seemed especially beautiful. Warm rays filtered down just far enough to illuminate the familiar sea of smog that wrapped around the faces of the buildings and cast a shimmering aura of brilliant gold across everything within view. Somewhere in the oblivion lay concrete streets, although Brian found it impossible to penetrate the majestic river of pollution coursing through his beloved city. As usual, he found himself consumed by the ethereal landscape. There were times when he still imagined the buildings as giants, dancing in an enchanted mist. But those childhood fantasies would have to die, along with his dreams of making a home among the clouds.

"Saying goodbye?"

Brian flinched in surprise, but didn't turn. He hadn't noticed the tall reflection take shape in the glass behind his own.

"Do you have all of your things packed?"

Brian still refused to answer.

"We don't have time for this. Everyone's waiting in the transport downstairs."

"I'm not going," Brian muttered, aware that such a statement was ridiculous. Teenagers don't dictate family policy. Still, it felt good to be difficult. To leave without a fight seemed like a betrayal. He could see the reaction in the glass. It wasn't a happy face.

"You'll adjust."

"I couldn't even pack all of my holobooks!" Brian complained, finally turning to face his father.

"You know the rules. Colony transports don't have much room onboard for personal items," David Bishop explained as he picked up the two small bags lying at his son's feet.

Angry at his father's lack of pity, Brian once again turned to face the window. The fading afternoon sun darkened the city view, allowing him to see his own reflection clearly in the glass. He still looked like a child. Many of his friends at school were beginning to show signs of growth, but Brian still bore the features of a young boy. His mother had a bad habit of ruffling his sandy blonde hair and commenting on how intelligent his deep brown eyes looked. "Just like your father," she'd laugh. All Brian saw was a short, skinny kid who excelled in Scriptural Studies Class, yet failed miserably when it came to geometry. He reached up to his forehead and ran his fingers over the familiar pattern embroidered on the soft, white skin, the symbol representing the Ever-Seeing Eye of God. *Better to be good at what really matters*, Brian reasoned smugly. *Math won't get me into heaven.*

"Brian. Now," his father demanded from the doorway.

Brian spun around quickly. The tone of his father's voice was tainted by a strange mixture of urgency, anger, and what sounded like fear. After having lived in the city for twenty years, why was his father so eager to leave? What was the hurry? Certainly the colony transport would wait for somebody as important as a High Council member. Brian examined his father with a critical glare.

"I'm sorry it has to be like this, son." David Bishop walked over and placed a firm hand on Brian's shoulder. "I wish we didn't have to rush such an important move."

"Why *do* we have to rush like this?"

A pained expression crossed his father's face. "We can't stay, Bri. There's been another attack—this time a Cathedral."

Brian couldn't believe the news. This had obviously been kept from the public, probably to avoid a panic. A stream of questions instantly washed away his lingering defiance. "How? Which one?"

"A suicide bomber hit the morning service at God's Grace. Lots of people were hurt."

"Isn't it safer for us here? There are Adherent soldiers stationed in every major building downtown," Brian added, hoping to convince himself as much as his father.

"I'm not sure it's safe for us anywhere," his father sighed, running his fingers over the mark on his son's forehead.

That thought terrified Brian. The terrorists of the Inter-City Liberation Front had gotten much more violent in recent months, although it was still hard to comprehend how other human beings could willingly, gladly attack everything Brian cherished. *They would pay eventually,* he reminded himself. *Just like every other Apostate.*

Brian and his father stood in silence in the rapidly descending elevator. His father's office was located on the upper levels of the Civil Industries Building, which essentially functioned as city hall. The massive structure housed the majority of Chicago's secular government, including the High Council, and its importance was clearly reflected by its great height. It would take a while to reach the bottom floor parking garage. Brian looked up at his father, wondering what outside events were being kept secret from him. It was painfully obvious that things were more serious than his father conceded, but a growing worry kept Brian from asking more questions.

"You're going to see some things during the next few weeks that are going to change your perspective drastically," his father noted, finally breaking the tense silence. He sounded depressed, almost sad. "I just want you to know that your mother and I love you."

This weary proclamation made Brian even more uncomfortable. Something was wrong, something more far-reaching than the day's terrorist attack. Just a couple of weeks before, Brian had been enjoying his final year at the North Chicago Junior Academy. In between the scripture readings and sermons that formed the basis of every good education in the twenty fourth century, Brian and his friends staged countless matches of holoball and competed mercilessly for the favor of the Ministers at the school. Between his father's work with the High Council and his mother's busy routine at the North Central Medical Center, Brian hadn't even seen much of his parents in the months preceding the "big announcement." Suddenly, though, his familiar routine had been interrupted. Brian would never forget the night his parents had walked into his bedroom and informed him of the move. Relocating to one of the Outer Colonies had been an increasingly popular trend for over a decade. Brian himself planned to one day travel to a colony, but only after completing school and becoming a full-fledged

Citizen. He had never contemplated leaving Earth at the age of thirteen, much less considered it a genuine possibility. Now there was no choice; he was going.

Brian tried to comfort himself by reciting Scripture. The *Final Testament* specifically stated that the job of every Adherent is to spread the new Gospels to worlds beyond Earth; to bring the Word of God to every corner of Creation, including the cosmos. Now Brian had the chance to complete this divine mission. He would try to make the best of his situation.

The elevator finally stopped, and the two occupants quickly donned their breathing masks. When the doors to the garage opened, the air immediately bathed Brian in its sweltering stickiness. Thankfully, a light afternoon rain was falling on the city's lower levels, cooling things off just enough to permit comfortable movement. This March had been the hottest on record, signaling yet another summer of heat alerts and severe storms.

The humble, four-wheeled family transport waited just a few meters away from the elevator doors. Brian got to the vehicle well ahead of his father, who still carried the bags without complaint. The side door of the transport swung open, revealing the familiar occupants inside.

In the front seat sat Bill Collins, a close friend and political ally of Brian's father. Bill was one of the most important trial lawyers in the city, a rich and powerful man respected even by the Ministers, despite his early retirement from political life. Brian simply knew him as "Uncle Bill." Bill's wife, Rachel, sat in the middle row of seats next to Brian's mother Jill and his older sister Jade.

Everyone greeted Brian cheerfully, everyone except the passenger sitting in the very back seat of the transport. She remained silent.

Brian automatically knew his place in the vehicle. He climbed in, still ignoring his father, the bags, and everyone else. He threw himself into the backseat, purposely slouching down to signal his anger at having been kidnapped in such a barbaric manner. Nobody seemed to notice his perturbation, not even the person sitting next to him. Brian looked over at his fellow passenger, Kim Collins. She was staring out the window, her dark eyes glazed over by a fine layer of tears. Her beautiful, brown hair poured down the center of her tiny back in a long, auburn wave. Like Brian, Kim was underdeveloped for her age, a common trait among children of their generation; although only a few months younger than Brian, she could have easily passed for eight or nine. As Brian surveyed his traveling companion, he couldn't help but feel comforted by her presence. It was nice to have a peer to share in the agony of a life cut short. Kim had been Brian's best friend since their earliest days of school. She was coming to the Colonies too.

David Bishop stowed the bags in the transport's cargo hold and hopped into the driver's seat. Brian looked over at Kim again. As the transport sped away, she finally turned from the window and greeted him with a beleaguered but sincere smile. Silent tears streamed down her pretty face.

CHAPTER 2

▼

GENESIS OF A JOURNEY

David Bishop activated his personal communicator as soon as the transport exited the parking garage. The rest of the adults began their own banal conversations, seemingly unaware of the magnitude of their coming journey. It was almost like they were purposely ignoring the rash decision they had made to leave behind their planet and their lives. Brian shifted his attention from his fellow passengers to the rapidly passing city outside. It had been a long time since he had ventured down to the street level of Chicago. Brian followed the steel and glass skyscrapers far up into the artificial clouds embracing the city. The setting sun, swollen and distorted by the haze, cast a final burst of heavenly light across the faces of the buildings. Such a grand sight made him feel small and insignificant. It was much more comforting to see the world from several hundred stories up.

The rain had dissipated much of the pollution at the city's bottom levels. Feeling the need to breathe the air of his home planet one last time, Brian lowered his window slightly before being scolded by Jade. The dank smell that permeated the streets and tickled his nostrils seemed out of place amid the billions of bright florescent lights that lit up the towering metropolis above. Plumes of steam rose from the cavernous sewers deep under the city, adding to the wet stink of the air.

"Brian, close that window!" Jade ordered again.

"Brian," his mother called, "Listen to your sister!" Her brisk tone echoed that of Brian's father, the uncharacteristic harshness demanding compliance. Brian quickly closed the window. Just as the glass resealed the vehicle, he noticed something strange: the normally busy streets were empty. Even though most people didn't own private transports, the city streets were usually inundated with pedestrians at all hours of the day.

"I had to leave Rusty at home," Kim whined to Brian, finally choosing to engage him in conversation. Brian's thoughts concerning the vacant streets were interrupted. Kim was referring to her robotic dog, Rusty, a baggage item that would have violated Colony Transport Protocol if she had brought it along.

"Is anyone going to take care of him?" Brian asked, trying to act concerned despite his preoccupation with the apparent emptiness of the city. He was also aware of the increasingly serious conversation his father was having on his communicator at the front of the transport. Brian thought he heard his father mention the word "Enclaves" several times. *Why was he talking about the Enclaves?* Enclaves were for those who refused to bear the Eye of God. All kinds of people lived in these communities. Atheists, Old Christians, Universalists, Neo-Hindus, Sudanites and even a few Jewish families made up the population of Apostates. Brian remembered hearing about the Enclave relocation programs as a child. Many Citizens insisted that the Apostates be removed from the city and "taken care of." It was Brian's father who had suggested housing them on the old lake bed. In the years since the relocation, the Church had enacted laws in cities around the world confining the Apostates to the Enclaves. Brian thought such laws were quite fair, considering how dangerous those people could be.

Brian looked down State Street towards the walls surrounding the Enclaves. Although he had no wish to venture near the walled city within a city, the most efficient route to the Spaceport ran parallel to the massive concrete barriers that enclosed the Apostates. "Aren't we supposed to go that way?" he blurted out, interrupting Kim's story about Rusty. His mother quickly turned in her seat. "Shhhh, Brian. We can't go that way right now."

"Why not?" he asked. "Is it flooded?" Brian had heard that the Enclaves would often flood terribly when it rained. Just 100 years ago, the last of the Great Lakes had covered the entire sector that housed the shoddily constructed concrete buildings. Realizing that he wasn't going to get an answer, Brian quieted down again, as asked. All of the adults in the transport went back to ignoring him.

"Brriiiaann!" Kim squealed, angry at having been cut off by her confidant.

"Oh, uh, sorry Kim," Brian apologized absent-mindedly. He tried to direct all of his attention back to Kim's complaints.

"Susan," Kim scoffed, clearly betraying her disdain for her pet's new handler.

"Susan's not bad," Brian insisted, trying to lighten Kim's mood.

"She's wanted him for years," Kim insisted. "She doesn't even care that I'm leaving, as long as she gets Rusty!"

"He *is* an expensive toy, and her dad doesn't make as much money as yours or mine."

"I still don't like it," Kim said, returning to her pouting glare out the window.

"It's okay, we'll find plenty of things to do on the Colony Transport," Brian assured. "Maybe you can even catch up on some of your scripture readi–" Brian stopped himself as his father's strained voice soared over their conversation. "What?" was the only word Brian caught, but it was a word loaded with concern.

David Bishop lowered his voice and continued to issue a battery of orders into his communicator. Brian couldn't pick up anything else from the back of the transport, but he knew the conversation was serious. He had spent his whole life studying the mannerisms of people in power. People like his father.

"Kim, honey, did you bring that dress you wore last year at the Cathedral banquet?" Brian's mother asked. Jill Bishop shifted in her seat and raised her voice in an obvious attempt to block out the increasingly heated exchange at the front of the transport. "You looked gorgeous in it."

"What's Dad talking about?" asked Brian coldly, ignoring his mother's ploy. He moved a few centimeters to the right as to reestablish a clear line of sight with his father.

Kim ignored the dress question, as well. "Mom?" she sputtered in a questioning tone.

"It's fine, Kim," Rachel assured. "Your father and Uncle David are just taking care of some business before we leave. Nothing too important." The nervous glance Rachel gave Brian's mother revealed this statement to be a lie.

Just as Brian was about to confront the adults in the transport about their behavior, the vehicle lurched forward and came to a violent stop at the corner. The door swung open, and two rain-soaked figures in trench coats dove into the vehicle. The women in the middle row of seats struggled to make room for the new passengers. One of the figures moved to the back row and forced Brian over toward Kim, who pressed herself up against the window in astonishment.

When the two men pulled down the hoods of their coats, only Brian and Kim seemed surprised. The man who took his place next to Brian was his cousin Luke, a soldier serving with the Adherent forces in Atlanta. Through his shock, Brain wondered why Luke wasn't with his unit. He wasn't scheduled for leave for at least another month or so. The other man was John Rodriguez, a friend of Luke's since their days at the Church's Senior Academy.

Luke spoke first: "They're not arresting this time, they're just killing," he groaned, as a trickle of blood ran down his face.

"Everyone?" Bill inquired with wild eyes.

"Yes," John confirmed.

Luke continued: "Martin's dead, I think me and John are the only ones from our group to escape."

"Those damn idiots," David Bishop cursed as he pressed down on the transport's accelerator. "Blowing up buildings sure accomplishes a lot. It just gives the Ministers an excuse to eliminate the remaining Enclaves!"

"The Church is sending more soldiers to the area from Houston and Atlanta. They're going to round up any suspected collaborators still living outside the Enclaves," Luke continued, as Brian's mother examined the cut on his hairline. "This is a huge operation, even bigger than we suspected. The Ministers have already managed to identify many of the ICLF leaders in Houston, and I wouldn't be surprised if they are moving in here too."

"From what I can tell, the ICLF is small and poorly organized," noted Bill. "The Church won't find any of the leadership in the Enclaves. Not that it will stop them from making examples. It never does. I'm sure we'll see some poor innocent bastards being paraded around on the news before the end of the day, though."

Innocent? The word could hardly be applied to any Apostate, at least none that Brian had ever heard about. Apostates were violent antisocials who resisted the Church's teachings, instead choosing to live as outcasts. They were all dangerous on some level and certainly not worth the risk they posed. Brian had always despised his father's inexplicable softness toward the Apostates and now felt disgusted by the continued show of sympathy for what was happening to them. Whatever operations the Adherent soldiers were carrying out in the city, Brian was sure they were justified in their actions. His father had no right to question the judgment of the Ministers, even if he was a High Council member. Brian's feelings of shame intensified as he looked over and surveyed the muscular frame of Luke's seated next to him. Ever since Brian could remember, he had tried to emulate his cousin. Now Brian eyed him with suspicion. Feeling sorry for the Apostates was bad enough, but helping them was unforgivable. Brian prayed Luke had a good reason for being here.

As the vehicle sped on, and the chaos of the moment lessoned, Brian pressed himself back into his seat and met his mother's worried eyes. "It's okay," she mouthed silently, as if he needed to be comforted. Brian's own eyes narrowed as he attempted to bore his gaze deep into her mind. *Tell me what's going on. Tell me*. After several seconds his icy glare proved too much for her to handle, and she nervously shifted her attention back to Luke's head. Brian inched farther away from his cousin toward Kim, who had placed her small hand in his own. In the glass, the heavy outline of concern clung heavily to her delicate features.

CHAPTER 3

▼

GOD'S DOORSTEP

Brian's father drove through the back streets of downtown Chicago toward the Spaceport in an attempt to avoid the conflict raging in the nearby Enclaves. "Why isn't there anyone around on the streets?" Brian finally questioned, breaking the silence that had once again gripped the vehicle. The adults seemed to have calmed down enough to produce a rational explanation.

"Before we left, the High Council ordered everyone to stay in their homes," his father answered tersely. "I wouldn't be surprised if the Ministers decided to assume total control of the city government at this point."

"Keeping everyone locked down will make it easier for the Adherent soldiers to do their job," Rachel muttered.

"Aren't we violating that order?" Kim asked.

Rachel smiled at her inquisitive daughter. "Your dad and Uncle David are allowed to break protocol, even during Code Orange. You know that, sweetheart."

"Oh," Kim sighed, obviously still concerned about skirting the rules so shamelessly.

"And Luke?" Brian asked his father as if his cousin weren't in the vehicle.

There was a brief pause as David Bishop turned to Bill Collins.

"Secret mission, buddy," Luke confessed jovially. "Can't tell you right now."

"Maybe you should," spat Brian.

"Maybe you should just shut up, Bri!" Jade suddenly yelled.

"You shut up!"

Brian's mother leaned over the back of seat. "Stop it. Both of you!"

Several loud thuds echoed in the distance from the general direction of the Enclave sectors, punctuating Jill Bishop's words with a dire exclamation point. The tense silence returned. Without warning, Brian's father swerved to avoid an Adherent cruiser darting out from a side street. The cruiser immediately activated its flashers, illuminating the area in a brilliant aura of red and white. Another cruiser pulled out several hundred meters ahead, blocking the route toward the Spaceport. Within seconds, half a dozen black, body armor-clad Adherent soldiers surrounded the transport.

"Damn!" Brian's father swore under his breath. "I thought we'd get there without running into this." He turned back to the other passengers. "Don't worry, it's gonna be fine. Just stay calm."

What do we have to worry about? Brian asked himself. Ever since he could remember, Brian had been taught to love and respect the friendly neighborhood Adherent soldiers who patrolled the streets and buildings of Chicago. "Maybe they're here to arrest you for being such a wench," he whispered to his sister.

Jade didn't turn around, but his mother did. Her gaze was deadly. Brian decided not to test her any further.

As a soldier approached the driver's side window, Luke and John bowed their heads guiltily, obviously trying to attract as little attention as possible. Maybe there was something to worry about after all.

"How can I help you, Sergeant?" Brian's father asked in his usual confident tone.

"License and Identification," the soldier demanded, not bothering to show David Bishop the slightest bit of courtesy. The other soldiers continued to surround the vehicle, pulse rifles raised. Brian didn't blame them for being cautious. His family's vehicle did look suspicious, especially in the middle of a city-wide alert. Code Orange was serious.

David and Bill calmly handed over their personal information. The soldier methodically scanned the color-coded passports, which immediately issued beeping sounds identifying the driver and passenger as important men.

"Sorry, sir," the soldier apologized, quickly returning the passports. "I've been ordered to stop every vehicle until we're downgraded from code orange."

"That's perfectly reasonable," Brian's father answered with a friendly chuckle. "You can't be too careful with so many crazies running around."

The soldier nodded his head in silent agreement, before adding, "In case you didn't know, the sectors around the eastern Enclaves are off limits due to a riot."

"Thanks, but we just came from that direction," Brian's father confessed. "It looks like we're taking the long way to the Spaceport today!"

"Understood," the soldier affirmed. Although an imposing black helmet obscured the soldier's facial expressions, he sounded much friendlier than before. "I'll notify the other patrols of your vehicle type so that you're not pulled over again. I'm sure you want to get out of here as soon as possible."

"You have no idea, Sergeant."

The soldiers immediately stepped away from the transport, and the Sergeant waved Brian's father on.

Several minutes later Brian could finally make out the technological monstrosity most Citizens referred to as the Spaceport. As the transport sped towards its destination, Brian got the distinct, wholly uncomfortable feeling that his family was entering the lair of a great beast. Ahead of them, the Spaceport's dark steel superstructure rose from the surrounding cityscape far up into the inky blackness and beyond. For safety reasons, no other buildings stood within one thousand meters of the Port. From the artificial concrete plain, four gargantuan pylons seemed to grow like tree trunks. The Spaceport itself rested on a platform supported by these massive legs, faint blinking lights offering the only clue as to the general outline of the building.

Brian had never been to the Spaceport, except for a class fieldtrip back in Bible school. At the time, Brian had been overwhelmed by boredom. Now, four years later, he was gripped by nervous apprehension. Seeing the Spaceport finally brought the prospect of leaving Earth into the realm of reality. If possible, he would have climbed out the transport window and run for the safety of home.

Brian's father stopped the transport in front of the main reception terminal located on the thin, central stalk that rose up into the belly of the Spaceport. True to the Sergeant's earlier words, there had been no more direct contact with Adherent soldiers until this point. As soon as the vehicle came to a halt, two soldiers and one baggage attendant approached.

"We're here! Everyone out," Bill announced.

Brian's father and Bill exited the car and immediately showed their identification and boarding passes to the soldiers. Meanwhile, Brian and Kim climbed out of the car with the rest of the passengers. This time, Brian picked up his own bags from the cargo hold. He didn't want to show any more juvenile behavior in front of Kim.

Although the others had put their breathing masks on prior to leaving the vehicle, Brian had forgotten to, as he often did. When the air was really bad, he usually noticed within seconds, but on this relatively mild night the smog didn't bother his lungs much. As they stood waiting for David and Bill to finish talking with the soldiers, Brian felt a sharp pinch on his left arm. "Put your mask on, Brian. Your asthma's already bad enough," Jade hissed in her typical motherly tone. Brian hated his sister's constant nagging. After all, she was only nineteen. How wise could she really be? During the last few weeks, he hadn't seen very much of his parents. Now he had Jade back from medical school, acting like she was in charge of him. He thought about making another "wench" comment or something worse, but put his mask on instead. No need to create even more drama in the first hour of the trip.

As Brian fixed the apparatus over his mouth he heard a familiar giggle: "Yeah, Brian, put your mask on," Kim snickered from behind, obviously delighted by his moment of weakness.

"Ha, ha!" Brian mocked. "Real funny, Collins!" He couldn't help but smile too. Kim loved these moments, and he loved to see her laugh.

"Come on, Bri," Luke urged, placing a hand on Brian's shoulder from behind. "The line's moving." Brian's smile faded at his cousin's gentle touch. Luke now seemed like a stranger to him. So did his parents, for that matter. As soon as things settled down, Brian had some serious questions for them. For now, though, he had little choice other than to allow his towering cousin to usher him through the sliding glass doors, a few more steps away from all he had ever known.

Upon entering the building, Brian was pummeled with a blast of crisp, cool air. He shivered as his body attempted to adjust to the controlled atmosphere. It was always a brisk sixty-eight degrees in the Spaceport, just like every other Adherent building.

Brian found that the intense, fluorescent lights lay a terrible strain on his eyes as they struggled to focus to the unfamiliar surroundings. Even though the ground floor terminal merely served as a security checkpoint before travelers ascended to the main terminal, the sheer scale of the entryway frequently stunned the unprepared. Brian wildly spun around as he took in the disorienting room. The black, marble floor of the terminal reflected the brilliant skylights hanging thirty meters above. Cold, dull, metallic surfaces sprouted out from the floor in every direction, forming walls, security scanners, computer terminals and attendant desks. Amongst this endless sea of metal, stone and glass, stood islands of green, potted plants placed at predetermined intervals to ensure the maximum amount of aesthetic value. Brian forced his eyes closed as vertigo overwhelmed his mind. He was much more comfortable in the dark, enclosed confines of his home, or better yet, the Cathedral. Brian succeeded in fighting back his bout of dizziness, but he couldn't block out the multitude of deafening sounds assaulting his ears.

"Brian, sweetheart," his mother's voice called from beyond the blackness.

Brian opened his eyes as his mother cupped both sides of his face.

"You're going to be fine," she assured. "Just breathe."

As his mother checked him over, Brian thought it strange that she acted so concerned about his problem with large spaces. Both of his parents had always seemed to laugh off this fear, insisting that he spend more time away from school and the Cathedral, perhaps in the botanical gardens or city museum. "Make sure you keep this out," she instructed, removing his identification necklace from inside his shirt. She sounded just like Jade. With her blonde hair, green eyes, and slight, yet athletic build, she looked like Jade too.

Brian noticed Rachel Collins going over the same routine with Kim just a couple of meters away. It was important to move through security checkpoints with the utmost efficiency. *Impeding the greater good was viewed as a sin in God's eyes*, Brian reminded himself. Once again, Kim wore an expression of concern as her mother turned away to talk to her father. She quickly shuffled over to Brian and grabbed his arm as the forming line of people moved forward through the security checkpoint.

The soldiers checking IDs at the main first floor checkpoint scrutinized everyone in the group, including Brian and Kim. Luke and John brought up the rear of the entourage, looking even more nervous than before. As Brian stepped up to one of the soldiers, the black figure bent down and ran a scanner across Brian's ID necklace. The soldier also examined the Eye of God on Brian's forehead with a laserscope, no doubt looking for a fake. Apostate terrorists were known to bear false marks to get past security checkpoints.

Once Brian and Kim passed through the gauntlet of soldiers and scanners, they turned around to watch how Luke and John dealt with the ordeal. Yet again, Brian witnessed a scene that challenged his confidence in Luke, not to mention his loyalty. As Luke held up his necklace for inspection, the soldier called out the name to another soldier sitting at a nearby computer. "Theodore Goldman," the soldier stated, Brian was sure of it. The other soldier at the computer paused for a moment, obviously checking his screen, before nodding that Luke was free to pass through the checkpoint.

Brian's cousin's last name was Bishop, not Goldman! Why did the nametag state otherwise? Brian began to step forward, intent on telling the soldiers they had made a mistake, when his father stepped in front of him. "Come on, Brian," he said, his voice once again terse and demanding. "Don't crowd the check-point."

"But–" Brian started, before stopping himself. Maybe saying something wasn't the best idea. If Luke was in trouble or something, maybe Brian would get into trouble just for being with him. Brian agonized over the dilemma. Conceal-ing the truth from Adherent soldiers was a sin. It was Brian's duty as a future Cit-izen to honor the Truth. But what exactly was the truth? Until Brian found out, he vowed to keep his thoughts to himself, praying that God wouldn't be upset.

CHAPTER 4

▼

A SHUTTLE TO HEAVEN

Following Brian's passage through the main terminal checkpoints, his father took him aside from the group. "Hey, son, how's it going?" he asked quietly, bending down to meet Brian at eye level.

"Fine, I guess," Brian lied.

"I know you're wondering what's going on with Luke, but sometimes, it's best just to go along with the flow."

"What do you mean?" Brian asked, silently pleading for his father to tell him the entire truth. He hated when his father used old clichés to explain things. It made him feel like a kid.

"What I mean is that even I don't know what Luke's orders are from the Church. I just know that he was permitted to come along with us to the colony."

"Is he on a mission or something?"

"Like I said, I'm not sure."

"But you're on the High Council; you could find out, Dad."

"I could, but I don't need to. I trust Luke. Don't you?"

Brian shrugged.

His father smiled, as if he found his son's critical analysis amusing. "The false name is probably an alias intelligence officers use while traveling. Wouldn't one of those ICLF maniacs just love to kill an important Citizen like Luke?"

"Yeah, you're right," Brian responded, pretending to see his father's logic.

"I'm sure once we get going on the colony ship, everything's going to return to normal," his father assured. "Like I said before, things are getting pretty bad down here on Earth. We're lucky to be leaving."

"Shouldn't you stay and try to fix things then? The Scriptures say that you shouldn't run from Evil, you should confront it," Brian lectured in the same confident tone he always adopted when reciting *The Final Testament*.

His father smiled again. "Maybe you'll understand when you have a family of your own someday."

Brian wasn't persuaded. His expression betrayed his lack of understanding.

"You'll just have to trust me, son. Now, go keep Kim company while we wait for the shuttle to start boarding."

As Brian walked over to Kim, he struggled to suppress his suspicions about his family. Kim was sitting in the waiting area next to the shuttle dock. She was watching something on the monitor. It looked like the news.

"How's it going, Kim?"

"Okay."

Brian sat down next to her, trying to appear in control.

"I saw you talking with your dad," she noted.

"It's pointless," Brian insisted. "I can't get any real answers out of him, just a bunch of well-rehearsed lines. Something's going on!" He quickly looked to his left and right, then leaned forward and lowered his voice to a whisper. "I don't care what they say. Luke's not supposed to be here. And what about the way everyone was acting in the transport? You saw my dad."

"Well, he has always tried to protect the Apostates from the Church," Kim pointed out. "It's not surprising that he's upset about what's happening in the Enclaves. Lots of people are probably dying right now, just like Luke said."

"It's more than that, Kim. I'm worried our parents might be protecting Luke. If he's helping out the Apostates he could get us all in trouble. My dad's a good Citizen, but I do think he'd betray the Church if Luke or somebody else needed his help. It's a weakness of his."

"Maybe, Bri, but I'm more concerned about why we're leaving for the colony. I've had a lot of questions over the past couple of weeks too, but every time I ask my parents about the move it seems like they're hiding stuff. You're right about that."

"What reason did they give?" Brian asked.

"Oh, just that we're going to live in a better place."

Brian shook his head and smiled knowingly. "Same here. It's the same story my parents have given. I think there's a connection between what's happening in the city with the Apostates and our moving to the colony."

"My mom made it sound like we'd be in danger if we stayed," Kim added.

Brian was surprised by her revelation, but remembered his father's earlier words about his family's safety. "From who, the ICLF?"

"Not just them," Kim replied, obviously thinking about the situation. "It sounded like certain people in the Church might want to hurt us too."

"The Church?" Brian repeated so loud that other people in the sitting area turned their heads. Why would anyone in the Church want to hurt his or Kim's family? His father had always been such a loyal Citizen, despite his irrational care for the plight of the Apostates. The only conflict Brian could remember between his father and the other Church officials had been back when the Church Ministers had demanded the removal of all Apostates from the Enclaves a few years earlier. Brian's father had passionately defended them, saying that they had nowhere else to go. This stance angered many in the Council and in the Ministry, but the tension had lessened in the time since that fight. As Brian thought about removing the Apostates, another memory floated into conscious thought. Brian remembered his mother getting upset with him one time for having suggested that the Apostates be eliminated outright. "Don't they teach you forgiveness in school?" she had asked passionately. Brian answered her as he had been taught. "Forgiveness is only for God's people and God's people alone," he had replied. The tears that welled up in his mother's emerald eyes upon hearing this condemnation signaled her disapproval. When Brian suggested that she was soft too, the tense conversation had abruptly ended. His mother had simply shaken her head, walked away and left Brian alone to ponder his convictions.

In the year since that argument, Brian worried often that his parents were drifting away from their religion. His religion. Did that have something to do with what Kim was revealing now? Purges were rare in the Church hierarchy, but they did happen. Is that what his parents feared? Getting purged?

"It's not right," insisted Kim, nodding towards the monitor in front of them.

Brian abandoned his flashback and followed Kim's gaze. The monitor displayed a scene of terrible devastation: the burning Enclaves of Chicago shot from a hovering news scout. Brian and Kim strained to hear the program over the steady drone of noise echoing through the terminal. "Adherent soldiers met fierce resistance from the ICLF terrorists," a woman's voice announced coolly. "Following a heated, four-hour battle, the High Council ordered the complete liquidation of Enclaves J7 and J9. Every possible precaution was taken to minimize collateral damage."

From the footage, it didn't look as if there was anything *but* collateral damage. Although the automated news scout hovered at a safe distance from the fires, Brian and Kim could still make out individual dwellings: homes standing in stark defiance of the inferno raging through the sector. Brian leaned closer to the monitor, attempting to focus on the details of the scene. There was movement in the scout's footage. Down on the ground, beneath the billowing black smoke, fuzzy outlines could be seen moving through the chaos. Just as Brian realized what these outlines were, who they were, a blaze of multiple muzzle flashes cut through the darkness, forever terminating the movement. The image on the monitor immediately shifted to the calm, attractive face of an Adherent Broadcast Network news anchor. "We'll have more coverage on the battle later, following sports and entertainment," she promised before the program cut to a commercial. As usual, it was a government-sponsored announcement assuring the faithful viewers of ABN that the Ministers and the Council: "care about the spiritual and financial well-being of every Citizen."

"What's not right?" Brian asked, finally addressing Kim's statement.

"Those people!" she cried, obviously frustrated with Brian's lack of understanding.

"What, the terrorists?"

"They're not all terrorists! What about the kids? What about the innocent civilians? They could be Saved, you know, made to see the light."

Now it was Brian's turn to feel frustrated. "Don't you remember what Minister Petrov said about them last week in school?" he asked rhetorically. "We can't let those people undermine the Church, no matter what excuses they give! They've got plenty of chances to convert; it's just that they choose not to!"

"Minister Petrov scares me," Kim sneered, wrinkling her nose in disgust. "My dad says he's bad. Just look at the way he carries himself. Minister Petrov tries to act like he's God or something."

Brian sat back in his seat, struck by Kim's harsh words of condemnation. Petrov, who never appeared in public without being shrouded in his crimson Church robes, did seem like a god to Brian. At over two meters tall, his shaven head towered above his students, while his sunken, black eyes surveyed all of Creation with their piercing stare.

"Minister Petrov's a good man, Kim," Brian retorted. "He promised me that he'd sponsor my entrance into the Adherent Military Academy if I did well in the

Senior Academy." Brian's voice shifted in tone. "That was before we were going to move, though. Now it'll never happen."

"It's a good thing," Kim added harshly. "I don't want you to become one of those soldiers who kills women and children in the name of God."

"Somebody's gotta keep the peace," Brian stated, mimicking a common slogan used by the Adherent military recruiters. Feeling that he had made his point, he stood up and walked over to the window overlooking the shuttle hanger bay. Kim didn't follow.

Not her too, Brian thought as he waited for the boarding signal.

As the passengers crowded into the confines of the docked shuttle, Brian ran ahead of his companions to secure a window seat. Kim sat down next to him, although her silence indicated that she was still mad about his insensitive comments regarding the Apostates. She didn't seem to mind sitting in the row's middle seat, away from the window. A window seat meant a good view of what lay below as the shuttle traveled into space. Heights bothered Kim just like open spaces bothered Brian. He found it strange that heights didn't bother him as well. After all, heights were technically just more wide open spaces.

Thankfully, the shuttle's interior lights were much dimmer than the blinding luminescence of the Spaceport. As Brian's eyes readjusted to their preferred environment, he surveyed the rest of the passengers onboard. His parents and Jade had found seats toward the front of the transport and were talking to a group of passengers Brian didn't recognize. Most of the shuttle's occupants would be traveling to the colony with Brian, although he didn't know any outside of his family or Kim's. His parents, on the other hand, looked like they knew many people, making Brian wonder why he had never met any of them before. In the short time they had waited in the Spaceport terminal, Brian had counted over twenty people approach his parents and address them like old acquaintances. It made him feel like an outsider.

As Brian raised himself to look over the seat in front of him, he saw his mother smile, then nod her head back in Brian and Kim's direction. The gray-haired woman she was chatting with looked at Brian and waved. Brian shot her a polite smile, forcing himself to mirror her wave. Kim didn't notice. She was looking down the aisle at the oncoming passengers, no doubt wondering who would fill the seat next to her. A large, balding man, who had introduced a young boy to Brian's father upon entering the shuttle, crammed himself into the vacant seat. A disgruntled sigh escaped from Kim's lips. She still wouldn't even look at Brian. *Fine*, he thought, *I'll just ignore her till she gives in and admits that she's wrong*. He raised himself up again, cocking his head back to view the rear half of the shuttle. Kim's parents were sitting a couple of rows back. Luke and John had split up and were now sitting on opposite sides of the cabin. Brian returned his posterior to the seat, strapped on his restraining harness, and watched Kim's new neighbor from the corner of his eye. The man's bulbous form had inadvertently spilled into Kim's designated space. He didn't seem to notice the intrusion. The man was talking across the aisle to the woman and young boy who had boarded the shuttle with him. Brian smirked and returned his face to the window.

Brian counted nine other shuttles docked in the bright, metallic hanger bay. He wondered how many others were loading passengers he would soon meet on the colony transport. Above the shuttles, Brian noticed that the dome of the bay had begun to separate, revealing the inky darkness of the night sky. He felt a sudden rush of nervous energy course through his veins as the shuttle's engines kicked on.

"This is the pilot speaking," a looming, disembodied voiced blared through the cabin. "Please fasten your restraint belts. If you refuse to follow safety protocol, Civil Industries will not be obligated to compensate you in the event of a catastrophe."

A catastrophe? Brian thought, reminding himself that this was his first flight on a shuttle. Did those happen often? He could feel Kim grip the armrest of the chair so hard that a vibration shuttered the entire row. She was obviously having similar concerns. Brian remembered Kim's fear of heights, and reluctantly placed a warm hand over hers. The shaking lessened. *I'm still not going to talk to her until we reach space*, Brian resolved.

The shuttle slowly backed away from the dock and floated lazily up through the open dome. Brian pressed his face to the duraglass and looked down at the Spaceport. It seemed so much smaller from the air. Below, the city began to take shape as the shuttle increased its altitude. It was ten o'clock, and there was very little haze left to obscure the glittering metropolis of skyscrapers, Cathedrals and factories crowding the landscape. The shuttle ascended just past the tips of the tallest city buildings, turned 180 degrees toward the west, and glided over Brian's former home. A few tears sneaked from his eyes, blurring the trillions of beautiful orange, green and blue hues that made up the dazzling urban kaleidoscope below. Brian strained to see the burning Enclaves to the southeast, but several enormous buildings blocked his view. The shuttle activated its main engines, and the scene in the window morphed into a rainbow of blurred color. Within seconds, the ship was traveling over the heat-parched wastes beyond the city, a land where nothing grew and nobody lived. When the shuttle began to ascend into the clouds, Brian couldn't even tell. All he saw was more blackness. He sat back in his seat and looked over at Kim. She still had her eyes closed as she silently recited a traveler's prayer.

"We estimate a smooth fifteen minute trip to the Starport," the pilot announced over the com system. "Please sit back and enjoy the ride."

Just as Brian began to contemplate dozing off, the first star appeared in his window, then another. The shuttle broke through the upper layers of clouds and was skirting the upper levels of Earth's atmosphere. At first, Brian was confused by the tiny twinkling dots piercing the night sky. He had never seen stars before, not real ones anyway, just on the ABN network or in school. As the shuttle continued to climb into space, more stars appeared. Suddenly, the sky exploded in a sea of light, even more intense than that of the city. "Wow," Brian muttered involuntarily. His reaction was immediately echoed by several other passengers. Even Kim opened a weary eye, curious to see what all the fuss was about.

The shuttle banked sharply to the right, and suddenly confronted Brian with the night-time Earth several hundred kilometers below. Kim whimpered, shutting her eyes again. Brian closed his eyes as well, terrified by the awesome sight. Slowly, he forced his eyes back open, drawn by the facade of his home planet. Brian could easily spot the faint glow given off by each city, even through the perpetual blanket of smog and clouds blindfolding humanity. *This must be how God sees the world*, Brian guessed.

"That's Las Vegas," the man next to Kim spoke up, motioning towards the most central light in the window.

"How can you tell?" Brian asked, his voice still wobbling from amazement.

"See all that darkness on either side of it?" the man asked.

"Yes."

"The dark on the left is the Pacific Ocean," the man revealed. Back when I was a boy, California used to be down there. Of course, that was before the Big One of 2292."

"Wow," Brian repeated, this time more out of respect than genuine wonder.

"Pretty soon we'll see Hawaii City coming up," the man added, before turning back to his wife and son.

Soon, just as the man had promised, Brian saw the glow given off by the massive, island city of Hawaii. Brian already knew that to the west of Hawaii there would be nothing until India. Where countries like China, Japan and Korea once stood, a black scar stretched for thousands of kilometers. Brian attempted to penetrate the clouds with his gaze. *What was really down there?* he pondered. Obviously not cities. He had learned in school that the region would not be habitable for centuries. Still, Brian wondered if there were people down there, somewhere in the void. Maybe some isolated groups of Apostates had somehow managed to adapt to the radiation. From time to time, Adherent soldiers still found nomads rooming the wastes back in America. Could there be the same kind of people down there? *Campfires could not be seen from space*, Brian reasoned. The thought of fire made Brian remember the burning Enclaves back in Chicago. In his mind, the evening's news footage merged with the charred swath of Earth down below. *That's the price of defying the Church*, Brian thought. *Good riddance.*

CHAPTER 5

▼

PILGRIM'S PATH

Spaceport, Starport, Brian never cared much about the differences between the two facilities. Both served the purpose of ushering Citizens away from the world he had always known and loved. Now, as the shuttle slowly crested over the receding shadow cast by the Earth, Brian finally understood the difference. An ethereal blast of sunlight erupted from behind the massive, turning planet, illuminating the technological wonder of Brian's lifetime.

The Starport looked tiny at first, almost like a floating model or toy. As the shuttle neared its destination, however, the baffling scale of the station became apparent. Rather than feeling as if he were approaching a beast or animal as in the case of the Spaceport, Brian got the distinct impression that he was nearing something alien, perhaps even divine. How could mankind build such a wondrous structure? Brian reminded himself that the project had taken the Church well over twenty years to complete, even with the aid of automated construction equipment and forced labor. Presently, there were two other Starports being constructed: one military facility near the moon, the other orbiting Mars in support of the mining operations. *Mankind truly was conquering the cosmos, just as the Final Testament prophecies ordained.* Brian felt a sudden sense of pride as he pondered this realization. He would help his people conquer the stars, winning a new planet for the Church.

In contrast to the Chicago Spaceport, which blended quite well into the city's drab, industrial architecture, the Starport resembled nothing Brian had ever seen, or imagined. The sheer size and complexity of the massive space station dictated that it be built entirely in space rather than by bringing up pre-assembled pieces from Earth. As a result of this building method, the Starport's appearance did not adhere to the modular, jigsaw puzzle profile of earlier space stations. Instead, the structure consisted of six large vertical pillars situated in two parallel rows of three. The 100 story pillars were connected to each other by two levels of docking shafts that outlined the station's perimeter. Coupled to these shafts, like pigs at a trough, floated several gargantuan colony transports and mining ships, one of which would take Brian to the stars.

"It's amazing," Kim finally spoke up, leaning over Brian's lap to get a better view. "Bigger than I ever expected!"

"I thought you were afraid of heights," Brian muttered, hoping that cool words would mask his delight at finally hearing her voice.

"As long as we're not looking down at anything," Kim explained. "Out here I can't even tell what's up or down. It's *not* like there's any ground!"

"Kimberly Collins, put that harness back on!" her mother ordered sternly from behind. Kim huffed in defiance, but quickly did as her mother asked.

"It is pretty strange," Brian agreed. "In a way, it just seems like we're flying through the air back on Earth." He realized that, thanks to the shuttle's artificial gravity system, the passengers didn't experience the weightlessness of space, just a slight lightening in their bodies. "Which ship do you think is ours?" he asked.

"Not sure," replied Kim as she re-buckled her harness. "There are so many. Plus, my dad never mentioned the name."

Brian had read old stories, ancient stories, about the importance of giving a ship a proper name. "As long as it's a good name," he said, voicing his thoughts.

"The Icarus," she giggled.

"The what?"

"The Icarus," Kim repeated, frustrated with her joke's loss of impact. "Don't you remember?"

Brian thought about the name for a moment, wondering why Kim found it funny. "Isn't that the story Minister Chang read to us when we were little kids?" he asked, confident that he remembered Kim's reference. The story was an old pagan myth, Greek or something. Minister Chang had been Brian and Kim's private tutor when they were young, hired by their parents to give them special religious and academic instruction. Chang was much different than the Ministers at the Junior Academy. He was kind, forgiving, and much more tolerant than most Adherent clergymen. Minister Petrov never would have allowed his students to read a pagan story, no matter how significant. "That's the one where the kid flew too close to the sun and melted his wings," Brian elaborated.

"Yeah, that's the one," Kim said, her face lighting up now that Brian got the meaning of her joke.

Brian looked out at the transports and thought about the significance of the name. "That's not funny, Kim!" he protested, laughter ruining any trace of conviction in his voice.

"Sure it is," she insisted. Her expression darkened slightly as another thought seemed to enter her mind. "Of course," she continued, "if you consider the story to be more about escaping than dying foolishly, I guess it's not so funny."

Brian didn't respond to this possible interpretation, although his laughter abruptly ceased. *I'm not escaping from anything, just going to another place,* he reminded himself. *It's more like I'm being taken away.*

The shuttle wove its way through a swarm of tiny, robotic utility ships and transports buzzing around the station. Finally, like a bee finding its favorite hole in the honey comb, the shuttle halted in front of one of the corner pillar's main docking bays. The solid outer doors of the bay parted, allowing the shuttle to enter. As the onboard computer slowly guided the shuttle into the open bay, several Adherent military fighters skirted past Brian's window.

"Now that's what I want to do," he proclaimed dreamily.

"What, work in the docking bay?" Kim asked, once again fidgeting with her restraint harness.

"No, fly one of those fighters that just went by!"

"Oh. Yeah, I guess that would be fun," Kim replied, her voice lacking enthusiasm.

"Just forget about it, Kim," Brian insisted, frustrated with her continued preoccupation with the harness.

"Sorry," she apologized. "This thing's just really bothering me. I can't wait to get it off!"

"Just wait another minute or two, and *we'll* be getting off," Brian reminded her. "You don't want to get yourself in trouble, do you?"

The inside of the hanger bay looked much like that of the Chicago Spaceport: cold, gray and metallic. Any sense of aesthetics was obviously superseded by a need to maintain efficiency and functionality onboard the station. Everywhere there were ships, technicians, cargo loaders and supply crates waiting to be carried off to different parts of the station. Brian's feet made a clanking noise as he stepped off the shuttle's exit ramp and onto the floor of the hanger. The hanger was large, too large for Brian's comfort. Besides the shuttle they had just arrived on, several other ships of varying size rested in the bay. The whole place smelled like grease, stale air and static electricity. Brian felt a small nudge as Kim bumped into his backside.

"Come on, Bri, go!" she urged. "You can look around in a second."

Brian didn't say anything, but stepped aside nonetheless. He and Kim waited next to the ramp for all of the adults to exit. In their typical polite manners, Brian's and Kim's parents waited for the other passengers to leave first before starting down the ramp. Just a minute before, while Brian had been pushing his way through the cabin and towards the exit ramp, his mother had grabbed his arm and told him to wait outside. Brian found this instruction to be unnecessary and annoying. Where else would he go? He didn't have the first clue as to where his family was going on the station or how they were going to get there. Most of the passengers from the shuttle filed through a door just a few meters from the ramp. There was no telling if this was the way correct route, however. Brian only knew that somewhere, at the end of this trip through the station, floated the colony ship and the inevitable journey that would follow.

"How was the ride, you two?" Luke asked, stepping off the ramp.

"Terrific," Brian muttered.

"Awesome!" exclaimed Kim. "The Starport looks like an angel from a distance!"

"Just wait until you see Saturn in a few weeks," Luke added, choosing to ignore, or failing to notice, Brian's sarcastic tone.

"We're going past Saturn?" Brian asked, not being able to maintain his icy demeanor upon hearing such a proposition.

"Yep, on our way out to the embarkation point," Luke confirmed. "It's right before we go into cryosleep. Sights like that lead to good dreams, huh?"

Brian got his emotions back under control. "Yeah, it'll be great Luke," he said in the most unenthusiastic voice possible. The prospect of seeing Saturn piqued Brian's interest, but he still found it hard to treat Luke like normal. Something in his cousin's voice made it seem to Brian like Luke was forcing conversation, avoiding the inevitable questions. Brian contemplated asking Luke about the strange alias, then thought better of the idea. There would be plenty of time later.

Luke obviously sensed the tension emanating from his little cousin. "Well buddy," he spoke up, sounding more nervous than Brian had ever heard him. "I'll go make sure all of our stuff came up on the transport alright."

Once Luke got a few paces away, Kim spoke up from Brian's side. "What's wrong Brian? Are you still worried about him?"

"I don't know," Brian confessed. "Like I said before, something's going on."

"Come on, it's Luke. He's still just the same Luke," Kim reminded her companion. "He's just a bit older now."

"I still need to know more," Brian stated, surprised even at his resolve to investigate the situation.

A moment later, the Bishops and Collins strode down the ramp, towards the two youngest members of their clans. Brian's father was talking on his personal communicator again, his face wearing an expression of serious authority. His mother was still talking to the older woman Brian had waved at earlier. "Make sure you get your bags from Luke," Bill Collins reminded Kim and Brian. "You don't want to leave anything in the hold, 'cause we're not coming back." He smiled at the kids.

Luke came around the side of the shuttle with several large bags loaded in his muscular arms. He tossed one at Brian, obviously confident that his younger cousin could handle the weight. Brian couldn't. The force of the flying bag knocked Brian onto the hanger floor as he attempted to catch it. "Oh, shhi–" Luke started to swear as he reassessed Brian's size in proportion to the bag. The fall didn't hurt so bad, at least, not as bad as Brian's decimated pride. Before anyone could help him up, he angrily thrust the bag off with an animalistic grunt. "Oh, Brian," his mother consoled as she rustled his hair. "Luke didn't mean it."

"Sorry about that Bri," Luke apologized as he lifted Brian from the floor. As Luke bent back down to pick up the bag, Brian grabbed his arm.

"Don't, I can get my own!"

"You sure?" Luke asked in a worried tone that made Brian flush with fury.

Brian didn't respond. Instead, he strained as the weight of the bag fought his arm, but he refused to drop it again.

"Suit yourself," Luke smiled as he continued to pass bags around to the family.

Brian's mother shot him a disapproving glance as she shook her head. She had never understood the pressures Brian placed on himself. Even worse, she didn't know how to confront the frustration he felt for being so small and powerless. Although his father remained too busy talking on his communicator to say anything, he gave his son a warm, reassuring smile.

When Brian turned, he expected to see Kim giggling at his clumsiness. She wasn't. "It looks pretty heavy, Brian," She pointed out earnestly.

"Sort of," Brian admitted. His left shoulder shook violently as he swung the bag towards the nearest exit. "Is that where we're going?" he asked, nodding his head in the door's general direction. "I'd like to get out of here."

"Oh, yeah," Bill responded. "You kids can go wait for us in the main reception area. Just don't go past the second security checkpoint. We'll be with you in a minute, as soon as David and I finish with some business."

Brian didn't wait for Bill to finish speaking. He simply started walking away from the group. The momentum of the swinging bag propelled him forward with increasing speed. Kim followed behind, torn between listening to the rest of her father's directions and following her friend. When faced with similar decisions throughout her life, Kim had always chosen Brian. He knew this and cherished her for it.

As Brian neared the exit, a firm hand clamped down on his left shoulder, almost making him lose the bag again. It definitely wasn't Kim's hand. She still lingered a meter back as Brian quickly shuffled out of the hanger.

"You're a spoiled brat, you know that, Brian?" a familiar voice spat from behind. Brain turned to meet Jade's eyes. "Blast-off, laser-brain," he muttered.

Surprisingly, Jade laughed at this verbal jab. "You've turned into quite the little militant while I've been away," she noted. "I better wait with you in the reception area. Wouldn't want you starting any trouble now, would we?"

"Don't you have something better to do, like heal the sick and dying?"

"For now, keeping your ego grounded is a big enough job, Bri."

CHAPTER 6

▼

THE SHEPHERD AND THE WOLF

"Minister Chang!" Kim yelled as she ran across the bustling reception area into the open arms of her former mentor. Chang's clergy robes enveloped Kim's tiny form, basking her in a sea of crimson. His face, which had always looked slightly weathered, now bore the deepening lines of old age. Brian noted as he approached, how white Chang's long hair had grown in the four and a half years since he had seen him last. Still, as the Minister embraced Kim, a warm smile melted these potentially harsh features away.

"How are you, my child?" Chang asked in his characteristically soothing voice. Despite Chang's many years spent in the Western Cities, a sharp Chinese accent still tinged his words.

"Fine," Kim answered as she pulled back from the curtains of robes. Her voice betrayed the stress caused by the tumultuous events of the previous two weeks. Chang frowned at her tone as he met Kim's eyes with a sincere look of concern.

"Why are you here?" she asked.

"I'll be going with you to the new colony," Chang revealed.

Kim's face lit up. "Really?"

"Even better, I'm going to be your teacher again."

Kim glanced around, obviously trying to locate Brian in order to gauge his reaction. Brian still hung back several meters. His response to Chang's revelation was much more reserved than Kim's. The soldiers at the first security checkpoint inside the reception area were having problems scanning Jade. It would be a moment before she got through. Brian used his sister's predicament as an excuse not to approach his former teacher.

"It's been hard to adjust to all of this commotion, hasn't it, Kim?" Chang inquired, drawing her attention back to their conversation.

It didn't take an empath to see that Kim was upset, but Chang did possess a certain empathetic charm that allowed him to comfort those around him. Kim simply nodded in response as she bit her lip. Brian rolled his eyes. Kim could be such a baby sometimes, especially when Chang was involved. Although Brian hadn't seen his old teacher since he entered the Junior Academy, Kim maintained a close relationship with the man, despite his relocation to Houston. Brian never bothered to contact Chang anymore. It was well known throughout the Church Academies that Minister Chang and Minister Petrov were longtime rivals. The older Brian got, the more he agreed with Petrov's assessment that Chang was too soft on his students and the Apostates. Nevertheless, Brian confessed that seeing Chang did give him a sense of comfort and security. At least he was a familiar sight.

Finally, Jade made it through the checkpoint after removing a small necklace that interfered with the scanners. She immediately pushed Brian from the safety of the crowd. "Come on, Brian. Aren't you glad to see him?"

Brian kept silent, waiting for the old man to acknowledge him.

"Mr. Bishop?" Chang asked in a formal manner. He slung one arm around Kim's shoulders and took a step in Brian's direction. He looked at Jade and winked. "Surely this young man standing in front of me isn't Brian Bishop!"

Brian smiled, knowing that Chang was trying to be funny. Despite the old man's claims to the contrary, Brian looked almost the same as he had four years before. Most adults who offered Brian such a forced compliment would have been thanked with a scowl. Chang, however, was different. It was hard not to be a little amused by the Minister's teasing words of kindness.

"Yeah, it's me," Brian confirmed.

"I've heard through some friends that you're quite the accomplished student, especially in scriptural matters," Chang noted, placing a hand on Brian's shoulder.

"You have no idea," Jade muttered sarcastically.

Suddenly Brian felt awkward. Did the Minister realize that he had been avoiding him these past few years? More importantly, did Chang resent Brian's growing closeness to Minister Petrov? Petrov's and Chang's views concerning the scriptures were totally incompatible. It was rumored that Petrov was partially responsible for sending Chang down to Houston, where his overly liberal views would be less corrosive on the Adherent Ministry. Houston's Ministers and High Council kept a much tighter grip on its religious dissenters than did Chicago's. Perhaps it was believed that he would do less damage there. As Brian scanned Chang's face, however, he detected no hostility toward himself or Petrov. He sheepishly shrugged his shoulders in response to the Minster's question, not wanting to appear too confident in his own intellectual prowess.

"Ever think of joining the clergy? We could use some Ministers with some intelligence!" Chang jested.

Brian winced. *There it is*, he thought. *Minister Chang can't resist criticizing his rivals. Minister Petrov always said that Chang's passive demeanor was simply a front for a liberal agenda. Just act like you don't care, Brian.* As Brian was about to answer the Minister's question, Kim interrupted.

"Brian wants to join the military," she said in a mocking tone. "He says somebody's gotta keep the peace!" Kim lowered her normally shrill voice as deep as possible, trying to sound like the Adherent recruiting commercials on ABN.

Minister Chang's eyebrows shot up, although he maintained his smile. The twinkle in his dark, brown eyes signaled mischief. "Ah, a soldier, huh?"

"Actually," Brian began to correct as he shot Kim a dirty look, "I really want to become a pilot."

"So you like math now? That's a drastic change from the last time I saw you!"

"You don't have to be great at math or physics to become a pilot," Brian insisted. "The new fighters don't require a lot of technical work, just good reflexes."

"Well, you always were a good holoball player," Chang pointed out.

"Thanks," Brian said, careful not to let the Minister's words lower his guard. The old man was definitely trying to challenge him, just as he always had. "I still can go into the Ministry after I complete my service," he pointed out. "Minister Petrov said he'd supp–" Brian stopped in mid sentence, aware that a reference to his new teacher amounted to profanity in front of Chang.

The old man's reaction surprised him, however. "Petrov's a good reference to have," Minister Chang agreed. "He's got a lot of power now in the Church. I always knew he'd be chosen to be on the Council of High Ministers; he has the ambition."

Brian attempted to detect hostility in Chang's voice, although none could be found. He sounded more defeated than anything else.

"Excuse me, sir," a voice spoke from behind. Brian, Jade, Kim and Minister Chang turned to confront an Adherent soldier who had wandered over from the checkpoint. "Your party is impeding traffic in this corridor," he pointed out. The soldier sounded nervous. Chang's red robes instantly identified him as an important man. Soldiers typically didn't question members of the clergy, although they were authorized to do so in valid situations. Apparently, impeding pedestrian traffic in the cramped confines of the reception area's corridor constituted a valid situation.

Chang glanced around quickly, as if he hadn't been aware of his surroundings before the soldier spoke. Most of the people moving around the reception area were from Brian's flight. It seemed silly to be so concerned about impeding their movement, since they all had to wait for directions on how to get to the colony transport anyway. Nevertheless, Chang played along with the soldier.

"Oh, please excuse us, Corporal," Chang humbly apologized. "You're absolutely right. Come on children."

They quickly stepped back from the moving commuters and found seats next to a viewport in a rectangular sitting area. Most of the seats were occupied by families who had ridden up on the shuttle. As Kim and Chang babbled on about school and the move to the colony, Brian surveyed his former teacher. *I know why Minister Petrov doesn't like Minister Chang*, Brian realized. *Chang thinks it's his job to bring out the good in everyone. He doesn't understand that caring too much encourages weakness.*

Within minutes, the others emerged from the hanger bay and passed through the first security checkpoint. Upon seeing the kids with Minister Chang, Brian's father waved and started walking over to the sitting area. *At least he's not still talking on that stupid communicator. Thank the Lord*, Brian thought. Halfway between the checkpoint and Brian, his father's movement was halted by a booming voice.

"It's him," Jade hissed, shaking her head in disgust.

"Who?" Brian asked.

"Fenner," Chang answered. His smile faded immediately. "Titus Fenner."

"Greetings, my friends," a tall, dark-haired man with a goatee bellowed as he approached Brian's family. The man wore the ornate black robes befitting a High Councilor. Although Brian's father wore the same attire at city High Council meetings, he frequently complained that those who wore the robes in public were merely flaunting their power.

"Titus," Brian's father greeted curtly as the man extended his hand.

"All are ready for the pilgrimage," Fenner announced. "My flock has been successfully shepherded onboard the transport. I trust your own flock is gathered as well, Bishop?"

"We'll be ready to go shortly," Bill answered for David. "We encountered some unexpected problems back on Earth, though. We'll be twelve short."

Fenner nodded in response. "Yes, yes, yes. A result of that terrible tragedy back on Earth. Those heinous attacks. I heard! The nerve of these terrorists!" he proclaimed, shaking his fist in the air in a dramatic display of outrage.

"They say it was ICLF," Brian's father added. "But I think they had some help from the inside this time. The Ministers have ordered the screening of every Citizen connected to the Council in Chicago."

Besides a shallow nod and moment of silence Fenner didn't react to the news. Instead, he lowered his fist and circled around David, Bill, Luke and John. Brian's and Kim's mothers seemed to be hiding behind their husbands. Within seconds, Brian knew why.

"And how do you two lovely ladies fare?" Fenner asked as he grasped Rachel Collins' right hand. Rachel seemed to wince, as if she wanted to recoil from Fenner's touch but couldn't. He bent down slowly and kissed the back of her hand.

"We're fine, Fenner," Brian's mother answered coldly. She brushed past his shoulder, not giving him the chance to show her a similar display of affection. As Brian's mother walked over to where Brian was sitting, Fenner followed her.

"Are these the wonderful children I've heard so much about?" he asked, referring to Brian, Kim and Jade.

"This would be them," Brian's mother confirmed, stepping in front of the kids like a mother ewe guarding her flock from a prowling wolf.

Kim eyed Fenner wearily as he patted her head. "Such a pretty girl, just like her mother."

"I didn't know you liked children so much, Fenner," Chang grumbled.

"Of course, Minister. Children are God's greatest gift. You of all people should know that."

Brian could feel the tension building in the small sitting area. *Fenner*, he tried to recall. *One of Houston's Council members.* Brian remembered the name being mentioned by his father several times over the years, always followed by harsh words. As Fenner turned his attention to Jade, Brian's father grabbed him on the shoulder.

"Come on," David Bishop insisted. "We've gotta register everyone with the station's computer before we can go."

"Of course," Fenner replied, grinning devilishly at Jade. "The stars await."

Brian's father led Fenner away in the direction of the waiting colony transport. Meanwhile, Rachel and Bill addressed the families waiting in the reception area.

"Okay, everyone, we're almost ready to go. Make sure you've got all your belongings and remember to have all of your identification tags ready. We don't want anyone getting left behind," Bill stated in a commanding tone.

With that, the reception area, which had grown silent following Fenner's arrival, exploded in a sea of commotion.

Brian sat for a moment, ignoring his mother's attempts to get him moving. *The Final Testament teaches that evil often disguises itself in grace*, he reminded himself. Never had the meaning of these words been so clear. Despite the disingenuous nature of Fenner's charm, though, Brian couldn't help but admire the power of his stride and the confidence in his tone. The man had power, and knew how to use it. Brian admired this trait, although he recognized that Fenner was not to be trusted. The High Councilor had to be added to the growing list of people to watch.

CHAPTER 7

▼

THE APOSTLE 4

"It looks ugly," complained Kim as she stared out the viewport.

As he looked at the docked colony transport for the first time, Brian couldn't help but agree. Thinking back, Brian didn't know exactly what he had expected. Surely, a vessel that could travel to the stars had to be incredibly beautiful, if not angelic. In truth, nothing about the bulky, functional starship could be described as being remotely beautiful. The dirty-gray ship's massive cluster of drive engines comprised at least half of its gargantuan mass. From where Brain and Kim stood, they couldn't even see where the engines stopped and the living quarters began. Brian followed the length of the ship with his eyes, moving from the stardrive and engineering sections to the massive cargo pods sprouting from the transport's sides. Four of the cargo pods contained equipment and supplies for the new colony, while two others housed the hundreds of cryotubes, which would accommodate the colonists once the ship had left the solar system. Contrary to the sleek, streamlined vision Brian had formulated in his head these past few days, the ship was anything but aerodynamic. In fact, it looked as if the delicate pods would snap off from the central trunk of the ship and float away into the void. On the central portion of the ship's main trunk, the name APOSTLE 4 could be deciphered in brilliant white letters. *At least it's got a strong name*, Brian thought.

"How big is it?" he asked his mother.

"Most colony transports these days measure about a thousand meters," she replied. "Of course, the part we'll actually be living in is only about half that."

Brain turned from the window to face the line of colonists waiting to board the transport. With over 500 colonists onboard, it was going to get crowded.

"How long are we going to ride in the ship before we go to sleep?" Kim asked.

"It'll take close to two months before we pass Saturn," Jill responded. "Then we'll hop in our beds and the computer will activate the stardrive."

"What are we supposed to do in that time?" Brian asked sarcastically.

His mother simply flashed him a disapproving glare.

Brian shrugged. He wasn't looking for an answer, just trying to be difficult. Nearly a week prior to leaving Earth, he had taken upon himself to study the itinerary of the entire trip to the Tau Ceti star system. Two months traveling out of the solar system, eight years spent in cryosleep, and one month traveling through the Tau Ceti system en route to the colony.

"Do we get separate quarters during the first part of the trip?" Kim asked hopefully.

"No honey, but you'll only be sharing a room with your family and ours," Jill explained.

Kim crinkled up her nose, trying to feign disgust. "You mean I've gotta share the same room with his attitude?" she moaned, nodding in Brian's direction.

Jill laughed. "I think we're just going to have to make him sleep in engineering."

"Hilarious," Brian muttered, trying not to smile.

After a lengthy journey, the Bishop and Collins' families finally located their quarters in the ship's dark, maze-like corridors. Brian felt an immediate surge of disappointment as he noticed that the room used the same metal grating for the floor as the rest of the ship. True to the rumors he had heard over the years, colony transports lacked any sort of amenities. *At least this room's got a window*, he reasoned.

The tiny, box-like quarters were lined on either side by two sets of bunk-beds, making eight beds altogether. In the middle of the room, a grimy old curtain hung, the only source of privacy for the two cramped families. Kim ran over and threw her bag on top of one of the lower beds closest to the window. Brian resisted the urge to choose the bed directly on top of her. Although there was one extra bed in the room, he knew that it would be most appropriate for him to sleep on his family's side. He and Kim were getting to the age when male/female sleeping arrangements attracted more scrutiny. Even though the bunk-beds separated their two occupants by a foot or more, the idea of a boy and girl sleeping together worried most adults. Brain felt confident that neither his parents nor

Kim's would complain about such an intimate arrangement; nevertheless, he still wanted to do the right thing, the kind of thing Minister Petrov would approve of.

Brian found the notion of being attracted to Kim "in that way" utterly ridiculous, anyway. Sure, Kim was a pretty girl and Brian loved her. But this love was the kind felt between siblings. *Besides, temptation outside of marriage was a sin in God's eyes*, Brian constantly reminded himself. *Better to keep such feelings suppressed, where they belong.* Sleeping across the room would be the safest method of accomplishing this task.

As the rest of the family members filtered in, Brian chose the upper bunk closest to the window on the left side of the room. From here, at least he could see Kim so long as the curtain wasn't drawn. His father threw his bag on the other top bunk and immediately headed back toward the door. "I've gotta get up to the bridge," he insisted. "John said that Fenner's already barking orders to the captain up there."

"Right," Bill acknowledged as he and Rachel stowed their bags. "I'll be up in a few minutes to look over the roster one last time."

"Jade and I should get to Medical," Jill added. "I haven't even had a chance to speak with Doctor Anderson yet." She turned to address Brian. "Are you all set here, Brian?"

"Yeah, I'll be fine," Brian assured as he cracked open a textbook from school. "I'm going to catch up on some reading."

"You know," his mother spoke up in a prodding tone that made Brian's blood pressure skyrocket, "Minister Chang said he's not even going to start lessons for another couple of days. You and Kim should take this opportunity to explore the ship a little. It's a lot bigger than you think."

"Maybe I'll do that," Brian muttered under his breath.

His mother responded to her son's sarcasm by issuing a familiar, fatigued sigh. Without another word, Jill and Jade left the room. Brian looked out of the corner of his eye to see if Bill and Rachel had noticed his disrespectful tone. They were too busy unpacking their things to notice much of anything. Kim was a different matter. She gave Brian a glare so hot it could have ignited a dead star. Careful not to show the slightest bit of surprise, Brian simply shrugged and returned to his reading.

After another minute or so, Bill and Rachel left for the bridge. As soon as the door closed behind them, Brian was jolted from his reading by a flying projectile. Stunned, he fumbled with the hardcover book which had sailed across the room with uncanny accuracy.

"What was that for?" he cried.

"I just thought you'd like something else to read, you jerk!" Kim hissed.

Brian examined the cover of the book that had impacted his cranium. It was a pocketsize version of the *Final Testament*. "You know, Kim, you shouldn't treat this book so disrespectfully!"

"Oh, but it's acceptable for you to treat your mom disrespectfully?" she shot back.

"That's different," Brian insisted.

"How?"

Brian thought for a minute. He failed to come up with an adequate excuse. "It just is."

"That's a pathetic answer."

The quarters were silent for several minutes as Brian and Kim continued their stand-off. She had a point, although Brian would be damned if he let her get the best of him. He struggled to return to the text a few centimeters in front of his eyes. *Johnson's Exobiology for Beginners* wasn't exactly a gripping read. His ears soon picked up the faint hum of the ship's reactor core and the steady clamor of passengers on other decks. Then they focused in on the sound of Kim's breathing. From across the room, Brian could tell she was inhaling and exhaling out her nose. This meant she was angry and wanted to show it. If he didn't call a truce now, it would be a long trip.

"I think you put a dent in my head," Brian complained, finally breaking the silence.

"You'll live, Bishop."

Brian rolled over on his side to face Kim. She was desperately trying to suppress a laugh as she pressed her face down into a book of her own. Brian stared at her some more, bugging out his eyes.

"Would you stop, Brian?" she pleaded, breaking down into a maniacal giggle. "You look freakish when you do that!"

"Do you wanna go look around the ship a little?" Brian asked. He wasn't merely trying to be diplomatic. Even though he had reeled at his mother's suggestion to explore his surroundings, part of him hoped that there were some other kids their age onboard. Most of the younger people Brian had seen on the shuttle and at the Starport were young children, too young to be considered potential friends. There had to be at least a few others who were old enough to be in the Junior Academy.

"Yeah," Kim answered as she ditched the book and sat up. "Let's go now."

"Were you even reading these last few minutes?"

"No. Were you?"

"No."

Brian and Kim made their way through the *Apostle 4*'s dim, cramped corridors in no particular direction. Just moving around the unfamiliar environment was enough of an adventure for the time being. Everywhere, colonists busily worked as they readied the ship for departure. Nobody seemed to show any interest in the two explorers, not even the armed Adherent soldiers patrolling the ship.

"Do you even know where we're going?" Brian asked after a few minutes of aimless wandering.

"No. Does it really matter though?"

"I guess not."

"Then don't worry, Brian. Just remember we're in Blue sector, Room 32A," Kim stated as she swerved to avoid a colonist carrying a box full of sensor equipment.

"We're in Yellow sector now," Brian reminded her. "I think there are five sectors altogether."

"I heard my mom saying that the Chicago colonists are in Blue and Green sectors, the London colonists are in Orange and Red sectors, and Fenner's Houston crowd are all in this sector," Kim noted.

Fenner, Brian thought. *Is he around right now, or still on the bridge?* Most likely he was still on the bridge, although Brian kept an eye out for his black, towering form. He didn't want any contact with Fenner, especially in the absence of another adult.

"Are you looking for Minister Chang's quarters, Kim?" he asked, noticing that Kim seemed to move with purpose.

"Maybe," she replied coyly, peeking her head into an open door as they passed by. "Excuse me," she started in the sweetest voice imaginable. Brian came up behind her, but couldn't quite see who she was talking to in the room. "Could you please tell me where Minister Chang's quarters are?" she asked politely.

A woman replied, "Oh, I believe he's located up the next corridor towards the bridge decks."

"Thank you very much," Kim responded, nodding her head. As she turned to leave, the woman called her back.

"Dear."

"Yep?"

"Could you come in for a moment," the woman asked. "Go ahead and invite your friend in."

Brian and Kim complied. The middle-aged woman sat on one of the room's bottom bunks, meticulously folding clothes into an open bag. Nobody else was in the room. The woman had dark brown skin and long, black hair, which was braided in four ornate loops behind her head. The tattoo on her forehead barely showed through the deep mahogany skin tone. The woman's facial features were so fine and delicate that it appeared as if her face was slightly out of focus. If not for the woman's voice, which seemed to carry the weight of age, Brian would have placed her in her twenties.

"You two just have to meet my son," she insisted. "You're about thirteen or fourteen, right?"

Brian was shocked. Nobody ever guessed his age right, much less overestimated it. In Kim's case, the feat was even more extraordinary.

"Yes," Kim replied in a surprised tone.

"So's Maleek." The woman looked around the room, as if her son was hiding in the cramped space. "He's around this ship somewhere, probably snooping around near engineering or something. That boy never could keep his hands off machines, no matter how big or small."

Brian was thrilled to hear of another kid on board his age. Still, he didn't know how to respond to the woman's revelation. He didn't even know her name.

"I'm Kim," Kim stated, as if picking up on Brian's feelings of awkwardness. "Kim Collins."

"Oh, you're Bill Collins' kid," the woman confirmed as she smiled warmly. "And this must be Brian Bishop."

"That's me," Brian said, astonished that the woman knew him simply for being with Kim.

"Minister Chang said you two are inseparable," the woman revealed. "You're going to be in class with Maleek starting Monday. Oh, I'm Alice Williams, by the way."

"Nice to meet you, Alice," Kim said as she took the woman's hand.

"Yeah," Brian added with a shy wave. He had never been any good at introductions. "Well, Kim and I are going to explore the rest of the ship. If we see Maleek, we'll introduce ourselves."

"He's a pretty tall boy for his age," Alice said. "His face is still very young looking, though. You can't mistake him for anyone else."

"Right," said Kim, nodding.

Brian witnessed a sad expression wash over Alice's face as he and Kim left the room.

"She seems lonely," Kim pointed out.

How could she be? Brian thought. *There are hundreds of people just a few meters away at all times.* Then he realized that she hadn't mentioned anything about Maleek's father.

CHAPTER 8

▼

EDGE OF ETERNITY

"Boring." Brian heard the word leave Kim's mouth at least a hundred times during their first month of travel through the solar system. There certainly wasn't much excitement onboard the ship, but Brian still found her complaints to be annoying. Despite the poor attitude he showed his parents, he didn't mind the predictable, "boring" routine nearly as much as Kim did. The downtime gave him time to think, and to pray. Now that he had left Earth, it really didn't seem to matter where he did these things, so long as he had the time.

The colonists' days were regulated by a seemingly endless cycle of food, talk, and Church. Due to space limitations, everyone ate and attended Church in small, separate groups organized by family and sector. Many colonists on the ship also had duties to fulfill, such as Brian's mother and sister in Medical. Brian's father, Bill and Rachel spent most of their time up on the bridge decks near the front of the ship. They worked alongside the gruff Adherent captain who officially commanded the ship, making sure that all of the colonists followed their prescribed routines. Once the ship finally reached Tau Ceti, Brian's father would join the colony's existing High Council. Bill would too, ending his brief retirement from public life. The captain, on the other hand, would leave a detachment of troops on the planet before making the long journey back to Earth. Brian wasn't sure of the captain's name, but knew the man to be a harsh authoritarian. Rachel instructed Brian and Kim to stay away from the bridge unless accompanied by an authorized adult. The Captain hated surprises and hated children even more.

As for the children, Brian and Kim included, school occupied a large chunk of time. True to his father's promise from a few weeks before, the familiar daily routine alleviated many of Brian's worries and suspicions for the time being. Along with Maleek, who rapidly befriended Brian and Kim, there were seven other students between the ages of eight and fifteen in Minister Chang's study sessions. Brian found this arrangement odd, considering there were upwards of seventy children traveling on the ship. When he had questioned Chang about the other children, the Minister responded by saying they were tutored by other colonists who worked for the Church. This answer made sense to Brian, since most of the children on the ship probably didn't attend the prestigious Church Academies anyway. Most Adherent Citizens were educated in large, public institutions run by Church Adepts rather than full-fledged Ministers. Only the offspring of the rich and powerful received Brian and Kim's level of education. Brian found it extremely comforting that things like social rank would be transported to the new colony.

One thing that did bother Brian was the strange stare he received from the other young people onboard the ship. They seemed to view Brian and his Academy school companions as pariahs more than peers. Several times during the first week of travel, Brian attempted to approach one of these kids. In almost every instance, the boy or girl had either ignored him or found a quick excuse to break off the conversation. *Maybe they're just intimidated by my social position*, Brian told himself. Still, being stared at and ignored by strangers made Brian feel inadequate. One day, while the class was discussing the results of The Great Unification Wars, he brought the subject up to Chang. "Why is it that the other kids seem to avoid us?" Brian blurted out, motioning with a hand to the other Academy students sitting around the Minister.

Chang put his holoprojector down, aware that the day's planned lesson would have to wait until Brian's question was answered. "Avoid you?" he responded, feigning ignorance.

"Yeah, they ignore us."

"I've noticed it too," Maleek spoke up.

The rest of the circle broke into a mild explosion of chatter as the rest of the students recounted their own experiences of being ostracized.

"I've heard some parents even telling their kids not to talk to us," Kim complained, her voice rising above the chatter. "It's like we've got a disease or something."

Chang silently raised a hand. The talking abruptly ceased. "Why do you think that is?" he asked. Chang liked to ask questions that challenged his students. This, Brian knew well.

"They're jealous," mocked a Korean girl named Suna who was about Brian and Kim's age.

The rest of the group seemed to agree with her assessment.

"Do you think it's as simple as that?" Chang asked, obviously searching for a deeper answer. His students pondered the question for few moments. Everyone seemed perplexed.

Finally, Kim fielded another guess: "They're scared of us?"

Brian leaned back in his seat and looked at Kim like she was crazy. *Scared of us?*

"That's definitely a possibility, Kim," Chang stated. "Most of the people traveling on this ship don't work for the Church, but they still have to live under its laws."

"So?" Brian sneered.

"So all of your families work for the Church, or at the very least, have close ties to it."

"I still don't see what that has to do with us," another student named Derrick insisted.

"Many of the colonists may see you as an extension of the government," Chang explained. "Your families' power intimidates some people."

"But the *Final Testament* teaches that we are all an extension of the government," Brian reminded his teacher. "If they're loyal Citizens and Believers, then they don't have to worry about anything!"

"But you can't deny, Brian, the High Councils have a long history of persecuting those who don't conform to the Church's laws and beliefs. Even people who thought they were good Citizens have been killed in God's name."

Nonsense, Brian thought. "There's a difference between persecuting innocents and eliminating dangerous people." Brian searched for a quick and easy example. "Just look at the Unification Wars, for instance."

"What about them?" Chang asked.

"Those countries were full of Apostates who wanted to destroy everything the Church was trying to build."

"That's right," Suna added. "My grandparents left their home to live in one of the Adherent cities. They made a choice—the right choice."

"So all those who didn't make this choice deserved to die?" Chang asked.

"Yes," Brian proclaimed confidently.

"Do all of you agree with Mr. Bishop?" Chang asked. He slowly scanned the faces of his students. A few nodded their heads in quiet agreement with Brian's statements.

"I don't agree," Kim said under her breath. Her words were loud enough for everyone to hear. Brian turned his head in disbelief. Aware that the class' eyes were on her, Kim spoke carefully. "The *New Testament* teaches that it's important to save, not kill your enemies," she began. "And since the *New Testament*'s still considered to be a holy book by the Church, we should follow its advice."

"That's a very well-reasoned argument, Kim," Chang noted with apparent delight.

"I agree," said Maleek. Nobody else in the group seemed to, but he continued anyway: "My dad was killed when I was eight by other Church officials. They said he had been collaborating with terrorists against the Church, even though he was a member of the Council."

"But the *Final Testament* says it's right to kill Apostates if they present a threat. The *Final Testament*'s God's last address to man. It overrides previous texts. If God says threats can be dealt with violently, then we should accept it," Brian argued.

"Who or what do you consider a threat?" Kim asked, assuming the role of her teacher. "Maleek's dad wasn't a threat."

"You don't know that," Brian argued. "He could have been ICLF. Those people definitely can't be Saved."

"Who says?" Kim asked Brian defiantly. "Maybe they have reasons for being violent."

"Maybe they don't like it when innocent people get murdered," Maleek added.

Careful not to let the debate get out of hand, Chang turned the issue back to the scriptural inconsistencies. "So does the *Final Testament* override all previous holy texts in every situation?"

"Of course," Brian insisted. "God had to amend his earlier messages to humanity. That's why we have the *Final Testament*."

"But didn't men write the *Final Testament*? Are they as infallible as God?" Chang questioned.

Brian couldn't take any more of this. *A Minister actually challenging the supremacy of the Final Testament?* It was blasphemy in its most devilish form. Minister Petrov was right: Chang was out of control. Brian stood up and pushed his chair back. "I've heard enough of this," he said before throwing down his holopad and storming out of the room. Nobody followed. The other students were conditioned to respect clergy members at all times, no matter how radical the discussion. In most cases, an outburst like Brian's in a Church setting would be punished by a whipping, or worse.

"Let him go," Brian heard Chang say as he distanced himself from the small storage area, which doubled as a classroom.

That's the last time I let that man poison my ears, Brian promised himself. *Forget Kim and Maleek, too.* Brian resented how close the two had become over the last month. The fact that jealousy was a sin didn't detract from his feelings of frustration and anger. If he no longer had Kim as a confidant, then what did he have? *Faith,* Brian thought. *I still have my faith.*

Titan drifted in front of its mother planet, obscuring all but the heavenly rings gracing Saturn's bulging waist like a fallen halo. Several more distant moons drifted in orbit, fulfilling their roles in the ancient gravitational ballet. Just as Titan's dark, cloudy mass took center-stage, its master's rings caught and refracted the faint sunlight, dazzling the scene with luminescence spewed forth from a trillion tiny prisms. Brian watched the celestial marvel unfold through Cryopod A's multi-paned octagonal viewport. Behind him lay row after row of soon-to-be occupied tubes. The dark, cavernous room offered the first true silence Brian had enjoyed for weeks. The entire area was supposed to be off-limits to the colonists prior to entering stasis, but some careless maintenance men had left the door open, allowing him to slip in undetected.

Brian kneeled down on the cold, metal floor and prayed in front of the window. He prayed for the ship's safe journey. He prayed for his parents and for Luke, who still acted like he was on the run from something. Most of all, Brian prayed for Kim. She was teetering dangerously close to heresy. Questioning Church doctrine was a serious offense, even for a young girl. Brian mostly blamed Chang for her transgressions. Kim had always been a bit liberal for an Academy student, but at least she had been respectful towards her faith. Maleek didn't make things any better. He shared Kim's doubts about the Church's righteousness and exploited this common bond to win her attention. Although Brian had liked the easy-going boy at first, he now viewed Maleek as a merciless competitor for Kim's soul. There had to be a way to win Kim back without appearing desperate, or even worse, weak.

Brian opened his eyes and scanned the darkness of Titan. Somewhere, below the thick layer of methane clouds, primordial life forms swam in icy, brown muck. This fact, scientists had known for over two centuries. Titan was one of the first planets found to sustain life besides Earth. Since that time, dozens of others had been discovered, although none that contained intelligent life like humans. *We are God's chosen creatures*, Brian thought. *Created to reign over all of Creation, just like in the scriptures.* Brian's mind wandered to the parched deserts of Tau Ceti 3, where wild packs of reptilian beasts combed the wastes in search of water. It would be difficult to adjust to a new world, but Brian felt confident that he could. Like the late twenty-second century prophet Jonathan, Brian would tame the wastes in the name of God. This time it would just be on a planet other than Earth.

Brian was so immersed in thoughts about the future he didn't hear the footsteps behind him.

"You aren't supposed to be here," a robotic-sounding voice said.

Shocked at this intrusion, Brian wheeled around. A fully-suited Adherent soldier towered above him, pulse rifle in hand.

"Uh, uh," Brian stammered. "Sorry."

The soldier gave what sounded like a muffled laugh and sat down on the nearest cryotube. He rested the pulse rifle against the bed and slowly removed his shiny black helmet. Brian eyed him wearily, not knowing what to do. Would he be punished for trespassing?

As the soldier placed the helmet on the ground next to his feet, he let out a fatigued sigh. At first glance, Brian thought it was Luke. The soldier had the same chiseled features, gaunt cheeks and closely cut hair as his cousin. On closer inspection, however, Brian could see gray streaks running through the man's otherwise brown hair.

"Don't worry about it, kid," the soldier reassured. "It's a great view from here, isn't it?"

"Yeah."

"Quiet, too."

"Yeah."

"How about this," the soldier proposed. "I won't tell if you don't."

"Sure," Brian agreed, still stuck on single word responses.

"Of course, we'll have to go in a few minutes. This section is supposed to be sealed off."

"It's nice though," Brian added, finally summoning enough courage to engage in a conversation. "I can actually hear myself pray."

"You're one of the Academy kids, aren't you?" the soldier asked. He wore a wry, knowing smile.

"How'd you know?"

"Ah, I just had a feeling. You look like you carry this emotional weight that other kids on the ship don't. I've never seen anything like it before. Maybe it's because this is the only place where I've ever seen Academy kids and normal kids together in such a confined area. It's easy to contrast you, I guess."

"Were you schooled in an Academy?" Brian asked. It was odd to interact with an Adherent soldier on such a personal level, especially one who was so inquisitive.

"Me? No. Are you kidding? I'm a Corporal for a reason. I joined up when I was only eighteen. My parents couldn't afford to keep me in the house any longer."

"I want to be a soldier someday, too," Brian proclaimed. "Being a pilot would be the best!"

"That's mighty patriotic of you," the soldier chuckled. He saw Brian eyeing the pulse rifle. "Ever held one of these?"

"No," Brian confessed. His eyes widened.

"Here, I'll teach you how it works." The soldier quickly showed Brian how the pulse rifle operated. Brian was surprised to find that the weight wasn't bad.

"It's so light," he noted.

"Yeah, but it kicks like a devil when you fire it on full-auto!"

"I can't wait to have one of my own," Brian said.

"Shouldn't you set your goals a little higher? I mean, if I were you, I'd go for a job on the Council, or in a Cathedral or something."

"It's not the same kind of service," Brian argued.

"That's right, it's not. You'll actually have an easy life!" The soldier took the weapon out of Brian's hands.

"Suffering is part of our spiritual penance," Brian said, quoting from scripture.

"Yeah, you're definitely an Academy kid," the soldier laughed. He stood up and put his helmet back on. "Time to resume my patrol," he said. "Come on, I'll walk you out of here."

Brian and the soldier quietly exited the restricted area, careful not to attract any attention.

"Oh, kid," the soldier said as Brian was walking away.

"What's that?"

"Anytime you want a tour of the bridge, just come and find me. I'm usually patrolling Green sector this time of day."

"Thanks, I'll have to do that sometime."

CHAPTER 9

▼

APOCALYPSE

It had been just under a week since Brian had stormed out of Chang's classroom. Despite his impassioned refusals to return, his parents had forced him to apologize and rejoin the class the day after the incident. Chang didn't seem to hold Brian's outburst against him. Brian suspected that his teacher actually found the exchange amusing. The rest of the students now held Brian in esteemed reverence. Few young people could summon up the bravery to argue with a Minister. It was obvious to all that Brian's apology to Chang was forced by higher powers. As usual, Kim and Maleek saw things differently. Now Brian felt farther away from his best friend than ever before. She may as well have been back on Earth for all the time they spent together in the days prior to entering cryosleep.

An eerie silence had fallen over the ship since the colonists began entering their cryotubes. Only a few families were still awake in the final hours before the computer engaged the stardrive. Soon, the *Apostle 4's* 586 passengers would be hurtling through space at over half the speed of light. When they woke up, they would be over twelve light years from Earth, in the Tau Ceti system. Although the trip onboard the ship would last just eight years, the time debt caused by the extreme velocity meant that to everyone back on Earth, forty years would pass. Of course, for the sleeping colonists, it would seem as if no time had passed at all. For all practical purposes, Brian would still be a thirteen-year-old boy in a ten-year-old body. For the people back on Earth, he would not even be a memory.

Brian lay on his bunk reading his favorite passages from *The Final Testament*. In case of a tube malfunction, which did occasionally happen, he wanted to be sure of his divine destination before going to sleep. As he read, his mother secured some belongings in containers under the bunks. She worked quietly and wore a serious expression. Brain wondered what her problem was, but not enough to ask.

Across the room, Kim and Maleek played some sort of holographic game on Jade's personal computer. Maleek was supposed to have accompanied his mother to Cryopod B over an hour ago, but he had somehow managed to sneak back out after she had entered stasis. This angered Brian immensely. He had wanted to set things right with Kim before they slept, just in case. With Maleek around, it wouldn't happen.

The door opened, and Brian's father entered the room.

"Hey, kids," he said. "Ready for a little nap?"

Kim and Maleek laughed. Brian didn't respond.

"I talked to your parents a minute ago," David Bishop said to Kim. "They're gonna come down here and see you before you go to sleep."

"Yeah, that's what my mom said earlier," Kim said as she giggled at her game.

Brian's father walked over to his mother and whispered something in her ear. It sounded like, "Everything's ready."

She nodded her head and frowned. When she turned to Brian she had an even more worried look on her face. "Ready to go, Bri? Everyone else is already asleep."

"Sure," Brian said. He handed her his holobook and hopped down from the bunk. Both of his parents placed their arms around him."

"We need to go to the bridge before we join you," his mother stated. "You, Kim, and Maleek know the way down to the pod. Jade's still awake and waiting for you. She'll help you with your cryotube."

"Right," Brian sighed.

Suddenly, the blaring sound of David Bishop's communicator filled the room. "Fenner's starting early," a strange voice hissed. "He's not following the timetable!"

"What?" Brian's father cried. "Not everyone's in their tubes yet! The children are still out!"

"Then you'd better come over here and stop him," the voice suggested. "He just shot one of the guards outside his quarters."

"Shit!" Brian's father swore. "Take care of them," he instructed Jill before running out of the room.

Brian's mother grabbed Kim and Brian by their shirts and pulled them close. "Come here, Maleek!" she urged, motioning with her eyes. Maleek cautiously approached her, not quite sure what to make of her frenzied voice.

"What's going on?" Brian demanded. If he had heard the voice on the communicator right, Fenner had just shot one of the Adherent soldiers. Brian's world collapsed as his mother's expression transmitted the severity of the situation.

"You kids need to stay in this room no matter what happens. No matter what, you hear? Got it?"

"No!" Brian yelled, managing to summon some courage. "Tell me what's going on!"

"Aunt J-Jill?"

Maleek still looked like he was in shock from hearing Brian's father scream the "S" word.

"No matter what, you hear me?" Jill Bishop yelled, shaking Brian and Kim with a force that seemed beyond the capacity of her small frame. The kids nodded, even Brian. "I love you sweetie," his mother said as she kissed him on the cheek. When she pulled back, Brian could see tears in her eyes. Kim started crying, too. Brian's mother put a hand on her head and said in her most compassionate voice, "It's going to be alright, honey. I'll find your parents."

With that, Jill Bishop spun around and followed her husband out of the room. After standing for a moment in stunned silence, Brian bolted to the door.

"She locked it!" he yelled, smashing his fist into the keypad. "I don't know which combination she used!"

"She said to stay here, Brian," Maleek said.

"Shut up!" Brian yelled back. "Just help me get this thing open!"

Maleek seemed to weigh his choices for a moment. Before he could step toward the keypad, though, the angry crack of a pulse rifle stopped him in mid-stride.

"What was that?" Kim screamed. The cold, metallic insides of the ship magnified the gunfire. Somebody was shooting on full-auto. The sound was deafening. It had to be coming from right outside the door. More shots could be heard echoing throughout the ship. It sounded like a battle was going on, more than just Fenner and a couple of guards.

"Open the door, Maleek!" Brian cried maniacally. He grabbed the tall kid by the shirt and shook him violently.

"No," Maleek managed to spit out.

"Aren't you worried about your mother, Maleek?" Brian asked, attempting to appeal to emotion. The tactic worked. Without further protest, Maleek broke free and started entering numbers on the keypad. Brian had little doubt that Maleek could easily hack into the door's CPU. Like him or not, the kid was a genius when it came to electronics.

After a tortuous minute of fiddling, Maleek got the door open. The two panels slid into either side of the wall, revealing a dead Adherent soldier lying in the corridor. Kim screamed. Brian gasped too, but maintained enough presence of mind to cover her mouth with his hand. Maleek, who had been closest to the body when the doors opened, stumbled back into the room and pressed himself partially under one of the bunks. Nobody spoke or moved for several seconds as the sounds of battle drifted farther away toward the front of the ship.

The acrid smell of plasma smoke soon drifted into the room, tempting Brian to investigate the danger. Shaking almost uncontrollably, he took a tentative step towards the body, but stopped as he felt the pinch of Kim's tiny hands on his arm.

"No, Bri. Don't," she whimpered. "I'm scared!"

"I know. Me too." He turned back to the relative safety of his quarters, before once again confronting the bloody darkness ahead. "But we can't stay here."

"What about Maleek?" Kim asked, pointing back into the room. From the looks of it, Maleek had passed out from shock and now lay peacefully under the bunk that provided him refuge.

"He'll be fine in there," Brian assured.

"What about our parents?"

"I don't know."

Kim started to cry again. Brian put his arm around her. Even in the terrifying chaos of the moment, her touch felt wonderful. "We should get to the bridge," Brian suggested in a forced tone that betrayed his continued fear. "Our parents are probably up there. If not, at least the ship's command crew can tell us what's going on."

"Do you think Fenner went crazy?" Kim asked as they walked cautiously around the dead smoldering body.

"I don't know what's going on, but I'm sure my dad's going to help fix things," Brian said. "He used to be an Adherent soldier way back before he even knew my mom. If they need help, he'll give it."

Brian and Kim slowly made their way through the embattled hallway, stepping over the dismembered bodies of colonists and soldiers on their way to the bridge. It was a scene out of Brian's worst nightmares. Blood splattered the wall.

Shot-out lights flickered menacingly, temporarily revealing the scope of the carnage. Hell had seeped over into his world.

Brian looked back to see that Kim's eyes were closed. *Good,* he thought. *She can't handle this kind of stuff.* Brian reminded himself just how close he was to losing control of his bladder and felt bad for putting down her capacity to endure trauma. As he stepped over a colonist body that lacked a head, Brian quickly looked down at the nametag to make sure it wasn't anyone he knew. It wasn't, but the sight of a human neck topped with unrecognizable gore churned his stomach. He started to feel like he was going to pass out, just like Maleek had only minutes before.

When Kim opened her eyes to find out why Brian was slouching over, she found herself staring directly at the beheaded colonist whose entrails leaked onto the deck plating. She broke free of Brian's grasp and let out the most unnerving wail he had ever heard. She covered her face with her hands and backed against the wall away from the headless body. Now that the sound of gunfire had faded, her cries echoed down the ship's corridors with terrible power. Brian, whose state of shock had been warded off by Kim's piercing cry, fumbled for her hand and pulled her close. "We've gotta keep moving, Kim!"

Brian moved along the wall toward the bridge careful to avoid any bodies lying in the middle of the corridor. Kim followed. Not because she wanted to, but because Brian pulled her arm with enough force to wrench it from its socket if met with resistance. As they neared the bridge, Brian bent down and picked up a pulse rifle from the stiff arm of a soldier's dead body. The glowing lights of the bridge could be seen up ahead through the darkness. Shouts could be heard as well, although Brian could not make out what was being said. He took a deep breath and walked towards the unknown. *God protect me,* he pleaded. *Give me the strength I need.* So far Brian had been pleased with his reaction to such a serious situation, although he still worried that fear may overwhelm his body at any moment. "Stay here," he ordered in a hushed voice to Kim. He didn't want her getting in the way up on the bridge. It may be a desperate struggle up there.

"No, I want to stay with you," she hissed back. Her face still streamed with tears, but she seemed to be lucid enough.

"Fine, but just stay back a bit."

Kim complied, tagging along behind Brian as he neared the commotion. Brian raised his weapon to the ready position, just like he had seen Adherent soldiers do a thousand times. As he thought about the Apostate terrorists who must be trying to take over the ship, an incredible surge of anger and adrenaline crashed through his body. Now it was his turn to punish them for defying God and attacking his family. Now Brian would become a soldier for the Church.

At this point, Brian was confident that he could face down a hundred ICLF terrorists and a thousand Fenners. But as he approached the open doorway leading up to the command deck, his father's voice disarmed him completely.

"Put it down," Brian heard his father say to an unknown enemy.

"D-Dad?" Brian stammered as he lowered his weapon and carelessly entered the bridge.

Brian's legs nearly buckled as his eyes took in the scene. Fenner stood at the ship's helm, pointing a blaster pistol at the captain's head. Beside the captain, three Adherent soldiers stood with their weapons raised. Just centimeters away from the barrels of these weapons stood four colonists. They, in turn, had their weapons raised at the soldiers. Aware that he was in the midst of a full-scale mutiny, Brian pointed his rifle at the back of the closest colonist and slowly entered the room. As the rest of the bridge came into Brian's left peripheral view, he noticed more figures pointing weapons at the soldiers. It was his father, mother, Luke and Rachel.

"Dad?" Brian yelled in a confused tone as he lingered near the doorway.

"Brian?" his father responded in the same, surprised pitch.

Brian lowered his weapon only slightly. Then, as he realized what was happening, raised it again, this time at his father's chest.

"Brian, get out of here," David Bishop yelled, still not taking his eyes off the soldiers. "Do it now!"

Brian's arms shook as they struggled to hold up the weapon. "No," he stated coldly, gritting his teeth.

Fenner's booming laugh filled the bridge. "Quite the little standoff we have here, huh Bishop?" He didn't seem to care that the Captain had a pistol pointed at his face.

"Shut up, Fenner!" Brian's father yelled. "This isn't funny!"

"Get out of here now, Brian!" Brian's mother and Rachel ordered simultaneously.

Kim, who had been lingering outside the bridge, was drawn to her mother's voice.

"Mom?" she cried, pushing past Brian into the room. The sudden movement surprised one of the Adherent soldiers, who had been pressing on the trigger of his rifle in anticipation of the death that was sure to come at any moment. He instinctively shot at the moving object.

Nobody expected such a reckless act under such dire circumstances. The soldiers and colonists watched in awe as a single blue bolt from the pulse rifle passed through the air and struck Kim squarely in the shoulder. Even Fenner turned his attention away from the soldiers for a moment.

A fine spray of red mist shot from Kim's back, hitting Brian in the side of the face. The blood took its time, floating through the air as if to signal the coming violence. Within a millisecond, Brian experienced an eternity of torture as Kim's small, fragile body fell against his own. His next action came without thought. Brian swung his rifle in the direction of the blue bolt and fired. It was on full-auto. The massive kick of the weapon threw him back against a blinking control panel. Blue lightning spat from the mouth of the gun like fire from a raging dragon. Through the flashing, Brian saw two of the soldiers explode in a cataclysm of armor, lightning and blood. The back of Brian's head slammed into the control panel and he fell to the floor next to Kim.

The colonists quickly capitalized on Brian's actions by shooting the surviving soldiers. Fenner smiled as he dispatched the Captain. As Brian began to slip out of consciousness, he saw his mother frantically working on Kim's wounded body.

"Rodriguez says all of the other sectors are secure," Brian heard a voice say. "We have three dead in Yellow sector." The words began to run together in jumbled, incoherent sounds. As his world was swallowed up by blackness, Brian felt two muscular arms slip under his back and lift him effortlessly into the air. It was his father. Sleep came next.

CHAPTER 10

▼

REVELATIONS

Traitors. Mutineers. Murderers. Of all the terrible labels Brian could think of, none stung harder than "Apostates." His parents were Apostates, and so was every other colonist onboard the *Apostle 4*. Only the Academy children and the Adherent soldiers, most of whom were dead, willingly bore the Eye of God. As his parents struggled to explain their treacherous secrets to Brian, all he could think of was his salvation. He had murdered two Adherent soldiers; Damnation was inevitable.

Four of the Academy students, Kim included, sat next to Brian in what used to be the Adherent captain's personal quarters. The rest of the Academy students had been put to sleep before the mutiny. They would awake to find their world drastically changed. As for the other children onboard, there wasn't a need to explain anything. Most were straight from the Enclaves. They had known about their status all along.

Brian's father explained that it had taken years to coordinate such a massive and secretive project. David Bishop, Bill Collins, Fenner, and several other High Council members had issued hundreds of fake IDs, work permits, and immigration forms in a well-organized attempt to fool the Church. So far, the plan had worked extremely well, apart from Fenner's refusal to follow the timetable for the mutiny. Brian and the Academy children had been raised in a world totally different from the one inhabited by their parents. Brian's recent suspicions had been justified.

"I'm sorry, Brian, there was no other way," his father apologized. "We had to raise you like a normal Citizen. Doing otherwise would have attracted a dangerous level of attention."

Brian said nothing. Kim, who wore a crisp, new sling around her wounded arm, leaned against his shoulder as they sat listening to their parents' excuses and apologies.

"We wanted to tell you eventually," Brian's mother continued. "We just never expected you to become," she paused for a moment, obviously struggling to find the right words, "such a *model* Citizen."

"That's what Minister Chang was for," Bill stated from the chair he was sitting in. He had been wounded in the leg while securing Blue sector with John and the other colonists prior to making his way to the bridge. "We wanted you to have a teacher who'd undermine Church doctrine without making it appear obvious. Kim? Do you understand what we're saying?"

Kim didn't show any signs of even hearing her father. Neither did Brian. They were both still in shock. Maleek, who had remained unconscious for close to an hour, was simply brought to his cryotube and put to sleep. He didn't even seem to remember the dead body or sounds of gunfire. Brian thought him to be the luckiest person in the universe at the moment.

"It's just too much, Bill," David whispered to his friend. "They can't deal with all of this right now."

Bill turned away from Brian and Kim and replied, "I know, but we can't delay this trip any longer. We have to put them to sleep soon. Johnson said he's already received a transmission from Space Command asking us about our status."

"They'll find you," Brian spoke. Everyone looked surprised to hear him break his stubborn silence.

"What was that, sweetie?" his mother asked, leaning closer.

"I said they'll find you," he repeated in an angry, yet controlled voice. Nobody seemed to know how to react to his threatening words.

"Brian," his father started.

"Don't," Brian said, cutting him off. "I don't want to hear any more excuses. You, I mean, *WE*, are going to pay for what we've done. I'm going to pay for what I've done. It's only right."

"You did the right thing, son."

"I killed them!" Brian screamed, suddenly breaking down. The yell startled Kim from her grief and painkiller-induced trance. She started sobbing again. Rachel immediately bent down to hug her daughter.

"Don't touch me!" Kim screamed in a frantic tone that echoed Brian's.

"We're sorry, baby," Bill pleaded as he knelt in front of Kim. "You've got to understand. It had to be this way."

"It didn't have to be this way," Brian argued. "Things could have been fine on the colony. You didn't have to take over the ship!"

"Sooner or later they would have discovered who these people actually are, who we are," his father insisted. "It was only a matter of time before they killed us, just like they killed everyone back in Chicago. And besides, we're not even going to Tau Ceti."

"Where are we going then?"

"Don't know," Brian's father confessed. "We're setting the ship's computer on autopilot and going to sleep. Right now, we've got several programmers making sure that it functions like it's supposed to. It's going to take a long trip to get us far enough away from Adherent space."

Upon hearing this new information, Brian's torment reached a new level of agony. He hated his life. He hated it even more than he hated his parents. Only three months before, everything had been great. He was well on his way to becoming a Citizen. More importantly, he was one of the Saved. Now, he was worse than an ICLF terrorist. Even if he were able to rejoin the Church somehow, God would never forgive him for being a traitorous murderer. He was damned for all of eternity, and it was all his parents' fault. They were worse than the colonists who were now sleeping in the cryotubes. Those colonists from the Enclaves had rejected the Church because they believed in their own God or gods. Brian's parents were atheists, the worst kind of Apostates. They didn't even have a god. That was why they had no qualms about posing as loyal Adherent Citizens. That's why they wanted to get as far away from the Church as possible.

At this moment, the worst possible moment for such an entrance, Fenner walked into the room. "So, how's my little hero?" he laughed, moving towards Brian. "Still a little upset I see. Well, as soon as we get this thing off your skull, I guarantee you'll feel a lot better!" Fenner bent down and attempted to run his long fingers over the tattoo on Brian's forehead. The Eye of God was the "thing" Fenner was referring to.

"Get away," Brian spat, as he slapped the hand.

"Is there a reason why you're here, Fenner?" Brian's father asked. He grabbed his colleague's outstretched arm and roughly pushed it away from Brian.

"Always about business, aren't you, Bishop?" Fenner sneered. "Well, for your information, I am here for a reason."

"Let's hear it," demanded Brian's mother.

"We've got three live Adherent soldiers in the armory. I'm just letting you know that I've decided to throw them out the airlock."

"You're what?" Bill asked.

"The airlock," Fenner matter-of-factly reiterated.

"No, you're not!" Brian's mother insisted.

"I'm afraid it's already been decided." Fenner spoke into his communicator, saying, "Go ahead and bring them to the bridge. I want to see them before they go."

"Fenner, you're not throwing them out the airlock," Brian's father commanded. "We'll put them on one of the life-pods and send them out into space. With any luck, a search and rescue ship should get to them in about a month. At least they'll get a chance to survive."

Fenner seemed to physically reel back at the idea of such a peaceful solution. "Unwise. I thought we were going to make it look like the ship was destroyed by a reactor breach. How are we supposed to do that if survivors inform the Church otherwise?"

"The reactor breach idea's unnecessary. By the time the Adherents get out here, we'll be too far out of the solar system to track anyway," David Bishop reasoned.

"I disagree," Fenner stated bluntly. His voice took on a more serious tone.

Luke, who had been sitting on the table a few paces away, visibly tightened the grip on his pulse rifle. Fenner was known to get violent when he got angry.

"We're not killing them," the others in the room insisted.

Fenner laughed. "I thought we all agreed to share command of this little expedition. Have I all of a sudden lost my say?"

"No, Fenner," the older woman Brian had seen back on the shuttle a few weeks ago replied. He now knew her to be Alice Kirkpatrick, an important Council member from London. She was an Apostate, just like his parents. The kind face, which had greeted Brian on an almost daily basis during the trip, now melted away under the crushing twin weights of stress and responsibility. "But you don't dictate policy without the consent of the group," she said, finishing her point to Fenner.

"You're lucky you haven't lost something else, Titus," Luke muttered from behind Fenner.

"That's right," Brian's father added. "It's your fault things got so bloody. We could have incapacitated the soldiers without much of a fight. You're lucky we don't push you out an airlock."

Brian expected Fenner to get angry at such an aggressive remark, but instead, the High Councilor just looked more amused. An armed colonist brought the captured Adherent soldiers to the doorway and Fenner dragged one inside. It was the man Brian had talked to in Cryopod A a few nights before. The soldier's leg was bleeding profusely. The bandage around it did little to cover the wound. Brian's mother immediately bent down to look at it. Although the soldier was obviously frightened, he didn't resist her inspection.

"I need to get him to Medical," she said. "He's lost a lot of blood."

"I'm glad you feel the need to treat these monsters with such compassion," Fenner said, addressing the room. "Tell me, Jill, do you think he'd show you the same courtesy if your roles were reversed?"

Nobody responded to Fenner's question. Everyone knew that the answer was probably a resounding "no." After a moment of silence, David Bishop spoke up. "It doesn't matter. We're not like them. That's why we're on this ship. We should take them with us. That way, we can still make it look like the ship's been destroyed. They won't cause a problem. Just put them in cryosleep."

Fenner surveyed his audience in an attempt to gauge their reactions to David Bishop's proposal. Quickly seeing that he had lost the argument, he let go of the soldier's collar and backed away. "Fine. Have it your way, Bishop. Just don't expect me to feel sorry for you if they become a problem." With that, Fenner pushed his way towards the door. Before exiting, he turned back. "We've got plenty of room for additional passengers. I hear there are twelve empty cryotubes in Pod A."

An hour later, Brian watched several colonists lower the wounded soldier into his cryotube several rows down from his own. His mother had treated the wounded leg extremely well. The soldier now slept peacefully under the powerful sedatives she had issued him. He had no knowledge of being put in a cryotube, a fact which Brian envied. As Brian sat on the edge of his own tube, Jade ran some last minute medical scans. On the tube next to him, Rachel silently brushed Kim's flowing brown hair. Both mother and daughter wore the simple white robes that were issued to passengers for cryosleep. Kim's robes were far too big for her. They completely covered her dangling feet.

"Hold still, Bri," Jade ordered as she checked his heart-rate.

Brian complied, although he said nothing to his sister.

"It's been quite a day for you, hasn't it?" she asked.

"You knew everything, didn't you?" Brian responded with a question of his own.

"Yes." Jade continued her work.

"How long?" he asked.

"Since I was about your age," she revealed. "Mom and Dad took a big risk when they told me. I could have gotten all of these people killed if I said anything."

"You should have said something," Brian stated coldly.

Jade slammed her scanner down on the cryotube. She looked like she was going to scold Brian, but as she confronted his guilt-ridden eyes, her posture relaxed. "I thought about it a lot."

"Why didn't you?"

Jade shrugged. "I don't know. I guess I just figured out that I loved Mom and Dad more than the Church."

"More than God?" Brian asked, pressing the issue.

"At first, no," Jade admitted. "But as time went on, I began to think like them. Now, I don't even think there is a God, at least not one like we were raised to believe in. Sure, maybe there is some divine being out there controlling everything, but it certainly wouldn't be like the *Final Testament* describes."

"It? Don't you mean He?" Brian attempted to correct his sister.

She smiled. "Whatever, Brian. My point is that, in time, I began to see the Church for what it is: a brutal regime that rules through fear more than faith. That's not the way of any divine being, Brian. That's the way of Evil."

"This is evil," Brian said. "What we're doing. What you're doing."

Jade stood up and gazed down at her younger brother. "I hope you change your mind," she said. "There's an entire universe out there that you're ignoring." She playfully rustled his hair. "You're a smart kid, Bishop, smarter than I was at your age. You'll come around."

No I won't, Brian thought. He looked past Jade, down towards the soldiers being put into the empty cryotubes. He desperately wanted to run over and free them. Together, Brian and the soldiers would take back the ship for the Church. Maybe that would atone for his sins.

"Take a couple of minutes, Brian," Jade said. "I'm going to get Mom and Dad. They'll want to talk to you one more time before you sleep."

"Don't bother," Brian muttered.

Jade either didn't hear him or chose to ignore his suggestion. Once she left, Kim shuffled over and sat next to him. "What are we going to do?" she asked.

"I don't know," he replied. "There's nothing we can do right now."

"My mom says it's time for me to go to sleep," she said.

Brian looked over her shoulder and saw Rachel watching them. She was smiling, although she turned away once Brian caught her eyes.

"I know. As soon as my parents come back with Jade, I'll have to go to sleep, too," he said.

"Thanks for saving me Brian," Kim said. "I love you." She wrapped her uninjured arm around Brian's neck and gently kissed him on the cheek.

Brian was too surprised to reciprocate her affection. *She loves me.* The thought of Kim's love filled Brian with a giddy warmth that chased away his feelings of hate, guilt and anxiety. Although he couldn't summon the courage to tell her that he loved her too, Brian managed enough presence of mind to throw his arms around her. After what had seemed like an eternity of bliss, Kim let go and pulled herself away. She gave Brian one last smile, then shuffled over to her cryotube. Brian watched as her mother lowered the tube's lid. Within seconds, Kim was sleeping the deep sleep of stasis.

When Brian's parents came to put him to sleep, he was already lying down in his cryotube. Brian didn't respond to his parents' continued attempts to sooth his wounded soul. He still thought of them as traitors to the Church as well as their son, but he no longer felt the worry that had plagued him in the hours since the mutiny. All he felt was the warmth. As long as Kim was next to him, Brian knew he could withstand any trials that came along. Even damnation. Even the uncertainty that came with being the child of Apostates.

A Dreamless Sleep

After rendezvousing with another hijacked colony transport named *The Righteous 1*, *The Apostle 4*, which the colonists quickly renamed *The Phoenix*, steadily picked up speed as its human cargo slept in a timeless, dreamless state. At the outer edges of the solar system, the two ships activated their stardrives and rapidly fled the iron grip of the Church. The sleeping colonists couldn't defend themselves if they were discovered, so the navigation computers were instructed to carefully avoid the inhabited systems closest to Sol. Once the ships traveled twenty light years beyond Adherent space, the onboard computers would begin searching for a suitable planet to colonize. The specifications programmed by the colonists were strict; the planet must be similar in size to Earth, have a suitable climate for agriculture, and most importantly, be void of intelligent life. The colonists would not be able to count on any supplies from Earth. Once landed, they would have to produce food and fend for themselves. A dry, dusty planet like Tau Ceti 3 would be too difficult to survive on.

The A.I. systems of two colony ships looked for 162 years before finding a planet that fit the rigid specifications set down by their sleeping masters. The time debt for such a trip was staggering: over 900 years. When the colonists awakened from their long sleep, nearly a millennium had passed back on Earth since they had left.

The colony ships began to slow down as they neared the fourth planet orbiting an average sized G class star. The star had been catalogued back in the twenty first century as J-64. It was almost 332 light years from Earth.

As the slowing transports neared the small, blue, white and green marble ahead, long-dormant heaters began to warm the interior of the ships. One by one, the colonists were awakened from their ancient slumber, starting with the members of the new Colonial Council. The children were the last to be revived. As Brian opened his eyes for the first time in centuries, he felt a sudden urge to vomit. He had cryosickness, a common ailment among those who had been in stasis too long. Brian struggled to fight back the overwhelming sense of nausea. After a few moments of agonizing concentration, he started to feel better. Then, as he slowly remembered the events that had transpired prior to his going to sleep, the sickness returned. Brian turned sharply and vomited into his bed.

CHAPTER 11

▼

RESURRECTION

The next thing Brian knew, his mother's soft hands were wrapped around his forehead. When he had finished throwing up, she pulled him to the side of the cryotube that had not been soiled. Brian didn't resist as her warm hands stroked his sweat-soaked hair. He felt as if at any moment consciousness would leave him again. In fact, he longed for the dark oblivion of cryosleep, where pain did not exist. Unable to return to that merciful state, Brian closed his eyes tightly and savored one blissful moment of weakness in the dark abyss of his mother's arms.

"Let's get him out of there, Jill," Brian heard a gruff male voice suggest. It was Dr. Anderson, the chief medical officer onboard the ship.

Brian felt himself being lifted out of the tube and laid on the cold floor. He still refused to open his eyes. Even the dim lights of Pod A seemed blinding compared to the total darkness Brian's eyes were used to.

"Just lay still and relax, Bri," his mother suggested. "You're sick from being asleep so long."

Brian replied with an incoherent grunt of affirmation, or at least he thought he did. His whole reality still seemed like some sort of cruel nightmare in which he was only a spectator. How long had they been asleep? Where was the ship now? A million questions swirled through Brian's spinning mind as Dr. Anderson ran body scans while his mother issued hyposprays packed with a multitude of medications. Out of all these questions, none motivated Brian to worry more than what had happened to Kim.

"Kim," Brian managed to spit out. The very effort made him want to vomit again.

"She's fine, Brian," his mother insisted. "Dr. Chen is just checking over her wound in Medical to make sure it's going to heal right.

The wound. Brian remembered it well. All cellular activity stopped in cryostasis, even healing. Kim's wound, although centuries old, would still be fresh and painful. As Brian fully came to his senses, the freshness of his own wounds began to plague his mind. He sat up.

"Whoa, take it easy there, Mr. Bishop," Dr. Anderson suggested. "Just lay back down."

Brian opened his eyes and fought against the pressure of the old man's hand on his chest. "Get off of me. I don't need your help."

"Brain," his mother said.

"I'm fine. Just leave me alone," Brian insisted. The time for weakness had passed.

"Suit yourself, soldier," Anderson relented, backing off to give his defiant patient some room. Brian's mother couldn't seem to let go of her son, even as he glared at the hand she had placed on his arm.

"I'm fine," Brian reiterated, bringing himself to his full height. He wobbled for a moment, trying to steady himself against the side of his cryotube. *Please, God, give me your strength*, he prayed. There was no telling if God would listen to a murderer and a traitor. Still, Brian hoped for the best. Maybe God would pity him.

Brian's eyes began to adjust to the dimmed lights of Pod A. Several colonists shuffled around in a disorientated state. They looked like Brian felt. A few more sat on the edge of their cryotubes, lacking the strength to walk. A few rows down, Maleek's mother quietly talked to her son. Brian couldn't hear the conversation, but judging from the boy's stoic facial expression, it pertained to his status as a child of Apostates. Prior to the hijacking, Brian had thought of Maleek as an adversary. Now he saw him as a kindred spirit.

Brian rested on the edge of his tube, gathering strength for the walk over to Maleek. Seeing as how Kim was in Medical with Jade, Maleek represented the only bastion of righteousness amid a sea of heresy. Hopefully, he did not accept his mother's beliefs.

As Brian rested, he noticed his mother still standing by in case he toppled back over. He refused to acknowledge her dutiful concern, though Dr. Anderson had already moved on to other patients.

The hushed silence of Pod A was suddenly broken by the harsh voice of a young colonist man carrying a pulse rifle. He stood over the open cryotube occupied by one of the captured soldiers.

"Come on, get out of there," the man ordered. "Move your ass before I shoot it off!"

The soldier he was yelling at gingerly lifted himself out of the tube. It was the Corporal with the wounded leg. The colonist man grabbed him by the collar of his white sleeping robes and attempted to yank him out of the tube.

The soldier cried in pain as he grabbed his leg. Brian wanted to rush the colonist man and kill him where he stood, but his mother beat him there.

"Get off of him!" she ordered the colonist.

The man complied without argument.

"Luke!" she yelled toward the opposite end of the room.

Brian didn't realize Luke had been around. He craned his neck in search of his cousin.

"What's up, Aunt Jill?" Luke asked from Brian's left.

"Help me get this soldier out of his tube. I need to look at his leg."

Luke glanced at the colonist holding the rifle and seemed to process what was going on. "Why don't you go help Harris in shuttle bay two," he suggested to the man.

The man glared at the Adherent solider, then did as he was asked. Once he had left the room, Luke and Brian's mother helped the wounded soldier out of his tube.

"Don't worry about it, Corporal," Luke mentioned as he gently set the man down. "Nobody's gonna hurt you. They're just angry."

"No kidding," the soldier snorted with a laugh. "I'm surprised I've made it this far."

"You shouldn't be," Brian's mother insisted. "We're not like that. Well, most of us aren't."

Brian wondered if by "most of us" his mother was trying to distinguish herself from Fenner. The High Councilor would have killed all three soldiers without hesitation. Even worse, he would have done it with glee.

"What about Decker and Murphy?" the Corporal inquired, referring to his comrades.

"They're locked up in one of the maintenance areas until we figure out what to do with them," Luke revealed.

The soldier laughed and shook his head. Brian couldn't understand why he thought it was funny. "If you're worried about us trying anything, don't," the soldier insisted. "I'm assuming we're not in Adherent space anymore."

"That's correct," Luke confirmed.

"How far out?"

"Not sure exactly," Luke admitted. "But we're far. They're trying to determine just where the A.I. system's dropped us. I haven't been up to the bridge yet to ask."

"Doesn't matter," the soldier said. "We've got nothing to gain by trying to take the ship back, if that's what you're worried about."

"I know that," Luke said. He smiled as he seemed to process the soldier's vulnerable predicament. "I'm a captain in an Adherent Intelligence Unit out of Atlanta. Unlike most of the people onboard this ship, I don't see you as faceless monsters."

"Don't be so sure," the soldier stated. "We … well, I've done some things over the years I'm not proud of."

"So have I," said Luke, his voice taking on a depressed tone.

Brian couldn't believe his ears. An Adherent soldier surrendering so easily? Agreeing with an enemy? It was unthinkable! Brian stood up and moved away from the conversation. He didn't want to hear any more fraternization between his cousin and the soldier. As Brian walked by Maleek toward Pod A's main viewport, he couldn't help noting how well the boy seemed to be dealing with his mother's news. Although Brian tried not to stare, he caught the icy look of resolve that crossed Maleek's face. In an instant, the clumsy, yet brilliant kid transformed from boy to man as he realized his entire existence had been a farce. Brian knew the feeling well, yet kept his distance until Maleek's mother left the room. As he waited for her to leave, Brian sat down in front of the viewport and attempted to block out the sounds of the other colonists in the room.

The twin moons outside the window seemed to hang motionless in orbit around an unseen planet off to the right. The closest moon was a bright, chalky gray, just like the one back home. The other was a dark smooth mass, which peeked out form behind the bulk of its larger sibling. The stars beyond formed alien shapes on the black canvas of space. Perhaps, at any moment, the thin, jagged outline of an Adherent warship would appear and rescue him from the ruthless hijackers who now controlled his destiny. Brian wondered if he could see the warm yellow glow of the sun somewhere among the unfamiliar points of light. Maybe the ship was too far away now to even see the sun. Maybe Brian was too far away to ever be rescued. The thought of being forever marooned on a godless alien planet populated by Apostates terrified him, although it seemed a fitting punishment for his sins. He felt an immediate need to determine what star system the ship had reached. The sick feeling had largely gone away now thanks to his mother's treatment, and Brian's rampant curiosity infused him with a new sense of strength. He stood up, turned away from the window, and walked through Pod A towards the door.

"Brain, honey, where are you going?" his mother asked in a concerned voice. She was still working on the soldier's leg.

"The bridge," he muttered in response. He didn't know why he even bothered to keep his mother informed. She didn't deserve to know his agenda. As Brian passed the now solitary Maleek, he asked, "Want to come with me?" The Academy children had to stay together now that they were the only faithful members of the Church within God knows how many light years of Earth. Brian was determined to keep them from becoming tainted by their parents' corrosive influence. Maleek, who looked emotionally intact, although a bit overwhelmed, nodded in affirmation and stood up to join Brian.

"You know what happened?" Brian asked coldly. There was no mistaking what he meant by the question.

"Maleek nodded again. This time it looked like he was going to start crying. Maybe he wasn't taking the news so well after all. Brian didn't blame him.

Come on," Brian urged in a commanding voice. Somebody had to maintain presence of mind between the two of them.

"Brian, just wait a minute and I'll join you," his mother called from behind. Brian continued walking, hoping that Maleek wouldn't look back in a moment of weakness.

"I told you, I'm fine," he muttered.

"Well, are you going to go up there with that robe on?" she asked.

Brain looked down at his white, flowing garb. He hadn't even noticed that Maleek and almost everyone else in the room had already changed into their normal clothes. Brian cursed himself. *I have to be reminded of everything*, he thought. "Where are my clothes?" he asked with a strained voice.

"They're still in a locker under your bunk," his mother replied. "It's unlocked if you don't want to wait for me."

Without so much as an affirmation, Brian turned and left the room.

Brian's hurried stride slowed to a shuffle as he retraced the path he and Kim had taken from their room to the bridge during the mutiny. Although he remembered wearing the comfortable, white cryosleep robes for only a few hours, his normal clothes now felt strange as he walked. It was as if his body somehow remembered wearing the cryosleep robes during the countless years he had slept. Brian looked down at the gray pants and jacket he now wore. They were what all Adherent children were required to wear, girls as well as boys. Once a student graduated to the Senior Academy, or in the case of most children, entered job training, he or she was permitted to wear more colorful clothing befitting of their social class. Only upper-level Academy students were allowed to wear black, the color worn by government officials and military personnel. Brian had always looked forward to the day when he would be allowed to wear black, the color that his father wore. Now, he didn't want to have anything in common with his father. Fenner wore black too. Red wasn't any better, since Chang's Minister robes were red. Brian sighed as he thought about it. His entire perception of reality was decimated thanks to the treachery of his parents. Every symbol of the Church had been desecrated by their deceit.

Brian looked over at Maleek as they continued toward the bridge. He wondered if Maleek was thinking about similar things. It was impossible to read his face.

"What are you thinking about?" Brian asked quietly as he suspiciously monitored two women passing by. He didn't want any of the Apostate colonists to hear him. He felt more like their enemy now than ever before, even though he had played an instrumental role in winning the ship for them.

"I don't know," confessed Maleek.

This cryptic response frustrated Brian. "How can you not know?"

"I mean, there's just so much to think about, I'm not sure quite how to answer."

"How about starting with what we're going to do next?" Brian suggested.

"There's nothing we can do, Brian!"

"Sure there is. We've just gotta be smart and wait for our chance. There has to be a way to contact the Church."

Maleek stopped in mid-stride and looked at Brian as if he were crazy. "What are you talking about? You aren't actually considering betraying our families, are you? How could you do that?"

"Would you shut up?" Brian demanded as he placed a firm hand over Maleek's mouth. "You're going to get us in trouble if you don't keep your voice down." Brian waited to speak again until two female colonists passed by them in the narrow corridor. "We can't just let them get away with what they did."

Maleek stepped back and swatted away Brian's hand. "If the Church somehow found us, they'd kill everyone onboard this ship, including me and you."

Brian paused for a moment and thought about the situation. Maleek was right. The Church would kill everyone onboard the ship, including the three captured soldiers. *So be it,* Brian thought. *If I have to die to pay for my sins, then fine.*

"It's the right thing to do," he argued.

"I don't know what's right or wrong anymore," admitted Maleek. "But I know that trying to contact the Church is a stupid idea."

Brian was getting tired of fighting with Maleek. It was apparent that he may not be such a great ally after all. "Let's just get to the bridge and find out where we are, first."

"Fine."

Brian half expected to see the bloodstains and pulse rifles littering the bridge floor, but as he entered the room, he noticed only the crowd of colonists diligently working at the computer terminals. Near the main communications terminal, three former High Council members, Alice Kirkpatrick, Keith Raasch and Ellena Yolanni, appeared to be discussing something important. Fenner wasn't on the bridge. Neither was Brian's father.

As Brian and Maleek sheepishly walked in, a few of the colonists looked up from their work and smiled warmly. Brian glared back at them. *They're only smiling at me because they know what I did up here,* he reasoned. *They probably think I'm one of them now.* Raasch, who Brian had seen talking to Maleek's mother on several occasions, noticed their entrance and broke off his conversation with his colleagues. Maleek immediately smiled and approached the man. Brian headed off in the opposite direction, toward the main viewport at the front of the bridge. Nobody followed him.

When faced with the breathtaking sight out the main viewport, Brian almost completely forgot about his anger. Ahead, just a few thousand kilometers away, the pristine blue and white facade of a virgin world looked back at him. Unlike the pictures Brian had seen of Earth from space, this alien world contained swirling, organic features wholly unfamiliar to him. Beneath the white clouds, green patches of land could be made out. They looked like emerald islands jutting outward from an endless sea of lapis. To the right side of the viewport, another colony ship could be seen hovering just a few kilometers ahead of the *Phoenix*. Brian had overheard one of the colonists say something about another ship before he entered cryosleep, but hadn't really processed the information until now. As he surveyed the other ship, Brian wondered if there was someone onboard like himself, someone whose entire existence had been destroyed by his or her parents' terrible secret. Brian also wondered how many Adherent soldiers had died onboard the other ship at the hands of the Apostates.

"Beautiful, isn't it?" a voice spoke up from behind. It was Brian's father. "We've decided to call it Elysium, like in the old Roman myths," David Bishop continued, placing his hands on his son's shoulders. Brian tensed, but didn't try to wiggle away.

"It figures that you'd choose a pagan name," Brian finally stated coldly.

His father sighed, but didn't seem angry. "We had a couple of votes for Eden, but most of us wanted a name that wouldn't remind us so much of the Church. They've been striving to create an Eden back on Earth for over a century, and have created nothing but Hell in the process."

Rather than snap back at his father's heretical remarks, Brian resolved to get the information he had come to the bridge for in the first place. "Where exactly are we?" he asked.

"We're about 332 light years from Earth and almost 300 from Adherent-controlled space."

The news dealt a killing blow to Brian's simmering hope. There was no chance for any justice now. The Apostates had successfully gotten away with murder. Even worse, Brian would never be able to return home from such a distance. He would be forever exiled.

Brian's father noticed his son's tear-streaked reflection in the viewport glass and hugged him from behind. "You'll see," he repeated several times. "You'll see that it was worth it, son. This is our home. It's meant to be."

Brian looked down at Elysium one last time before shutting his eyes and fighting off his father's embrace. No home, not even a paradise, could alleviate the Hellish agony of guilt tearing apart his conscience. *Never.*

CHAPTER 12

▼

PLANETFALL

"My mom says that there are these huge bird things that walk on two legs and eat off the tops of the highest trees," Kim said to Brian as they took their seats on the planetary shuttle docked in the *Phoenix's* main hanger bay. Despite the interesting nature of the information, Kim's voice contained none of its usual excitement. Brian nodded as he made sure not to bump her left arm, which was cradled in a crisp white sling. In the week since awakening from cryosleep, Brian and Kim had not talked much, although they spent almost every waking hour together. Even though the rest of the children onboard the ship had come by several times to visit, Brian and Kim had refused to even leave their quarters, despite their parents' suggestions that they get out and enjoy their peers. Minister Chang too, had unsuccessfully tried to get them to leave their room and failed. Brain had felt proud when Kim refused to even come out into the corridor to greet her former mentor.

Kim's father, Fenner, John Rodriguez and several other colonists from both colony transports had been the first to visit the surface of the new planet. Although several probes had been previously sent by both colony transports, the colonists didn't feel comfortable relocating to the planet's surface until a scouting party had reported it to be suitable for habitation.

Elysium was a world very much like Earth, although it had a slightly smaller mass and fewer large bodies of land. Countless rivers crisscrossed the four major continents located in the temperate zones around the equator, resulting in an incredibly lush ecosystem dominated by sweeping grasslands and forests of giant conifers and ferns. The gravitational difference between Elysium and Earth wasn't extreme, but many colonists would report feeling slightly lighter for the first few weeks they spent on-planet. Brian had already heard many rumors about the flocks of giant reptiles that glided through the air like birds, and the herds of enormous plant-eating mammals that grazed the open grasslands. Perhaps in a few generations the colonists too would see a slight effect on their height.

Before the colonists had even been awaken from their sleep, the A.I. systems onboard the ships had determined that no advanced civilizations lived on the planet. Nevertheless, the colonists breathed a sigh of relief when they concluded that nothing smarter than a lemur back on Earth lived on Elysium. The most intelligent creatures encountered so far were some squirrel-like mammals that lived in the forests and seemed to be equivalent to lower primates in terms of intellectual skills. Normally, the prospect of encountering new species of animals on an alien planet would have thrilled Brian and Kim. There hadn't been a wild animal living on Earth for over a century. But now, as they boarded the shuttle that would carry them down to their new home on a mid-sized continent in the southern part of the northern hemisphere, they could think of nothing besides the safe confines of their Cathedral back home.

After Kim's statement about the bird creatures, she and Brian returned to silence. Everyone else onboard the shuttle was chatting excitedly about what lay ahead. Brian simply blocked out the noise. A few rows in front of him sat Murphy and Decker, two of the former Adherent soldiers. The Corporal, Hudson was his last name, was already on the planet's surface with Luke. The colonists had decided to let the soldiers roam freely after determining that they would not present a threat. Still, Brian noticed several colonists who were seated around the shuttle eyeing the men suspiciously, as if at any moment the soldiers were going to stand up and demand that the shuttle fly them back to Earth.

Brian felt a jolt as the shuttle powered up in the hanger. It slowly rose and proceeded to exit the open bay doors into space. As the glowing planet neared his window, Brian noticed that Kim was beginning to shake. Although she had been numbed by recent events, she still retained her fear of heights. Not wanting to hurt her arm, Brian put his hand on her shaking leg. Kim giggled a little at the gesture. She had always been ticklish, especially when it came to her legs and feet. Brian remembered the time back when he and his friend Marcus had held her down and tickled her until she wet her pants. Later, Kim had gotten Brian back by shaving his eyebrows while he slept on her parents' couch. Brian would never forget the look on Minister Petrov's face the next morning when he saw his star pupil staring back at him with no eyebrows. The memory made Brian smile. It was the first time he had smiled since the mutiny.

As the shuttle neared the outer atmosphere of Elysium, Brian caught a glimpse of the planet's third moon on the horizon. Unlike the benign appearance of its brethren, this third, smaller moon bore a rusty tint, almost as vivid as the color of blood. In keeping with the Roman theme, many of the colonists had already started calling it Ares. Brian found the idea of a blood-red moon fitting, considering all of the blood that was on the colonists' hands. He hoped that every night they would look up toward the sky and be reminded of their grievous sins.

The redness of the moon was immediately overwhelmed by the red flames that shot past Brian's window as the shuttle entered the atmosphere. Kim's leg started shaking again as the ship bounced from turbulence. Within seconds, the flames and violent shaking stopped, and Brian's eyes were greeted by a deep blue sky streaked with feathery clouds of icy water vapor. On the other side of the shuttle, the sun's rays filtered in through the viewports, bathing the cabin in a warm, celestial light. Before the passengers had time to squint, the muffled whiteness of a cloud blanketed the window. A hushed silence fell over the cabin as the passengers eagerly awaited their first view of their new home. Even Brian held his breath, not quite sure what to expect on the planet's surface.

As the shuttle cleared the large cloud through which it had plummeted, the planet's facade was finally revealed to its new inhabitants. The first impression Brian got was one dominated by the greenest green his eyes could process. Below, a vast plain carpeted the floor of a broad valley. Far off in the distance, rocky, jagged peaks burst upward from the sapphire-colored horizon line, framing the awesome sight below. Although the shuttle was still thousands of meters above the ground, Brian began to make out individual features dotting the landscape. A lone, meandering river cut through the sea of grass, making its way slowly towards the mountains. Throughout the plain, at random intervals, towered huge cylindrical rock formations that looked as if they had been carved millions of years before by some immensely tall architect. *God*, Brian supposed.

The shuttle swooped sharply downward, so quickly that it seemed as if it would scrape its belly on the tall grass. It banked to the left, giving Brian a view of several large beasts plucking leaves from the tips of the tallest trees along the riverbank. The creatures seemed to fit Kim's earlier description of the bird-things. Brian tapped Kim's leg in an attempt to get her attention, but she simply shook her head in a blind refusal to open her eyes.

"Look, Kim. Are those the things your dad was talking about?"

She still refused to open her eyes, but gave a faint "probably" anyway.

A couple of the animals, whatever they were, looked up from their meal to inspect the shuttle as it whizzed by overhead. Brian's eyes stayed fixed on them until he noticed the sheer face of a rocky plateau rapidly approaching his window. At two points in the gray cliff, water spewed over the side, covering the wall in a spray of wet mist. At the last possible moment, the shuttle ascended just enough to clear the plateau's edge, giving Brian a view of the settlement that would serve as the heart of the new colony for the first years of its existence. Although the small cluster of prefabricated metal buildings were intended to be the base of operations for the new colony, it still looked like little more than a rough encampment. It would be another two weeks or so before all of the cargo pods were offloaded from the orbiting colony transports. Once this feat was accomplished, the colonists would leave the ships in a high, steady orbit around one of the moons just in case they were ever needed again.

The group of buildings Brian's shuttle was landing at constituted one of two initial settlements on Elysium. The other settlement, which was populated mostly by colonists from *The Righteous*, was located on the plain at the bottom of the plateau just a few kilometers to the east. Both settlements were situated in close proximity to broad streams running through rich, arable land. The decision to build one of the encampments on top of the plateau was based largely on a concern for the large predatory animals that had been observed stalking the regions to the north. If the predators insisted on attacking the camp on the floor of the valley, the residents could simply retreat to the upper camp until the problem had been dealt with. Once the area had been fully groomed for human habitation, the leaders of the new colony envisioned that the entire valley below would be converted into farmland, although the process would likely take several years or more. In the meantime, the colonists would continue to live off their rations from the ships and attempt to discern exactly what plants and animals could be eaten on Elysium.

Brian's shuttle touched down at the far north end of the bustling *Phoenix* camp, far away from the treacherous drop of the plateau at the southern end of town. Brian immediately noticed that the tall, wavy grass came almost as high as his viewport, and wondered if he would be able to find his way to the camp once off the ship. Thankfully, it looked as if some of the colonists had already cut multiple paths through the grass towards the main encampment. Brian watched out the window as the first colonists from his shuttle got off and made their way down the paths. He was content to stay onboard until everyone had exited. From the safely of the shuttle, it was easy to look out across the large, wide-open spaces. Actually venturing out into such vastness was a different story, however.

"Come on, Brian," urged Kim, who now had her eyes open and appeared eager to explore her surroundings. Brian simply longed to be back onboard the transport in the relative darkness of space.

"Fine, I'm coming," he groaned as she pulled on his jacket with her fully functional arm.

The line of colonists exiting the shuttle politely made room for Brian and Kim in the central aisle. Kim nodded to them in thanks, but Brian simply took his place in line and stared straight ahead. Many of the colonists onboard the shuttle had already gotten their Eyes of God removed from their foreheads, confirming their status as defiant Apostates. Every time Brian looked at the bare forehead of one of his shipmates, it reminded him that he was among people who hated everything he stood for. What made it worse was that they treated him so kindly, as if he were a creature to be pitied. *You're the ones who should be pitied*, he thought whenever he looked at one of them. Even as Brian walked down the aisle toward the open exit hatch of the shuttle, he vowed silently never to allow them to remove his own Eye of God, or Kim's for that matter. He would die before it happened, even if he was already damned for his crimes against the Church.

Brian's thoughts were interrupted by the sounds of Kim sniffing loudly behind him. At first, he thought she was having some sort of allergic reaction to the planet's atmosphere. Perhaps there were microscopic particles in the air the colonist scientists and doctors had missed. Brian turned quickly to examine Kim's face.

"What?" she asked, looking at him like he was crazy.

"Why are you doing that?" he asked.

"Don't you smell that?"

"Smell what?"

"The air."

Brian frowned. Then, in an effort to mimic Kim, he took in the deepest breath his nostrils would allow. The sweet, moist smell in the air next to the door totally overwhelmed his senses, almost knocking him down. Panicked, Brian held his breath as he attempted to process the unfamiliar sensation of breathing clean, non-treated air. As he exited the door and stepped down onto the matted grass surrounding the shuttle, he slowly allowed himself to take the air fully into his lungs. He also felt the warm shroud of sunlight envelop his body for the first time in his life. Apart from Kim's profession of love before they had entered cryosleep, it was the most exhilarating moment Brian had ever experienced. Every pore and cell in his body seemed to soak up new energy as a soft breeze carried the scent of the Elysian spring. He felt as if he had been rewarded with heaven despite his sins. As a new wave of guilt suddenly threatened to emerge, Kim grabbed Brian's arm again. "Everyone's heading toward the town," she noted, motioning toward the closest path through the grass. A few stragglers still hovered around the shuttle, crying and kneeling on the grass as if they were at the feet of God Himself.

Brian turned his gaze upward up at the sky, which was dominated by the red glare of Ares even through the midday's blueness. Without a word, he took Kim's hand and walked through the tunnel of grass toward the camp.

PART II

▼

CHAPTER 13

▼

LIFE AFTER THE FALL

Leafy ferns brushed the face of the creature as it hunted its unsuspecting prey. The rapidly darkening forest enveloped its form as it sped from tree to tree, pausing momentarily to scan its surroundings. The prey was close. The creature closed its eyes and breathed in the sweet Elysian breeze that bathed the twilight hour in a familiar blanket of crisp coolness. A quick glance upward through the dense canopy revealed a pinkish sky that was quickly giving way to a deep violet hue. Soon, the twin gray moons would be gone, having been chased from the sky by their smaller red sibling. Not content to lose the advantage of surprise, the creature took to running again. It loved to run, especially at night. Skimming through the forest at such a pace created a feeling of primal euphoria. To run in the wild was to be free, a feeling the creature had not always been familiar with. Now, as it reached maturity, it craved this feeling of freedom. It had grown strong in recent years, its power having been fed by the wilds in which it spent its time.

As it neared the edge of the thicket, it came upon its primary objective. Perched precariously on the edge of a rocky cliff, sat another creature, this one beyond all descriptions of beauty. The creature inched forward, careful not to make a sound or take its eyes off its prey for even a moment. The prey was facing away from the forest, out over the valley that lay below the sheer cliff face. It was a human woman. She was short for her size, although more perfectly proportioned than any other human the predator had yet encountered. The baggy, unflattering jacket draped over the woman's shoulders obscured the tight, hour-glass form underneath. Long, brown hair, which seemed to shimmer even in the dimming light, fell down the middle of her back as gracefully as a waterfall. He moved closer, within striking distance of the woman. Soon, it would be too late for her to react. She was his. Closer. Closer.

"Nice try, Brian, I know it's you," Kim said playfully.

Brian kept silent, hoping to at least make her turn around.

"You're way too noisy to be a wraith hound," she noted. "We haven't even seen one near the valley for almost a year now!"

Brian sighed. He could never seem to get the better of her. "It was worth a try," he said, dropping the act and standing beside her.

Kim didn't look up. She didn't even open her eyes. Whenever she came to this spot to pray, she always sat in the same cross-legged position. Chang had taught her this position a couple of years before. He referred to it as "the mediation posture."

Brian felt strange for a second. Perhaps he was intruding. As he looked down at Kim's face, he noticed the faint outline of a smile. It was an entirely serene smile, as if she could see something that he couldn't, even through her closed eyelids. It made him uneasy. "Sit down, Bri," she suggested, patting the grass-matted ground beside her.

Brian complied. Standing up so close to the edge of the cliff was making him dizzy anyway. He tried to assume Kim's astute posture for a moment, but then settled for a more haphazard legs-out approach. Kim smiled, a definite smile this time. "You should come here more often."

"I don't want to intrude. I know how important this place is to you."

"It *is* important. That's why you should come here more often," she insisted, eyes still closed. "I feel different here than anywhere else around the valley. Just look at the sky over the mountains. Have you ever seen such a vibrant orange? It looks like the clouds are on fire. I feel like I'm right next to heaven up here, looking down at the entire world." Kim paused for a second, adding "And soon Ares will be out."

Brian shuddered at the mention of the blood-red moon. "Have you had any-more of those dreams?"

"Not for a while," Kim answered, her voice taking on a more serious tone.

Since their earliest days on Elysium, Kim had talked of strange dreams involving the moon. She now called them visions. Normally, these visions came at night while she was asleep, but occasionally, they came during the day. When this happened, Kim would often seem to lose contact with reality. Always, the image was the same: the glowing red disk of Ares surrounded by a void blacker than the darkest night. Kim said that it seemed like there was more to the dreams than she could remember. It was as if somebody was trying to talk to her, but she couldn't quite understand the language. In fact, she insisted that there was no sound in these dreams at all, just the image of a burning red disk.

Brian found the whole situation with the "visions" disturbing, especially considering the strange nature of the moon itself. For years, the colonists had attempted to study the moon. At first, they assumed that it got its color from the same iron-oxide that Mars did back home, but whenever they attempted to run scans of the moon's surface, they either got no readings at all, or readings that didn't make any sense. It was as if the moon wasn't even there at times, at least on the scanners. It didn't even exert any noticeable gravitational pull on the planet itself, despite having a closer orbit than the other two moons circling Elysium. The general consensus was that it had an unstable gravitational field that fooled the planet-based scientific instruments, but this was only a theory. In truth, nobody knew anything concrete about the moon, other than the fact that it hovered over the colony every night like a watchful eye.

Brian forced the thoughts of Ares out of his mind and looked out toward the horizon. The setting sun was beautiful, he had to admit. Far below on the dark valley floor, several large redwing geckos gave a final chorus of cries before ceding their valley to the creatures of the night. Brian's eyes quickly drifted back to Kim. He detected a silent quiver on her lips as she mouthed the final lines to a private prayer. After a moment of silence, she bowed her head and opened her eyes. The receding sun gave off one last burst of light before falling behind the mountains, bestowing Kim's deep brown eyes with a temporary, captivating fire.

"What did you say?" Brian asked.

"Just saying thanks."

"For what?"

She laughed, then quickly leaned over and kissed him on the lips. Brian kissed back. He ran his hand over Kim's cold cheek, and she leaned into him. Once again, Brian felt a wave of primal energy wash over him, far more intense than when he was running through the woods just a few minutes before. They had been as this point countless times before, locked in a passionate kiss that could so easily lead to more. But Brian knew better than to pressure Kim into something she wasn't ready for. Old rules took even longer to die than habits, especially when the punishment for breaking them had always been so severe. Although much of the Church's doctrine had been demolished in the five years since the colonists had fled to Elysium, many still had a hard time letting go of their old ways. Kim, especially, had insisted on maintaining many key features of her faith, even after Brian had long since discarded his own. As she hastily pulled back from Brian's embrace, the embroidered Eye on her forehead reminded him of this fact.

Kim shivered, her flushed cheeks disguising how cold she really was.

"We should get back," Brian said. "It's getting late."

"So why did you decide to come tonight?" she asked. "Why tonight out of all nights?"

"I wanted to warn you."

"Warn me of what?"

"They're planning something back in town," he revealed. "I shouldn't be telling you this, but I figured I'd let you know."

Kim looked perplexed for a moment, then, suddenly, lit up. "A birthday party?"

"Yeah," Brian confirmed. "I tried to tell them that you wouldn't like it, but you know how they are."

"It's just awkward," Kim admitted. "It still feels strange, no matter what they say."

Back on Earth, the Church had banned all personal celebrations several decades before Brian and Kim were even born. Since arriving on Elysium, the parents in the colony had reinstated the timeless tradition called a "birthday" for all citizens. Although the adult birthdays were rather minor affairs in the community, the birthdays of the children were considered major events. Brian figured that the parents felt they were making up for time lost or something. He still remembered how explosively he had resisted his parent's first attempt to give him a birthday over four years before.

Things had been tough for Brian those first couple of years, especially in the months following the colonists' arrival. While everyone struggled to establish a foothold on a wild, untamed world, Brian had been content to brood away his time in the cramped confines of his family's shelter, fantasizing about an escape he knew would never come. Brian refused to eat meals with his fellow colonists, or even speak to his neighbors. His parents, who had tried to be supportive at first, eventually grew frustrated with their son's subversive demeanor. Years later, Brian still remembered many of the arguments he had deliberately started with his father during this period. Often, Brian would attack his mother for some petty reason, since he considered her an easier target. This, predictably, would upset his father, and so on. Finally, the tension became too much for even Brian to bear, and he soon sought refuge outside of the house.

In those early days, the colonists still knew very little about Elysium and the wonders it contained. The wilderness surrounding the small settlements was full of exotic animals that had very little fear of creatures as small and helpless as humans. The leaders of the colony set up a perimeter inside the valley that nobody was permitted to leave without an armed escort. Brian, who in those days still thought of the colonial leadership as a gang of murderous heathens, made sure to violate the order as much as possible. Looking back, he wasn't sure why he took such a risk. Maybe he subconsciously hoped that a vicious predator would end his marred existence and save him the pain of having to live on away from the Church. Maybe he felt that God would protect him. Most likely, he just wanted to escape in whatever way he could, be it by distance or death.

Whenever he could, Brian would slip away from the house, usually in the early morning while his parents were meeting with the Colonial Council. At first, his forays into the wilderness were rather short. Gradually, as he became more comfortable with his surroundings, he began to disappear for longer periods of time. His parents just assumed that he was wandering the village or visiting Kim. They had no idea that he was undertaking such dangerous journeys on an almost daily basis.

The only person Brian couldn't escape from was Kim. She soon discovered where he was going and made a point to tag along. Although Brian loved her company, he hated always having to worry about her safety. He even considered taking a pulse rifle along for a time, but could never bring himself to actually take one from the weapons locker.

During their explorations away from the settlements, Brian and Kim would usually just walk together in silence. Brian liked it that way. He liked having silence to contemplate his situation, but he also liked the comfort of Kim's presence. Besides, the unspoken bond that existed between them often made speech unnecessary. As for the danger of predators, Brian and Kim rarely encountered anything truly menacing in the wilderness. Many of the animals on Elysium were harmless plant eaters or small carnivores. Kim always suggested that the really dangerous creatures, like the packs of wraith hounds that hunted on the northern edge of the valley, didn't even view humans as food since they seemed to prefer the large bird-like creatures that grazed in the fields bordering the forests. Brian had a different take on their luck; he attributed it to God's protection. The way Brian saw it, if God truly wanted him punished, He would have allowed Brian's death within a week. Still, despite Brian's continued confidence in his Supreme Creator, he made sure to be back in the village well before dark, when the largest and most dangerous animals roamed the forests and plains.

Before long, Brian became so used to the wilderness that he forgot all about its potential dangers. Instead, he was confronted by a new, more terrifying revelation. Out in the wild, cut off from the feelings of hatred generated by the colony, Brian began to notice something about Elysium he had initially ignored: its beauty. The most disturbing part was that the overwhelming majesty of this world was unlike anything Brian had ever encountered, even in the words of Scripture. The intense, emerald greenery covering the forest floor; the towering trees that stretched over fifty meters into the tangled canopy above; the rushing brooks that suddenly dropped hundreds of meters down to the plains below; the bird-like reptiles whose spread wings resembled the most brilliant rainbow imaginable. The blue sky; the red moon and twinkling stars: once Brian began to notice these things, it seemed as if his eyes would overwhelm his mind's ability to comprehend such beauty. It was beyond anything he had ever known up until this point. The choking, dark confines of his existence back on Earth, the surroundings that had been so comforting in the past, gradually faded into memory as Elysium became home.

Meanwhile, Brian's faith in the Church began to waver as he realized how inadequate human words were when describing the sights and smells. He eventually came to the conclusion that God didn't reside in the dim cathedral corridors or in the convoluted scriptures of the Church. God was here, on Elysium. Everywhere. Once, long before Brian had been born, there had been a paradise like this on Earth. It had been man, namely the Church that had transformed it into something else, something less perfect. Back on Earth, the Church claimed to offer people hope, an escape from the world that had been destroyed. Now that Brian had a new world, one unlike anything any other human had ever imagined, he felt a new sense of hope, a genuine sense of hope. The Church, whose message of hope he had embraced his entire life, began to look more and more like a threat as this new reality materialized. Brian shuddered to think what it would look like if a factory or Cathedral were suddenly erected on the floor of the green valley below his home. Even if the colonists deserved to pay for their crimes, the last thing Brian wanted to see were black military ships descending from space onto the unblemished face of his planet.

Of course, Brian didn't mention anything about his spiritual crisis to the other colonists, not even Kim. Although he began to understand more and more why they had fled the Church, he refused to give them the satisfaction of seeing him abandon his faith. Instead, he merely softened his stance toward them, especially his parents. By his fourteenth birthday, Brian participated fully in the day-to-day activities of the colonists. He even attended school on a daily basis with Chang and the other students. Contrary to Brian's fears, nobody mentioned his obvious shift away from his earlier ideology. The colonists simply accepted him as part of the community. Brian's mother seemed particularly glad to have her son back, although she too made a point to avoid mentioning this fact to Brian. If and when Brian was ready to discuss his feelings, his parents would listen.

That time came just before his sixteenth birthday, on the very day he would have been accepted into military training back on Earth. Brian remembered that he had been helping his father and several other colonists construct a new grain silo on the valley floor near the river when he suddenly mentioned that he wanted his Eye of God removed as soon as possible. Although several bystanders momentarily stopped hammering, David Bishop merely nodded his head in affirmation and promised that Brian could get it taken off by nightfall. That was it. No dramatics and no revelations. After that point, Brian considered himself a full-fledged member of the community. A minor procedure performed by Dr. Anderson erased the embroidered symbol from Brian's head permanently. His faith, which had been such a guiding force in childhood, was now an unknown factor. Brian wasn't sure if he believed in God anymore, but he definitely knew that if He existed, He wasn't like anything accepted by Adherent canon. Brian realized that his new views were similar to what Jade had described years before on the colony transport following the mutiny. He still hated when his sister was right.

Kim's faith was a different matter, however. As they walked back to her surprise eighteenth birthday party, Brian contemplated for the thousandth time why Kim, who had always doubted the Church's tactics and motives, still chose to bear its most powerful symbol over two years after he had rid himself of it. "Because wherever and whatever God is, he, she or it still watches us," she always replied before adding: "That's one thing the Church *was* right about."

CHAPTER 14

▼

THE CEREMONY

After only several months on Elysium, the initial two settlements had split into five smaller communities spread throughout the valley. This division was due to the high projected growth of the colony during the first generation on Elysium. Contrary to early fears, Earth crops adapted well to the somewhat alien environment, and the indigenous predators kept their distance from the colony most of the time. Within less than a year, many of the young couples were already expecting children, despite Dr. Anderson's insistence that the colonists refrain from excessive reproduction until the colony proved stable at its current size.

The makeup of each community was determined largely by each colonist's home city back on Earth. The Chicago colonists, Brian and Kim included, had opted to stay at the original settlement on top of the plateau overlooking the valley. Fenner had taken his Houston flock to the far south of the valley at the foot of the mountains. Raasch's people had moved northwest of the Chicago settlement, beyond the large forest at the opposite end of the plateau. The London group of colonists still resided in a settlement at the southern base of the plateau. The colonists had named these settlements *Independence, Little Houston, Sanctuary, and New London* respectively, although they still officially functioned as one large colony. By far, the largest and most diverse settlement sat in the middle of the valley floor and was made up of colonists from several Earth cities. It was called *New Haven*. Dotting the landscape in between the settlements were large farms, each producing food for the nearest community. Although each settlement was run semi-autonomously, the leaders from all five villages would meet on an almost daily basis in New Haven to discuss issues that impacted the Elysian colony as a whole. Chang's school was also located in the central settlement and was filled with students from every village four days out of the week. During the peek of winter, when heavy rains often made travel through the valley difficult, children would often receive schooling in their home village. During most of the year, however, they were schooled as one large group by Chang and several other former Ministers and teachers. Chang claimed that despite the occasional inconvenience of having to travel to New Haven, the students needed to feel part of a larger community.

Even before Brian and Kim could see their own village, they could detect the faint orangish glow given off by the multitude of small fires burning at the center of the settlement. Although each village had several hydrogen generators on permanent loan from the Adherent military, most colonists seemed to prefer the comforting light of the fire. As they walked the path along the steep edge of the plateau toward the warm, growing light, Brian could see a similar glow from New London far below on the valley floor. Since the early days of prefabricated metal housing, the colonists had replaced many of these cramped, awkward structures with smooth, organic homes molded from the brownish clay extracted from the river beds around the valley. Many of these homes were quite elaborate, and Brian found their rounded silhouettes to be much more visually appealing than the old buildings. Apart from several large grain silos and a fairly ornate meeting hall at the center of the village, both of which were constructed of wood, New London could have easily been mistaken for a primitive settlement built by a stone-age people. From the top of the ridge, Brian couldn't even make out any signs of machinery. Besides the small flashlight he held in his right hand, there was nothing to remind him that his people had come from a world dominated by technology.

"So what exactly do they have planned?" Kim asked.

"Not sure," Brian admitted. "They didn't tell me much."

"They probably knew you'd squeal."

"They'd be right," he agreed.

"I hope they don't give me some sort of present. That just seems so childish."

"It depends on what the present is, though."

Kim looked at Brian and rolled her eyes. "Remember that doll Mrs. Echani gave me last year? I mean, I appreciate the time and effort she put into making it, but I'd rather she have spared herself from the torture."

"Mrs. Echani's old, Kim," Brian reminded her. "She still remembers what it was like to get birthday presents as a little girl, so that's what she gives."

"Good point."

"And don't forget that she lost her only daughter in the Houston uprising," Brian added.

"Alright, alright, don't make me feel so bad!" Kim whined. "I'm just saying that I feel guilty that she has to work so hard on a present I never wanted in the first place."

"I think in some ways birthday presents are just as much for the person giving the gift," Brian pointed out logically.

"This coming from the person who makes a point to avoid the entire village on his own birthdays," she laughed.

Brian nodded and raised his eyebrows. "Look, I didn't say I understand or even like the whole idea. I'm merely pointing out some things I've noticed."

"I just think it's a strange custom. I'm not sure why they insist on going through it every year for every kid in the village. I mean, I like the whole idea of everyone taking time out of their daily routine to gather together; I understand that. I just don't get the whole present thing."

"Well, you're eighteen now, Kim. Maybe they'll do something different this year."

"Let's hope."

As Brian and Kim rounded the last cluster of trees, Independence came fully into view. The extremely tall grass that had enveloped the colonists when they had first arrived on Elysium had long since been cut down and replaced by small gardens and neatly constructed stone pathways and terraces. The homes at the edge of town were dark, as if abandoned. At any moment, Brian expected every-one to jump out and yell some absurdity, scaring him to death all in the name of fun. He braced himself for the inevitable onslaught of noise and chaos. Kim grasped his hand tightly, obviously expecting the same thing. As they passed the Bishop and Collins residences, Brian and Kim noticed a dark, solitary figure coming toward them. The figure was tall, obviously well-built and had a rifle slung over his right shoulder. Brian showed the flashlight on the man's face.

"Hi, Luke," Kim greeted.

Luke looked up. "Hey, you two!"

Brian had realized lately how much Luke had matured. Although his cousin had always been older and stronger, he had grown into a capable leader who now assumed the task of providing security for the entire community. Along with Corporal Hudson and several other colonists who were young and physically fit,

Luke had established the first Elysian police force. Not that one was needed all that much, but it was still nice to have a group of armed men who could stop someone like Fenner from doing anything too rash should a dangerous situation arise. Most of the time the small police force simply provided security against the few dangerous animals that still occasionally made their way into the valley. They also accompanied the survey missions and science teams that traveled around the lower continents during the summer months.

"They were getting a little worried about you. You know your parents don't like it when you're out this late," Luke explained.

Brian felt a sting to his pride. "We can take care of ourselves. And besides, it's not that late." Brian wanted to remind Luke that he had asked his younger cousin only months before to join the police force, an offer that Brian had flatly refused. Still, Luke had offered, demonstrating that he recognized Brian wasn't a kid anymore.

"Hey, I know you can," Luke chuckled as he held both hands up in a gesture of surrender, "but when Rachel Collins gives me an order to go out and look for her daughter, I don't argue."

Brian nodded and shrugged in agreement.

"Anyway, we should get going. Everyone's waiting in front of the meeting hall."

Why was everyone gathered there? Brian asked himself. He looked over at Kim's perplexed face. She was obviously asking herself the same thing.

Brian, Kim and Luke came to the middle of the village, in front of the building that served as town hall. It was eerie seeing what looked to be the entire village standing silently around several large bonfires in anticipation of the guest of honor's arrival. At the center of the crowd, in front of the largest fire, stood Kim's parents, the Bishops and Minister Chang. A quick survey of the other faces revealed a mixture of young people and adults from every settlement. Maleek, Suna and several other students from Chang's school stood alongside their parents and elders. It was clear that almost everyone who knew Kim on a personal level was present at the event.

Luke stepped forward from Brian and Kim and took his place next to his uncle David. Brian felt Kim stiffen beside him. She was obviously uncomfortable from all the attention. Brian was uncomfortable too. He hadn't been told about any of this before hand. The serious atmosphere generated by the silence of the group was lessened only by the faint outline of a smile on the face of Minister

Chang. Brian also thought he detected a look of pride on the faces of Kim's parents. *What was this all about?*

Several seconds later Chang broke the silence. "Kimberly Collins, please step forward."

Kim gingerly complied with the request. Brian, feeling suddenly like he was in the way, sought refuge in the crowd. Kim still didn't say a word as she waited to find out why the village had orchestrated such an elaborate ceremony. Chang continued speaking as he approached his student. Although he addressed Kim directly, he spoke loud enough for the entire crowd to hear. "Kim, I have known you since you were barely able to walk. Over the years, I have had the privilege of seeing you grow as student and as a person. During my career as a Minister and teacher, I have encountered many bright young minds, some of the ablest, most eager and most intelligent humanity ever offered. But never have I seen a young person who possesses such a firm, unwavering moral compass, even in the most difficult of circumstances."

As Chang spoke to Kim, tears began to moisten her eyes. The Minister put his hand on her shoulder and turned to face the crowd. Brian suddenly understood what the ceremony was about.

"There are many among us who believe that the ways of the Church have no place here on Elysium, but we must be careful not to forsake our heritage or our souls simply because people within the Church chose to misuse their power. Whether you are religious or not, I believe it is important to remember the hope that brought us here to this distant paradise. It wasn't merely a desire to improve our material lives. Many sacrificed their fortunes, their careers and their safety to travel here and live in freedom."

Brian immediately thought of Fenner as he heard Chang's statements about religion. Not surprisingly, the High Counselor's tall, menacing figure was absent among the crowd. Few, if any, of the colonists practiced the old religion, although many still attended the Minister's nondenominational services at the makeshift Church down in New Haven. Fenner was the leader of a small, yet increasingly vocal, group of colonists who objected to such public displays of faith. Some parents in this faction had even threatened to pull their children out of Chang's school, despite the Minister's assurances that there was no trace of religious instruction in the curriculum. Brian found the objections ridiculous, considering how much the former clergy members had distanced themselves from Adherent doctrine. They too had risked everything to come to Elysium and had sacrificed lives of power in order to do so. Furthermore, there was nothing threatening in Chang's message of faith or his position within community. For all of the respect the Minister commanded, he was little more than a traditional figurehead, a familiar source of knowledge, wisdom and stability the colonists could look to in an age of uncertainty. Perhaps if he were younger, his vitality would ensure a more important role, but as it stood, Chang's life seemed to be winding down. Nevertheless, part of Brian was beginning to view his onetime mentor as an anachronism better suited to the classroom than the pulpit. Fenner's views, although harsh, had some credibility considering the colonists' past experiences living under the Church.

Chang smiled as if he had just thought of something funny. His head bowed as he abandoned his normally statuesque posture. Before the eyes of the entire village, Chang shrunk into the kind, humble, elderly man he really was beneath the robes of a Minister. "I am old," he continued, stepping back away from Kim and towards the crowd. "I only have a few years left here on Elysium." He held his head up high again. "And although we have several excellent Ministers and teachers among our growing communities, more are needed if we are to raise a new generation of intellectually, morally and spiritually competent citizens." Chang motioned back toward Kim, as if he were presenting her as a prize. "Kim Collins is the first of this new order. She will be my direct successor, if she so chooses."

Following Chang's announcement, the crowd immediately broke into thunderous applause and enveloped Kim in a blanket of embraces and congratulations. Brian stood back as the sea of people rushed passed him. *As if she would say no, Chang*, Brian thought as he smiled. *Nobody deserves an honor like this more than Kim.* Brian realized, as most of the colonists did, that Chang was right: Kim was the best of what they had to offer.

Brian looked up and watched as Bill Collins hugged his daughter. It was a happy sight, yet Brian suddenly noticed a knot forming in his stomach, one that superseded the more positive feelings of pride. He had felt at home on Elysium for years now, but had yet to find what he considered to be complete contentment. He really only felt happy around Kim, and now she seemed further away than ever. She had a place in the community, a defined path. In the following months, she would no doubt take on many new responsibilities within the community, especially with the younger students at the school. Kim's new path was a special honor. Despite his lack of traditional political power, Chang still represented knowledge and wisdom, two forces that transcended politics. Some day, Kim too would command this deep reservoir of loyalty and respect. Her youth also afforded her potential power that Chang lacked.

Kim's birthday "gift" now placed her on Brian's growing list of friends with adult responsibilities. Maleek had been working with several of the colonial engineers for months in order to ensure that he was familiar with every piece of machinery on Elysium. In time, this machinery would age and need to be repaired on a regular basis. Even though the colonists had adapted to living off the land, nobody wanted to be without power in an emergency. Suna, on the other hand, had begun work with Serena Kufa, the colony's leading exobotanist. Even Derrick, who was generally considered to be the most irresponsible of the bunch, had taken a recent interest in medicine and now frequently assisted Jade on house calls around the colony. As Brian stood alone and watched the celebrations for Kim, he realized with utter horror that out of all his peers, he was the only one without a role in the community. Sure, he helped out with odd jobs or chores whenever he was needed, but he had no path. Luke's offer for Brian to join the security force may have seemed ridiculous to Brian at the time, but he realized that it might have been his family's attempt to give him a place. Brian thought back to Chang's speech just a few minutes before. Once, Brian had been the star pupil, the one slated for greatness. Alongside his feelings of pride for Kim, he suddenly felt a nagging sense that he had been cheated. Perhaps he had merely cheated himself. In the absence of the Church, Brian had no place. No position of importance. If he wasn't careful, in time, he would become just as irrelevant as the Church.

CHAPTER 15

▼

A TASTE OF CLARITY

Brian shivered as the chill of the night began to gnaw at his exposed skin. He contemplated going home and getting a jacket, but decided it was too much work. If he went home now, he may as well stay there and go to bed. Instead, he huddled closer to the dying fire. His eyes fixated on the reddened coals. They were the same color as Ares, a crimson blood color tinged with a hint of orange. Brian tore his gaze from the entrancing glow and looked up at the cold night sky. As was usual during the Elysian autumn, it was a clear night sky dominated by the red glare of Ares to the north. Brian tried to keep his mind clear, devoid of any thoughts involving his future or his destiny. Right now, he just wanted to absorb the simple placidity offered by a night sky powdered with stars.

A sudden, muffled outburst of laughter from Kim's house brought him back to reality. Brian checked his timepiece. It was well past midnight. Most of the villagers had gone to sleep, but Kim's family and a few close friends, including Brian's family, were obviously determined to continue the celebration. Earlier Brian had made a point to join the festivities, although he quickly grew tired of standing around in Kim's crowded house with half the village. Kim had shot him a few frazzled looks as she was swarmed by the mass of people, but couldn't even get close enough to Brian to talk to him. After an hour or so, Brian had sought refuge outside. Kim would understand. She probably wanted to do the same. And besides, he would see her again in the morning.

Brian looked back toward the noise just a few houses down from where he was sitting. *Things aren't as cramped in there now*, he reasoned. *They're probably wondering where I am. I should at least say goodnight to everyone.* Just as he began to stand up, however, Maleek's tall form exited Kim's house and started walking his way. Derrick, who was much shorter and somewhat heavier, followed closely behind.

"Sounds like quite the party in there," Brian commented as they approached.

Maleek looked up and grinned.

"We knew you'd be out here, Bishop," Derrick said. "Your parents thought you went home or something."

"I was thinking about it."

"Ah, come on, you can't go to bed already!" Maleek complained as he sat down next to the fire. "How often do we come here to actually spend the night?"

"Where are you staying?" Brian asked.

"Your house," Derrick answered. "Your mom said we could just set up a couple of fold away cots in your room."

"What do I get in return for the use of these glorious accommodations?" Brian chided.

"The pleasure of out esteemed company, of course," Derrick laughed as he punched Brian in the arm.

Brian laughed too. It had been a while since the three of them had spent any time together outside of school. Even though Brian spent more time with Kim than anyone else, he still craved some time alone with his buddies. All of the students at Chang's school who were of approximate age knew each other quite well, but small cliques still formed. Maleek, Derrick and Tim Tailor, who couldn't make it to Kim's birthday tonight, were Brian's clique. Kim had Suna and Molly Johnson, who were both still in the house with her.

Another burst of laughter, this time from Bill Collins, cut through the air. The three friends smiled, but said nothing. It was obvious that everyone was thinking. Finally, Maleek spoke: "Things have changed so much lately," he said. "I've been so busy that I don't even have time to think."

The other two nodded their heads in agreement.

"They're going to change even more now," Derrick added thoughtfully, nodding back in the direction of Kim's house. "She's going to be even busier than we are. Kind of makes you wish we weren't finishing school in a couple of months, huh?"

"No kidding," said Maleek. "Fenner's been on my ass lately about making sure I'm this expert mechanic. I don't know why, since we have several engineers over in Little Houston. I think he just likes applying the pressure."

Brian still remained silent. The other two looked at him, as if waiting for his opinion.

"I heard your cousin asked you to join the security force," Derrick said, trying to prod him out of his trance.

"Yeah," Brian confirmed, not feeling the need to elaborate. He had resumed staring at the burning coals.

"Well, don't leave us in suspense. Did you take the offer?" Maleek asked.

"Nope."

"Why not?"

"It just didn't feel like the right decision."

"What's that mean?"

"I don't know. It just didn't seem right for me," Brian repeated, shrugging his shoulders. He expected a sarcastic response from Derrick for giving such a cryptic answer, but received none. Perhaps his friend knew how useless Brian was feeling and empathized.

Maleek, ever the optimist, said cheerfully, "Don't worry, you'll find something, Brian."

"Yeah," muttered Brian.

"Hey," Derrick interjected, making it clear that he wanted to change the subject. "We should plan something before the winter rains come. A trip or something."

Brian perked his head up. That actually sounded like a good idea. "What do you have in mind?"

"Kim said that Chang's taking some of the primary students up to Lake Clarity on the north continent for a field trip," Derrick said.

"Yeah, she mentioned something about that," noted Brian. "They're going up next week, right?"

"They are. I think we should go along."

Brian shook his head. "I don't know. Minister Poole asked me if I could teach a couple of classes to the junior students while he's gone on the trip. Plus, I promised the Lei's that I'd help them fix their roof."

"Forget that!" Derrick scoffed. "There are plenty of people around here who can do that kind of stuff!"

"Yeah, Bri," Maleek chimed in. "Don't cut out on us with some stupid excuses. Besides, Kim told me to get you to do something like this. She thinks you're in a slump lately. Or was it a rut?"

"A rut," Derrick confirmed.

"A what?" Brian raised his eyebrows.

Maleek ignored his question. "Hey, remember that time we ran Molly's dad's landspeeder through Mrs. Lei's garden?"

"She came to my house and knocked on the door with a shovel, like she was going to beat me with it," Derrick laughed. He always turned beat red when he started laughing. "She started yelling so fast in Chinese that my dad thought Mr. Lei had died or something!" Derrick stood up and raised his hands over his head, as if he held an invisible hoe ready to strike. "Finally she just started yelling: 'You damn boys! You bad! Very bad!'" In the glowing light of the fire, Derrick looked more like a deranged ape shaking its fists at the night sky than an angry Mrs. Lei. Maleek broke into hysterics, rolling on the ground holding his stomach. Even Brian couldn't help but laugh at the sight of his friend making an idiot out of himself.

"Are you boys enjoying yourselves?" a sultry voice spoke up from the darkness. It was Suna.

Derrick jumped from surprise and almost fell over into the fire. This made Maleek laugh even harder. He kept pointing to his face in an attempt to draw attention to the look of sheer stupidity that adorned Derrick's own.

Suna walked up to the fire and pushed Derrick, who had recovered rather well from his moment of embarrassment. This time he gave up and fell back to the ground in an exaggerated motion. "Easy there, Soong."

"Shut up," Suna hissed. She gracefully sat down next to him and caressed his back in a rare show of affection.

Watching them, Brian realized how close Suna and Derrick had grown over the past year. In fact, they were rarely seen apart, even outside of school. *What a pair*, Brian thought. *Derrick the perpetual joker and Suna the stoic pragmatist.* It was strange how the two had influenced each other. Derrick now exhibited signs of taking some responsibility while Suna, who had been so critically serious as a child, now cracked the occasional smile or even joke.

"How is it in there?" asked Maleek.

"Winding down," Suna answered. "I think everyone's getting tired, especially Kim."

"Does she seem happy about it?" Brian asked.

"A little overwhelmed at the moment, but I can't imagine her turning Chang's offer down."

"I can't either," agreed Brian.

Silence overcame the group once again as a stiff breeze invigorated the fire. Brian noticed people starting to leave the Collins residence, but couldn't make out who it was in the dark. Maleek, who was looking in the same direction, noticed too.

"Time for bed," he yawned, standing up on his long, spindly legs and stretching to his full height.

"Good idea," noted Suna, who stood up as well. Derrick followed suit.

"Coming, Bishop? If you don't hurry, you'll be the one sleeping on a cot tonight!"

"Yeah, just tell my parents I'll be there in a minute."

"Sure thing," Derrick said as he and the rest of the group headed toward the dark shapes leaving Kim's.

Brian heard Derrick call out to his mother before slipping back into a trance-like state. He closed his eyes and breathed in the strong, smoky air from the fire. A wave of relaxation swept over him, turning the seconds he had planned to stay at the fire into several minutes.

Lake Clarity. On a world teeming with pristine lakes, rivers and oceans, few bodies of water rivaled the sheer beauty of it. The lake sat nestled in a cul-de-sac of rocky, limestone peaks rising sharply from the crystal blue water's edge. On the lake's western shore, sheer, jagged cliffs loomed over the thin, stone-covered beach. The cliffs extended far up to the north end of the lake, where they eventually gave way to the more gradual, forest-covered slopes of the eastern shore. The only easy access to the lake was through a gap in the rocks to the south, where the imposing topography of the region gave way to a lush, alpine meadow that stretched for several square kilometers. The soft, constant flow of the meadow grass was broken only by the frequent, large boulders that had been left by a passing glacier eons before and the occasional conifer or meandering creek that sprouted from the ground.

Brian had been to the lake on two previous trips. When he was fifteen, he had accompanied his father, somewhat unwillingly, up to the region on an expedition to scout the northern continent. Having grown accustomed to the endless fields, forests and rivers that graced the valley around the colony, Brian didn't find the northern regions very special. What did take him back was the color of the lake itself, a deep blue sapphire, which looked almost artificial in its intensity. The air was different up here too. It had a harshness to it that the southern continents lacked. Farther away from Elysium's equator, the seasons actually changed drastically, perpetuating an eternal cycle of life and death. The whole region intrigued Brian, and he soon felt himself compelled to return.

On his second visit, Brian had come up to the lake with Chang and several of his classmates on a fieldtrip. During that trip, Brian actually had time to explore some of the areas around the lake, including the dark, pine-scented forests that splashed down the rocky peaks onto the surrounding landscape. On the day before the students left to come home, Brian had spotted several openings in the cliff face on the western side of the lake, no doubt the entrances to caverns. Although he had no idea how far the crevices extended into the darkness, Brian longed to explore them on a future visit. This new trip would give him the opportunity to do so.

Brian felt a little surprised that there was another field trip to the lake so soon. After all, Elysium was a planet of many natural wonders, few of which had been explored. Then Brian remembered how excited the colony's three geologists had been when they heard about the region. Unlike the land surrounding the colony, the Lake Clarity region was shaped relatively recently by glaciers rather than ancient volcanoes. The scientists claimed that it provided them with a unique opportunity to study the planet's more recent history. Brian supposed that it was easier to get a fieldtrip approved by the Council if it served more than one purpose.

With his mind made up, Brian returned to present reality and opened his eyes. As his vision adjusted to the warm, smoky atmosphere, he saw Kim standing on the opposite side of the flames watching him intently.

"How long have you been there?" he asked.

"A minute or two," she smiled wearily.

"Long night, huh?"

She nodded. "A strange one, too."

"Well, you said it yourself, birthdays are a strange custom."

"This was a little more than a birthday," she sighed, walking over to where Brian was sitting. She slumped down beside him and rested her head on his left shoulder.

"What now?" he asked.

"You mean tonight?"

"No, in general. What does Chang want you to do?"

"Nothing too drastic, at least not yet. He wants me to stay on at the school though, even after I'm done with classes."

Brian felt a sinking sensation in the pit of his stomach. "Will you be moving down to New Haven then?" he asked, trying not to sound too disturbed by the prospect.

Kim took her head off Brian's shoulder and gave him a look that made him feel stupid. "Yeah, but it's only a half an hour walk, Brian. It's not like I'm moving halfway across the universe!"

"Well, no kidding!"

"Hey, don't get upset. Things aren't going to change between us."

"But things are already changing."

Kim pursed her lips and looked deep into his eyes, as if she were examining his soul. "Come with me up to Lake Clarity this weekend. It'll do you some good to get out of here for a few days."

"Maleek said you thought I'd fallen into a rut."

Kim began to smile, but successfully fought back the urge to laugh. "Something to that effect. I think that getting out of here for a few days will help you out."

"Fine, I'll go," Brian relented.

"That was easy," she said.

"Well, your minions already did a good job trying to persuade me."

This time Kim did laugh. She took his hand as the conversation fell silent again. Brian looked back over at her after a stretch of several minutes, thinking she had fallen asleep. He was dismayed to find her wide awake, staring up at the sky, toward Ares. Once again, he felt as if she were a million kilometers away.

Without turning to face Brian, Kim began to speak in a calm, knowing voice. "Don't worry, Brian. You'll find your way soon enough. I promise."

CHAPTER 16

▼

FROM CLARITY TO CONFLAGRATION

"Got everything you need there?" David Bishop asked Kim cheerfully as she tossed her bag into the belly of the waiting shuttle.

"I hope so," she replied. "We'll be gone for at least five days."

"I'm sure some of the parents around here wouldn't mind if you took these kids off their hands for a little longer than that," David added. "They're getting antsy now that the rains have come."

Brian, who had been waiting patiently behind Kim to throw his own bag into the cargo hold, looked up at the gray sky. He hated the Elysian winter. At least up North it snowed. Down on the lower continents it just rained for two months straight. He was surprised it wasn't raining at this very moment.

"Well, you two have yourselves a good time."

"Thanks," said Kim.

"We will," added Brian, finally relieving himself of his bag. He had packed too much, as usual.

Kim gave a wave and walked up the boarding ramp into the shuttle, leaving Brian and his father alone.

"I noticed Luke's coming along," Brian noted.

"Yeah. He, Murphy and Sonia."

"Are they worried about predators? I saw them carrying rifles."

"You know Luke. He doesn't take any chances."

"I think it's because he's bored around here. Nothing ever happens."

"True," Brian's father agreed. "But that's a good thing."

"I guess you're right."

Brian turned to follow Kim's lead up the boarding ramp, but his father's voice stopped him.

"Son,"

"Yeah?"

"Seriously, have a good time."

"I will."

"Love you."

"Love you, too."

With that, Brian turned and entered the shuttle.

It had been well over a year since Brian had ridden in anything mechanical. Of the eight shuttles from the two colony ships, only four were used regularly, and these only for emergencies and official business. The prevailing philosophy among the colonial leaders was that sooner or later, the mechanical devices they relied on, including the shuttles, would get old and fail. To help deal with this problem, the colonists made a point to become self-sufficient as quickly as possible. The colonists also prepared for this day by storing much of the nonessential equipment, including the other four shuttles, onboard the two colony ships, which were programmed to orbit between Ares and Phobos on standby should they ever be needed. Having these resources available may someday be necessary for the long-term survival of the colony. It certainly made for a good insurance policy should they ever have to leave the planet.

Of the sixty-two students from the colony's primary school, about half were onboard Brian's shuttle. In addition to the children, there were several parent chaperones and two additional teachers besides Chang present. The other shuttle, which was leaving from Little Houston, carried a few of the older students who couldn't make it to New Haven where the other shuttle initially boarded. Derrick, Maleek, Molly and several older students from Brian's class were on this shuttle. Tim was absent yet again, having gone on a trip to the coast with a small group of colonists who were investigating possible volcanic activity. The Little Houston shuttle also carried most of the equipment needed for the trip, along with a few adult colonists who were tasked with studying and mapping out features on the northern continent. Although the colonists had made a point to explore much of their planet, it would take several lifetimes for them to even scratch the surface of Elysium's secrets.

Brian sat up in front of the shuttle between Luke and Jade. Brian's mother had sent her along as the chief medical officer for the trip. This was yet another precaution taken by the colonial leadership. The potential for an outbreak on an alien world such as Elysium was always a concern. Just two years before, several colonists had died from a flu-like virus that attacked the lungs. The colony's medical personal eventually devised an effective serum, but the whole event made everyone aware of just how dangerous contact with new strains of illnesses could be. Brian felt glad to have his sister along. He hadn't seen her much since she had accepted a medical position over in Sanctuary where her new husband lived. Brian looked down at the restraint that hung lazily across her mid section. Jade was pregnant, yet still showed no outward signs of her condition. Brian leaned over to ask her about her new house when his leg bumped Luke's rifle, which was leaning against the left side of the seat.

"Get this damn thing out of here," Brian spat, kicking the rifle violently.

Luke, who had been talking to Murphy in the seat next to him, looked stunned.

"Easy, Bri," Jade soothed, grabbing his arm. "Just relax."

"Sorry, bud," Luke apologized. "You're right, I should keep it stowed properly.

Brian suddenly realized how badly he had overreacted. Then he felt like a tyrant. He couldn't recall a time in his entire life when his cousin had said or done anything bad to him. Even now, after facing Brian's raging temper, Luke played the part of diplomat. "I'm sorry," he began. "It's just—"

"Don't worry about it," Luke said in his characteristically nonchalant voice. "Back when I was in boot camp about ten years ago, I saw another cadet get fifty lashes for not stowing his weapon in his locker."

Brian shuddered. "Scary."

"Yeah."

Confident that Luke wasn't angry, Brian arched his head back to see if Kim had heard his little outburst. She hadn't. The group of children swarming around her shielded any incoming stimuli, especially when half of the children were refusing to sit in their seats properly. Finally, Chang stepped back from the cabin and the chaos instantly transformed into a model of order. Brian thought Kim looked relieved, and the beleaguered sigh she let out in his direction confirmed that he was right in this assumption. As Chang sat down, the shuttle's engines roared to life, and it slowly lifted off from the dusty landing zone in the middle of town. Brian, who wasn't seated near a window, leaned his head back and rested it on his seat. Sleep came fast.

Unlike Kim, Brian rarely dreamed. And when he did, his dreams certainly weren't as deep as hers. There were never any visions and certainly no answers, just incoherent images and words. When he awoke, the first thing he noticed was sunlight bathing the interior of the cabin. Outside the window a few seats to Brian's left, an icy blue sky could be seen clearly. Up in the northern highlands it rarely rained, and when it did, the storms were short and violent.

Brian saw several of the younger children straining to see the jagged peaks out the windows. A few seconds later, Kim's voice filled the cabin, reminding her charges not to undo their restraints until the ship had landed. Knowing the trip would be over soon, Brian struggled to jolt himself out of his grogginess.

The shuttle landed on the edge of the flat meadow on the southern shore. As soon as the passengers began to stand up, Brian shot out of his seat and bolted down the exit ramp. He didn't want to be caught in the inevitable stampede of children that was sure to follow. Kim and the other adults could handle the younger students. Brian had never considered himself to be good with kids, anyway. He grabbed his bag from the cargo hold and quickly made his way over to the other shuttle that had landed several dozen meters away next to one of the short, yet bulky, conifers dotting the mountainous landscape. Brian had agreed to come to Clarity so that he could have some fun with his friends. Beyond that, he felt little responsibility to assist Chang with the fieldtrip. He only hoped that Kim's duties wouldn't keep her from him the whole time.

The rest of the first day was spent unpacking the shuttles and setting up camp at the base of a chalky-white cliff face near the water. On the second day, Chang led the students up into the surrounding hills to examine the exotic rock formations that had been carved by glaciers tens of thousands of years before. Diego Cruz, a geologist from Sanctuary and teacher at the New Haven school, did most of the talking, while Kim played the role of chaperone. Brian and the rest of his friends, who had traveled to Lake Clarity on two previous occasions and had heard more lectures on rock formations than they could stand, went off to explore the wooded area on the far side of the five-kilometer-wide lake. Brian wanted to visit the caves he had seen on the previous trip, but agreed to let Maleek and Derrick plan the day's activities. Brian needed time to explore the caves and didn't want to hear any whining from unwilling companions. And besides, a light snow had fallen the night before, and although most of it had melted in the early hours of the morning, they hoped to find some deeper patches in the shade created by the trees and rocky slopes.

Following an intense snowball fight, Brian, Derrick, Molly, Maleek, Suna and four kids from the class below began the long, difficult trek back towards camp as it began to grow dark. Halfway through the trip, Brian had given his outer jacket to a sixteen-year-old girl named Lisa, who had neglected to bring her own. As light, fluffy snowflakes began to fall from the dimming, late autumn sky, Brian wished that he could instantly transport himself back to camp where he could bask in the warm glow of the fire.

"It didn't seem this far earlier today," Derrick pointed out as they trudged alongside the gently lapping shoreline of the mirror-like lake.

"It's always more fun when you're going somewhere new," Maleek reasoned.

"Great. Thanks for the insight," Derrick muttered.

"Maybe if you didn't roll around in the snow so much, you wouldn't be so cold," Suna pointed out in a tone as frosty as the air.

"Yeah, Derrick," Molly added. "I didn't hear any complaining when you pushed Maleek's face into that drift by the creek."

"He had it coming," laughed Derrick.

Maleek said nothing to defend himself, opting instead to show his disapproval by flashing an obscene hand gesture in his friend's direction.

"Me?" Derrick shrugged innocently.

Brian, who had begun to shiver, ignored the ongoing banter. Instead he stared down at the frozen, white, sandy strip of beach, and concentrated on getting back to the camp.

The younger kids also seemed to be focused on getting back to warmth. The group of four, three girls and one boy, seemed to move together as one body as they struggled to feed off each other's heat. Brian knew all of them well, and realized that they didn't have much experience with real cold. Most of the colonists younger than Brian and his friends had spent a large chunk of their lives on the small, warm continent on which the colony was situated. To them, the Lake Clarity region, beautiful as it was, must have seemed like a frozen alien wasteland compared to their warm, inviting valley. Even in the dead of winter, the colonists rarely experienced temperatures even close to freezing.

Just as Brian began to see the faint signs of fire from the camp, he heard several large booming sounds echo over the lake. He looked up at the sky, puzzled as to why it was thundering on such a clear, cold night. Another loud clap shattered the nocturnal calm that had settled in around the lake. Brian turned and looked at his friends. They were curious as well. Then, as a third, more prolonged barrage sounded out, the group's demeanor changed. It was gunfire.

Without hesitation, Brian started running toward the camp. He felt footsteps close behind, and soon heard Derrick begin to swear. He swore a lot when he got excited or scared. Maleek was back there too, although his long, clumsy legs had difficulty navigating the dark, featureless underbrush. He soon fell behind. *They'd better not just be shooting their rifles for practice or fun*, Brian thought. Then he remembered that Luke had strict rules about when and where to hold target practice. This had to be a legitimate crisis. Brian steadily increased his speed.

As Brian bounded over a fallen log and entered the camp, he was greeted by a scene of total chaos. Equipment was overturned. Tents were shredded. Everywhere, debris was strewn about, as if some unknown attacker had ransacked the camp. Several younger children ran around screaming, looking for some adult to take charge and save them from the phantom horror tearing through the camp.

After a moment of searching, Brian's eyes fell upon the cause of the disturbance. Through the dusky twilight, he saw the sleek, powerful white forms of several adult Equestriars running around in confusion. The animals were Elysium's answer to Earth's horses, although they were a foot or two taller and a couple of hundred kilograms heavier than full-grown Clydesdales. Just as Brian's mind processed what was going on, a blue bolt from Murphy's pulse rifle shot past one of the raging beasts and into a cluster of rocks to the west of the camp. *What's he shooting at?* Brian asked himself. *Murphy usually doesn't miss.*

Brian felt his companions bump into the back of him and he spun around. "Stay here. Find some cover behind one of the trees," he ordered sternly.

"What's going on?" asked Susan Breton, a fifteen year old from New London who had accompanied Brian to the forest.

"I don't know, but stay here," Brian reiterated.

"Where are you going?" Suna asked.

"I've gotta find out what's going on."

"Not without us," Maleek insisted.

Brian thought about it for a moment. "Fine," he relented. "but just watch out for the Equestriars. They'll run you right over without even knowing it."

Brian turned back toward the camp again and made his way over to the nearest tent that was still standing. The group followed closely behind. Brian didn't mind having his friends at his back, but hated feeling responsible for the safety of his four younger companions. Brian and Derrick quickly snatched up two kids who were running around and ferried them to the relative safety of the tent.

Brian stuck his head into the flap and found Sonia Carter, a member of Luke's security force, trying desperately to calm down a group of younger children.

"Brian," she started, looking somewhat surprised to see him. "Take this group over behind the boulders in the southeastern corner of camp. Do you know which ones I'm talking about?"

"Forget that!" Brian yelled, trying to make himself heard over the crying children and stampeding animals. "Molly or somebody else can do it. I can help you and Luke, just tell me what's going—"

Brian didn't have time to finish his sentence. At that moment, Susan screamed louder than seemed humanly possible. Behind Brian, near the rocks that Murphy had fired at, two hulking forms emerged at terrifying speed. They were the apex predators of Elysium's northern continents; large, two legged beasts towering five or six meters above the ground. The closest comparison Brian had come up with to describe them during past observations were Tyrannosaurus Rexes with a thin layer of gray, downy feathers over their incredibly thick hides. The females, which were larger than the males, sported a large, bony, sail-like structure down the middle of their arched backs. Normally, they seemed to make a point to stay far away from human activity, but the herd of Equestriars had obviously allowed them to overcome their fear.

The smaller of the two beasts, no doubt the male, ran into the middle of camp and sunk its menacing rows of serrated teeth into the side of a fleeing Equestriar. The prey let out a painful scream, not unlike the one Susan had issued only seconds before. As the wounded Eequstriar fought for its life, the other beast broke for the opposite end of the camp beyond Brian's view. Brian instinctively pushed his younger companions into the tent and shut the flap, hoping that it would conceal them from the roaming eyes of the excited predators. Sonia immediately threw back the flap and joined Brian. "We can't just stay here," she said in a frustrated tone.

"It's too late to move the kids," Maleek said. "They'll have to stay in the tent."

"Where's your pulse rifle?" Derrick asked, staring down at Sonia's empty hands.

"I don't know," she confessed. "It was in my tent."

Brian looked around. Everything was in shambles. The rifle could be anywhere.

"How about Kim or Chang? Where'd they go?"

Sonia shook her head again.

"Come on," Brian said, pointing to the cluster of trees by the shoreline that separated the two halves of the encampment. "Molly, Suna," he yelled back to the tent. Molly poked her head out wearily. "As soon as you see that thing leave, get to the shuttles!"

Molly nodded, although Brian wasn't sure she would carry out the plan. Hopefully, Suna would take charge if Molly froze up.

Brian led Sonia, Maleek and Derrick over to the trees and lay down in the short, but dense underbrush. To their right they heard two more shots ring out through the darkness. They could also here more yelling, which was barely audible over deafening sound of stamping hooves on the dry, frosty ground. Ahead, about twenty meters away, the smaller predator tore into its recently deceased prey.

"Derrick, Maleek." Brian whispered. "Run back to the tent and get them to the shuttles. They won't make a move as long as that thing's over there. You're going to have to drag them."

"What if it sees us?" Maleek asked. "We can't outrun that, especially not with a bunch of kids."

"Just do it!" Brian yelled through gritted teeth. "It won't notice as long as it's eating. Besides, we'll be making a lot more noise for it to focus on."

Derrick and Maleek seemed to hesitate for a moment.

"Go, damn it!"

Brian watched his two friends get up and slink quietly back to the tent.

"What do you have in mind, Brian?" Sonia asked. Although she had been a security soldier for more than two years, Sonia wasn't much older than Brian, maybe in her early twenties at the most. Brian didn't know her well, but was confident that she was brave enough to charge recklessly into a situation like this.

"We're going to find out where everyone else is," he said with an icy resolve.

"I can't see what's going on up there," Sonia noted, motioning toward the far side of camp.

"Neither can I, but we're not doing anything by sitting here. Ready?"

Sonia nodded.

Brian jumped to his feet and ran out of the cluster of trees into the other section of camp. In the light of the fires, which still burned as if nothing had happened, Brian saw the faint outlines of people moving on the outskirts of the camp. He started over to one of the larger tents, one that had remained untouched by the chaos, but a familiar voice stopped him.

"Brian!"

"Kim?"

Brian stopped as he attempted to locate the source of the whisper.

"Over here," Kim yelled as Brian caught a glimpse of an outstretched hand behind a rock. He ran over to it, and found Kim huddled with ten of the children and two of the parents.

"Where's everyone else?" Brian asked.

"Luke and Murphy managed to chase off most of the Equestriars, but then we saw one of those huge monsters."

"How about Chang?"

Kim motioned over to a ditch on the far western side of camp, near some of the boulders. "He and the others are somewhere over there. I think they're okay, but I haven't seen any of them for a few minutes. Jade's back at the shuttle with Diego and Maria, so they should be fine too."

Brian perked his head up. The chase seemed to be moving farther away. "I need to find Luke."

"No, Bri. Stay here and wait for him to come back!"

"I've gotta go, Kim!" Brian stood up again and started toward the noise beyond the boulders.

"Brian, be careful," Sonia ordered.

"I will, just stay here and watch the kids!"

Brian made his way quickly through camp, not quite sure where he was going or what he should do when he got there. Suddenly, he heard Luke's voice coming from the corridor of boulders up ahead. His cousin emerged in full retreat with Murphy at his side. Behind them charged the larger of the two beasts. It wasn't hunting for Equestriars anymore.

Brian stood motionless as the chase got closer to him. He was standing exposed, in the middle of a circle of crumbled tents and roaring campfires. Just as the predator came within striking distance of Luke, he turned, hastily aimed his pulse rifle and fired. The shot grazed off the animal's thick hide as it let out a roar of rage and pain. It swung its head in a grazing motion and knocked Luke several meters back on the rough surface of a boulder. Brian thought he heard the air leave his cousin's body, even from a fair distance away. As the animal bore down on its comparatively tiny prey, Murphy picked up a tent pole and jabbed the animal in the leg. The predator instinctively kicked back toward the annoyance, knocking Murphy to the ground as well.

From his peripheral, Brian saw the sleek, dark form of the second predator come into view. It had no doubt responded to the cries of its mate. Brian frantically looked around for some sort of weapon to use against the beasts. He settled on a tent pole, not unlike the one Murphy had tried to use. But Brian had a different idea in mind for striking the animal. He ran around to Luke's side to get a better view of the beast's front. As the creature bent down to deliver the killing blow to Luke's body, Brian shifted the pole in his hand, found its center of gravity and hurled the makeshift javelin at the animal's head.

The creature must have seen the object coming, since it jerked its head back in surprise. The pole missed Brian's intended target, but still managed to strike the animal in the neck, attaching itself to the skin like a giant acupuncture needle. This time the creature's scream of pain dwarfed anything any human could ever muster. It reared back in agony as it shook its neck and head violently back and forth. After a few seconds, the pole came loose from its flesh and fell to the ground.

Mistake, was the only word that came to Brian's mind. He hadn't thought of a plan beyond throwing the pole. Both creatures seemed to stare at him for a second, obviously wondering how such a puny creature could dare to challenge them. Brian knew what was coming. He turned and ran. Far behind, he heard the receding sound of Kim's voice cry out to him.

The western shore of Lake Clarity that extended north of the camp was much rockier and difficult to navigate than the open meadow to the south. As Brian cut around each rock and jumped from crevice to crevice as fast as his feet could carry him, he anticipated the sharp bite of teeth on his exposed backside. He could hear the two enraged predators running closely behind him. He could even smell their musky stench, a sweaty, pungent aroma that stoked a dormant, primate instinct hiding deep within his subconscious. Brian no longer felt the fear that had kept his feet immobile when the creatures had first emerged behind Luke and Murphy. He had an idea: *The caves.* He only hoped his memory was good enough to lead him to the openings in the pale moonlight of Phobos.

The pursuing creatures grunted often; Brian supposed they were having trouble moving their large bodies around the thousands of shattered pieces of the limestone cliff face that had fallen down over the centuries. Brian felt a sharp pain as his own legs scrapped the sharp surface of a jagged rock. He hobbled for a moment, just long enough for the smaller predator to come with striking distance. Brian ducked as its teeth snapped just centimeters from his face. He smelled rotting meat on its breath. Brian forced himself through a thin crevice that he was confident was too small to be negotiated by his pursuers. The action bought him some time. On the other side of the crevice he saw a rocky outcropping that marked the entrance to one of the caves. Brian ducked and cut quickly to his left into the safety of the cave. A wave of elation swept through his adrenaline-wracked body. He had made it. But no sooner did he enter the apparent safety of the shelter then he realized that he had chosen the wrong crevice to hide in. Unlike many of the other cracks in the limestone, the one Brian had chosen did not open up into an actual cavern. It didn't even extend far enough into the cliff to save him from the probing jaws of the predators.

Brian pressed his back against the dark, moist rock, away from the large opening of the crevice. *Maybe they won't find me in here*, he hoped. *It's dark and they did lose me a second ago.* Then he remembered the large nostrils that adorned the heads of the predators. It was only a matter of time.

The loud, wet sound of sniffing could soon be heard out in the moonlight. Brian tried to become one with the wall, pressing his back into the rock so hard that it began to cut into his skin. The snout of the smaller beast hovered outside the crevice for a moment, before poking into the opening. Brian was suddenly greeted by the large, featureless eyes of a killer. The beast saw him, and let out a deafening cry. It sounded like satisfaction. The other predator appeared at the crevice's opening and forced its smaller mate out of the way.

This is it, Brian told himself. He was comforted only by the hope that everyone in the camp had escaped to the safety of the shuttles. Brian's only regret was that he hadn't spent enough time with Kim during the day, and that he hadn't seen his mother the day before he had left to go on the trip.

Brian forced his eyes to stay open. He wanted to see his death coming. If there was a God, Brian hoped that it was the kind, gentle entity that Kim envisioned. The female predator lowered herself down enough so she could reach inside the crevice with her jaws and moved on Brian. He dodged, somehow finding enough room in the cramped confines of his surroundings to avoid being hit by the creature's knife-filled mouth. The beast hit the wall with her snout and shook her head, apparently stunned from the blow. Brian's stomach brushed against the side of her ghastly face. The contact with the rough, merciless jawbone of the creature added to the strange concoction of fear and fatigue brewing in his mind, and immediately produced a new sensation of primal rage. Brian looked down at his attacker and gritted his teeth. He picked up a holoball-sized rock that had broken off the crevice wall and brought it down on the tip of the beast's blunt, slimy snout. This time she recoiled from the blow, snorting and sneezing uncontrollably. The male, which had been waiting patiently on the side, stared dumbfounded at the display.

Anticipating another attack, Brian stood squarely in the center of the crevice opening, rock in hand. But the attack never came. The female predator let out a long, anguished whine and retreated off into the darkness. After another minute or two of confusion, the other beast followed.

Brian waited until he was sure they were gone before letting his body collapse onto the floor of the crevice. He forced himself up after a moment and made his way several dozen meters down to another opening, one that actually penetrated deeply into the cliff face. Confident that he was finally safe in his new hiding place, Brian collapsed again, this time for the night.

CHAPTER 17

▼

THE CATHEDRAL

Brian awoke to the sound of his mother's voice calling his name. It reminded him of back when she used to get him up for school as a child. He forced his eyes open and tried to lift his body out of bed. To his dismay, he found himself lying on a cold, wet floor. *The cave*, he thought. *I must have fallen asleep, or passed out.* Brian's side and leg hurt terribly. Even worse, he shivered from the cold breeze whipping through the crevice a few meters away. He rolled over, groaning loudly, and propped himself up on the rocky wall near the cavern's tiny opening. Warm rays of sunlight penetrated the murky darkness around him, bathing his filth-covered face in heavenly illumination. Still feeling too weak to call out, he listened for the voice.

"Briiiaannn," he heard again. It wasn't his mother's voice. It was Jade. She had a worried sound in her voice, a panicked tone that transcended her usual level of neuroticism.

"I'm here," he called out, wincing from the pain in his side.

"Brian?" a multitude of voices echoed all at once. They seemed perplexed as to where he was.

"In the cave!" Brian screamed as loudly as possible. He was a little perturbed at having to repeat such a painful action.

"Wait, up there, in the cliff face," he heard Murphy say to the others.

No kidding, he thought.

"Hey Bishop, you alive in there?" Derrick asked as he poked his head into the cave.

"Kind of," Brian answered. "There's no way I'm moving anytime soon, though."

Jade brushed roughly past Derrick and into the cave.

"Oh God," she sighed, pouncing on Brian with an open bio-scanner. "You had us so worried." Brian relaxed as Jade pawed at him. "Are you bitten? Are you hurt?" she asked in rapid succession.

"I don't know," Brian said, shrugging. "My side hurts. So does my leg."

As Jade continued to check Brian over, a small crowd gathered at the cave's entrance.

"We've been looking for you all night, Brian!" said Maleek. "Chang's leading another search party up on the other side of the lake. We weren't even sure which direction you were going!"

Brian thought about it for a moment. At the time, it hadn't seemed like the chase had gone on very long. But as he thought about where the caves were in the cliff face, Brian realized that he must have run for at least ten minutes or more. The caves were easily two kilometers from the camp, on the far northwestern side of the lake.

"Where's Luke?" Brian asked as he attempted to lift himself from the floor. The last time he had seen his cousin, Luke looked as if he may be mortally wounded.

"Just relax," Jade ordered, pushing him down. "Luke's fine. He's just got a couple of broken ribs. I've got him resting in the medical bay in one of the shuttles. I had to sedate him in order to keep him from coming with us to look for you." Jade stood up and told the people who were standing outside of the cave to get a stretcher from the camp. She turned back to Brian. "You've got a sprained knee and some bad cuts and bruises on your side. Nothing serious, but I don't want you moving too much until I run some more scans on the shuttle."

That's fine, Brian thought. He was content to lie there all day if needed. He rested his head against a makeshift pillow Maleek had fashioned from a blanket and surrendered completely to Jade's examination. He overheard Murphy radio Chang about the rescue, and the Minister's excited response to the news. Now all Brian wanted to do was sleep. He used his right arm, which didn't cause any pain when moved, to pull one of the blankets his sister had given him fully over his body and tried to block out the noise of the growing crowd around him.

"So how'd you get away from those things?" Derrick asked.

Everyone quieted as they waited for an answer.

Brian opened a weary eye. "I ran into one of the smaller caves and tried to hide," he muttered carelessly, hoping his answer would suffice. It didn't.

"So then what," Maleek jumped in. "Did they find you?"

"Yeah, were you scared?" asked Molly from outside the cave.

"They found me."

"Then what?"

Brian let out a frustrated sigh. "I hit the big one's nose with a rock when it stuck its face in to get me."

"And then?" someone else asked.

"And then it ran away. I think it figured I wasn't worth the effort."

A collective gasp ran through the group.

"That was some brave maneuver," Murphy spoke up. "You thought pretty fast on your feet, kid."

"I didn't really think it through at all," Brian confessed.

"What flash of inspiration made you decide to come here?" Jade asked.

Brian gave her a scowl. She knew quite well that he wasn't in the mood to recount the story. Her wry smile confirmed that she was having some fun with her little brother.

"I don't know," he answered again. "I remembered seeing some of the cave entrances last time we were here a couple of years ago. I was going to come explore them before we left this time."

"Well, it looks like you got to explore them a bit sooner than expected, eh?" Murphy chuckled, shinning his flashlight toward the infinite blackness of the cave.

"Wow, I bet this system goes on for kilometers," Maleek said, as if just realizing he was in a cave.

Brian rolled his eyes.

The ever-impulsive Derrick grabbed Maleek by the arm and charged off in the direction of Murphy' beam.

"Where are you two going?" Jade asked in her motherly tone.

"Where does it look like, Bishop?" Derrick shot back, before continuing onward.

Now it was Jade's turn to roll her eyes. "Well, don't kill yourselves or get lost down there!"

"What?" a fading voice called back from the darkness.

A part of Brian wanted to join his friends on their spelunking adventure, but the rest of him was content to sleep for the remainder of the trip. With the crowd's attention now on the cave system itself, he was free from answering any more questions about his minor act of heroism. Brian wasn't sure if he had run from the predators the night before out of fear or a sincere desire to lead them away from the camp. The only thing he was sure of was that he didn't appreciate the extra attention. He had worked very hard over the last few years to avoid distinguishing himself in a group of people who came from positions in society so very different from his own. He could still remember back to when some colonists referred to him as "That Adherent kid."

Brian closed his eyes again and tried to drift off to sleep as he waited for the stretcher to arrive to bring him back to camp. He also hoped that Kim would make it over to the cave before he was moved back. She was one person whom he did want the extra attention from. At this point in the trip, he had totally given up competing with the children for her time. Brian understood why she had such responsibility. He just couldn't understand why she had wanted him to come up to the lake so badly if all she planned to do was play teacher and chaperone.

Brian's ears perked as he heard echoes emanating from deep within the cave. At first, he assumed that Derrick was being loud like usual, or perhaps Maleek was showing off for Molly. As the shouts grew louder, however, Brian realized that something was wrong. He turned his head to face the darkness and began to shake from yet another stream of adrenaline crashing through his body. At this point, he half expected a three-headed purple dragon to storm out of the cave depths and incinerate him with fire.

"What are they yelling?" Jade asked Murphy, who continued to shine the beam of light into the void.

"Come here," he answered. "I think they want us to come there."

"Dammit," swore Jade, standing up from Brian's side. "This better not be a stupid prank or something." She looked back down at Brian. "Think you'll survive, Bri?"

Brain didn't respond. He was starring into the darkness, wondering what his friends had found.

"Can you watch him?" Jade asked Maria Sanchez, one of the colony's geologists who had come along on the trip. The kind, young woman pulled her attention from the stalagmites on the floor near the cave entrance and nodded in affirmation. As she took Jade's place, Brian's sister and Murphy started in the direction of the yelling.

Derrick's going to get in so much trouble if this is a joke, Brian thought to himself. *If Luke hears about it, he won't let him leave the shuttle until the end of the trip!* Brian gazed up at Maria's face. "Three to one odds he's playing a prank," he said. But upon hearing another muffled yell, Brian began to doubt that possibility.

Maria smiled weakly. Brian remembered that she rarely said anything if it didn't have to do with sedimentary rocks or erosion rates.

Brian soon made a second attempt to stand up. He felt quite a bit better now, in part due to the painkillers Jade had given him a few minutes before.

"Brian, Jade said to—" Maria started, before Brian cut her off.

"I know, but I'm feeling a little better now."

He stood up all the way, propping himself up on the rocky interior of the cave. Maria stepped back, apparently helpless to stop him. He looked at her again. "I'm fine."

She nodded in understanding. "What do you think's going on?"

"Don't know, but like I said, Derrick's probably fooling around."

Outside the cave, Brian heard several members of the search party milling around, talking about the previous night's adventure. They were apparently unaware of the potential drama that was unfolding in the bowels of the cliff. "What's taking them so long?" Brian asked out loud, more to himself than Maria.

She didn't answer, although the worried look on her face signaled that she wanted to know the same. The cave had grown deathly silent.

Brian's ears were so tuned to the sounds of the cave that he failed to notice the growing noise outside the crevice entrance. Chang's search party had arrived and was being filled in on Brian's rescue. Kim was the first to pop her head through the opening.

"Bri!" she squealed, almost tackling his wounded body. Brian grunted in agony, but reasoned that the pain was worth it.

"Oh, sorry," Kim apologized, pulling back.

"I'm fine," he lied.

Kim hugged him again, this time more gently. She pulled back again and kissed him several times on the lips in rapid succession. Now Brian felt positively great.

"Good show, Mr. Bishop," Chang s announced from the cave entrance. He was flanked by several of the younger students who had tagged along. Upon seeing her teacher and students, Kim immediately pulled back from Brian. He hated how reserved she became around them, as if showing Brian physical affection was some sort of sin. Of course, in their past lives, it had been.

"Thanks," Brian responded, attempting to cover up any presence of hostility in his voice. Although he got along with Chang much better than he had five years before, the old man still managed to spawn many negative emotions. Even Brian wasn't sure where these feelings all came from. Perhaps he merely felt resentful for Kim's constant devotion to her mentor. Perhaps it was because Brian had long ago given up on modeling himself on a mentor of his own.

Chang's gaze shifted from Brian's face to the darkness beyond. Brian turned to see Murphy emerge with a drawn flashlight, slung pulse rifle, and a look of utter astonishment. Brian felt a wave of relief until he noticed this expression. Jade wasn't with him. Nobody was with him. Murphy silently passed right by Brian and took Chang aside. He whispered something into the Minister's ear that Brian couldn't discern, and Chang's face instantly mirrored Murphy's.

"What's going on? Is everyone safe?" Brian asked.

Murphy shot Chang a glance, and the Minister nodded, as if signaling his approval.

"Tell me," Brian demanded. He hated being treated like a kid, especially now.

"Come with me," Murphy said in a stern voice. He looked at Kim. "Tell Maria to come back in and check if Dr. Cruz is around too. They need to see this."

Kim began toward entrance.

"And Kim," Murphy said. "Don't let the others know about it. Keep things quiet."

Kim looked puzzled. So did Brian. After a few confused seconds, she turned and did as Murphy asked. Once she was out of the cave, Chang handed Brian an extra flashlight and the trio began walking down the dark tunnel. The Minister, seeing that Brian was limping slightly, placed an arm around him and attempted to help shoulder the weight. Murphy walked quickly a few paces ahead, as if driven by some unseen force.

As Brian made his way down the dark, moist tunnel, he felt Chang's bony, aged form begin to shake. Brian wasn't sure if it was because of the added weight, or because of what Murphy had revealed to him.

After several minutes of walking, Brian finally heard the excited voices of his friends and sister up ahead. At this point in his journey, he was quite annoyed with anyone who wanted to pursue a new adventure. The only thing driving him on was a lingering curiosity over what exactly lay at the end of the tunnel. Upon hearing another battery of yells, this round much louder than the last, he disengaged himself from Chang and charged ahead next to Murphy. In the meager beams of the flashlights, Brian could only see that the tunnel opened up into a larger room. He immediately felt a rush of air against his face, a telltale sign that the chasm in front of him was enormous. Far ahead, like three distant beacons on the rocky shore of an Earthly ocean, Brian could see the lights they were walking toward. *They have to be at least a hundred meters away*, Brian thought. The lights also looked like they were several meters below where Brian was walking, as if there was some sort of drop-off or slope in front of him. He slowed.

"Don't worry, it's a ramp," Murphy mentioned as if he had read Brian's mind.

Brian didn't take the word "ramp" literally, just as a description of a sloping floor. Like Murphy had predicted, Brian soon felt himself descending toward the three flashlights, which were waving around in every possible direction. The chasm, or whatever they were in, was so large that the beams didn't even reach to the opposite ends of the walls. For all Brian knew, they were in an endless void.

Brian stopped again. Chang stopped too. Murphy, who had already made it to Derrick, Maleek and Jade, put his backpack down on the cave floor and began to fish through its contents.

"What is this place?" Brian asked, looking down at his feet. Murphy's ramp description was uncanny. It really looked as if they were standing on a structure that had been carved by hand. It seemed far too smooth to have occurred naturally. Unlike the cave entrance, and the tunnel, there were no asymmetrical rock formations or stalagmites protruding from the ground. Also, the cavern now felt dry and warm, as if it were immune to the outside elements.

"You think that's weird, Bishop, just wait until you see this!" Derrick exclaimed from several meters away.

Brian looked up just in time to see Murphy remove two illumination flares from his pack and ignite them. Brian recoiled from the blast of light and shielded his eyes instinctively. Murphy threw both flares far out into the darkness and they exploded again, this time into their second, more intense phase.

Even when Brian's eyes adjusted to the light, it seemed as if they were playing tricks with his imagination. The room in which he now stood dwarfed anything he had ever seen, even the great Cathedrals back on Earth. And yet, the word "cathedral" was the most accurate description Brian's disbelieving mind could fathom at this extraordinary moment, one of the most astounding in his young life.

It stood there, just a few meters ahead of Maleek, at what looked to be the very center of the vast, spherical chasm; an octet of obelisks standing two meters tall and spaced evenly about ten meters apart in a circle. At the center of the formation sat a stone dais adorned with a large spherical object, its perfectly smooth surface interrupted only by a small, missing chunk on the top side. The sphere was about level with Brian's head and seemed to absorb all light directed toward it. It offered no reflection in response to inspection, yet its surface seemed to shimmer from some inner source.

Brian walked past his friends, toward the closest obelisk. On its impossibly flawless, onyx surface he could make out an intricate, interlocking system of designs and marks. It looked like some sort of writing, although no human mind could comprehend the intended meaning. But to Brian the message was clear: Elysium was inhabited. Brian and his people had made their home on a world that was not their own.

Whoever or whatever built the monument must have died out long ago, Brian kept telling himself in the hours following the discovery. Surely, if the builders were still alive somewhere on the planet, the colonists would have found evidence prior to discovery in the cave. After some debate between Chang, Jade, a newly resurrected Luke, and the scientists on the trip, they had come to the conclusion that there was no harm in letting everyone know what had been found, whatever *it* was. As the day stretched into what was sure to be a very long night, nobody could yet agree on an answer to that fundamental question.

A religious icon? An astronomical tool? A written history of a dead species? Brian felt as perplexed as the others. As he rested on what looked to be an altar situated next to the main ramp in the chasm, Brian tiredly watched the increasingly heated debate amongst his companions. His eyelids were getting heavy. He checked his timepiece. It was close to midnight, and nobody showed signs of wanting to leave the cave. Those who had been sent back to camp to guard the younger children and contact the colony about the discovery did so only after being ordered by Luke, who had taken command of the situation. It was clear that this discovery had the potential to cause hysteria among the colonists if handled poorly.

To aid in the initial analysis of the cave, the three scientists had taken a set of emergency floodlights from one of the shuttles and had arranged them around the room. It still looked impossibly large; at least one hundred meters from the ultra-smooth floor to design-strewn ceiling.

Finally it became quiet in the room as the crowd of adults surveyed each obelisk meticulously. Kim, who surprisingly enough hadn't gone back to camp to be with the children stood motionless as she examined the inner sphere in the middle of the formation. Brian began to get concerned as he watched her from afar. She hadn't moved in several minutes and now appeared to be mouthing silent words.

"Kim?" he called out.

The others, startled by the sudden noise, gave Brian a look of annoyance, but then followed his gaze back to Kim.

"Kim, honey?" Jade spoke as she approached from behind.

"I know what this is," Kim said in an almost catatonic voice. "It's Ares."

"That's certainly a possibility, Kim" Dr. Cruz interjected in a doubting tone, "but there's no way to be sure. It could be the sun, or Elysium itself. Perhaps even Phobos or Demos."

"Some of the markings on the pillars look like constellations," Maria added with excitement. She was in her element now: scientific theory.

"You're right, Maria" Kim said, in the same, calm voice. "It is a representation of the night sky. This formation represents their entire universe.

"It may take years of study before we determine anything," Cruz quickly added. "We need to get some more of the scientific staff from the colony. It also wouldn't hurt if we found similar ruins to compare."

"When I contacted the colony, Raasch said that they'd send a team back up here as soon possible," Luke said. "Right now they just want us to record as much data as possible and leave. There's a severe storm brewing on the southern coast that could make the return trip a little bumpy if it grows. Plus, some of the parents back home are worried about their kids. I told them about the attack last night."

Brian continued to watch Kim. She still hadn't taken her eyes off the sphere.

"How do you know it's Ares?" he asked her.

Kim said nothing in response. Everyone looked at her with renewed concern. Then she spoke: "Because it's in the center where it can see everything. And the Eye of God sees all."

CHAPTER 18

▼

SHARDS OF THE PAST

"The Eye of God sees all," Brian repeated several times as he lay on his back in his dark tent. "What the hell does that mean?"

Nobody in the cave had acknowledged Kim's statement about the spherical object, but everyone had heard it. The statement terrified them. It was an unwelcome reminder of the past. Many times, looking up at the night sky over the colony, they had seen the red moon and shuttered at its harsh, unwavering glare. It did look like an eye, an eye that watched everything the colonists did every day of their lives, much as the Church had back on Earth.

Although Brian had accompanied Kim back to the camp after Jade suggested that they get some rest, the two didn't speak much. Kim had absent-mindedly asked Brian how he felt, and he responded "fine" just as carelessly. He wanted to penetrate the icy exterior she had begun to erect during the past few weeks and see into her mind. The process had been gradual, but as they walked toward camp through the cold darkness, Brian couldn't hide from the fact that Kim was different now than she had been. She was no longer the playful, kind friend with whom he had weathered the storms of childhood. Everything seemed different, and Brian didn't know why. Kim no longer shared her thoughts with him as she had in the past, and the few details she did give him were cryptic and unsettling. When she kissed him lately, the action seemed to lack passion, barring the previous morning when she had found him alive in the cave. When they talked, she seemed to hold back, as if she knew something that Brian didn't and believed he was incapable of handling the truth. It was strange; he now felt more like a burden than her companion, as if he were a student trying to learn a lesson. The worst part of it all for Brian was that it seemed like Kim didn't need him anymore.

After telling Kim goodnight without so much as a kiss, Brian had reluctantly returned to his tent, which had been moved to the relative safety of the wooded area on the lake's eastern shore. Maleek and Derrick, who shared the tent with him, had asked if he wanted to come along to gather some things from the shuttle's cargo hold to start a fire. Brian, feeling close to passing out while standing up, declined the offer, opting instead to dive into his warm sleeping bag.

Brain replayed the day's incredible events over in his mind a few times, then thought some more about Kim. He had to ask her what was going on, no matter how she reacted. If things kept going the way they were, there was a chance that she would drift even further away from him. What if she took the Vow of Celibacy, as the female members of the Church had always done back on Earth? The idea was ridiculous, but he shuddered anyway. With Kim acting the way she had been the last few months, anything seemed possible. Brian decided to confront her about it tomorrow, before they left for the colony. Until then, he decided that such weighty issues could be put on hold until he got the rest he had been craving for what seemed like eternity.

Just as he was drifting off into the merciful oblivion of sleep, Brian heard the noise of someone fiddling with the hatch on his tent. "Shut up, you two," Brian commanded in a lazy voice. His voice was muffled by the supple fluff of his sleeping bag, which had fallen over his mouth.

The fiddling continued.

"I said I don't want to go to the shuttle!" Brian yelled, this time sitting up in frustration. To his surprise, the flap opened, revealing Kim.

Brian no longer felt tired. In fact, his heart was pounding. *Why was she here?* Brian thought of a few possibilities.

"Hi," Kim said as she slipped through the hatch and closed it behind her.

"Hi," Brian responded, not wanting to sound too alarmed.

"Don't worry, I told Maleek and Derrick to go build the fire away from the tent. They won't bother us."

Brian reached over and turned on the small lamp next to his sleeping bag. Kim took a seat on his bag and leaned over his outstretched legs. Brian closed the gap between their bodies and kissed her passionately on the lips.

But before Brian even reached the point of arousal, he realized something was wrong. Kim still felt cold and distant, even though she didn't fight him off. He pulled back.

"What's wrong?"

Kim bit her lip and looked away from him. Her eyes were beginning to tear up.

"Kim, what's the matter? What's with you lately?" Brian's voice carried the pent-up frustration that had festered over the preceding weeks. He wanted an answer, now.

"Bri," she began, not in her usual, confident tone.

"Yeah?"

"Remember when I told you a few nights ago that nothing was going to change between us when I move to New Haven in the spring?"

"Yeah."

"Well," Tears began to run down her face. "I think I lied to you."

"What do you mean?"

"I don't know," she confessed.

"What do you mean you don't know?"

"I mean," Kim continued, obviously struggling to put emotion into words. "I mean that I think things will change. I need them to change."

"How? Why?" Brian was beginning to raise his voice. *What was she talking about?*

"I feel different lately. It's like I know I should be doing something, but I don't know what or how."

Brian forced himself to listen to what he interpreted as babble. He reminded himself that this was what he had wanted: some sort of answer to Kim's strange behavior.

She continued: "I just need some time to sort things out, Bri. This trip, the kids, the cave—it's all made me realize how badly I want to work at the school and continue my studies under Minister Chang. It doesn't help that I'm having these stupid dreams."

"No kidding, Kim. I could have told you that!"

"It's not that simple, Brian. I wish I could explain, but it's hard."

"Try."

"It's like there's this voice inside my head telling me that there's something else that I need to do, something more important." Kim tried desperately not to look up and meet Brian's perplexed look of confusion. "I need time to sort things out."

"Then take the time," Brian suggested. "I'll help you out however I can."

"That's the problem. I need to do this alone."

Alone?

"I think I need some time away from you. You're too much of a distraction."

"Why?" Brian asked as he stood up. His skyrocketing blood pressure felt like it was going to propel him straight through the ceiling of the tent.

"For as long as I can remember, I've relied on you, Bri."

"That's good. That's how it should be, Kim."

"You're right," she said as a wistful smile crossed her lips. "I know you love me. But right now, those feelings are making it harder for me to figure out what I'm supposed to do. I need some time alone at the school this spring. There's a reason why young Ministers have always undergone a period of isolation. It's the only way they could really find their faith. I should be able to sort things out with some time."

"For how long?" Brian asked fearfully. *What was she saying?*

"I don't know. It could take a while. And I understand that it's not fair for me to expect you to wait around forever. You need to live your life, Bri. Don't worry about me."

Thinking back, Brian had no doubt that Kim meant that statement to be a gift rather than a wound, but at the moment, her words pushed him past the point of reason.

"Fuck this!" Brian growled, storming past Kim and out of the tent. She tried to grab his arm on the way out, but her tiny hands slipped off.

"Wait, Brian!" she yelled, chasing after him into the forest. Several of the others in the camp looked up from their fires in awe. Kim, who was usually a model of calm, a young woman for all children to look up to, was the last person they expected to see in such a heated battle.

Brian, for his part, kept walking silently up the eastern shore of the lake, not sure quite where he was headed. It didn't matter as long as it was away from Kim.

"Wait, Brian. I love you!" Kim cried. Her tears had transformed into twin waterfalls.

"Great," he muttered, not bothering to slow his stride.

Kim broke into a full run and quickly caught up to his side. This time she wrenched onto his right arm and refused to let go. Brian stopped.

"Please understand," she cried. "I don't want to hurt you. It's not *you* that's the problem."

At this point, Brian didn't care *who* was the problem. He just wanted to strike back and tell Kim his own interpretation of the situation. He had been diplomatic enough up until this point, and it had gotten him nowhere.

"I'll tell you what the problem is, Kim," he began, starring into her eyes with an anger she had never seen him direct against her. "It's this," he declared as he poked the Eye on her forehead with an outstretched finger.

Kim stepped back and ran her own finger over the tattoo. She clearly failed to understand what he meant, so Brian elaborated: "It's Chang. It's the school. It's all of this God nonsense that you, for some strange reason, seem to love more than anything else! It's all bullshit, Kim. No wonder you're confused. It's a joke."

Kim was in shock. Brian had never spoken to her like this. He continued the assault: "I can't believe that after all this time, you, the person who questioned the Church more than any of us, insists on keeping that thing on your forehead. I can't believe that you still look up at the sky and see God, that lie they pushed down our throats as kids. Look around, do you see God here? Do you think if God exists He really gives a shit about whether you become a Minister or not? Do you really think it matters?"

"You sound like Fenner," Kim spat angrily.

"Maybe I do. Maybe Fenner's right. Maybe the old religion doesn't have any place here on Elysium. If you asked most of the colonists, they'd agree. Just look at what it did back on Earth."

"It doesn't have to be like that," Kim argued. "I never said I wanted it to be like it was back on Earth."

"It will be, Kim. Someday, our ancestors will forget about why we came here in the first place and wreck this planet with some stupid ideas about God. I'm sure those creatures who built the monument in the cave believed in a god too, and now they're long dead. A lotta help their god was to them, huh?"

"Stop it!"

Brian decided it was time to deliver the killing blow: "And just look at yourself, Kim. Look at what it's done to you. So high and mighty, running around with Minister Chang like you know something about the universe the rest of us don't. You've changed so much I don't even know you anymore. I may not know what to do with my life, but at least I know who I am. You're a fake."

"Stop it! Stop it!" Kim cried as she put her hands over her ears, as if attempting to block out words that had already been spoken. She stumbled away from Brian like he was some animal intent on devouring her. As she made her way back to camp, Brian turned quickly in the opposite direction, hoping that by removing the sight of her from his eyes, he could avoid going after her and apologizing. *I said what needed to be said*, he reasoned.

Brian found a large boulder about a kilometer from the camp that he could sit on and look out over the water. A stiff breeze kicked up, forcing Brian to shrink down into his heavy thermal jacket. Light snow began to fall, the white flakes mixing with the sea of stars far above. Across the dark, choppy lake, Brian could make out the faint glow of a flood lamp as it lit the entranceway to the cave. Inside, Jade and the others were no doubt still trying to determine the purpose of the ruins.

So much had happened in one day. *Kim was right; things will never be the same, for us or anybody else on this planet.* Brian thought back to what he had said to Kim. He had been cruel, to say the least. But he was confident that he had wounded her no more than she had unwittingly wounded him. She had made a gray situation out of one that was once black and white. Since childhood, Brian had imagined that he and Kim would grow up and eventually go through the Adherent marriage ceremony together. Even when he had arrived on Elysium with all of the fear and anger of the time, Brian still envisioned Kim at his side no matter what happened. Now he wasn't so sure. In a way, he longed for the days when she was the only thing in his life he could count on, the only thing that ultimately mattered.

Brian looked back up at the sky and cursed Fate, or whatever it was that kept him from finding contentment. The pale glow of Demos stared back at him, uncaring and utterly removed from the dealings of mankind. Brian turned his head in an attempt to catch the red glare of Ares to the southeast, but he could see nothing. The moon was too low in the sky to eclipse the rocky peaks surrounding the lake. What Brian did see was a tiny dot of light making its way through a constellation the colonists had named Justine, after the ancient Byzantine Empress. *A shooting star*, Brian thought as he watched it glide downward to its inevitable disintegration.

But the dot of light did not fade. It grew bigger. As Brian tracked its movement northward with growing amazement, he realized that it wasn't a meteor at all, but a ship. Brian found it odd that the colonists had decided to send a shuttle up here in the middle of the night, unless, of course, it was because of the cave. Maybe the Council decided it was too important of a discovery to put off exploration, even for a few days. Brian stood up on the boulder, forgetting about the cold wind lashing against his face. *It's going fast*, he noted. *I didn't think the shuttles could go that fast. I wonder who the pilot is.*

As the ship passed the rocky peaks on the western side of the lake and proceeded to loop around back toward the camp, Brian understood why it was going
so fast and so dangerously close to the mountains: it wasn't a colonial shuttle at
all. It wasn't anything Brian had ever seen before.

CHAPTER 19

▼

PARADISE LOST

Brian went over the image in his head a thousand times as he ran at top speed back to camp: a large, black, arrow-shaped vessel with glowing red lights on what appeared to be two sets of external drive engines, silently darting through the sky toward camp. There was no way that he could have mistaken the ship for something the colonists possessed. Unlike the bulky planetary shuttles the colonists used, this ship looked sleek and aggressive, almost like a fighter, but larger. But if it wasn't something from the colony, then what was it? Brian ran through the two most likely possibilities, neither of which provided much comfort. If other humans had discovered Elysium, then the colonists' private paradise would be forever compromised. Others would want to live on such a beautiful world. The other possibility was that the ship wasn't human at all, but alien in design. This idea scared Brian even more. He thought back to the cave at the base of the cliff and wondered if the ancient architects of the monument had returned home only to find their Cathedral desecrated. Brian suddenly felt stupid for mocking them in front of Kim. It was entirely possible that they, whoever *they* were, still thrived in a nearby star system.

The ship Brian had seen pass over the lake had disappeared behind a veil of trees. Had it landed? He didn't know. Maybe it was just scouting the area, having no intention of landing at all. Brian had to get to the camp as fast as possible. Unlike the previous night, though, his heightened levels of adrenaline failed to erase his physical limitations. His side wound was screaming out, protesting the rough jostling caused by the up-and-down motion. His knee hurt too, and he was getting tired. The sight of the first campfire came just as fatigue and pain began to slow him down to a stumble. He was close. If the others had not seen the ship, they could be in danger without ever knowing it. He had to warn them.

Before Brian could reach the flickering light ahead, he was greeted by a much larger signal as a fiery explosion lit up the outskirts of the forest. The flames rose over the tops of the trees and bathed the entire southern half of the lake in a warm, orange glow. It was one of the shuttles. It had to be. There was no other piece of equipment near the camp that could have produced such a display if destroyed.

Brian came to a complete stop and stood mesmerized by the flames shooting skyward. Even though every instinct told him to run in the opposite direction, Brian forced himself to resume his perilous trek toward the camp. There was little he could do to fight off an advanced alien ship, but he decided that it would be better if he died with his friends and loved ones rather than alone in a freezing, dark forest. But for all he knew, everyone could be dead already.

Moments later, as Brian bounded into the camp, the sound of frightened shouting assured him that there were still people alive. He looked around for Kim and the others. Several of the adults herded the children into small groups. All of them were crying hysterically, unaware of the danger they were truly in. The whole scene was eerily reminiscent of the previous night's attack by the predators, except that the tents themselves looked unmolested. Brian came to a complete stop yet again, this time, to get his bearings. Debris from the exploded shuttle littered the ground around the tents and hung from the outstretched limbs of the trees. It looked as if heaven had rained its furry down upon them. The scene jogged another image from Brian's mind, one that he had long forgotten: the burning Enclaves of Chicago.

Brian buried the disturbing memory and saw Kim at the center of a group of children several meters to his right. As she looked up, Brian met her eyes and saw the fear that she was attempting to conceal. He said nothing and moved on, confident that she was safe for the time being.

Brian made his way to the far end of camp near the tree-line that bordered the meadow. Around the burning husk of the destroyed shuttle, Sonia, several of the older students and two teachers from Chang's school attempted to quell the blaze. Beside them, the other shuttle sat in silence, as if waiting for its turn to explode. Brian looked up at the sky, but saw nothing. The ship must have destroyed the shuttle then moved on. He lowered his gaze in time to see Luke emerge from the boulders on the western side of the lake with the rest of the group from the cave. Brian went to them.

"What the hell happened?" asked Jade. "Diego said he saw something over the lake, so we decided to come back and see what it was. Then we heard an explosion!"

"Did one of the shuttles crash?" Murphy asked, dumbfounded.

Brian was astonished that nobody had put the evidence together. Perhaps they had not seen what he had.

"It's not one of ours," he yelled into the group.

They stared at him, apparently more confused than before.

"What?" asked Luke.

"It's a ship!" Brian yelled again. "But it's not one of our shuttles."

Luke's expression, which had been confused but controlled up until this point, hardened into a pained grimace as he processed Brian's revelation. His voice took on a sudden, surprising calm. "Where did it go, Brian? Did you see it?"

"It went south, over the meadow."

"Did it land?"

"I don't know."

"Murphy, get Sonia, and break out four additional pulse rifles from the locker. Hand them out to any of the adults who are willing to take one."

Murphy nodded in response to Luke's order.

"I'll take one," Cruz volunteered.

"So will I," said Tom Johnson, one of the shuttle pilots who had been at the cave.

"If you need, Luke, I will come with you too," Chang said. It was a noble gesture, but Brian doubted Luke would let the elderly man actually put himself in harm's way unless every other able-bodied adult was dead or incapacitated.

Luke nodded in response to the offers and addressed Jade. "Hurry up and get some medical supplies and the radio from the shuttle. Run! We don't know if they'll come back for the other one too."

Jade broke away toward the shuttle.

"And Jade," Luke called after her, "as soon as you get the radio, find an empty tent and contact New Haven. Tell them Situation Omega has occurred."

Brian knew what that term meant. It was the universal code in the colony for contact with an outside element, be it human or alien. Although no one took it very seriously, every colonist knew that there might come a day when they were discovered on Elysium. What Brian wasn't sure what the contingency plans were for such an event.

Luke quickly got the attention of the adults in the camp and unveiled his plan. Chang would lead the students and the rest of the adults back up toward the caves, away from the open meadow area. If the ship had landed, it would have to be in the field; there were no other suitable locations near the lake. Luke would lead a small group of armed adults into the meadow to investigate if, in fact, the ship had landed. Beyond these simple directions, there was nothing else that could be done.

Despite the utter lack of options, Brian thought his cousin's plan sounded risky. There was no telling what awaited them out in the dark, flowing grasses of the meadow. Even worse, if the pilots of the unidentified ship knew about the caves, there would be nowhere for the students to run if they were cornered. Brian scoured his mind for alternatives, but found none. As long as there was a hostile ship in the area, the colonists could not flee in the other shuttle. It was dangerous to even go near it. Already, a pilot and two parent chaperones had been killed onboard the other shuttle when it had exploded.

As Luke and his makeshift posse set off for the meadow with their pulse rifles drawn, Brian hesitatingly followed Chang's group toward the caves. He felt like he was abandoning his cousin, instead choosing to flee with the children. It certainly didn't seem like a very noble way to confront a dangerous situation.

"Luke," Brian called out.

"No, Bri," Luke turned and answered, as if he already knew what Brian was going to offer. "Get to the cave and help the others. Make sure Derrick and Maleek go with you. I don't want them following us!"

"Bu—"

"Just do it and don't worry!"

"Fine."

"Come on, Brian, we need to go, now!" Jade insisted, pulling at his arm.

Brian reluctantly came along, although he couldn't help looking back over his shoulder at Luke and the others as they marched off into the night.

Chang's flock moved silently up the shore to the caves. A few of the children whimpered, but Kim managed to quiet them with her soothing voice. Brian trailed far behind the group, keeping his ears perked for the sound of rifle shots. Jade, who had assumed a central position in the moving formation, continued trying to contact New Haven on the radio.

"It's the damn storm," she hissed at Maria, who dutifully held the boxy transmitter while Maleek adjusted the settings. "I can't get through as long as it's moving along the coast. It must be directly over the main northern relay tower right now."

Brian thought about the colony. *Did they know what was going on? Did they have unwanted visitors of their own?* He shuttered. *Was there a colony left?*

Molly, who also shuffled toward the back of the formation with Suna and Derrick, dropped back all the way to Brian's side.

"What's going on, Brian? Nobody's told me or Suna anything!"

"We don't know what's going on, that's why Luke's searching the meadow for the ship," he said, a little annoyed at having to deal with Molly's anxiety in addition to his own. *Why should I have all the answers? I'm not in charge of anything*, he reminded himself.

Brian's answer looked like it made Molly feel even worse.

"Don't worry," he assured. "The ship's probably long gone by now. It was just flying recon, I'm sure of it."

"Really?"

"Yeah, don't worry. We're still here, aren't we? If they wanted us dead, they would have gotten us already."

He saw a slight look of relief pass over Molly's pretty face. She was a nice girl, even though her constant absent-mindedness had driven Brian to the brink of insanity several times during their school career together.

Brian turned his attention to Derrick, who had been listening in on the conversation. *Good thing Suna's here*, Brian thought. *He'd charge right down into the meadow without even a rifle if she weren't.* Brian stopped again. *What's holding me back from going with Luke?* Kim? Jade? Fear? Even though Luke had insisted that Brian flee with Chang and the rest of the group, Brian knew that his cousin couldn't stop him from coming along.

Ahead, the crowd of children passed out of sight behind a large rock. Nobody noticed his absence. Brian was alone. He reminded himself that Luke was wounded and four of his six companions were untrained volunteers. If there were hostile soldiers onboard the ship, there was a good chance that his cousin's small posse would be overwhelmed. Brian turned back toward the camp and started walking. After a few steps, he broke into a trot.

"Where are you headed, Bishop?" Derrick's voice rang out from behind.

Brian stopped in mid-stride. "I'm going back," he answered.

"Then we're coming, too."

Behind Derrick stood Maleek, Suna and Fred Willis, one of the students just a couple of years behind Brian and his friends.

"Yeah, we're not going to let you pull some stupid stunt like you did last night," Suna proclaimed.

Brian thought it over. There wasn't time to debate the subject. Plus, he could use the extra help. He was sure his friends were more than capable with a pulse rifle, although he didn't know Fred well enough to know how he'd react in a crisis. Brian was about to relent and let his friends come along when he saw another shadowy form emerge from the rocks. It was Jade.

"What the hell are you doing? All of you get moving! This isn't a game!" she yelled.

Nobody moved. Brian stared at his sister and shrugged his shoulders.

"Damn it!" Jade swore.

"Do you have keys to the weapons locker?" Brian asked.

Jade didn't answer. She returned his defiant gaze for a moment before reluctantly digging into her pocket and pulling out what Brian had asked for. She tossed the keys at Brian, and he caught them in mid-flight.

"Careful," she murmured lightly. Her voice sounded like it was beginning to buckle.

Brian shifted the keys in his hand for a moment and wondered if Kim knew where he was. *She's probably too busy with the kids to notice I'm gone*, he reasoned. Still, he wanted to see her. He wanted to apologize and say that he loved her in case he was walking to his doom. He wanted just one last time to hear her voice. But she wasn't there. In the moments that came after Jade had given him the keys, only the steady whisper of the wind bid him good luck.

"Let's go," Brian said to the group. He turned back toward camp for the last time and left his sister alone on the rocky shore of the lake.

The fires in the camp still burned when Brian and his companions arrived. He immediately ran to Luke's tent and opened the large, black container that held the pulse rifles and blasters. As he silently handed them out, he listened again for the sound of blaster fire in the distance. It had been at least fifteen minutes since Luke had set out for the meadow. If the ship had landed anywhere near the camp, they would find it shortly.

In addition to the rifles and blaster pistols, Brian handed out several flashlights to his comrades. Although the twin moons of Phobos and Demos were both out, their ghostly light was dimmed by a thin veil of dark winter clouds that had rolled in.

The irony of the situation struck Brian as he handed out the weapons to his friends. A year before, when Luke had suggested that the older children in the colony be trained how to use them, Brian thought the idea paranoid, not to mention ridiculous. When the Colonial Council approved Luke's plan, Brian refused to even attend the training sessions, much to Luke's dismay. At the time, Brain had also made a point to reiterate how stupid he felt the idea was to his peers, who all dutifully underwent the weapons instruction anyway. Now Brian was relying on the very training he had condemned.

He pulled out the last of the rifles, the one he would be using, and activated its energy cell. The weapon made a high pitched humming noise as it powered up its lethal payload. The action made Brian feel guilty, like he was doing something he shouldn't. The rifle itself felt awkward in his arms. It was the first time he had held one in over five years. Still, training or no, he remembered how to use it and how it felt to pull the trigger in anger. He also remembered what it felt like to kill.

Brian became aware that he had been starring at the rifle for several seconds, and quickly stood up, trying to mask any traces of self-doubt or fear.

"What are we doing, Bri?" Maleek asked as he fingered his pulse rifle nervously.

"We're going to find Luke. I'll lead the way. Derrick and Maleek, you stay behind me and to the sides about ten meters apart."

Brian looked at Suna and Fred, who eagerly awaited his command.

"You two stay behind a bit and watch our backs. If we start shooting at something, make sure we're not in the way if you start shooting too."

Brian felt a rush as they nodded in affirmation. He was surprised to see how readily his peers listened to him. In school, he had always made a point to outdo his fellow students academically, no matter how hard he had to work. In recent years, however, Brian had become much more introverted. He rarely revealed his opinion anymore, and almost never got involved in classroom debates. Brian often felt that his path to leadership had ended onboard the *Apostle 4*'s bridge, and he tried to distance himself from it whenever possible. At times, he wasn't even sure his friends took him seriously. But now, in the most serious of situations, he realized that the respect he had commanded as a young Academy student still held tremendous sway over their actions.

The group quietly left camp and wove their way through a series of rocky outcroppings next to the remaining shuttle. When they emerged on the other side of this natural barrier, they were greeted by the dark, swaying grass of the meadow. In the summer, the grass was pliant and green, but now, as it brushed past his legs, Brian felt the toll that an early winter had exacted on the plants. Out in the open, the cold breeze turned into a stiff wind that made Brian's eyes water and his hands begin to chap. He would have given anything to be back home in the warm embrace of his valley.

Brian looked back through darkness and saw that his companions were moving just as he had instructed. They even adjusted their speed to keep spread out as Brian hastened or slowed his movement. Luke had trained them well. It was hard to move at a steady pace through the darkness. Brian didn't want to use the flashlights unless he had to for fear that they would create an easier target. He lowered himself down so that his upper torso and head barley crested the normally waist-high grass. His heart pounded. Somewhere, out in the night, Luke and the search party still moved.

Behind, Brian could hear the wind whistling through the corridors of rocks close to the lake. The rustling sound of the grass also filled the air. Brian slowed, aware that he and his friends were totally exposed in the open spaces of the meadow, darkness or no. He raised his hand and made a downward motion. Everyone knelt into the safety of the grass.

"Do you see something?" Maleek whispered.

"No, but I'm going to check."

Brian took out a set of night-vision binoculars from the backpack he had collected from Luke's tent. He turned them on and scanned outward to a point in the meadow about two hundred meters away, where the land sloped down toward a meandering creek. Brian focused in on a cluster of small boulders and trees at the edge of the slope. There was movement.

"Do you see something?" Maleek asked again.

"Shut up!" Brian hissed. He turned back to his other companions. "Watch the rocks, but don't shoot," he whispered just loud enough to be heard over the breeze. It was clear from the expression on Suna's face that she already saw what Brian did.

There were two figures. Brian zoomed in more. *No, three figures, two standing closely together.* They looked to be human. One of the shadowy forms was leaning against the other, as if it was hurt. Brian zoomed in on the heads. It was Sonia with Luke's arm thrown around her shoulder. She was trying to carry him. Beside them stumbled Tom Johnson. He also looked like he was wounded, although not as badly as Luke.

Brian carelessly threw down the binoculars and ran toward them. After a few seconds of hesitation, the others followed.

"What happened?" Brian yelled as he approached the limping figures. Sonia's head shot up quickly. Her eyes were filled with fear. If she still had her pulse rifle with her, she may have shot Brian out of fright. Luckily, she must have dropped it somewhere.

"What happened?" Brian asked again, grabbing at Luke as his seemingly life-less body slipped off Sonia's shoulder into the grass. Sonia sat down next to him, curled up in a ball and started to cry.

"We need to get out of here," Tom Johnson groaned. He was still on his feet, hobbling in the general direction of camp. Brian noticed a steady stream of blood running down his pant leg into his boot. "They're coming."

Brian ignored Johnson's warning and attempted to flip Luke over. When Brian put his hands around Luke's chest to get a hold of his body, he felt a warm, moist sensation on his hands. It was blood. Brian gripped Luke's jacket and flipped his cousin over onto his back. The others arrived at his side and pro-ceeded to ask Sonia what had happened. Brian ignored them too. Of the adults who had set off for the meadow, these seemed to be the only three survivors. The rest were probably dead, or wounded even more than Luke was. Even Murphy must have fallen. *What could have happened?*

"Luke?" Brian whimpered. He tried not to look down at the massive wound in his cousin's chest. Instead he looked at his face, into his friendly brown eyes. The life was draining quickly. Luke's eyes darted around in confusion. His face was a pale gray, not unlike that of the twin moons high above.

"Bri," he grunted with a smile. Brain wasn't sure if Luke knew where he was.

"Who did this?" Brian asked.

Luke's eyes suddenly focused on Brian and he seemed to regain coherence. "Bri, get out of here. They're coming."

"Who's coming?" Brian yelled.

Luke didn't have a chance to answer. At that moment, Brian heard a low gut-tural sound echo from the direction of the creek bed. The sound sent a series of chills through his body that felt like a thousand knives sticking into his nerve endings. He froze.

The sound echoed again. It was a yell, a voice of some kind, but nothing any of Brian or his companions had heard before. Whoever or whatever was making it was getting closer.

Brian grabbed his rifle and slammed himself up against the closest rock so hard it felt like he had fractured his skull. The others in the group did the same. Derrick had enough sense to grab Sonia and pull her with them, making sure to cover her mouth to muffle the scream they all saw coming. Tom Johnson had other ideas. He raced off in the opposite direction as fast as his wounded leg would carry him. After a few pained steps, however, he fell face first into the grass and stayed there. Brian sat huddled against the rock shaking for a moment. Then he looked at the others and realized that they expected him to do something. Anything.

Slowly, methodically, Brian checked his pulse rifle and slid down to the ground, so that he lay on his stomach in the prone position. A few meters away, Maleek did the same, and the two snaked toward each other until both could see through a break in the rocks overlooking the ridge and creek.

Several hundred meters or so ahead on the bluffs just west of a large, thick cluster of trees, Brian once again detected movement. Maleek, who had been smart enough to pick up the binoculars Brian had dropped, handed them to his friend. Was it the wind swaying the grass? Brian couldn't tell. *Where did that noise come from*? He asked himself as he scanned the area through the green-tinted night vision mode.

As Brian turned to ask Maleek if he saw anything, a terrible screeching sound cut through the night air. The look of sheer terror on Maleek's face mirrored Brian's own. Brian's trembling thumb switched the rifle to semi-automatic mode and he strained his eyes to find where the shot had come from.

An unfortunate deer-like creature, which had emerged from the woods with its herd only a few seconds before, now lay dead in the swaying sea of grass. The intact portion of its upper body lay quivering near the crest of a small hill beyond the creek. Even through the greenish tint of the binoculars, Brian could see that the bottom portion of its body painted the field a deep red color, accented by the occasional bit of white bone and yellow cartilage. The bipedal humanoid who had robbed the creature of its life soon emerged. It hovered over the kill for a moment, before being joined by its companions. Brian was horrified. They were not men or aliens. They were monsters.

The tall, bulky figures appeared one by one at the top of the small hill on which the dead herbivore lay. They looked to be wearing breathing masks, although it was difficult to distinguish between the individual pieces of grotesque, interlocking systems of black body armor that seemed to grow out of their rough, leathery bodies. The creatures' knee joints were bent totally opposite of a human's and it gave their walk an oscillating, mechanical appearance. The most disturbing aspect of these creatures was by far their eyes: glowing, featureless bulbs that Brian immediately assumed could see in the dark just as well as the light. Their weapons, the ghastly creations that had issued the screaming sound only seconds before, appeared to grow out of the creature's long, mechanical arms.

The patrol of four creatures funneled down into the creek bed and began to walk along the trail that bordered the woods. Brian regained his composure enough to aim his rifle at one that was positioned in the center of the formation. Brian's gnawing anxiety had faded now and was replaced by a feeling of intense hatred. These creatures, these things, whatever they were, had invaded his home and would kill everyone he loved if he let them. Brian only hoped that his companions would overcome their own fear through similar feelings of aggression.

Brian readied himself. He leaned forward slightly and braced his body for the inevitable kick his weapon would issue once he pulled its trigger. Brian's breath slowed to a halt, as did his heart. But even as his heartbeat's frequency decreased, his arteries throbbed painfully, as if someone was squeezing his aorta with two iron-fisted hands. His face pressed hard against the cold metal of his weapon, Brian made extra sure that his shooting eye was aligned perfectly with the sights in his scope. He moved his weapon to the left as the formation passed by. He zoomed in slightly on the lead creature in the formation, just in time to see the alien's chest explode and expel a fine red mist into the cool air. Derrick had struck first and hit his mark. Brian pulled the trigger himself and unleashed his fury upon the unsuspecting squad of creatures. The first few well aimed shots of his assault quickly gave way to a hail of approximate saturation fire as the weapon violently wrestled its master for control. The loud violence and pounding rhythm gave Brian a newfound sense of power. His companions apparently felt the same way and showed their appreciation for their weapon's capabilities by mercilessly cutting down the surprised creatures.

The one-sided battle lasted mere seconds. Brian's and his companions' weapons fell silent as they realized that all four of the creatures had fallen during the first moments of the barrage. Brian sat frozen for a moment as he surveyed the destruction. *It worked*, he thought. *We did it.* Despite the extreme trauma of the situation, he and his friends had killed the monsters. The bodies themselves still smoldered on the cold ground next to the creek. Brian stood up and looked around at his comrades. They seemed to be stunned, but at least they hadn't hesitated once the ambush started.

"Are they dead?" asked Fred, his voice shaking slightly.

"I think so," Brian answered.

"There could be more," Suna added.

As Brian contemplated that possibility, he crouched back down behind the boulder. He glanced in the direction of where Luke was laying and wondered if he was still alive. Out in the grass by Luke's wounded body, Brian saw Sonia poke her head up cautiously. She had slowly made her way back toward camp during the barrage of gunfire. Brian didn't see Tom Johnson anywhere, not that it mattered much at this point.

"We need to get Luke out of here," Brian stated.

"Suna's right. What if there are more of those things?" asked Maleek, who still lay on the ground with his weapon pointed out beyond the creek bed.

Brian thought about it for a moment. "There could be more, but I doubt they'd be stupid enough to walk into another trap. We need to pull back toward the cave. The longer we stay here the more danger we're in."

"And just wait for them to come and attack us?" Derrick added in a defiant tone. "Forget that!"

"There can't be that many. The ship wasn't that big. I think we can handle a few more if they try to follow us back to the lake," Brian stated in a confident tone.

"Where *is* that ship?" Suna asked.

"Probably over the ridge where they came from," Brian reasoned.

"I say we go hit that damn thing now," Derrick said. "If there are any more of those things we can kill them."

"No way!" yelled Fred as he got to his feet. "Brian's right, we should get back!"

Although Brian appreciated the support, he cringed at the sound of Fred's voice echoing through the meadow.

"Shut up," Brian and Suna hissed simultaneously.

But it was too late. Fred's expression changed from a look of fear to one of shock. Brian stared into the younger kid's light blue eyes as they lost focus. Brian hadn't remembered hearing a shot. Nevertheless, Fred quivered slightly as his body began to react to the large hole that had suddenly been created in his upper chest cavity. After a second or two, Fred slumped down to his knees, before falling to the ground with a muffled thud.

Brian stared at the lifeless body in terror. He rolled over and looked out between the boulders toward the wooded area where the shot must have come from. The twin moons had grown in brilliance overhead and their soft gray light illuminated the foreboding silhouette of the alien thicket as the ancient trees swayed gently in the wind. The long, intricate outlines of the needle-covered trees intertwined and moved together as if they were a single organism taking in a deep breath after a long nap. It was inside this elegant beast of nature that Brian's eyes began to filter out a more subtle, less rhythmic pattern of shadows. The shadows moved in an erratic, intelligent manner contrary to the wind's direction. *There are more of them.*

"In the trees!" Brian screamed at the top of his lungs before being cut off by a deafening roar of fire let loose from the swaying thicket.

Brian grabbed for his weapon, which he had momentarily placed against the rock, but in his frenzied rush he knocked it over onto the ground. He crawled on his stomach and grabbed the rifle, intent on rising to his feet and returning fire. As he began to rise, however, he sensed a solid ceiling of heat just above the top of his rock and was forced to stay down to avoid getting his head ripped off. He heard Derrick cry out, and looked over to see his friend clutching his leg in agony. Suna, who had blindly fired a few shots over the rocks, dropped her weapon and attempted to examine the wound. Maleek, who was the closest to Fred when he had been killed, stared at the body as he leaned against the boulder to Brian's right. They were trapped. There was no way to fight back against such an overwhelming onslaught. The only emotion Brian felt at that moment was one of shame. He was stupid for letting overconfidence influence his actions. His gung-ho arrogance was going to get all of his friends killed. There was no way he was ever going to see Kim or his family again.

A few red-colored bolts of light shot through the small opening in the boulders through which Brian had looked only moments before, jolting him from his extreme state of fear. Despite the risk, they had to make an escape, fast. Every moment that passed, Brian imagined a swarm of creatures emerging from the thicket, closer and closer to their position on top of the ridge. Derrick seemed to read Brian's thoughts: "We need to get the fuck out of here!" he yelled, still clutching his bleeding leg. Beside him, Suna was crying, a sight Brian had never seen. That spectacle, perhaps more than anything else that was going on, filled him with a sense of dread.

"What about Luke?" Brian yelled, motioning toward the grass a few meters behind him. "We can't just leave him!"

"You and Maleek are going to have to drag him," Derrick yelled back, "but we're dead if we stay here!"

Brian weighed the possibility of rescuing his cousin against getting killed himself and reasoned that it was worth a try, if Luke was still alive.

"Let's go!" he yelled, crawling away from the boulders on his hands and knees through the grass back toward camp. Within a few paces of the rocks, Brian came upon Luke's body. He looked at his cousin's chest and saw that it was still rising, albeit raggedly. "Grab his jacket, Maleek," Brian yelled, slapping his friend on the shoulder.

Maleek did as Brian ordered. As they struggled to pull the dead weight of Luke's unconscious body, Brian could still hear a whizzing sound cutting just above the tips of the grass. The creatures were relentless in their attack. Brian realized that he and his friends were going to have to crawl back to camp if they wanted to survive. He gritted his teeth and dug his feet into the cold dirt of the meadow, trying desperately to propel himself and his load toward safety as quickly as possible. After only a few meters, Brian realized that this task was impossible. There was no way to pull Luke back to camp in time. Even if he and Maleek stood up and carried his cousin, Brian estimated it would take several minutes to reach the rocky cover surrounding the lake, and that was assuming the creatures weren't gaining on them every step of the way.

"Damn!" Brian swore as he let go of Luke's jacket and rocked back into the grass.

Maleek gave Luke a couple more tugs before giving up too. He gave Brian a perplexed glance as if to ask how they were going to escape. Though the moonlight illuminated Maleek's face, Brian still couldn't see more than a foot or two in any direction in the grass. Derrick and Suna were absent. Brian hoped that they had somehow made it back to the lake.

Brian put his hands on his face in frustration and listened for some sign of his other comrades. The sound of weapons fire had dissipated and the lethal ceiling of energy no longer pressed down on the flowing grass in which he and Maleek lay. *Maybe the creatures pulled back*, Brian tried to convince himself. They had taken several dead; perhaps there were only a handful left.

"What now?" Maleek whispered.

Although the voice could barely be heard above the sound of the wind, Brian cringed. He put a shaking finger up to his lips and motioned with his eyes back toward the rocky ridge from which they had retreated.

There were more sounds. The creatures hadn't left. Brian could hear their rough, unintelligible voices just a few meters behind them. The language was unlike anything he had ever encountered, an oscillating pattern of rough, guttural choking noises. Panic overtook him. He frantically looked around in a vain attempt to find some means of escape. Short of getting up and running away, an act which would certainly get him killed, there were none. The voices were getting closer.

Brian rolled over and whispered in Maleek's ear. "Spread out and put your head down. Try not to make any noise."

Maleek nodded. Brian was amazed that he could still function despite the paralyzing fear he felt shooting through his body. It was just as amazing that high-strung Maleek could as well.

Brian rolled away as quietly as possible and pushed himself down into the grass a meter or two from Luke. Maleek did the same, and soon Brian lost sight of his friend amid the thick shadows cast by the swaying blades of green. He was alone now, waiting to find out how perceptive and motivated his hunters really were. Brian's shaking hand found the butt of his pulse rifle, which had been slung over his shoulder while trying to move Luke. With great effort, he lifted the strap over his head and slowly, torturously, placed it at his side. If the creatures did find him, he wanted to put up a fight before he died. Until then, he would hide.

Brian pushed his face against the cold wetness of the ground and stared into the shifting shadows of the grass forest around him. As the sounds of the creatures approached, Brian's eyes focused in on several yellow, circular disks penetrating the murky darkness. The eyes belonged to several of the deer-like creatures, similar to the one he had seen killed a few minutes before. Like Brian, they were hiding from death. As Brian met their terrified eyes, he felt even weaker than before, as if the realization that he had been reduced to game somehow made his predicament more dangerous. Brian shuddered at the thought of the gruesome creatures gloating over his dead body. He also wondered if the deer back on the bluffs had felt any pain as it had its insides ripped out within the span of a millisecond.

The rustling sound of grass called Brian's attention back to the present. A meter in front of him, a large, booted foot could be made out. One of the creatures was close. *Does he see me?* Brian wondered in terror. He readied his pulse rifle, but fought back the urge to fire. Once he made the decision to shoot, the other creatures would know exactly where he was.

After taking a few more steps towards where Brian lay, the creature's face became visible through the thick vegetation. It was even more horrible up close than Brian had imagined. Veins protruded from its leathery facial skin like tubes running from a machine. They seemed to converge on the cold, featureless lights that served as its eyes. The eyes themselves were focused on a point beyond where Brian hid, perhaps at the area around the camp. The creature took another step forward, but it was a cautious one. Brian readied himself.

Without warning, Brian heard a crashing sound behind him as one of his companions broke cover, stood up and ran. Brian struggled to find the strength to fire his weapon at the creature in front of him. In another second or two, it would lock onto the running target and kill whoever it was. As hard as he tried, however, Brian couldn't do it. Fear had totally taken control. A sharp human cry cut through the night air. It was an older voice, probably Tom Johnson. Brian looked into the creature's eyes as it slowly raised its weapon in Johnson's direction and fired a single shot. Two more screeching blasts rang out from beyond Brian's view. Then came the same terrible laugh he had heard the creatures issue when they had killed the deer-like creature.

Brian buried his face down into the dirt as tears ran down his cheeks in tiny streams, forming small puddles of agony. He was helpless, the worst feeling in the entire universe. As the creature took two more steps in his direction, Brian began to think about death and God again. He remembered hearing Fenner complain a couple of years before about how some people who claim to find the idea of God ridiculous always return to Him in the final moments before their death. Brian had come to agree with Fenner's assessment that this was a sign of weakness, or at the very least, convenience. Then he remembered Chang's response. "It's never too late," the old Minister used to say. Brian wondered if this applied to the last thirty seconds of life. Even if it did, he felt like a coward for filling his mind with fearful questions about death and eternity at a moment when decisive action was needed. Nevertheless, he couldn't seem to break himself out of the ontological grid-lock. Instead of firing at the oncoming enemy, he lay there and waited for death. *If there is a God, I hope He's like the one Kim believes in*, he thought again.

Following another eerie moment of silence, Brian looked up. His gaze was met by the twin glaring lights towering two and a quarter meters above him. The creature had found him. Brian thought he detected the outline of a faint smile grace the monster's charred lips as it gleefully pointed its weapon only centimeters from his face. Fear. Shock. Terror. Dread. There were no words that could describe the feeling that ripped through Brian's gut at that moment. Hope certainly wasn't one of them. *This is it*, a voice in Brian's head managed to scream out amid the turmoil of his frightened animal mind.

Brian never expected to hear the sound of the blast that would kill him, but it came shortly after he had closed his eyes in anticipation of the End. It seemed far away, as if it were in a different room of a large house. He felt no pain, then felt relief for that simple fact. The blast that accompanied the shot lit the scene beyond Brian's closed eyelids so brightly that his retinas burned from the shock. Still, there was no pain. Even more amazingly, Brian was still conscious. He opened his eyes in dazed confusion.

The dark form above him was still pointing its weapon at his face, but it hadn't fired. Instead, it clutched a glowing, blue divot that had been made in its black chest armor. The creature let out what sounded like a groan of pain, before being struck twice more by blue bolts of energy. It fell backward into the grass away from Brian.

As Brian's taxed psyche began to admit more stimuli, he was able to make out the unmistakable sounds of battle around him. His friends were fighting back. Maybe it was Derrick and Suna. The sensation of surprise temporarily overrode Brian's fear and he was able to grab his pulse rifle and rise to his knees so that he could just see over the tips of the grass.

Brian ducked again as several more blue bolts shot through the air from behind him and hit their marks near the boulders at the edge of the ridge. He raised himself slowly and took aim at the remaining two creatures that had taken cover behind the lip of the ridge. Brian could make out the tips of the creatures' hairless skulls from where he was. He aimed and fired at the one on the left. The first shot struck the ground in front of the ridge, but the second blasted a hole in the creature's skull. The other creature, upon seeing its last comrade fall, turned and retreated back down to the creek.

Before Brian even regained enough courage to consider a pursuit, three figures brushed past him in the darkness. They reached the edge of the ridge and fired down at the creature. From where he was, Brian couldn't see the kill, but he did hear the muffled groan that signaled it.

Silence accompanied the moments immediately following the battle. The entire area was bathed in smoke that rose from the bodies of the fallen creatures. Brian also noticed the smell, a hot burning scent of flesh and wiring that sickened him instantly. He suppressed the urge to vomit as he swiveled his head around in an attempt to make sense of what had happened. One by one, he saw his friends poke their heads up from the grass. Maleek, Suna and Derrick were all still alive, although Derrick quickly slumped back down into the grass to nurse his wound. Sonia, who had attempted to hide in the grass near Tom Johnson, could be seen rocking back and forth as she sobbed. Brian was stunned to see Minister Chang at her side, providing consul with his calm, soothing voice. There was a pulse rifle slung over his shoulder, although Brian wasn't sure if Chang had actually been involved in the firefight. Behind the Minister stood two of the adult colonists who had initially sought refuge in the cave. They also carried rifles. Upon seeing that Derrick was wounded, they rushed over to help him.

Brian turned his head back toward the ridge and saw the three figures that had run past him in the chaos. Although it was impossible to make out their faces in the darkness, the silhouette of two of the figures betrayed their identities. It was Jade and Kim. After hovering at the ridge for another few seconds, they turned and approached Brian.

"Luke," Brian managed to spit out just before Jade stepped on her cousin's body.

Brian heard her gasp as she bent down to examine Luke. "Suna," she called out. "Run and get my kit from camp! Hurry!"

Suna complied without hesitation. She seemed to be in better shape mentally than Brian.

"Are you hurt, Brian?" Kim asked as she bent down in front of him. It was obvious from her pained expression that she was intentionally ignoring Luke's body just a few meters away. She lay her pulse rifle down on the ground and put her hands on Brian's face.

"I'm fine," he muttered, rising to his feet. He felt grateful for being saved, but more than a little embarrassed. He had underestimated Kim and his sister, not to mention Chang. Even worse, he had overestimated himself. What could he say? Certainly not thanks.

"That was brave, but stupid," Kim said with an icy glare. "You should have told me you were going!"

"There wasn't time," Brian responded flippantly as he moved away from Kim toward Luke. He noticed that Jade's movements were becoming more and more rushed and desperate looking as she worked on Luke's body. Even at a distance of a meter, Brian couldn't see what Jade's hands were doing under the concealment of the grass, but he could make out the steady, up and down motion of her arms. At that moment, he realized that no matter how fast Suna retrieved the life-support module from camp, Luke would die. He was probably dead already.

The scene was too much for Brian to handle. He had been too late to help his cousin. If he had only gone with Luke in the first place, then maybe they could have fought off the creatures together. Tears came again, but this time they were tears of anger instead of fear. Brian clenched his fists and spun around. Kim attempted to calm him down by placing her soft hands on his right arm. He violently shook her off and stormed over to the closest dead carcass.

"Bri, wait."

Brian wasn't sure what he wanted to do to the dead creature's body, but he knew that lashing out, however pointless, would make him feel better. He didn't care that everyone was watching him. He didn't care about anything but revenge.

Brian stood over the smoking body and pointed his pulse rifle at its hideously deformed face. He wanted it gone, erased forever from his sight and his memory. But as he aimed at the black, blood-covered object of his hatred, his eyes focused on the white design adorning its twisted, metallic breastplate. He should have noticed it before. The symbol was large, unmistakable. *It's funny the way impor-*

tant things get overlooked in a crisis situation, he told himself later. As Brian stared down at the creature's chest, a chest belonging to a monster that exceeded any nightmare vision of an alien any human being could have conjured, his gaze was met by the most familiar of sights: The Ever-Seeing Eye of God.

They've found us.

CHAPTER 20

▼

DUE SUFFERING

900 years. Brian thought about it over and over again as he sat onboard the quiet shuttle. Although the colonists had spent less than 300 in cryosleep, the time-debt they experienced while traveling at over half the speed of light meant that over 900 years had passed back on Earth since they had left. The general consensus among the colonists had been that the Church, and humanity for that matter, would die long before the turn of the thirty second century. Already, things had been bad enough in the twenty fourth century. Starvation, war, over-population, disease, lack of resources: the list of insurmountable problems seemed endless at the time. Even if things had gotten better, nobody would have expected such a cruel, oppressive government to last for the better part of the mil-lennium. But somehow the Church had endured, at least in some capacity. Per-haps one of the far-flung colonies had prospered enough to carry on Earth's legacy to other star systems. There simply was no way to glean any information from the dead Adherent bodies, or from the strange craft they had arrived in. They may as well have been aliens. Even the writing on the ship's computers was entirely foreign. 900 years was a long time for the development of a culture. But judging from the intense cruelty of the Adherent soldiers, Brian realized that at least some things had remained the same.

They had found the bodies, Murphy and the others, in a ghastly pile near where the Adherent scout ship had landed. There wasn't much left. Brian supposed they had been ambushed as soon as they had mounted the grassy meadow bluffs. The fight must have been quick and brutal. The creatures or soldiers, whatever they were, had shot each of the bodies multiple times with horrifying precision. Brian wondered how Luke, Sonia and Tom had even managed to initially escape the fate of their companions. *Maybe they wanted some sport*, Brian thought, as he remembered how much the Adherent soldiers seemed to enjoy killing their prey. The creatures certainly didn't act like soldiers. Judging by their murderous, chaotic behavior, it was difficult to determine what, if anything, motivated them.

After a brief survey of the Adherent ship, a heated debate ensued over what to do next. Chang and Jade insisted that returning to the colony, however dangerous, was the only option considering the circumstances. The opposition, led by a parent chaperone named Linda Marcos, argued that it was foolish to risk a shuttle full of children on a return trip until the situation had been explored. She demanded to stay behind in the caves with the students while another group took the shuttle back on a reconnaissance mission. The other members of the small, weary group of adults simply avoided casting a vote either way. Without Luke, there was nobody left who was used to making serious life and death decisions. Brian had stayed out of the fight, but watched from just a few meters away as he sat next to the fresh grave of his cousin. Luke had always remarked how beautiful the lake was. Brian found it fitting that he would now rest forever on its rocky shore.

Of course, it was foolish for the children to stay behind and wait for the situation to be resolved. If the colony had indeed been attacked and destroyed, it would mean certain death for any survivors. There was no way a small isolated group of humans could survive on Elysium without the support of the larger community, especially a group comprised mainly of young kids. Brian knew this, yet kept quiet. He was confident that Chang's powers of persuasion would win the argument, despite the polarizing effect Jade's angry tone was obviously having on the opposition. After a few more minutes of arguing, Marcos finally ceded to the Minister's position and stormed off in the direction of where the children were being held near camp. With the dispute settled, Brian stepped in and helped plan the return trip to the colony. The camp and most of the equipment would be abandoned for now in order to make room for everyone on the remaining shuttle. Everyone was to board immediately. It was far too risky to linger near the Adherent ship. There was no telling who or what would come looking for it.

With Tom Johnson and the other pilot dead, Sonia had to pull herself together enough to fly the shuttle back to the colony. She was still extremely shaken from her ordeal, but Brian felt that Chang calmed her down well enough to fly. Jade, who had some experience as a pilot thanks to Luke's instruction, could assist in an emergency situation. The agreed-upon flight plan would take the ship on a long arc around the severe storm that was pounding the coastline. It would be a much longer trip than it had been on the way up, but it served the dual purpose of getting back to the colony in the stealthiest way possible while still avoiding the weather. Brian suspected that the Adherents had detection equipment far more sensitive that what the colonists possessed. It may not matter how careful they were. Nevertheless, it couldn't hurt to try to remain discrete on the way home.

Kim, Chang, and the rest of the school group quickly got the children onboard the shuttle while Brian and his friends helped Jade load up some essential supplies from the camp. Nobody talked about the attack or the deaths. Derrick, the only person who would have had the audacity to do so, was already fast asleep in the shuttle's tiny medical bay. Brian envied him. Digging the graves had not been an easy task, mentally or physically. For once, Brian had been confident that Derrick wouldn't complain about missing out on an activity.

Brian's thoughts drifted back to the impromptu funeral on the shoreline just a few hours before. It had been a surreal scene, one he would never forget. In the dim coldness of the predawn morning, Chang had stood over the seven fresh graves as he recited a short prayer for the dead. Kim had been at his side, as if she were attempting to memorize the Minister's every action for the day when she would be the one reciting the morbid chant. On the opposite side of the graves, with the water to their backs, stood Brian, Jade, and several of the adults. None of the younger children attended the service. They had been raised in a world vastly different from Earth. On Elysium, death was a natural event, not the end result of calculated human cruelty. Unlike Brian and his peers, they had never witnessed, much less experienced, such a traumatizing event as the attack.

As he sat in the shuttle, Brian forcibly cleared his mind and rolled his head back on the seat. His heavy eyelids immediately began to close. The rest of the passengers onboard the now crowded shuttle seemed to be succumbing to fatigue as well. Apart from the steady hum of the ship's engines and a few muffled sobs from the children, everything was silent.

Brian sat in the same seat he had on the trip up to Lake Clarity, but was now flanked by Molly and Maleek rather than Luke and his sister. Ahead of Brian, in the pilot's cabin, Jade was attempting to help Sonia fly the shuttle. Although Sonia was still shaken from the previous night's events, she seemed to be lucid enough to perform her duties. The shuttle glided through the air as smoothly as ever, so much so that Brian almost forgot about the dire circumstances under which they were returning. Even through his closed eyelids, he could see that the inside of the ship's cabin glowed with a magenta light cast from the morning sun. It was still early, just past daybreak. Nobody had slept since the attack. Under a fury of jumbled concerns, excited questions and a host of other emotions he struggled to process, Brian felt a sudden sinking sensation overwhelm his body. Sleep came fast.

Out of all the times Brian had slept and wished to dream, this was not one of them. He would have preferred the sweet, familiar oblivion that usually characterized his slumber. But now an image came. It was hazy at first, hard to make out. Gradually, the muffled sounds and jumbled pictures coalesced into a single, coherent scene. Brian looked around and found that he was standing in the Cathedral back home on Earth. Before him, the massive, shadowy cavern of the main hall began to take shape. High above, he could see stars through the large ceiling windows. It was night, and the pale glow of the solitary moon cast its ghostly light down upon the rows of pews, which flanked the long red carpet leading up to the altar at the front of the room. *Impossible*, Brian thought. *The moon's light can never be seen on the ground from Earth.* The sight of stars dotting the black night was even more unsettling.

Brian suddenly felt a chill as he realized he wasn't alone. Even from the other end of the room he could make out a small figure crouched down in front of the main altar in prayer. Whoever it was, he or she was alone. The Cathedral was quiet, as it usually was after dark. It had always seemed more of a tomb than a place of worship, anyway. But still, Brian couldn't recall ever seeing it empty. The realization that he was in fact dreaming did little to stem his uneasiness. The whole experience felt unnatural, almost wrong. Compelled by some unknown force, Brian started walking down the crimson path toward the lone figure. The person took no notice of him, despite his heavy breathing. He wanted desperately to turn and run in the opposite direction, yet couldn't seem to control his feet. As he neared the hunched figure, Brian realized who it was. "K-Kim?"

There was no answer.

Brian felt more like running now than before. It was similar to the fear he had felt when being hunted by the Adherent soldiers during the night, only more arbitrary. As intense as the emotion was, Brian didn't know why he felt so afraid. It was definitely Kim at the altar, and she looked perfectly fine underneath the crimson red robe. He shouldn't be afraid, but was.

"Kim?" Brian called out again, this time in a more confident tone.

Still, no answer.

Damn her, Brian thought angrily. His fear instantly melted away as he felt a wave of hostility. She was ignoring him. "This has got to stop," he said, approaching her with an outstretched hand. He wanted to grab her and shake her back to her senses. She offered no resistance as his hands wrapped around her shoulders. Brian pulled her back towards him and opened his mouth to issue a reprimand. Then, he stopped himself. Kim's head fell limply back. As he looked into her face he saw that her eyes were closed. Hadn't she just been conscious? It didn't make sense.

"Kim!" Brian yelled, this time in a worried tone. Her eyes instantly opened. But instead of their usually deep brown, they were a featureless, glowing red. Brian cried out in terror and frantically tried to let go, but his muscles refused to obey. His arms, slaves to the same unknown force that drove his legs to walk toward the altar, held Kim's body close as her hideous eyes bore into his consciousness. Just as Brian thought he couldn't stand the sight any longer, Kim's mouth opened and let out a series of moans far too deep for her own body to conjure. All around him, Brian felt the pale light of the moon transform into the familiar red glow that had accompanied him on many Elysian nights. This time Brian managed a full-fledged scream as the scene fell away into blackness. In place of Kim and the cathedral was the burning disk of Ares surrounded by the endless void she had described on numerous occasions. Before Brian had time to fully grasp the new image, the scene morphed for the final time. In the brief second before Brian awoke, he found himself on the shore of Lake Clarity surrounded by the seven dead bodies he had recently helped bury. They were all standing and looking at him with the same red eyes he had seen only moments before on Kim.

"Bri!" a familiar voice called out.

Brian flailed in his seat as his terrified mind climbed back into reality. Kim was kneeling in front of him, shaking his legs. Her eyes were now brown and the crimson red of his dream had been replaced by the gray light of the Elysian winter afternoon.

"You're sweating like a faucet!" Kim pointed out in a concerned tone as she wiped his face with a cloth.

Brian looked at her with wild eyes and realized he had been dreaming. The sight of her concerned face made him feel safe. A familiar feeling of warmth soon replaced his terror. He wasn't conscience enough yet to remember the recent tension with her. "Sorry," Brian apologized, his voice still shaking slightly. He straightened himself up, trying to mask any trace of fear or weakness. As an added measure, Brian patted her hand, as if *he* were the one comforting *her*.

"I was getting worried ..." Kim began.

"It's nothing," Brian said, cutting her off. But Kim finished anyway: "Your thrashing around was beginning to scare the children!"

Brian shot up out of his seat and quickly wiped his brow. "I'm fine," he reiterated in a tense, yet restrained tone. His anger was still apparent. The comment was directed to the passengers behind him as well as Kim. He didn't bother turning to see if his words had any impact on them. He was still feeling embarrassed, not quite sure how much noise he had made during his nightmare.

"Of course you are," Kim said in a low voice as she walked away and found a seat near the back of the shuttle.

Brian let out a long, protracted sigh and turned his attention to Maleek, who had obviously witnessed the exchange with Kim, yet pretended to be distracted with the closest window. "Where are we?" Brian asked.

"Close. Jade just came back a minute ago and said we're only a hundred kilometers out."

"Are they following the flight plan we talked about?"

Maleek shrugged. "She didn't say."

Brian looked out the starboard window. "It looks like we're too high."

"Don't worry, Bri," a sleepy-eyed Molly said from beside Maleek. "Jade and Sonia know what they're doing."

Brian didn't respond to Molly. Instead, he plowed through the door leading up to the cockpit. Up front, he found Jade and Sonia at the controls, as expected, with Chang seated at the small navigation console to the right of the cramped space. Through the duraglass shell Brian saw the tips of the tallest trees passing just underneath the speeding ship. Every so often the ship would bank slightly to avoid a rocky peak.

"Checking on things?" Jade asked, without looking up from the controls.

"Yeah."

"Are you all right, Brian?" Chang asked. "Kim said you were having a nightmare when she came up here a few minutes ago."

"I'm fine," Brian said in a much calmer tone than he had to his other comrades. It was much easier to admit weakness in front of Chang than in front of his peers. "I'm just not used to dreaming."

"You can tell me about it later, if you want."

"Thanks." Brain wanted to change the subject. "Where are we landing?"

"At the southern end of Olympia Gorge."

"That's close."

Jade swiveled around in her seat and gave Brian a frustrated scowl. "You won't think that when we have to walk all night just to get to the colony."

"If those things pick up on our power signature, we're done," Brian pointed out.

"If their scanners were that sensitive, they would have detected us already," Jade responded. "We've been running on the lowest power setting possible since we left Clarity."

"Maybe everything's normal back at the colony. Maybe those things only came after us," Sonia interjected nervously. She was obviously trying to play the optimist. Brian supposed that someone had to.

"If that's the case, then we'll look pretty stupid sneaking back home, won't we?" Chang added, trying to introduce some humor into the somber cabin. Nobody laughed. Not even the Minister. Even if things were normal back home, the colony was now in danger. Chances were that something was seriously wrong. All of the adults onboard the ship were aware that Jade still couldn't make radio contact with the colony, even though the ship was now only a few dozen kilometers away. The static that had greeted her repeated efforts was ominous.

Sonia and Jade skillfully nestled the shuttle down into the southern portion of the massive cut in the land named Olympia. The gorge itself was much less hospitable to humans than the valley where the colony was situated. Sheer, slate walls tumbled hundreds of meters down into the primeval forest below, where aggressive packs of wraith hounds roamed unopposed. Outside the windows, the scene became dark as the dull light from the opaque sky struggled to penetrate the green canopy that permanently obscured the ground.

When Brian had pictured his homecoming the previous night, he hadn't expected it to be like this. As he stepped off the shuttle, he was rudely bombarded by the cool, dank wetness of the forest. Everywhere, the wild, cackling sounds seemed to dare him to step far enough away from the shuttle to be swallowed whole. There was nothing unfamiliar about the forest itself. Brian had made the trek to Olympia many times before, even in the heavy, uncomfortable winter rains. But the realization that he must trek through the wilderness toward an uncertain future added a feeling of danger to his journey.

In all, Brian, Maleek, Kim Jade, and Maria would be making the trip back to the colony. Once they determined the situation there, the others could be retrieved. None of the school children even left the safety of the ship, nor did the injured Derrick, although he protested vehemently. Chang and the remaining adults would stay with the ship as well. Most didn't relish the idea of hiking nearly twenty kilometers over rough terrain, and Brian was glad they were staying behind. More people would just slow down the journey. It was already late afternoon. They would have to hurry if they were to reach the valley by morning.

Nobody spoke as the small party trudged along through the darkness. The stealth wasn't so much out of fear of being seen or heard by Adherent soldiers. Compared to the almost deafening sounds of rain and wildlife echoing through the forest, a few hushed voices meant very little. Instead, it was the painful reality that there was simply nothing to say. Following such traumatic events, small talk sounded ridiculous and none of Brian's comrades seemed willing to discuss the more relevant problems they faced. Plus, talking wasted precious energy, especially during the difficult climb through the rocky crevices surrounding Olympia. Despite the relatively good shape his companions were in, Brian repeatedly found it necessary to stop and wait for them to catch up. Kim was the only one who constantly stayed at his side, although she too remained silent. He found it difficult to determine her feelings towards him, whether she was angry or not, although he appreciated her being there all the same. It reminded Brian of when they used to go for their hikes years before, back when they had first arrived on Elysium.

Just past the ten kilometer mark, Jade broke the silence and called out to Brian. He stopped and checked his timepiece. It was well past midnight. The ridge they were walking along was more sparsely wooded than the surrounding areas, which allowed the now driving rain to exert its full force upon their backs. He looked up at Kim and saw that she was as soaked as he was.

"What is it?" Brian asked, a little perturbed at having to stop in such an uncomfortable spot. The rest of the group closed the gap and approached Brian and Kim.

"We should slow down," Jade suggested. "We're making good time, and I don't want to be too exhausted when we reach the valley."

Brian surveyed his sister for a moment. She wore a somber expression, but that was typical for her even in relatively benign situations. In the chaos of the last couple of nights, Brian had almost forgotten that she was pregnant. Even worse, she had a husband whose fate she now had to worry about in addition to her mother and father's. Despite the physical and mental stress, though, Jade showed no outward signs of breaking down. Brian had always admired his sister's strength. Even in the tumultuous days following planetfall five years before, he couldn't bring himself to shut her out as he had his parents. Besides Kim and his parents, Jade was his most sturdy pillar of support, perhaps even more now that Kim seemed so distant and his parents' fate was a mystery.

He thought about it for a moment. Jade was right about slowing down. If the colony had been attacked or overrun, it wouldn't provide a safe haven for rest. Even worse, there may be Adherent patrols around the valley. They would have to be more careful the closer they got to home. "I agree," he said. "But if we're going to rest, we should find some cover."

"How about the Winthrop cottage?" Maleek asked. "It's not too far from here, is it?"

"That's right," Jade exclaimed, her expression lightening just a bit. "I didn't even think about that."

Brian hadn't thought about it either. Old man Winthrop was a retired engineer who had a history of eccentric behavior. He had moved away from the valley settlements two years earlier, claiming that he needed "peace and quiet" to write some sort of novel. Although the colonists had found the move odd, they helped Winthrop build his isolated cottage several kilometers from the valley. Novels that were not approved by the Church had been banned back on Earth. Many colonists were intrigued by the prospect of someone producing original literature, regardless of the eccentricities that were known to be inherent to the writing process. Although nobody knew whether Winthrop had actually written anything during his time away from the settlement, his home had become a stopping place for the hunting parties and survey teams that frequently ventured north of the colony. Even though a trip to the cottage would take Brian and his comrades off their original path, it was a good place to rest. More importantly, Winthrop may be able to provide some information about what was going on.

"It's only about two kilometers from here," Brian answered. "But, we'll have to backtrack once we leave. The path from the cottage to the valley leads to Sanctuary, and it usually gets washed out in the rain. Either way, we're going to lose time."

Jade stood there for a moment in silence as she pondered the choices.

"What's it going to be, Jade?" Brian asked in an authoritative tone. His father often asked the same question whenever Brian or Jade seemed indecisive. At this point, Brian just wanted to keep moving.

"Let's head to the cottage," she decided. "Unless there are any objections."

"I don't care as long as we get out of the rain!" Maleek whined.

"Same here," Brian added. He looked around at the faces of his other companions. Maria shook her head in compliance, but Kim wore a deep, concerned expression on her face that no one else seemed to notice. Brian didn't say anything to her or the group. *Who knows what's on her mind*, he reasoned. But still, her demeanor worried him. Perhaps she sensed something that he did not.

Despite Jade's insistence that they slow down, the walk to the cottage went much faster than the rest of the trip had. Brian, who had actually been to Winthrop's before, craved the warm, cozy fire the old man frequently kept burning during the winter, and unwittingly hastened his step to reach it. The others matched his pace, apparently forgetting that they were supposed to be cautious now that they were so close to the colony. As they neared the cottage, however, it was Brian who held his hand up and brought them to a halt. Even though he wanted to run up onto the small rickety porch of the building, he knew better than to jeopardize the group's safety simply because he was wet, cold and tired.

Brian lowered himself into the underbrush next to the path and flipped off the small lamp attached to the strap of his backpack. They were still a few hundred meters from the clearing that surrounded the cottage, and it was impossible to see anything in the dreary blackness.

"Stay here while we check things out," Brain hissed back to his comrades, who had kneeled down behind him. He met Kim's eyes and she nodded. Brian wondered if she resented being volunteered to go with him, but cared more about having her at his side than having her approval.

Brian winced as he lowered himself even further down into the wet, cold bed of leaves that matted the forest floor. Although Elysium was blessed not to have any poisonous snakes, there were other reptilian creatures that made their home in the muck. Brian tried not to think about them. Instead, he slowly inched his way in the general direction of the thicket, careful not to make any noise. After several minutes of creeping forward, Brian sensed that he had reached the tree-line surrounding the clearing in which the cottage and its companion buildings were situated.

"I'm going to look," he whispered to Kim, before pushing his face through the grass.

There seemed to be nothing out of the ordinary about the property. The quaint, yet primitive dwelling could have easily been mistaken for a home from seventeenth-century colonial America had it not been located on an alien world hundreds of light years from Earth. The cottage itself was dark, but that wasn't surprising considering how late at night it was. A small lamp hung on the edge of the shed in back of the cottage and provided just enough light for Brian to see that everything was as it should be. He stood up and hastily made his way across the clearing to the shed. Kim followed.

"We shouldn't look so suspicious," Kim mentioned as she and Brian pushed their backs up to the shed. "Old Man Winthrop has guns, and he's the kind of person who would use them if he thought he were in danger."

"You're right," said Brian. "We should just go to the front door and knock. Everything looks fine around here anyway."

As Brian started around the side of the cottage, however, Kim grabbed his arm. "Be careful, Bri. Something still doesn't feel right."

"Don't be so paranoid," Brian said. Nevertheless, he charged up his pulse rifle to the maximum setting as he neared the front of the home.

A shrill creaking noise suddenly cut through the air, sending Brian and Kim against the wall once again. Brian felt the now familiar feeling of terror sweep over his body as he remembered the weapons fired by the Adherent soldiers the previous night. But his nerves instantly eased as he heard the noise again, this time in tandem with the breeze. He felt stupid for being so jumpy, and quickly masked his fear by standing up and peering around the corner of the building. The front door was open slightly and was being pushed by the steady wind that had kicked up now that the rain had ceased. Brian shook his head and smiled as he stepped onto the side of the front porch. Then he stopped as fear gripped him again. *Why is the front door open?*

CHAPTER 21

▼

AN UNEXPECTED SAVIOR

Brian desperately wished that he could have taken back the first two noisy steps he had ventured up onto the porch. He quickly pulled away from the small, living room window he had clumsily stumbled in front of. At the same time his eyes darted out into the night, as he anticipated an attack from trees at the edge of the clearing. He waited. A soft, whispy mist was beginning to roll in across the clearing, lending a macabre atmosphere to the setting. Although the nocturnal sounds of the forest were as intense as ever, Brian heard his heart beating loudest of all. He looked back at Kim, who had been smart enough not to rush up toward the door with him. She also scanned the area, her pulse rifle pointed out toward the darkness of the forest. Brian leaned over and tapped her on the shoulder.

"I don't see anything," she whispered without taking her eyes off the woods.

Brian tugged on her shirt this time and motioned with his head toward the door. Despite the need to investigate the cottage, Brian felt uneasy about just sneaking in. He also felt a little scared. Kim seemed to understand his need for reassurance, and she stepped up behind him as he peered into the window.

The inside of the living room looked as Brian had remembered it. There were a couple of simple wooden chairs at the fireplace, with a small table sitting in between. Papers, presumably for writing, were scattered everywhere, as usual, especially on the ornate desk situated near the far window. The fireplace looked cool, save for a few orange embers that poked through the soot. The only real light in the front portion of the cottage was a lone gas lamp that illuminated a small area near the kitchen. *Maybe Winthrop's just asleep*, Brian reasoned. The man was getting old. He may have simply forgotten to latch the front door properly. Brian snapped on the small light attached to the barrel of his rifle and nudged his way in past the swinging door. Kim knelt down and continued to watch the area as he searched the cottage.

Winthrop's bedroom was located in back of the cottage through a door in the kitchen. Another door just a few meters away led to a small guestroom the old man used for storage. After determining that there was nothing of interest in the living room or kitchen, Brian reluctantly approached the bedroom door. *It's best to knock*, Brian thought. *Chances are that I'm going to scare him no matter what I do, but at least I can try to be polite.* Winthrop was known to have a severe temper, although Brian had never encountered it on his previous visits to the cabin.

Kim, who was now standing just inside the front door, watched Brian as he stood in the kitchen and listened for sounds. There was nothing. *The old man must be a heavy sleeper. Then again, it's possible that he died in his sleep.* Brian thought about that possibility for a moment. No, it was too coincidental. What were the chances that Winthrop died within a night of the attack at Lake Clarity? He had to be in his room sleeping. Brian took a deep breath and knocked three times, then put his head against the door and listened. Again, there was nothing.

"Mr. Winthrop?" Kim called out from across the room. "It's Kim Collins and Brian Bishop. Are you all right?"

Brian stepped back and stared at the door. He didn't want to go in. He didn't want to find out why the old man was silent. He had already suffered through enough surprises. He felt perfectly content to stand around in the kitchen all night. Finally, it was Kim who grew impatient. She brushed past Brian and opened the door. Despite Brian's fear, he was sharp enough to raise his pulse rifle as the door creaked open. Kim already had her rifle raised.

The inside the bedroom was as placid as the rest of the cottage. Another small lamp burned on a nightstand next to the bed, bathing the scene in a warm, inviting light. The multi-colored patchwork quilt Mrs. Novich had constructed as a present years before had obviously been used recently, but there was no sign of the bed's usual occupant. Now totally confused, Brian lowered his guard and charged into the room, taking in as many details from the perplexing circumstances as possible. "Where in Hell is he?" Brian asked brashly. "The outhouse?"

Kim shook her head. "Nope. I peeked in when we came up to the house. It was empty."

It didn't make sense. There was no sign of struggle. No indication of anything out of the ordinary. Brian walked around the edge of the bed and peeked out the lone, small window that looked out back toward the south side of the storage shed. He saw that the fog outside was getting worse.

"We should go back and tell the others," he said to Kim as she stepped into the room.

"Right," she nodded, scanning her surroundings from the floor to the ceiling. She walked to the opposite side of the small room from Brian and pawed through some of the papers and artifacts strewn about on top of Winthrop's dresser.

Brian returned his attention to the window and noticed a small, round hole in the bottom of one of the panes. He ran his finger around the outer edges of the smooth, perfect circle and looked back at Kim perplexed. She hadn't noticed the hole and was still busy examining the rest of the room. Brian was just about to say something about his peculiar find when she spoke up.

"Hey look, it's a picture of Winthrop's wife. This had to be way before she died," Kim noted. She reached out toward the framed image, which was slightly obscured by the open door. "I wonder how old she—"

Kim stopped in mid sentence as she pulled the door away from the picture. The shadows in the room shifted, revealing a massive crimson splatter extending from the left half of the picture to the doorframe. It was blood. The mystery of Winthrop's whereabouts had been solved, at least partially. Without thinking, Brian charged forward and grabbed Kim by the arm. They had to get out of the cabin, away from whatever it was that had gotten the old man. The front portion of the cabin's interior flew past Brian as he and Kim made their way toward the front door. There could be a division of Adherent soldiers waiting for them outside, but Brian was willing to take that chance as long as it meant leaving the now-tainted refuge.

In the thick, choking mist, Brian could barely see more than a meter in any direction. He put his right hand on the side of the cabin and felt his way toward where he thought they had initially come from. Kim, who had not said a word since seeing the bloodstain, had broken free of his grasp, although she followed so closely that she almost tripped Brian up.

The fog effectively stifled any ambient sounds coming from the forest. Now all Brian could hear was his own ragged breathing. He had planned on keeping his light off all the way back to his comrades, but realized after only a few steps away from the building that it would be impossible to see through the dark blanket that swirled around his face. He switched his lamp on and hoped that he didn't get shot in the process. The light did little to guide his steps, although it was strong enough to reveal the sharp branches that marked the tree-line. Without slowing, he and Kim hit the forest. Brian winced as the branches swatted at his face, but any pain he may have felt was dulled by shock and fear. There was no fooling himself any longer. The colony had been overrun.

Brian's forward movement was suddenly terminated by Kim, who pulled hard on his arm in the direction from which they had come. He looked at her harshly, then realized that they had run past their waiting companions several meters back. Once Brian stopped and listened, he heard Jade's rasping whisper calling out from the darkness.

"What's going on?" she hissed.

Brian didn't answer her right away. Instead, he followed the sound of her voice and pulled her up from the ground. "We have to leave. Winthrop's gone."

The confused look on Jade's face indicated that she didn't understand exactly what "gone" meant.

"They're here, they got him!" Kim clarified.

"What do we do?" Maria cried out, far too loud for Brian's comfort. He immediately pounced on her and covered her mouth with his hand. He looked right into her terrified eyes as he spoke.

"We stick with our original plan. We still don't know what the situation is back at the colony."

"What about the shuttle?" Maleek asked.

"It's too late to go back now. And they're safer back in the gorge than they would be here," Jade insisted.

"That's right," Brian agreed, slowly lowering his hand from Maria's mouth. "We'll go back to the path that leads to Little Houston and make our way toward the colony. Hopefully, this fog will give us some cover."

There was no debate. The others knew Brian's plan was the soundest option they had for survival. They filed in behind him as he started back toward the path they had originally agreed upon. Kim followed right behind, while Jade brought up the rear. As the guide, Brian was the only one who kept a light on. It was the one located on the end of his rifle. *One light's a smaller target than five*, he reasoned.

As he neared the path that swung around the east end of the valley, Brian began to slow down again. Although they still managed to hug his backside at a decent speed, he could tell that his companions were tiring. He also needed to check his bearings. The fog had managed to penetrate deep into the woods, and it was making visual navigation difficult. Brian scanned his surroundings for a moment as he came to a halt. Then he pulled out the small navigational computer in his backpack and proceeded to check his position.

The other group members realized what he was doing and took the opportunity to rest, with the exception of Jade, who leaned against a tree and attempted to pierce the darkness in search of potential enemies. There still wasn't any sign of Adherent soldiers, and the lack of regular sounds in the forest only contributed to the sense of tension that everyone felt.

Brian was bringing up the computer's longitudinal readings when he heard the crackle in the underbrush. He paused for a moment, flipping off his light. The others had heard it too, and raised their rifles toward the noise. Brian slowly put the nav computer back in his pack and raised his own rifle. He adjusted his aim slightly as another sound rang out a few meters away. Just as Brian's heart felt like it was going to explode from suspense, a small, furry pikabat ran out from the underbrush past his feet. Behind, Maria let out a muffled scream as she jumped back in terror. For a brief second, Brian thought that she might lose control and begin firing wildly in his direction, but a calming hand from Kim got her to loosen her grip on the trigger. Brian let out a deep breath and flipped his light back on. *Maybe I should take Maria's rifle*, he thought, stepping toward the unnerved woman. Unlike his other party members, she had not been trained very thoroughly in the use of firearms.

He stepped toward her, intent on taking the rifle, but suddenly dropped in painful agony as a blue bolt shot through the darkness and struck him in the chest. Several more shots rang out from the trees. In the moments before he lost consciousness, Brian saw the blurred outlines of his fallen companions lying at his side. Then he heard a familiar voice. "You're lucky we're out here looking for survivors, Bishop," the tall, menacing figure leered. "I normally don't set my rifle on stun."

CHAPTER 22

▼

UNDER THE HAMMER

Brian listened as Fenner explained the situation. In the cramped confines of the cave, the High Councilor's voice boomed with its characteristic power. Fenner was excited. In fact, it was evident that he lived for this type of excitement. Brian reminded himself that it had been years since Fenner had been given a chance to demonstrate any real leadership or grab for the power he constantly craved.

Besides Brian and his companions, there were several armed colonists seated around the dark interior of the cavern. Hudson was there, as well as another man from the colonial security force. They looked tired, and seemed to take little notice of Fenner's animated grandstanding.

"There are three ships that we know about," Fenner began. "Two smaller scout craft and one cruiser. They came two nights ago after most of us had gone to sleep. We wouldn't have been alerted at all, but Jan Thompson intercepted some sort of radio transmission from the science party over on the coast. Apparently they had been attacked, but the message got cut off before she could get any relevant information. It just sounded like static-muffled shouting."

Brian thought about it for a moment. Tim. The same thing must have happened to Tim that happened to the fieldtrip up in Lake Clarity. *He may still be alive*, Brian hoped. There was still a possibility.

Fenner continued, ignoring Brian's pained expression. "A few of us were woken up following the message. We were planning to call a general assembly when we heard the first explosions. It was impossible to see in the dark, but it looked like two of the scout ships had knocked out the generator over in New London. They must have picked up on its power signature, because none of our generators were running. The sound woke most of the people up in our village. Nobody knew what was going on. They ran out of their houses in a panic. Even I couldn't get them calmed down."

"So what'd you do?" Jade asked.

"I did my best to round up enough colonists for a defense of the village and handed out pulse rifles. I assume the other villages did the same, because within a minute or two we heard shots echoing through the valley. I think we were the last village to get hit. When I got into the watch tower all I saw was the cruiser swoop down from the sky over Independence and Sanctuary and start firing. The fight didn't last long. I don't think any of those creatures even had to leave their ships. The cruiser landed down on the valley floor and started offloading troops. Then one of the scout ships started attacking our village. It was pointless to fight back against that, so I ordered everyone to head into the peaks. I figured the mountains could provide some protection until we figured out what was going on. A few colonists insisted on staying behind. Some fought back when the Adherents came into the village. I watched it happen from a distance. They should have listened to my orders, because nobody who fought back survived. The creatures took everyone else they found prisoner."

"What about survivors?" Brian asked in a frantic tone. All he could think about was his parents.

"So far from what we've observed, the Adherents have kept everyone they've captured alive," Fenner revealed. "It's strange, considering how violent their initial assault was."

"Then they're being held prisoner?" Jade asked.

"Hudson said he's counted six large holding pens down on the valley floor. Almost everyone in the entire colony seems to be held there under guard."

"The Adherents are even feeding them," Hudson added in a voice that sounded almost amused. "It doesn't seem to fit what we know about them."

"My guess is that they are waiting for orders from their command, wherever that's located," Fenner supposed.

"What makes you think that?" Jade asked. Brian thought she was doing an excellent job of keeping herself together, despite the possibility that their parents were dead. Only the fire in her eyes hinted at the simmering concern she felt for her loved ones down in the valley.

"Think about it, Doctor," Fenner snorted. "Who knew that we were here, on this planet?" He didn't wait for a reply. "No one! They don't know what to do with us."

"It was the same at the lake," Brian noted. "They only blew up one of the shuttles then tried to move in on foot. It was like they were trying to capture us, not just kill us. It doesn't make sense."

Fenner turned to meet Brian's eyes. The look he gave sent chills through Brian's body. "Sure it does, Bishop. Does a blaster fire without someone pulling the trigger? They won't take any actions without receiving proper authorizations, just like a computer. I'd say their level of sentience is somewhat lacking. Since the attack, they've been searching for us methodically, but their search patterns have been very easy to predict. It's been relatively easy to avoid their patrols the last couple of days, which is good, since the last thing we want is to be added to that herd of cattle down on the valley floor."

"Mind you, all of this is just a theory," Hudson interjected. "We've only been able to observe things from a distance. It's too dangerous to get close."

Fenner seemed annoyed by the interruption, but didn't address the Corporal. "Regardless of *why* they haven't killed the rest of the colonists, it's only a matter of time before they receive the orders they're waiting for. The sooner we act, the better."

Now Kim spoke up. Her voice was tinged with a sarcasm that Brian hadn't heard from her in years. "And what are we going to do, Fenner, charge right down there and take back the colony in a hail of gunfire?"

"If necessary, Ms. Collins, we will. Maybe you can pray for us."

Normally Brian would have defended Kim from Fenner's remark, but the High Councilor was right. He was also their only chance for survival at this point. "What do we do?" Brian asked, ignoring Kim's indignation.

"First, we need to rest," Fenner insisted. It wasn't the answer Brian had expected. Fenner explained: "None of us has slept in two days. We've been on a constant state of alert since the initial attack. I'm sure you've been under similar conditions."

Brian nodded his head in affirmation.

"We'll get some sleep, then plan out our assault in the morning."

For the second time in three nights, Brian found himself sleeping on the hard, rocky floor of a cave. At least now he had a thin thermal bag to cushion his aching body. Sleep had come fast following Fenner's briefing, but it didn't last for long. Brian awoke with a violent jerk less than an hour after having fallen asleep.

Immediately, he was overwhelmed by a feeling of tremendous dread as he pondered the fate of his parents and friends just a few kilometers away. Losing Luke had been bad enough, but losing his parents would be unbearable. It scared Brian even more to realize how dependent on them he still was. The sheer darkness of his surroundings intensified his feelings of despair. He thought about reaching over and flicking on one of the lamps sitting to his left, but decided against it. *If I break down and cry, I don't want anyone to see it*, he reasoned.

As Brian fought to retain his composure in the darkness, he felt a stirring sensation near his feet. It was Kim. His worrisome feelings faded slightly. He leaned forward and put a gentle hand on her side as she rolled over in her bag. Brian detected faint, indecipherable whimpers coming from her mouth and suspected that she was having another one of her dreams. The fight they had had three nights before replayed itself in his mind as he watched her. *What's happening to you, Kim? Why are you experiencing all of this?* Brian suddenly wished that it was he who was being ravaged by visions. At least then he could understand what was plaguing her mind. The dream that had come to him on the transport the previous night offered no hint to Kim's affliction. He hated being powerless to help her.

Kim rolled over again and fell silent. Brian, now obsessed with his seemingly insurmountable problems, decided that fresh air would do him better than sleep. He stood up as quietly as possible and made his way toward the faint moonlight marking the exit from the cave.

A cool, light mist greeted Brian as he stepped into the night. Within seconds his face felt wet from thousands of little pinpricks of water. Brian wiped the moisture off his cheeks and struggled to make sense of his surroundings. As his eyes adjusted, Brian could see that several armed colonists sat perched around the rocky outcroppings surrounding the caves, yet they took no apparent notice of him. Instead, they scanned the murky darkness for the unmistakable forms of Adherent soldiers. Brian scanned too, wondering if the Adherents were searching for him and his companions.

"Funny how things turn out, isn't it?" a voice spoke up from behind.

Brian wheeled around and saw Fenner's shadowy form sitting on large boulder next to the cave's entrance.

"What do you mean?" Brian asked, a little shaken at the surprise.

Fenner gave what sounded like a laugh. "I mean that after hundreds of years and trillions of kilometers, we're still being hunted by the same predator."

Brian didn't respond to the observation, although the man had his attention.

"Can't sleep, huh?" Fenner asked.

"No."

"You're a typical Bishop. Always got something on your mind."

Brian gave Fenner a puzzled look.

In one swift motion, Fenner propelled himself off the boulder and landed on the ground in front of Brian. The movement was entirely silent, and it looked for a moment as if Fenner's black poncho would envelope Brian in its dark embrace.

"Come with me," the High Councilor ordered, as he started away from the cave toward the rocky labyrinth that cut through the mountains and down into the valley.

Brian followed tentatively. Even under these circumstances, he didn't trust Fenner. In fact, Brian felt like he was doing something wrong just by being alone with the man, as if he were defying the directions his mother had given him so many years before. *Never trust Fenner*, she had said. *There is nothing good in that man*. But still, Brian followed, curious as to where he was being led.

After about five minutes of walking, Fenner spoke again. "I remember the night before every major operation your father would have trouble sleeping too. It was strange, because as soon as the bullets started to fly he'd be the most composed out of all of us. But the night before, you'd think he had the weight of the world on his shoulders."

Once again, Fenner's words had grabbed Brian's attention, so much so that he picked up his pace in order to close the gap that had formed between him and the High Councilor. Brian had known for years that his father and Kim's father had both served in the Adherent military with Fenner as young men, although neither had ever seemed willing to discuss their service in any capacity. Once, when Brian had asked what his father had done during the Houston Insurrection of 2370, his mother had gotten so upset that she had to leave the room. His father had simply replied that it wasn't a good time to tell him the story. Now here was Fenner, an open, if not entirely trustworthy, link to his father's past.

Fenner came to a halt and lay his pulse rifle down next to a fallen tree.

"Have a seat, Bishop," he instructed, motioning toward the space on the tree closest to him.

As Brian came around the other side of the tree, he noticed that there were large, yet dim lights showing through the sea of mist and fog in front of him. It was the colony, several kilometers away. Despite this distance, the lights still seemed terribly close to Brian, and he wondered how safe he and Fenner really were out on their own.

Fenner seemed to read Brian's mind. "Don't worry, the Adherents make a lot of noise during their patrols. We'll hear them coming from a kilometer away."

"What did you do with my father?" Brian asked, returning to his subject of interest.

"In the Intelligence Service?"

"You guys were in Intel?" Brian exclaimed loudly.

Fenner seemed amused by Brian's ignorance. "I can see he's managed to keep a lot from you. I'm sure Collins is the same way with his daughter." Fenner sighed, indicating that he was about to give Brian the in-depth answer he had been looking for. "Your father, Bill Collins and several others, including myself, were all assigned to the Invasive Ops division of Intel following our graduation from the Academy. We were considered to be the best and brightest of the Adherents, and we did our job extremely well."

"What did you do?"

"We specialized in large scale urban pacification and counter-insurgency tactics. My specialty was interrogation, although we were all cross-trained. Your father was chief of operations for our unit."

Brian couldn't believe what he was hearing. His father had been an instrumental part of the destruction of resistance to Church rule. He must have orchestrated the deaths of hundreds, if not thousands of Apostates. "But–" Brian began, before Fenner cut him off.

"But what? Are you wondering how your father could have done those things even though he had the same belief system he does now?"

Brian didn't answer, but Fenner had once again guessed correctly.

"Simply the means to an end, Brian," Fenner stated casually.

Brian was almost as shocked to hear the High Councilor use his first name as he was to hear about his father's past. Fenner continued: "Working in Invasive Ops was a bloody assignment, but it was short. It also gave us the power and influence, not to mention the skills we needed to get to this planet. Soon after we graduated from the Academy, we came to the conclusion that there was no other way to destroy or escape the Church. We had to go along with the act, at least for a while. Being a loyal Adherent officer tortured your father's conscience, but I always reasoned that the end would justify the means. Initially, we planned to aid one of the resistance movements and fight the Church from within. After several years, though, things changed. Bill and your father got married and had kids. Their priorities changed. Maybe if I had a family of my own, I'd feel the same way." Fenner's eyes seemed to glaze over for a moment in contemplation. "Anyway, I couldn't do things alone, so I went along with their new plan. We got ourselves appointed to the High Councils and began our preparations to leave Earth."

"Elysium," Brian muttered, as he finally placed the missing pieces of the puzzle.

"This is the end I'm talking about Brian, the dream you see below you."

Brian looked down at the valley as Fenner's words crystallized in his mind.

"There are two types of people in this world, Brian: People of talk and people of action. Your father has always been a man of action, even if we haven't always agreed on what kind of action should be taken. Like it or not, you're a man of action too. I know Chang, not to mention your mother, have always tried to suppress that trait in you, but it's a trait you've kept, regardless. Tomorrow, when we're planning to retake the valley from the Adherents, I'm going to need another man of action to back me up. Don't be afraid to embrace those leadership skills; we both know you've suppressed them long enough."

Fenner abruptly ended the conversation by standing up before Brian had a chance to respond. "Try to get some sleep, Bishop, you'll need it," he said before starting back toward the cave.

Although it seemed pointless now, Brian felt compelled to tell someone, even if it was Fenner, about the discovery made at Lake Clarity. "A few nights ago, up at the lake, we found something in one of the caves," he blurted out awkwardly.

"Something?" Fenner asked, his voice carrying a tone that was more condescending than inquisitive. Brian continued anyway: "There was a Cathedral or something ... we weren't sure what it was, exactly, but it looked old."

"No doubt left by our predecessors,"

"Our predecessors?"

Fenner let out a sigh that signaled his intention to release more information. "Yet another secret I'll let you in on, Brian: Elysium was once inhabited. By whom, we don't know, but it's a safe bet they weren't human."

"You knew?"

"All of the Councilors have known since our earliest days on this planet. There are signs everywhere, but they're well-hidden. The leadership, including myself, decided that the possibility of alien contact was a concern the rest of the colonists shouldn't have to add to their current list."

"Do you know what happened to them?"

"Who knows. They didn't leave much behind, just scattered ruins. Maybe they died out or killed each other off." Fenner shrugged and checked his timepiece. He was getting impatient. "Let's make sure the same thing doesn't happen to us."

Fenner once again resumed his stride back toward camp. Just as his back began to fade into the darkness, Brian managed to spit out one last question. "So why did you go along with my father's plan? Why not just fight on with the ICLF?"

Fenner paused in mid-stride and stood there silently. His odd reaction scared Brian a little, who hadn't meant his question to be an insult.

"Get some sleep," Fenner finally replied, before leaving Brian alone to ponder his thoughts.

CHAPTER 23

▼

A WILLING SACRIFICE

The next morning Brian woke to the sound of exited discussion at the mouth of the cave. He groggily shook his head, realizing that he had only slept a couple of full hours since coming back to camp during the night. After a few more moments of confusion, he threw off his thermal bag and dragged himself up and toward the dim light. At the front of the cave, the colonists had congregated around two men Brian didn't recognize. Eager for information, Brian took his place in the hushed crowd next to Kim, who listened attentively to the men as they recounted their story.

"By the time we got there, the Adherents had already rounded up the people from the shuttle," one of the men said. Although he directed his comments toward Fenner and Hudson, his eyes frequently darted between the members of the audience. Brian, like everyone else, remained silent. It was already clear by the man's expression what the content of the report would be.

The other man from the patrol spoke up. "It didn't look like anyone had tried to fight back. We even heard Chang try to talk to the Adherent that seemed to be in charge, but he was just herded into a line like the rest of them."

"What about the shuttle?" Fenner asked. He looked mildly concerned.

"After the Adherents escorted the prisoners back toward the colony, a couple stayed behind and blew up the damn thing! We left as soon as the ship exploded. The return trip took us about twice as long as it should have. We couldn't risk taking the south trail back; there were too many patrols."

"Shit," Fenner swore. "We could have used that shuttle."

"What about Chang and the others?" Jade asked angrily. "Don't you care about them?"

"They're safer now than they were," Fenner retorted. "Now you don't have to worry about them getting ambushed. We'll free them along with the others." He stood for a moment and stared ponderously at the ground before finally adding, "This proves that we need to act immediately. It's only a matter of time before one of those patrols stumbles onto us in the night." Following his analysis, Fenner quickly broke from the congregation and went back into the cave. Although he said nothing, the other followed him, save for three of the colonists who returned to their sentry posts in the surrounding crags.

Fenner switched on a small lamp that illuminated the murky surroundings. He knelt down in on the rocky floor several meters away from the sleeping area and unveiled a crude representation of the valley made out of rocks and sticks. If everything else about the situation hadn't been so serious, the whole scene would have looked comical. Brian and his companions repositioned themselves around Fenner's model.

"So what's the plan?" Jade asked, her voice betraying her distrust of Fenner's leadership skills.

"As Miss Collins pointed out so eloquently last night, charging down into the valley would be foolish," he answered. "Nevertheless, we must take the Adherents by force."

Hudson interjected: "We've discussed several plans that would isolate smaller groups of Adherents so we could deal with them in manageably-sized groups, but we kept running into the same problems: time and numbers. We simply don't have enough people to fight the Adherents in several different locations at once, and it would only be a matter of time before they got their ships off the ground and blasted us to pieces. We don't have any weapons that can counter that kind of air power."

Brian looked around the cave and thought about it for a moment. Including Jade, himself, Kim, Maleek and Maria, there were still only twenty of them to oppose perhaps as many as eighty to one hundred Adherent soldiers. Even worse, most of the colonists around him had little or no military training whatsoever. The odds weren't bad, they were ridiculous. The only advantage the group of colonists had was the lack of children among their company. It was obvious that Fenner had rescued only those who would be useful in the coming fight.

"So I came up with a solution to both problems at once," Fenner proclaimed confidently, to no one's surprise. "There is a way we can eliminate their air power and negate their larger numbers with one attack."

"How?" a middle-aged colonist woman asked.

Fenner seemed pleased to have a cue to explain his plan. "We'll use one of the shuttles from the colony transports in orbit around Ares."

"What?" the group seemed to ask all at once. Jade's voice rang loudest of all.

Fenner held his hands up in an attempt to calm them. The look on his face indicated that he had expected this reaction. "It's simple. We'll remote pilot it down at full speed and use it as a missile against their command ship. It's just sitting there, asking to be attacked."

"You've gotta be joking, Fenner," Jade huffed as she stood up and pointed a finger at him. "We're better off just attacking the camp directly and hoping things work out for the best! We don't even know if the colony transports are still in orbit. The Adherents could have gotten to them as soon as they entered the system."

"No," corrected Hudson in his typically calm voice. "I snuck into Little Houston two nights ago and grabbed one of the remote uplink systems. The beacon on both ships is still active. The Adherent sensors probably didn't pick up the ships because of Ares' gravitation variations. I was only able to connect to them because I knew the specific transponder frequency to look for."

Jade's confrontational stance lessened a little in the face of Hudson's words. She respected the man, as did many in the colony. If he supported Fenner's plan, then there may actually be some credibility to it.

"There's just one problem," Fenner stated.

"Only one?" Jade asked with her eyebrows raised.

"The only computer console that can actually connect to the ships and remote pilot one of the shuttles is down in New Haven. One of us is going to have to go down there, activate the console, and remote pilot the shuttle down to its target."

"That's suicide with those things down there!" Maria exclaimed.

"She's right," one of the men agreed. "The com station you're talking about is right next to their main encampment. There's no way anyone could sneak down there."

"Even if they could," Kim added, "you still have the other attack ships to worry about."

"That's where the rest of us come in," Fenner smiled. "When the shuttle hits its mark, we'll attack the village in two groups. One group will focus on attacking the main force of Adherents, while the other group will break for our remaining two shuttles on the ground in New Haven."

"They haven't destroyed them?" Kim asked doubtingly.

"No, they're still intact. I don't think the Adherents are expecting an outside threat at this point, maybe just a few stragglers who escaped the initial round-up."

"That's not too far from the truth, Fenner," Jade said. "And just who are you going to volunteer to go on this little suicide mission to pilot the shuttle?"

Fenner seemed to think about it for a moment even though Brian already knew he had an answer. "Well, there is only one of us who has the technical proficiency to get the console running and program the shuttle from the ground."

Brian felt Maleek tense up next to him. It was clear who Fenner was referring to.

"No way," said Jade. "Maleek, you are not going down there by yourself. I don't car—"

"I'll go with him." Brian said eagerly, cutting off his sister. So far, he had remained quiet during the debate. By making such a bold statement, though, he was essentially endorsing Fenner's plan.

The High Councilor's eyes twinkled with delight and approval. Jade's mouth gaped in surprise. Kim turned and walked out of the cave. Brian pretended to ignore all of these reactions. He put a hand on Maleek's shoulder. "We can make it. No problem."

Fenner's words from the night before replayed themselves in Brian's mind. He wasn't going along with the plan just to win the High Councilor's approval. He was going along with the plan because he believed in it.

CHAPTER 24

▼

MEN OF ACTION

Brian tried not to think too hard as he and Maleek quietly made their way down into the valley. Even though his mind was working at full capacity, calculating the most tactical route possible, he tried not to think about the bigger issues at hand, like why he was going into the valley or what awaited him there. Try as he may, though, Brian couldn't seem to center himself.

Maleek said little. He definitely didn't seem aware of Brian's inner turmoil. Brian couldn't figure out if his friend was just trying to be stealthy, or was angry at having been volunteered for such a dangerous task. *Is he upset because I went along with Fenner's plan?* Brian asked himself. *He shouldn't be.* After all, Brian was just trying to be assertive, a leader.

Leader. The word echoed through Brian's mind. The last time he had tried to be a leader his reckless actions had almost ended in disaster. Lying helpless in the bloodstained meadow near Lake Clarity had been one of the worst experiences of his life. The fear, though, had been the least painful part of that experience. Much worse had been the feeling that he was going to get all of his friends killed chasing after Luke, trying to be a hero, trying to be a leader. If it hadn't been for Kim, Jade and the others, his fears would have come true. He would have gotten his friends killed. Now, here he was, trying to be a leader again by following the lead of another. The only question was whether or not Fenner's plan was as reckless as Brian's had been. Kim and Jade certainly didn't trust Fenner. Perhaps they were right not to.

The thought of the girls sent Brian's mind spiraling in a different direction. Following the meeting in the cave, Brian had fully expected Kim and Jade, especially Jade, to assault him with a barrage of chastisements for going along with Fenner's plan. To his surprise, however, neither had given him any sort of problem. During the long hours that had passed before nightfall, they had quietly helped with preparations for the assault, making an obvious effort not to discuss what Brian was doing. When night fell and Brian and Maleek received their final instructions from Fenner and Hudson, Kim and Jade's guarded facade crumbled. Although both women remained relatively composed, their final words of caution and encouragement were accompanied by tear-filled eyes and shaky voices. As Brian and Maleek slipped out of camp, he spotted Kim in the murky twilight perched on a large boulder in the meditative position, no doubt praying for his safety. Brian realized that she would soon be joining him in the jaws of danger. That was his only regret about Fenner's plan; it required that everyone be involved at some stage. If only there was a way for Kim and Jade to remain behind in the relative safety of the cave, Brian would have chosen it. He reminded himself that they would have refused to stay behind, even if doing so would have been an option, but that knowledge did little to ease his mind.

Brian heard a sharp sound that instantly brought him back to the present. It was Maleek calling his name.

"What?" Brian whispered back.

"You're going way too fast. I think I hear something."

Brian deliberately slowed down his pace and checked his timepiece. He *had* been going too fast. They had hiked over four kilometers through the crags in just under an hour. The realization that he was being careless instantly sobered Brian up. He pushed his tortured thoughts back into the recesses of his mind and refocused his senses on the brisk night.

It was unusually crisp for this time of year. There were very few clouds out, and Phobos could just barely be seen over the ridges to the northwest of the valley. Ares and Demos still hadn't risen yet, making it difficult to see the surrounding areas.

Brian perked his ears, listening for the sound Maleek was talking about. A strong, cool breeze filtered through the rocky corridor through which they were walking. Brian listened closer. Just above the steady howling of the wind, he could make out voices, or something that sounded like muffled voices at a distance. The sounds were coming from the general direction of Little Houston, whose outskirts were now only a few hundred meters to the north of their position. Brian's heart began to race, but he was careful not to show any sign of anxiety in front of Maleek. Judging by the look on his friend's face, Brian supposed that it wouldn't take much to send him running in the opposite direction. If that happened, Brian would probably follow.

"Which way are we going to go?" Maleek asked nervously. His eyes were darting back and forth between Brian and the source of the noises.

Brian thought about it. "We'll take the western-most pass into the valley. I know Fenner wanted us to go closer to the village, but this will be safer."

Maleek nodded his head in affirmation. He knew the area around Little Houston even better than Brian, and apparently agreed with his friend's appraisal of the situation. They slipped quietly around the outskirts of the village, keeping their ears perked for the low guttural sounds of the Adherents' speech. Slowly they moved, careful not to kick any of the loose rocks lying in front of them on the path. In the almost total darkness of the crags, it was an almost impossible task, and Brian winced each time his feet made a sound. Each time, though, he kept moving, knowing that they were still on a time-table.

Just as he and Maleek cleared the south grain storehouse that marked the border of the village proper, they heard the Adherents again. This time the creatures were close. Now Brian and Maleek did stop as they tried to ascertain where the enemy was. Brian, who had slumped down behind a small rock, lifted himself up just enough to see into the village. Although he and Maleek were still on the elevated path that swung around the back of the village, he felt terribly exposed. Brian could see a small group of Adherents about seventy-five meters away in front of the main generator building. They appeared to be huddled around a sensor array of some sort, which looked to be connected to the generator housed in the building.

"Are they tapping into the generator?" Brian asked.

Maleek raised himself up to Brian's level and surveyed the scene for a moment. His breathing was elevated, but his voice was clear. "I don't think the generator is even on. They may just be examining it. Maybe they plan on using it later, or something. I can't tell."

Suddenly, Brian's radio crackled and cut Maleek off. In the relative silence of the night, the noise sounded like an explosion. Brian instinctively tried to muffle the sound with his hand as he and Maleek pressed themselves down behind the rock. Fenner's voice came over the radio. "How's your progress coming?" he asked.

"We're moving around the edge of Little Houston right now," Brian answered.

"Just make sure you keep moving!" Fenner hissed. "Are there Adherent soldiers in your path?"

"There are several in the village."

"Are they *in* your path?" Fenner asked again in an annoyed tone.

Brian looked to his left down the dark, lifeless corridor of rocks that led down to the valley. He couldn't see more than twenty meters in that direction, but gave Fenner the answer he was looking for. "I don't think so."

"Then move."

Brian looked at Maleek, who wore an expression of perturbation. He was all too familiar with Fenner's demanding personality.

Although Brian was sure that his face mirrored Maleek's, he knew that Fenner was right. They had to reach New Haven well before dawn if the attack was to be a success. The longer they stayed in one location, the greater the chances they would be discovered.

"Understood." Brian answered, before cutting the transmission off. "Let's go, Maleek."

Apart from the Adherent squad in Little Houston, Brian and Maleek didn't come across any more soldiers on their way down into the valley. The path they had chosen took them on a large arc that intersected the valley almost a kilometer west of Little Houston, next to the clear, babbling creek that cut its way across the length of the valley.

As Brian and Maleek emerged from the rocks, they were greeted by the familiar, flowing grasses of the valley floor, which had grown tall and fat during the cold, yet wet, Elysian winter. Unlike many of the areas around the valley, the grass along the river had not been cleared, save for a couple of small areas next to colonist farms. For the first time in several days, Brian felt like he was home. He was also struck by a newly strengthened resolved to defend that home.

"Hold on," Brian said as he retrieved the binoculars from his backpack. Maleek complied and kneeled down next to Brian so that his head barely poked out over the tips of the grass blades. Now that they were out of the rocks, on the flat, open spaces of the valley floor, they were much more exposed. The only break in the terrain came in the form of the ancient rock formations punctuating the otherwise flat landscape.

Brian followed the creek with his binoculars to the northwest, where the running lights of the main Adherent dropship could faintly be seen in the distance. The ship seemed small to Brian, almost like a child's toy. He reminded himself that it was several kilometers away, and that it could spit out instant death if awakened from its seemingly docile state.

"Our best bet is to follow the creek to New Haven," he noted. "If we run across any Adherent patrols we can just hide in the grass."

"Can you see the holding pens?" Maleek asked.

Brian squinted, and attempted to zoom past the glow created by New Haven and the Adherent ship. "No, they must be on the far side of the village, closer to Independence." Brian put the binoculars away and checked his pulse rifle to make sure it was charged. *Now comes the really dangerous part.*

The steady rushing sound of the creek helped mask Brian and Maleek's approach as they moved at a brisk jog toward the village. From time to time, they would stop, and Brian would scan the area for soldiers. There were none, and the dark, lifeless farm houses and silos scattered around the valley gave little hint as to where danger lay. Every indication suggested that they had made their way into the valley undetected.

At about one in the morning, Brian suddenly came to a halt and turned in the direction of the Peterson farm just a few meters from the creek. "I'm going to update Fenner on our progress. We've moved pretty far in the last hour."

Maleek nodded and followed Brian toward the small, yet well-kept, farmhouse, which now sat in murky silence.

Brian lowered his body towards the ground and raised his pulse rifle. Even though the house looked to be unoccupied, his recent experience at the Winthrop cottage had made him wary. Maleek stayed in the relative safety of the grass as Brian approached the front door. Brian turned the handle, and the heavy wooden door creaked open. The light on his pulse rifle would have made the search of the house much quicker, but Brian feared giving his position away to anyone or anything that may be looking around the valley. A lone light in a supposedly empty house would invite an instant response from the Adherent soldiers.

Following a brief search of the building, Brian stuck his arm out and motioned for Maleek to come inside. Both sat down on the floor as Brian took out his radio and switched on the transmitter. Within seconds, Fenner's voice filled the dark room. "How's your progress?"

"We're in the Peterson house," Brian answered.

"Good. We've just moved down to the edge of the valley and should be there in a couple hours. I want you two to stay put for a while, then move into the village by three. Maleek?"

"Here," Maleek answered.

"I want you to bring down the shuttle at exactly half past three, just like we planned. Remember, you must hit the main dropship. That's what they seem to be relying on for their command and communication. We'll deal with the two scout craft when that big one is taken care of, understand?"

"Yes."

"Good. Fenner out."

The radio transmission snapped off, leaving Brian and Maleek to rest in the black silence of the house.

"Well," Brian said, checking his timepiece, "I guess we wait." Trying to set an example of calmness, he stretched out on the floor and rested his head on one of the chairs Mr. Peterson had carved by hand.

Maleek did they same, and let out a long, strained breath that broke into a stifled laugh. Brian let out a nervous chuckle too. "I can't believe we're doing this."

"Listening to Fenner, or just the fact that we're going on a suicide mission?" Maleek asked.

"Both," Brian answered, turning his gaze out the small, rough glass window that faced the creek.

"Do you think everyone is safe, Brian?" Maleek asked, his tone and expression turning serious again.

"Sure, Maleek. Don't worry about it."

"You're a good leader, Brian. You lie well, just like Fenner."

Brian took Maleek's remark as a compliment, even though he disagreed with the comparison. "Thanks."

They sat in silence for the better part of an hour, preparing themselves mentally for what could prove to be the most difficult task of their lives. Finally, Brian broke the silence, aware that there was no excuse to stall any longer.

"Well, let's go. It's still going to take us—"

Brian was just about to give a time estimate, when he caught a glimpse of an Adherent soldier walking up from the creek. Brian dove down onto the floor and began to crawl toward the main bedroom, away from the front door. Maleek followed without question. It was obvious to him what Brian had seen. Within seconds, they could hear the harsh voices of the soldiers as they scattered across the Peterson's property, no doubt looking for whatever creatures they had seen or tracked alongside the wet, muddy bank.

Brian desperately wished he could understand what the soldiers were saying; whether or not they knew of his and Maleek's presence. It was clear by the sound of their voices and movement outside that they were at the house for a reason. He looked into Maleek's terrified eyes. "We need to get out of here before we get trapped."

"How?"

Brian motioned with his eyes up toward the bedroom window. There wasn't time for a debate. The voices sounded like they were right outside the front door, and there were footsteps coming around the side of the house. Within moments, they were going to be trapped on all sides. Just as Brian began to reach for the window, however, he heard the front door crash open.

"Shit," Maleek hissed, pressing himself against the side wall. Brian did the same, and raised his pulse rifle toward the door leading from the living room into the bedroom. Just as the footsteps outside the door became deafening, they heard a sharp, crying sound outside. It was the call of a redwing gecko. The footsteps outside the door immediately shifted as the Adherent soldiers ran outside after the noise. Brian raised himself up just enough to see the soldiers pass by in the rays of moonlight bathing the Peterson's main field. A few moments later, they heard the screeching sounds of the soldiers' weapons, and then, silence.

Brian didn't waste any time. "Come on," he said, grabbing Maleek by the shirt collar. He threw open the bedroom window and jumped out into the cold grass next to the crude porch. Maleek followed. They quickly brushed themselves off and broke into a full run toward the thick, tall grass down by the creek.

At any moment, Brian expected to be shot in the back, but he refused to turn around. The excited voices of the soldiers could be heard far behind, but they seemed not to be following. After another few hundred meters, he dropped to his stomach and pulled the radio out. "Fenner, Fenner, come in."

The radio crackled, and Fenner's voice emerged. "What?"

"We just ran into an Adherent patrol at the Peterson house. I think they tracked us from Little Houston."

"Are they following you still?"

Brian looked around and strained to hear the sound of heavy footsteps. He heard nothing, except for the strong breeze blowing the sea of grass around them. "No, they're still back by the house."

"Where are you now?" Fenner asked.

"Just outside of New Haven." Brian lifted his head up slightly. "I can see some of the storehouses a few hundred meters away."

"Any more soldiers in the area?"

"I don't think so," Brian guessed. He didn't feel too comfortable exposing himself for another look.

"We're taking a longer route than you did," Fenner noted. "Stay with the plan. Don't activate the shuttle until after three; otherwise, you'll be facing the Adherents on your own. Fenner out."

Brian checked his timepiece again. "Great, we still have another hour to wait."

"We can't stay here," Maleek insisted. "Those things will find us."

"I agree. We have to find a better place to hide." Brian winced as he lifted himself up for another look. His eyes focused on the soft glow in the sky on the north side of the village. The light was being cast by the main Adherent dropship dominating the flat valley floor from this vantage point. The holding pens were over by the ship, and for a moment, Brian seriously considered a route which would take him close enough to get a look at how his family and friends were coping with their confinement. Not knowing their status was eating away at his attention span. In fact, their well-being was all he could think about. Just one look at his mother or father might give him the strength he needed to carry out his end of the mission. Then again, it may make him weaker. He shook his head, getting rid of the notion. Most of the Adherents were probably located around the command ship and the holding pens. Staying as far away as possible would be the best strategy. Brian searched around the immediate vicinity for a more practical approach.

The closest building was one of the storage sheds on the outskirts of the village. There didn't appear to be any soldiers in their path to the shed. "We'll have to hide in there for a while. I don't think the Adherents will think to look for us back in the village. They'll probably look for us out around the other farms, if they're even looking for us. I just hope that they don't run across the others."

"Fenner knows they're out there."

"I know. Fenner won't let himself get ambushed, at least I hope."

"Me too."

CHAPTER 25

▼

HOLY WAR

Waiting in the cramped confines of the utility shed wasn't like it had been in the Peterson house. The brief, yet terrifying, encounter with the Adherent patrol had rattled Brian's nerves and made the current lull all the more unbearable. As he sat with Maleek, silently waiting as the minutes passed by, a sick, leaden feeling began to take hold of his entrails. Brian thought back. The last time he had felt this way had been back aboard the colony transport on the day of the mutiny, as he and Kim had made their way toward their fateful encounter with their parents on the bridge. It was the feeling that something terrible was going to happen, something out of Brian's control. In the excitement and confusion of Lake Clarity, Brian had not been given time to contemplate his actions. But now, as the moment of action was getting closer, he was afforded all the time his mind needed to dredge up the horrors of battles past.

Brian fought to keep his nerves at bay. He reached deep inside and latched onto the intense feelings of anger and indignation he felt for those who had invaded his home. Kim would have chastised him for embracing such dark, potentially volatile emotions, but Brian nurtured them, cherished them until they once again consumed his body. *They have to be punished. They have to pay for what they've done!*

His confidence partially restored, Brian looked into Maleek's face. He could gather little from his friend's outward appearance. Aside from an apparently elevated rate of breathing, Maleek appeared relatively collected, although serious, as if resigned to whatever fate awaited him. A ruby-red shard of light reflected off of his ebony skin, enhancing his dire expression. Ares had risen.

Brian shifted slightly on the dirt floor of the shed and was greeted by the full glare of the blood moon. The light grew in intensity as the moon rose above the surrounding peaks and assumed its supreme position in the comforting shroud of the Elysian night. He checked his timepiece. It was almost three. Another minute or two and they would have to make their run for the communication station in the center of town. Surprisingly, this realization did not stir up more feelings of fearful apprehension in Brian. He now felt calm and collected, as if he was about to take a nocturnal stroll through the peaceful fields of the valley. He thought about it for a moment, amazed at the sudden transformation occurring inside of him. *Why am I so calm?* Brian instinctively scanned his surroundings, as if the answer somehow lay in the dusty shed. His eyes finally settled on the small window overhead. It was the moon, or specifically, the light coming for it. The familiar red hue that had accompanied him on many nighttime walks through the colony now filled him with a warm, safe feeling. The light reminded him that Elysium was his world, and that the creatures, those things which had invaded his domain, were merely intruders, trespassers who needed to be expelled at all costs.

Brian thought of Kim as he came to this revelation. He wondered if she now prayed to this heavenly body, just as the ancient inhabitants of Elysium had done. Did she somehow see God in the crimson red eye that hung above the colony every night? Did she receive the same sense of comfort from it that Brian did? The questions swirled in Brian's mind like a torrent. It was as if he had begun to understand what had been consuming Kim's attention for the last year or so. Ares was just a rust-colored rock hurdling around in orbit, and yet, Brian felt a trace of something telling him that it was more, at least for the colonists.

Brian looked down at his timepiece. It was two minutes past three. He pulled himself up to a crouching position and inched his way over to the shed's rickety door.

"Do you see anything?" Maleek whispered.

Brian didn't answer right away. He opened the door a few centimeters, placing one eye against the crack. There was nothing. Not a thing. Even in the dead silence of the shed, he couldn't hear the Adherent soldiers. "We should move now," Brian urged suddenly, well aware that there could be a squad of Adherents just around the corner of the nearest building. Still, waiting in the shed was pointless. They had come this far for a reason: the communications station. Maleek joined Brian at the door. His elevated breathing was now the loudest noise in the area.

"This should be easy," Brian said, trying to sound confident. "The com station's only a hundred meters away, just behind Dan Kolowski's shop." Brian stuck his arm out the door and pointed toward that long, simple building that served as a workshop for New Haven's most skilled blacksmith. Although usually lit by the warm streetlights of the village center, the building now lay dark and cold in the night, as if hiding from the invaders. Brian was right; sneaking over to the com station would be easy, even if there were soldiers nearby. There were plenty of small buildings and piles of debris to hide behind on the way.

Before the gnawing anxiety returned, Brian resolved to spring into action. It was the equivalent of tearing a bandage off quickly rather than thinking about how bad it would hurt at every jerk. He shot up and trotted silently over to the back of Kolowski's, slinking down next to the corner of the building nearest to the open area between the neighboring structures. Maleek, who had obviously been caught off guard by Brian's sudden sprint, followed behind a few moments later, glancing wildly in every direction as he moved. He slumped down next to Brian and waited for the next move.

Brian paused for a moment before gathering the courage to peek around the side of the building. He fished his night vision goggles out of his pack and slowly lowered himself on his belly. Initially, it appeared as if the entire village was deserted. The dark buildings gave no hint as to recent activity. Still, Brian felt as if there was movement somewhere in the darkness. He increased the resolution and meticulously scanned every aspect of his surroundings. *There they are*, he thought as he focused in on the colony's main governmental building on the far side of the village. Although partially obscured by several other large buildings, Brian spotted a small group of Adherent soldiers lurking at the end of a street about 300 meters away. It was a sight he had fully expected to encounter, and he immediately changed his initial plan of approach. He rolled back behind the building and stood up against the metal siding. Maleek's blank expression changed as soon as he realized what Brian had seen. "Where are they?" he asked.

"A ways away," Brian answered. "Come on." He pulled at Maleek's shoulder strap and led his friend around the back of the building down a completely dark corridor of trees that bordered the village center. They carefully avoided the thin rays of pale red moonlight filtering down through the tree branches like translucent celestial arteries. Brian looked only a few meters ahead, skillfully choosing his cover as he made his way toward the small building housing the com station. There was a backdoor to the building, which, if opened, would allow them access on the side facing away from the area where he had spotted the soldiers.

Somewhere in the back of Brian's mind registered the dark mass of the schoolhouse that stood just south of where they were moving. He had traveled this way many times, always in a hurry to leave the artificial confines of the classroom in favor of the open plains surrounding the village. He would have traded anything to be in those safe confines now, hidden from the inhuman eyes scanning the village. Even in the cover of the trees and the dark alleys he felt dangerously exposed. He didn't even want to plan for the possibility that he and Maleek would bump into an Adherent patrol in the darkness. No amount of planning would get them out of that serious a mess.

Brian's heart fluttered one last time as he reached the back door of the com station. He pressed himself against the wall next to the door and cautiously peeked through the darkened window. Apart from the soft blue glow of the com station computer screens, the room was dark, and silent. Brian could barely detect the calm hum of the building's small generator over the steady night breeze. The building itself was the only one in the entire colony that was powered all day every day by artificial means. New Haven's technically minded citizens were tasked with maintaining the building for the rest of the colony. Besides the actual communications equipment, the building housed an electronic database, refrigerated DNA samples, and medications, and a host of smaller, more specialized pieces of equipment that were deemed essential by the leaders of the colony. Before this night, Brian had taken little interest in the cramped, yet orderly building. Maleek, however, was intimately familiar with its contents, not to mention the inner-workings of every electronic device contained within.

"Does everything look like it should?" asked Brian as quietly as possible. The small group of Adherents was just on the other side of the building, across the street. Maleek peeked through the pane of glass next to Brian's face.

"Yeah," just like Mr. Andalla usually keeps it.

Richard Andalla was the engineer who was normally in charge of the building. Brian wondered if he was still alive somewhere in the holding pens.

"Is the door open?" asked Maleek, apparently eager to get at the equipment.

Brian reached down and slowly twisted the door handle. To his surprise, it turned easily. Perhaps there had still been people working in the building when the Adherents had attacked. Brian didn't really care at this point. What was important was the he and Maleek could get in without a struggle.

The door drifted open, and Brian and Maleek swiftly slipped in. Brian closed the door behind them, as if that would somehow protect them from a squad of angry Adherents. Brian thought about turning on a small flashlight in his bag, but realized it would light up the entire building. "Can you see?" he asked

Maleek, aware that the faint light cast by the surrounding equipment would have to suffice.

"It's good enough," answered Maleek. He was looking around at the room, no doubt checking to see if everything was as if should be.

"Any ideas on why the Adherents left this room alone?" asked Brian.

"No reason to do otherwise," noted Maleek. "From what I've seen of their technology so far, they probably consider our technology insignificant."

Maleek's words sparked a sudden pang of doubt in Brian's mind. He was right; the Adherents were ridiculously advanced. The idea of relying on a shuttle that was centuries old to fight those things was almost laughable, and would have been if the situation hadn't been so grave. Still, it was their only chance.

Maleek sat down in front of one of the monitors and began to access the system.

"Is it working?" Brian asked, nervously looking around from a crouched position on the floor.

"Yeah, the system's intact. I'll need about ten minutes or so to get the shuttle prepped and on its way."

"Just hurry." Brian felt like they were on borrowed time as it was. He could hear one of the smaller Adherent ships landing in the distance, near the command dropship. He hadn't realized one of the shuttles had been out patrolling somewhere around the colony. Brian was suddenly gripped by a terrible thought. *What if Fenner and the others had gotten captured?* He hadn't heard anything from them for well over an hour. Brian pulled his radio out and stared at it for a moment. Fenner would be angry if he broke radio silence, but the reassurance would be worth the tongue lashing.

"Fenner, Fenner, come in."

Brian was greeted by a burst of static that lasted for several torturous seconds.

"What? Is there a problem?" Fenner finally responded. "We're a little busy here. The trip into the valley took a little longer than expected."

"Nothing's wrong, I just wanted to let you know that we're at the com station. Maleek's tapping into the colony ship's computer right now." Filling Fenner in on their progress was the best reason Brian could come up with.

"That's it? Don't contact me again," Fenner spat. "We don't want the Adherents to intercept any transmissions, Bishop, you know that."

"I know, but—"

"You'll know when we start the attack. Just keep up your end of this!"

With that, the transmission cut out, leaving Brian and Maleek in silence.

"I've got it, Brian," Maleek spoke up.

Brian knelt down beside his friend and examined the computer screen. He saw a rough, three dimensional model of the Phoenix surrounded by a labyrinthine structure of seemingly incomprehensible codes and numbers. A flashing yellow light began to blink, indicating that the main hangerbay had been accessed remotely. Brian recognized the shuttle identification numbers on the side of the screen as Maleek took control of them too. Brian imagined the lifeless colony ships orbiting near the glowing, featureless face of Ares. In the cold vacuum of space they had been kept in perfect condition, unchanged from the day when he had traveled down to the surface of Elysium over five years before.

"It'll take fifteen minutes or so before it reaches the surface. I'll try to program in the coordinates Fenner gave me for the Adherent command ship. The shuttle should be able to just follow the path on auto pilot, but I'll monitor its progress."

"That's fine. We're stuck here until Fenner starts the attack anyway," noted Brian.

He sat back and tried to relax as Maleek hovered over the computer. A soft rain had begun to fall, signaling its arrival by the familiar pattering sound on the roof. The light from Ares had dissipated substantially as the moon slipped behind the incoming storm clouds. A few scattered thunderclaps roared in the distance. Brian closed his eyes and tried to will the seconds by faster. He looked down at his timepiece after what had seemed several minutes, and saw, depressingly, that it had been less than five. Maleek was still hunched over the computer screen, totally immersed by his task. A feeling of uselessness overcame Brian as he watched his friend. He may have been the supposed leader, but he felt more like the hired gun, whose only job was to provide security for the real brains in the room. That was fine, though. He didn't envy the endless hours of technical study which consumed most of Maleek's time. And to think, Brian had wanted to be a pilot as a kid. *How things change.*

Brian became more nervous as another minute passed. He didn't want to be stiff or feel groggy when it was time to move. He stood up to his full height and made his way from window to window, surveying the surrounding buildings. The rain was now coming down in a steady shower and small streams were beginning to form in the rough, clay streets. He slowed slightly as he reached the window facing the village center. When he peeked outside, he found that the small group of Adherents had left their position. In fact, Brian could find no evidence of enemy activity anywhere, even though the cold glow from their ship now dominated the heavy, wet air. Brian would have preferred that the soldiers were still within view. At least then he would know where they were.

Another thunderclap, this one much closer, sounded overhead as the wind picked up. A loud creaking sound accompanied the lightning that followed, causing Brian to jump back from the window. He wheeled wildly, frantically looking for the source of the loud sound in the otherwise silent room. His eyes settled on the back door through which he and Maleek had entered minutes before. He must have left it open slightly, as it was now blowing open under the force of the storm. *Careless.* Brian ran over to the door and grabbed the handle, unaware of the large, foreboding shadow that had risen to fill the thin, wooden doorframe.

Brian didn't see the Adherent soldier so much as bumped into it. Luckily, the creature was standing with its back toward the doorway. As Brian fell back from the mass of tangled flesh and machinery, he instinctively raised his pulse rifle and squeezed the trigger. It was a twitch kill, totally lacking in any skill or marksmanship. Brian hadn't even thought about pulling the trigger; it just happened. The surprised Adherent had barely begun to turn as it was struck in the side with the blue bolt of plasma. It groaned in pain, and reeled back into the downpour. Brian hit the ground and fired again, this time consciously intending to kill his target.

The Adherent gave one last groan as it collapsed into a pile of smoking black armor. Brian looked over at Maleek, who wore the same look of shock as he did. Within seconds, they heard indecipherable, yet obviously angry, yelling as other soldiers began to converge on their position. Once again, Brian acted without thinking. "Stay here. Make sure the shuttle hits its mark." Before Maleek even had a chance to respond, Brian stood up and ran out the door, shutting it tightly behind him this time. He stepped over the dead body and began to sprint.

The first thing Brian sensed as his body hit the rain were the multiple objects closing in on him in the dark. He instinctively turned to his right and fired several shots toward the closest shadow that moved toward him although there was no indication that he hit anything. The response was swift and harsh. A multitude of screeching blasts shot in his direction, one searing the outer edge of his backpack. Brian dove headfirst over a pile of storage boxes near a tree, just in time to avoid another volley of shots. Aware that the soldiers were right on him, Brian crawled around the corner of one of the boxes and shot wildly in the direction of the com station building. A shower of sparks exploded from one of the Adherent soldiers, signaling that Brian had hit his mark. The intense flash of light revealed at least three more forms near the building about ten meters from Brian. They didn't even bother to seek cover; they simply raised their rifles in a robotic fashion and returned fire. Brian rolled away from the storage boxes as they were shredded under the assault. He somehow managed to roll out of his backpack too, freeing himself of the weight that had prevented him from entering into a full sprint. As he rose to his feet he stumbled back into an alleyway between two food warehouses. The bolts of energy from the soldiers' weapons ricocheted off the metal sides of the building, framing Brian in a sea of death. The only thing that saved him were the piles of equipment and supplies that had been sloppily discarded between the two buildings. Brian fired his pulse rifle with his right hand while he used his left to clear away any debris that lay in his path. As soon as he cleared the alley, he broke into a full run towards the open fields behind the school.

Brian tensed up as he anticipated being shot in the back. He could hear and see the shots whizzing past him, some close enough for him to feel the heat. He could also hear more yelling as the Adherent soldiers gave chase in increasingly large numbers. Finally, as Brian hit the taller grass outside of the main village center, he felt as if he had created a gap. He stopped and kneeled at the grass' edge. The Adherent soldiers were still following him, he could tell by the direction of their voices, but they had slowed down. Even though Brian wanted to head into the relative safety of the grass and hide until Fenner arrived, he knew he had to prolong the chase. As long as the soldiers were following him, they probably wouldn't take the time to search the com building. Hopefully, Maleek would be smart enough to keep a low profile.

Brian checked his timepiece. There were still several minutes left until the shuttle reached its objective and Fenner began the assault. He looked around the village outskirts for some sort of advantage he could use against the Adherents. Most of the surrounding buildings were houses, with little in the way of solid defenses. Bottling himself up inside one would be suicide. The only other idea he could come up with was running back into the village and catching the attention of the soldiers, then somehow making his way toward the command ship. That may prevent reinforcements from arriving in the area and searching the com station. At least it would keep the soldiers occupied for another minute or two. Brian realized it was the same, relatively simple plan he had used on the predators up at Lake Clarity. Unlike that situation, however, Brian didn't expect to outwit or escape his adversaries. He only hoped to buy some time before they killed him. Fenner had been right; he had to keep his end of the plan. The only thing that mattered was getting the shuttle to hit its target. It was the only way he could give his friends and family a chance. It was the only way Kim would have a chance. Brian closed his eyes for a moment and pictured her face, the way it had been a few months before, carefree and beautiful. He gripped his pulse rifle and started moving back in the direction from which he had come.

The street that ran down the center of the village from north to south was Brian's chosen avenue of advance. He circled around the closest house and fired blindly toward the darkened grove of trees near the grain warehouses. The Adherents were closer than Brian had expected. They emerged from a nearby alleyway and opened fire. Brian ignored the shots and continued running as fast as he could. He weaved toward the left side of the street, hoping to gain some cover from the small stone walls separating an interlocking series of gardens in front of the town hall. As Brian passed the steps of the hall, he hopped over a thin, wooden fence that closed off a tight alleyway. He fired off another burst of shots to ensure his hunters didn't lose interest in their prey and realized with horror that the opposite was true: an entire squad of soldiers was making their way down the street after him, firing as they advanced. The fence in front of him disintegrated in seconds. Brian felt a sharp burning pain on his left arm as a shot grazed him. He also took a glancing hit in the leg, although it didn't seem to hurt as much. He threw himself against the clay bricks of the building's foundation and resumed his flight out of the village center.

The first clear glimpse of the Adherent command ship almost stopped Brian in mid-stride. It loomed over the surrounding plain like one of the Cathedrals back on Earth. Its long torpedo shape looked like a bullet that stood poised ready to strike at the heart of any Apostate who dared to challenge the Church. The sight enraged him more than any of the soldiers, and he felt ready to charge toward the main body of Adherent troops and kill every last one of them. A stray bolt of energy suddenly whizzed past Brian's face from behind, forcing him to duck into the tall grass outside the village and continue toward the hulking mass of lights and metal ahead.

The creek that snaked through the eastern portion of the valley ran past the outskirts of New Haven and around a series of rocky pillars before widening into a river and straightening out near the Adherent encampment to the west of the valley. The plan Brian was rapidly formulating called for him to take cover behind the pillar closest to the camp, near the holding pens housing the colonists. The pillar sat atop a small, circular hill, which provided a view of the surrounding terrain; it would be the perfect defensive position. Moments later, Brian's heart lightened slightly as he hit the cold water of the creek. He was almost there. The shuttle would arrive soon, blowing the command ship to pieces. Fenner and the others would be there as well. Brian continued along the bank toward the pillar between his position and the command ship. The soldiers who had chased him through the village were still charging through the grass about 100 meters behind. If not for the protection offered by the sloping river bank, Brian was sure he would have already been killed.

The mass of the ancient, stone pillar soon towered overhead, even higher than the Adherent ship. Brian slipped into the pillar's shadow and away from the muddy bank. He was just about to reach the relative safety of the rocks when he tripped and fell in the mud. The fall into the cool muck stunned him, and for several crucial seconds he stayed on his knees and attempted to shake off the pain of the impact. His wounded leg, which had been dulled by shock and adrenaline during the chase, now exerted itself in full-force. Brian winced in pain as he lifted himself up. As he rose, he was instantly greeted by a new group of Adherents emerging from the other side of the pillar about 200 meters to his right. The entire contingent of soldiers must have been aware of his presence at this point. His plan had worked a little too well. Brian looked back down toward the water and saw the group that had been chasing him close the gap that he had built between New Haven and the pillar. *Shit, I'm trapped.*

Brian fired down toward the river at the Adherent soldiers, betraying his exact location. He dove behind the largest boulder within reach and wedged himself into a crevice in the rock. *Last stand,* were the only words his mind latched onto in the chaos. Sensing that the soldiers from the camp were closer than those coming up from the river, he turned and fired over the tops of the boulders toward the pillar. One of the soldiers fell, but the rest kept coming. Brian turned and ducked down into the rocks again, only to see that the group coming up from the river was shooting at him too. He held down the trigger and sprayed the entire area in a mad fury. Although he couldn't see the soldiers well over his tiny stone fortress, he was sure that he had killed at least some of them. Regardless of how many lucky shots he made, though, he would be overtaken within seconds. Brian lay down on his belly and crawled between the tightest spot between the rocks, leaving only one opening through which the Adherents could get to him. This ensured that he could shoot a couple more before being killed.

As he readied himself, he noticed the large, brightly lit square located alongside the river to the northwest. It took a moment for the image to register in his mind, although once it did, the scene consumed him. It was the holding pens, just a few hundred meters downstream, partially visible around the side of the rocky tower. Below stood Brian's parents and friends, no doubt watching his last moments unfold in heated suspense. Of course, from such a distance they had no idea that it was Brian Bishop heroically fighting off the Adherent soldiers; nevertheless, the friendly audience made Brian feel at ease. At least he wouldn't die alone. He ran his finger along the trigger of his rifle as he heard the soldiers' armored boots scrapping along the rocks next to his hiding place. It was time.

Just as Brian readied himself to fire a volley at the first soldier who came in front of him, he was almost knocked unconscious by a massive wave of heat and sound that blasted through the rocks. Brian checked himself for a moment, thinking that he had been killed by a grenade or explosive, but found that he was very much alive. The initial blast was followed by another, this one even more powerful. He heard the awful cries of the soldiers overhead as their bodies were thrown against rocks like dolls. The intensity of the second blast almost drove Brian mad with terror as his rocky fortress trembled around him. Regardless of the consequences, he wanted to get out of his cramped hiding place. Before he could remove himself from the rocks, however, the source of the blasts blew past the pillar. It was a shuttle, a colonial shuttle. The ship's plasma cannons blazed and its missile tubes fired volley after volley at targets on the other side of the pillar.

Brian pulled himself from his hiding spot and stumbled around the rocky outcroppings at the base of the pillar. He rounded the corner just in time to see one of the smaller Adherent ships explode in a spectacular ball of fire on the valley floor. It had been hit by a flaming missile from above: another one of the colonial shuttles. The holocaust was astounding in its scope; the bodies of dead Adherent soldiers lay everywhere, many blown to pieces. Burning shuttle wreckage merged with Adherent ship parts in a fiery mixture of debris. The surviving Adherents could be discerned by the flashes emitted by their weapons. They were firing at the remaining shuttle and at other targets that Brian couldn't make out from a distance.

As his eyes and ears attempted to absorb the chaos of battle, Brian realized what had happened: Maleek had somehow managed to take direct control of multiple shuttles, crashing the first into one of the smaller Adherent scout ships. The surviving colonial shuttle was being controlled remotely. Maleek looked to be doing an excellent job too, maneuvering the craft with the skill of a seasoned pilot. Although the Adherent command ship appeared unscathed, despite Fenner's explicit orders to destroy it, the attack seemed to have totally decimated the Adherent garrison beyond the point of mounting an effective defense. Unable to hold back his feelings of bloodlust any longer, Brian let out a bellowing war cry that somehow managed to rise above the turmoil. The rain continued its relentless assault as he started hobbling down toward the battle, although the red light of Ares still managed to penetrate the storm clouds with an unnatural intensity. Now it was time to punish the Adherent soldiers for invading Elysium.

As he descended the hill on which the pillar was located, Brian spotted several flashes of blue on the outer edge of the camp, past the command ship. *Fenner*, he realized. Fenner and the others were attacking the camp from the south. Kim was somewhere over there too. He had to help them. He had to find Kim. Brian, knowing where she'd be headed, began limping toward the holding pens near the command ship, trying to ignore the Adherent soldiers who scrambled through the burning wreckage of the scout ship in the darkness. Luckily, they seemed wholly unable to deal with the swift brutality of a guerilla attack and paid no attention to the lone human heading through their ranks toward the pens.

"Don't touch that fence, Brian," a colonist yelled from behind the confines of the humming fence. "It's electrically charged."

Brian didn't recognize or stop to acknowledge the man who had given the advice. In fact, he blocked out all of the yelling, pleas and encouragement shouted by his fellow colonists. The power to the holding pens had to be fed by a generator somewhere, but there was no indication of any power lines along the perimeter. Brian tore himself away from the pens for a moment and charged into the middle of the Adherent camp. He took up a position among the large, white, dome-like structures that housed the weapons and equipment used by the Adherents. From this vantage point, he was able to fire at several Adherent soldiers who had their backs turned to him. Once they fell, Brian saw a human hand shoot up from the wreckage of the Adherent scout ship that had been destroyed.

Brian looked around and reasoned that it was safe enough to cross the open area between his position and the shuttle wreckage. As soon as he stepped out, however, he realized how slow his wounds had made him. It was like a bad dream as he ran toward his comrades. The look on Jade's face told him that he was in danger, but the harder he ran, the slower he seemed to move. The others rose from behind their hiding spots and shot past Brian's face at his unseen attackers. Finally, as he smashed into part of the ship's shattered hull, Jade and Hudson pulled him behind cover.

"Damn, Brian, you're hit," Jade gasped as she immediately went to work on his leg. Brian looked to his left as he lay on his back and saw the dead face of a colonist woman staring back at him, her hair caked in blood. He pulled his head up and attempted to examine his own wounds under Jade's hurried hands. Another explosion rocked the entire area. "There goes the other shuttle," Hudson grunted as he let off a volley of shots toward the command ship. Brian's earlier feeling of elation died as he realized the hopelessness of their situation. There were still many more Adherent soldiers out there and no way for the dwindling colonist attack force to replace their casualties. Brian put his head back and closed his eyes as Jade injected his leg with some sort of medication. The shot stopped the pain although it instantly made him feel groggy. Brian also felt a new set of hands slip behind his head. He could tell they were Kim's, even though his eyes remained close. She said nothing; just cradled his head and held his hand. He could have died happy at that moment. Only the sound of Fenner's voice kept him from going unconscious. "What's the situation? I can't see anything and we're pinned!" yelled the High Councilor over the surrounding noise.

"Wilkins and the others have taken up a position east of the command ship. They should be able to hold it for a while," noted Hudson, who had just gotten off the radio with the other group of attackers.

"Then what? We've already lost almost half our number, and almost everyone else is wounded, Fenner," Jade pointed out.

"She's right," said Hudson, "Without air support it's only a matter of time. We should have told Maleek to just destroy the command ship."

"No, this can still work," Fenner said confidently.

Even in Brian's nearly unconscious state, he could tell Fenner had a plan that he hadn't been informed of prior to risking his life. The anger Brian felt at having been kept partially ignorant gave him a new wave of strength. He sat up. "What can work, Fenner?" he rasped.

"We need to storm the command ship and end this!"

"We don't have enough people," complained Hudson. "What we need to do is rethink this before we all get killed. There has to be an override switch for the holding pens somewhere in this camp."

"It's in the command ship," said Fenner.

"How do you know?"

"Because we've damaged both of the smaller ships and there's no other external power source in this camp. And–" Fenner cut himself off, stood up and blasted an approaching Adherent in the chest. He looked down at Brian and the rest of the group with wild eyes. "It seemed to be powering up as we passed by. If it gets off the ground it'll kill us all!"

Nobody argued with Fenner's claim. It made sense that the Adherent soldiers would use their greatest asset once they discovered the nature of their threat.

"Hudson, Collins, you come with me. Doctor, you hold out here and kill anything that moves toward that ship."

Kim kissed Brian on the top of the head, a gesture which indicated that she planned to follow Fenner up into the command ship. Jade didn't argue with Fenner's orders either; she would stay and treat the wounded, providing cover if needed. Brian began to get up, but Kim and his sister held him down.

"No, Bri, you're hurt." Kim pleaded. "You need to stay here."

Fenner noticed Brian's pathetic attempt to follow. "She's right, Bishop. You've done your part, we'll finish it."

Brian wasn't sure if the remark had been intended to calm or rouse him, but it had the latter effect. He broke through Kim and Jade's grasp and clumsily got to his feet beside Fenner. The High Councilor smiled knowingly. "Let's go!"

CHAPTER 26

▼

THE WRATH OF GOD

The frantic run between the wrecked Adherent shuttle and the command ship was surprisingly easy to make. The other group of attacking colonists had done an excellent job of creating chaos on the outskirts of camp, and many of the Adherent soldiers were tied up in the massive firefight. As Fenner reached the downed loading ramp in the back of the command ship, he blasted two waiting soldiers before they had a chance to respond. Brian thought it strange that creatures so fearsome looking were dispatched so easily, but supposed that maybe it was because they weren't used to fighting an enemy as nimble and resourceful as the colonists. Still, despite the danger and losses, the fight seemed almost too easy.

Hudson helped Brian up the ramp as his wounded body shook from the stress. Kim ran right in front of them, with Fenner and another colonist in front of her. It was a pitiful boarding party, and Brian realized the stupidity of such a rash action under the murderous circumstances. It was only Fenner's intense certainty that kept them going; a drive to accomplish the impossible.

The moment they entered the Adherent ship, it became clear that they were in an alien environment. The metallic walls seemed organic, as if the entire ship was a living entity. The tight twisting corridors on the outer edges of the ship gave little hint to form or structure, although Fenner continued to move quickly, as if he knew the proper direction. The first sign of resistance they encountered were three soldiers crowded around a display sensor in a larger, circular room in the interior of the ship. Although unarmed, one of them lunged at Fenner as he entered the room. Fenner fell back against the wall, allowing Hudson a clear shot at the creature. Brian and Kim shot the other two without hesitation, even though neither made an attempt at escape or attack.

Hudson seemed perplexed by the sensor array. "We need somebody like Maleek in here," he noted.

"We'll have plenty of time to examine the ship once we eliminate the rest of the Adherents," Fenner assured.

Suddenly, Fenner's plan became clear to Brian: *He must have told Maleek to spare the command ship because he wanted it for himself.* Fenner was an intelligence officer by training. It made sense that he'd want to squeeze every bit of information out of the captured ship. Brian could understand that, although he questioned the risks involved in keeping the ship intact.

After examining the circular room for another moment, Fenner resumed the search for the bridge, or reactor, or whatever he was looking for. Brian couldn't tell. All he cared about at this point was safely ending the battle and getting everyone out of the holding pens.

Once they had exited the sensor room, the interior of the ship opened up into larger arteries of travel. The entire thing seemed to pulse with energy, and Brian swore that he could hear a faint breathing sound echo throughout the corridors. The worst part of the whole experience was that it was dark and hot inside the ship, traits that made navigation all the more difficult. Following a brief firefight with two more Adherents, the boarding party entered what appeared to be the command center of the ship.

Surprisingly, the bridge didn't look all that different from those Brian remembered from childhood. Apart from the indecipherable writing on the monitors, and the omnipresent pulsing of the walls, it seemed perfectly human. Brian wondered if human beings actually built the ship. Or, had it been creatures like the ones they were fighting? *Were there human beings left at all?* Perhaps those were the questions Fenner sought to answer with his investigation of the vessel.

"I can't read any of this shit!" yelled Hudson back at Fenner. "Even if the override for the pens was here, we'd never find it! I say we just blast this place and take out their whole network. It's gotta do something!"

Fenner didn't respond to Hudson's suggestions. Instead, he stood apart from the group with his back turned. He was fiddling with one of the visual displays on a board of blinking lights that looked like some sort of computer. He obviously didn't know what he was doing, but pressed buttons nonetheless.

"Fenner!" Kim called, trying to get his attention. When Fenner finally responded, it was in a calm, yet chilly voice. "I believe this is an engineering station."

"What makes you say that?"

"Because this screen is displaying a diagnostic of the entire ship."

Brian and the others crowded around Fenner at the display.

"The generator?" postulated Hudson, pointing at a bulge near the rear.

"I'm sure it is," Fenner said, "but I'm more interested in this compartment over here. Notice how all of these little lines that run throughout the ship schematic all converge on this room?"

"Like its heart?" Brian asked.

"Precisely."

Fenner's radio blared, filling the bridge with static and the sounds of battle. It was one of the colonists from the other group. "Fenner, come in," he said. The transmission was terrible even though it was coming from just a few hundred meters away. It was a miracle that the transmission could penetrate the command ship's hull at all. "Madie and Taylor are dead," the voice said. "The four of us have pulled back to the outskirts of *New Haven*, but Jade and the others are still down in encampment. Whatever you're going to do you need to do now!"

"Understood," said Fenner in the same calm, cool voice. He turned to Brian and the others. "Come on."

One would expect the heart of the command ship to be heavily guarded, but Brian and his comrades found that their path from the bridge was totally clear of obstacles. Although there were clearly automated weapons blisters protruding from the walls surrounding the center of the ship, they were silently pointed at the ground, as if offline. Nevertheless, Fenner slowed as he entered the spherical room that had attracted so much attention on the schematic, careful not to rush these last crucial moments of the assault. If Fenner had given any sort of reaction whatsoever, Brian would have been somewhat prepared for the ghastly sight dominating the room, but it was clear that even the High Counselor was caught off guard by the black, inhuman eyes that greeted him.

Brian's gaze followed the intricate pattern of cables and wires across the ceiling and down to the bloated, grotesque figure through whose body they entered. The creature, if that's what it truly was since it didn't look like anything that lived, hung motionless in the center of the room, its eyes open and its lipless mouth slightly gaping. Kim gasped as she saw its mangled body, a mess of flesh and metal that made the creature look like the victim of a terrible shuttle wreck. Its skin was moist and fleshy, and veins could be seen running just under its pale gray surface. The face was almost skeletal in nature. It was not unlike the Adherent soldiers, although this thing, this monstrosity, was far more disturbing to Brian. It looked like it was being perpetually tortured in the bowels of this hellish ship, its eyes giving only a faint indication of the true pain it suffered on a constant basis.

Fenner approached the creature, laughing quietly under his breath. "And here we have the brain of the ship, if you will. What a joke." He rifle butted the creature in the head, just enough to show the others that it still had life in it. Although it remained silent, its mouth opened and closed, as if trying to communicate the pain it was experiencing.

"Stop it, Fenner," Kim cried, as if anticipating the torture Fenner was planning to unleash on the creature. "It's already sick and dying. Just do what you have to do and get it over with."

Nobody argued against Kim's reasoning. Although it was unclear how she knew the creature's health status, her voice carried a conviction that stifled any dispute, even from Fenner. The creature was a thing to be pitied, regardless of the atrocities it was responsible for. That much was clear.

Fenner smiled and nodded at Kim. Then he put the muzzle of his rifle to its skull and pulled the trigger. The blast separated much of the creature's head from the wires and circuitry in the ceiling and its black, lifeless eyes seemed to glaze over slightly in the dim light of the room. It was dead, and so was the ship. The generator, which had been left untouched, still pumped energy to the needed systems, although the brain that had monitored and controlled its higher functions, including the ninety-two Adherent soldiers still fighting outside, was dead.

A few silent seconds ticked by as they stood around the creature's dangling carcass before Fenner's radio chimed in, much to Brian's relief. "This is Wilkins, here. Whatever you guys did it worked, 'cause those things just fell over dead a few seconds ago."

"Copy that," replied Fenner. "Go find Maleek and bring him onboard the command ship. We need to find out how to control the primary systems. Also, get one of the shuttles in New Haven's bay prepped. We may have to airlift the others out of the holding pens if we can't get them powered down in the next few hours." He turned to Kim and nodded toward the dead creature at the center of the room. "You said this thing was sick?"

She nodded silently.

"How?"

"I don't know. I just sensed it. It was almost like I could feel that it was in distress, even before you hit it."

Fenner looked at her suspiciously. "Go get Jade and bring her in here. I want this thing examined as soon as possible."

"You should sit down somewhere and rest, Brian," Kim suggested, running her hand across his cheek. She looked at him with a concerned expression, but did as Fenner asked and left the room to find his sister.

"She's right, Bishop, you look terrible," Fenner snorted, punching in a new frequency on his radio. "Hudson, do a quick sweep of the rest of the ship. I want to make sure that none of those things is still alive, roaming around."

"Understood, Fenner," Hudson responded.

Brian rested against the wall and tried to sit down slowly. Half way down, though, he began to feel weak and slid the rest of the distance. As he hit the hard, yet smooth, metallic floor, his entire body began to throb, especially his bandaged leg. He couldn't even feel most of his arm anymore. Jade's medication was wearing off already. Brian couldn't wait until she arrived.

In the only show of compassion Brian had ever witnessed from him, Fenner knelt down and picked his body up off the floor. The next thing Brian knew he was being whisked toward the command ship bridge by Fenner's strong arms. He felt himself being propped up against a buzzing computer console, then saw Fenner's dark, fuzzy mass leave the room.

When Brian came to, he saw several people standing around him, all busy analyzing the various controls and screens on the bridge. His body felt much better than it had; Jade must have given him more medication. Fenner stood a few meters away, still barking orders through his radio. The bridge's shutters were up, and the pale morning light sifted in through the crystal clear windows. Brian was just about to ask the High Councilor how much time had passed, when he saw Jade emerge from the closest corridor. Although her voice was hushed, Brian could clearly hear her. She seemed perplexed.

"Have you finished the exam?" Fenner asked, discarding his radio. He seemed intensely interested in her report.

"I've done all I can without the rest of my equipment," she confessed. "Kim was right; it was definitely dying from an infection."

"What kind?"

"Bacterial."

Fenner's eyes widened. "Are we in danger?"

Jade shook her head back and forth. "That's the strange part. The bacterial species is one of the most common strains on Elysium. We knew about it before even setting down on-planet, and it's pretty much harmless to us, even in large quantities."

"And it was killing this thing?"

"Apparently. What's strange is that these Adherents seem physically superior to us in every way. They should be more resistant to infection than us, not more susceptible. The tissue sample I took from the body, what was left of it, showed a massive intrusion on the cellular level. I'm surprised it didn't die sooner."

"Well, that thing's sickness explains much of the lethargic behavior we've observed in the other troops over the last few days. Under normal circumstances we never should have been able to evade them like we have. They must've relied entirely on that thing for higher brain functions," noted Fenner thoughtfully.

"It's a miracle for us that it got sick then," Jade said.

"Yes, it is," Fenner agreed, his voice trailing off slightly as he thought about her words. His searching eyes fell on Brian's. He was obviously thinking the same thing: *Kim*. She knew it was sick. Perhaps she knew *how* it had gotten sick too, since Jade seemed unable, with all her knowledge, to find an easily accessible answer.

After a long pause Jade spoke up in her usual, impatient tone. "Well, the shuttles have begun evacuating everyone from the holding pens. I should go help out the wounded."

"Yes, of course." Fenner nodded. He still seemed distracted. "Tell your parents to join me up here when they're ready. Brian can stay up here until he's ready to move."

Jade had left the bridge before Fenner had even finished speaking. Brian readied himself for the inevitable questions being generated in the High Councilor's calculating mind. After another long pause, Brian decided to meet Fenner head on. "Wondering how Kim knew?" Brian asked.

"How far have her abilities progressed?" Fenner asked.

Brian thought about it for a moment. "Not sure. All I know is that she's been having strange dreams for a long time."

"What kind?"

"Dreams about Ares. About this planet. I think it may have something to do with the ruins we found."

Fenner frowned and motioned to the colonists in the room behind him. Brian had been talking quite loud. The High Councilor put his hands behind his back, lowered his head and began pacing back and forth over Brian. "I think at this point it's safe to assume that there is something going on here beyond our control."

"Like God?" Brian laughed. It was ridiculous to see Fenner, the most militant atheist he had ever met, pondering forces greater than himself.

"No, but it may be something beyond our understanding. I'm not sure, but Kim seems to be the link."

"I don't think even she understands it," Brian insisted, trying to get her out of Fenner's focus.

"Maybe not, but she could be a valuable asset to us in the future," Fenner stated thoughtfully. "Keep your eyes on her, Bishop."

The High Counselor's words made Brian uncomfortable. He didn't like thinking about the girl he loved as an asset, some tool to be used. He pictured Kim outside in the New Haven landing zone worriedly helping the colonists get from the shuttle to the hospital.

Fenner turned his attention to a colonist who was attempting to access one of the computer terminals. Brian, eager to see his family, yet too exhausted to follow Jade outside, leaned back and waited anxiously. A feeling of relief washed over him as he realized that everything was over. He had proved himself in the most dangerous of circumstances. Even more importantly, the Adherents had been defeated. Regardless of what trials awaited him in the future, Brian felt as though the worst was behind him.

After another long stretch of waiting, Fenner received another call on his radio. Brian looked up to find the High Councilor's armed outstretched, holding the radio in his face. "It's your sister," he said. "Don't take too long on that thing, I need it."

Brian took the radio. "Did you find them?"

Jade's voice sounded weak on the other side. There were a multitude of voices in the background, including one that Brian recognized as her husband. Brian was relieved to find that he was unharmed. Jade had suffered enough over the course of the last week. Perhaps that's why she sounded so bad. "I-I've got mom right here, Bri," she responded. "We'll be up on the bridge in a minute."

"Great," Brian said, rising to his feet. He couldn't wait to see the look on his parents' faces when they saw him, especially the look of pride on his father's face. "Is Dad there?" Brian asked. There was a good possibility that his father was off helping unload the colonists, the ever-present leader that he was. Brian waited for Jade's response. She was obviously still on the other end. "Jade?"

"Yeah, Bri."

"Where's Dad?"

She didn't respond.

"Jade. WHERE IS DAD?" Brian yelled, so loud that everyone on the bridge, including Fenner, turned to see what the problem was.

Brian's question was met only with a muffled sob. As the terrible truth presented itself in all its horror, Fenner stared at Brian gravely. Now they both knew the answer to the question: David Bishop was dead.

CHAPTER 27

▼

FROM DUST TO DUST

Brian let the soft, warm, spring breeze wash over his face as he absorbed the multitude of colors that burst forth from the green land surrounding his father's grave. The brief, rainy winter months had passed, and now the valley decorated itself in preparation for the long, bountiful Elysian summer. When they had first arrived on-planet, Brian had found it odd that his fellow colonists insisted on burying the dead, just as the pagans had in centuries past. Back on Earth, he had only known the ritualistic cremations held in the basement of the Cathedrals, each one being followed by the prompt disposal of the remains in a communal repository under the city. Since that time, Brian had come to understand the power attached to a monument as simple, yet meaningful, as a grave. In the weeks since the Adherent invasion, Brian had made a point to visit the small cemetery on the edge of the Independence plateau several times a week. He found that it helped him come to terms with his father's death. More than that, though, it also was a place of peace, where he could gaze out across the entire valley his father had fought to protect.

There were other, less obvious reasons why Brian visited the grave, ones that even he didn't totally understand. Deep down, he agonized over the last months he had spent with his father. Not because they had a bad relationship; far from it. In the years since arriving on Elysium Brian had become quite close to his father. He had nothing to regret as far as the relationship was concerned. They had been on good terms when he had left for Lake Clarity. Instead, it was the nagging feeling that his father missed his maturation, his transformation into the person he now felt like. Brian was confident that his father truly believed in him, but recognizing potential and seeing it come to fruition are two different things. Even worse was the fear that he somehow hadn't lived up to his father's expectations, despite his new status as a hero of the colony. Having his mother around for support helped, but Brian had never been as concerned with pleasing her. She was his mother; she loved him and that was enough. But David Bishop was somebody else entirely. He was a model for Brian to emulate, the leader that he had always wished to become; loved and respected. Although details surrounding his father's death were vague, one thing was clear: he had fought the Adherent soldiers to the death as they had invaded his home. David Bishop never surrendered.

Brian angled his head back and raised his gaze above the gravestone, down toward the valley below. The early afternoon sun lit the emerald landscape, creating a soft glow that seemed to blanket everything within view. Millions of blossoms, similar to those adorning the gravesites, peppered the valley in a stunning array of shifting colors. The impossibly tall, thin grazing creatures Brian had misidentified as birds the first time he had seen them, had recently returned to the valley to graze. They seemed totally oblivious to the large, black Adherent ship still sitting like a blight upon the otherwise unblemished landscape. Although Brian couldn't see them from his vantage point on the high plateau, he knew the ship was swarming with colonists who had been hand-chosen by Fenner to literally take the ship apart for examination. Maleek was down there too, probably tinkering with the same computer terminal Brian had seen him at the previous morning.

Brian wasn't sure what Fenner's plans were regarding the ship, but he knew few people in the colony would oppose what the High Councilor had to say. That night Fenner planned to present his findings on the ship to the colonists at a town hall meeting down in New Haven. Brian hoped the meeting would alleviate, rather than stoke, the rampant fear pulsing through the colony since the invasion. At any moment the colonists expected the skies to blacken and rain down more Adherent ships, this time ones that wouldn't succumb to a simple microbe and a determined group of amateur soldiers.

Fenner recognized this fear and capitalized on it. Without David Bishop to act as a counterweight, the High Councilor had managed to grasp every scrap of political power in the colony. Other leaders, such as Bill Collins and Councilor Raasch, seemed too tired, too drained to step up to their former level of prominence. Even Chang seemed diminished, although his age had begun to show long before the Adherent ships. Fenner, along with Brian and his friends, were heroes, somehow set apart from the other colonists. They had fought a small war and survived. Without them, the colony, with all its hopes and dreams, would have ended. There was only one person who had power that rivaled Fenner's, although she had neither the ambition, nor aggression of the High Councilor.

Brian craned his neck just enough to see the rough path leading up the side of the plateau from the valley. Right away, he could see a growing silhouette approaching up the path, only a little past schedule. As Kim neared, Brian couldn't help but notice the strength of her stride, the physical power somehow imbued in her tiny physical stature. The sheer charisma of her personality, her adult personality, created an invisible aura around her that intoxicated everyone in her presence. Despite these subtle, yet substantial, changes in Kim, Brian had never felt closer to her. Since the invasion, she had made a point to spend all of her free time with Brian, even when she had pressing duties back at the school or in the church. She had seemingly cast off the stress and concerns that had corroded their relationship in the months prior to the Church's arrival. It was as if she had made a conscious decision to put her love for Brian ahead of everything else. Brian hadn't come to a decision on why he thought she had changed. Obviously, the sincere threat of death had made her reprioritize her personal life, but Brian was convinced that it was more than that. Perhaps it was because Kim's visions were getting better, or maybe they had even gone away altogether. Perhaps it was because she had achieved the status in the colony she had been seeking for years and now felt it was her right to sit back and enjoy her life a bit. Brian certainly didn't mind, and neither did any of the other colonists. They admired Kim almost to the point of worship, coming to her for spiritual, as well as practical, advice on almost every conceivable matter. Fenner may have had the political power, but Kim had the power that really mattered: the power of belief. The colonists believed in her, and for whatever reason, she had become the heart of the colony.

"Sorry I'm late," she apologized, wiping a bead of sweat from her thin brow. "Everyone kept asking me if I was going to the meeting tonight. It took fifteen minutes just to get out of the village."

Brian looked down at his wrist, then remembered that he hadn't worn a timepiece in weeks. Apart from looking after his mother and helping keep Derrick occupied while his leg healed, Brian had avoided any significant measure of responsibility. Fenner was the primary reason behind this lack of participation in the community. No sooner had Brian learned of his father's death than the High Councilor had begun to incorporate him into his schemes. Fenner wanted Brian to take his father's place on the Colonial Council, an idea that Brian was sure the other colonists would have supported without hesitation.

The problem was that there was more to the invitation than Fenner let on. Brian knew that as soon as he got onto the Council Fenner would treat him as a clone, a tool to be used to gain an advantage over his political adversaries. To avoid this fate, Brian had merely stated to Fenner that he wished to take Luke's place on the security force and work with Hudson, a job that required little in the way of political know-how, or for that matter, interest. Fenner had initially seemed angry about Brian's refusal to play along, but was now too involved in the examination of the Adherent ship to actively continue any sort of grudge. He simply went back to ignoring Brian just as he had done before the attack.

Brian smiled at Kim. "Don't worry about it. I didn't even know you were late." He stood up and kissed her quickly on the lips.

"Where are you going?" she asked.

"I thought we'd head over to my house for a while. My mom said that Mrs. Chen was bringing over some sort of stew she made."

"I hope it's not that stuff she made out of Pikabat a couple of weeks ago. I just can't get used to the taste of that meat."

"No, I think she got the hint when nobody asked for seconds," Brian snickered. He turned to leave, but Kim abruptly took his hand and pulled him down into the soft, matted grass.

"Let's just sit for a couple of minutes. I'm exhausted."

Brian fought back the complaints of his empty stomach, reasoning that he owed Kim a short rest for making such a quick trip up from the valley.

"I saw Jade today. She was coming out of the hospital."

"She's looking pretty big now, isn't she?"

"Yeah. When's the baby due?"

"It's still going to be a couple of months," Brian noted, unsure as to the exact date. Despite the importance of a new child in the community, he didn't concern himself too much with the specifics. He still wasn't comfortable around small children, at least, not like Kim was. However, Brian did want to be a good uncle when the time arrived.

"She have any ideas for names?" Kim asked.

"Well, Matt's said he likes the name Serenity if it's a girl, but I think Jade has other ideas. She's always been pretty conservative and Serenity's kind of a bold name."

"What if it's a boy?"

"I think she'll name it after our dad." Brian looked down into the grass after revealing the answer. The thought of his father's legacy made the air heavy with grief. He could feel Kim's empathetic gaze peering through his soul, even without the benefit of eye contact. Brian anticipated that she would try to say something profound or helpful, as if he was one of the colonists who constantly bombarded her with questions about their lives. He should have known better by now. "Wouldn't it be really weird if it turned out to be a boy and they stilled named it Serenity?" she asked devilishly.

Brian smiled and looked over at Kim. She was biting her lip, looking up at the sky, as if seriously contemplating the possibility. "That has to be the stupidest thing I've heard all day," Brian said, letting out a brief, perplexed laugh.

"You think it's ridiculous, but do you remember that boy named Faith who was in third grade with us?"

"Uh! How could I forget?" Brian remembered that there had been a craze back on Earth to name children after religious words or traits. The older he got, the more thankful he became for his rather pedestrian name. He would rather be a Brian or a Bill, or just about any other name before he'd want to be a Faith. "At least his parents could have named him Faithful, or something a little more masculine!" he pointed out.

"Faithful? Like Minister Chang's old dog?" Kim said as she broke into hysterics. "Remember how it would pee all over the Cathedral floor when it got excited? It lived to be like a hundred years old in dog years!"

"Yeah. Do you remember that time it peed on Minister Petrov's ceremonial robes after he left them in Chang's office?"

"YES! Do you remember the look on Petrov's face when he noticed how bad he smelled?"

Now Brian began to laugh. The event had seemed totally serious to them as loyal little eight year olds, but now, the image of Petrov wearing a urine-soaked robe, then blaming it on one of his students seemed hilarious. After a few more minutes of pointless conversation, they got up and headed toward the Bishop residence for dinner, which turned out to be Mrs. Chen's infamous stew, after all.

CHAPTER 28

▼

HELPING THOSE WHO
HELP THEMSELVES

The twilight hour had always been Brian's favorite time of day since arriving on Elysium. As the hot, summer sun began to dip below the horizon, a hidden world seemed to reveal itself under the fiery sky. Even though Brian felt quite full from devouring so many of his mother's rolls at dinner, a wave of invigoration swept over him as he stepped outside into the cool, evening air. Kim was close behind, although she immediately ran back inside his house to grab her jacket. Brian paced in front of the door a minute before passing in front of the small window looking in on the house's simple kitchen. He caught a glimpse of his mother clearing the table. She looked tired and sad, just as she had for the last several months. Kim had urged her to go to the town meeting, but Dr. Jill Bishop had steadily refused all attempts at being dislodged. She had only recently begun seeing patients again, and rarely attended public events. Brian noted how much pain she had endured while trying to recover from his father's death. It wasn't surprising, really. Although Jill Bishop had always been a strong person, much of that strength had come from her relationship with her husband of over twenty years. In order to understand, Brian imagined what it would be like to lose Kim when he reached middle age. It was only this reference point that allowed him to fathom the depths of his mother's sorrow.

"I tried one last time," Kim said as she emerged from the house again.

"That's fine. Let her stay. She seems a little better than before."

"Yeah, but it would be nice to have her there tonight. Somebody needs to keep Fenner contained."

"I'm sure your parents will do the job," Brian suggested.

"I don't know. It's weird; my dad seems to be cooperating with everything Fenner's been doing lately. It's almost like they're buddies."

"I doubt that," Brian laughed.

"I'm serious. My mom's been the same way. They've both given him way too much power. They're already down at the town hall, probably chatting things up with Fenner right now."

"Well, he did save the colony," Brian pointed out, for some reason feeling the need to defend the High Councilor. "I don't know what we would have done without him."

"There's a danger in letting that man get too much power," Kim reiterated.

Brian noticed how serious she'd become and tried to lighten to mood. "Derrick and Suna will be there," he said cheerfully.

The ploy worked. Kim's faced lit up. "Can you believe he asked her to marry him?" she asked.

"A year ago I would have said no, but he's grown up a lot."

"They're still pretty young," Kim pointed out.

"Same age as we are," Brian said, not fully aware of what he was implying.

Kim looked at him and smiled. "That's true," she conceded. She took his hand in her own. An awkward silence set in as Brian thought about marriage. The idea did seem strange. It was as if considering it was akin to killing the last vestiges of youth, a prospect Brian found frightening despite the profundity of his recent life experiences. Back on Earth, Adherent students normally chose mates by their last year at the Senior Academy, often before the age of eighteen. Brian wondered for a moment whether Kim would have been his mate if they had stayed.

The conversation turned playful again as Brian and Kim joined the steady stream of colonists who were making the journey from Independence down to New Haven. A few older colonists loaded up in one of the land speeders, but most walked the entire kilometer and a half down the steep path into the valley. It was a nice night, and the hundreds of burning torches along the path beckoned to all those who were capable of making the trip on foot.

As Brian and Kim reached the small bridge that crossed the river near the Adherent command ship, they heard a familiar voice.

"Hey, guys!" Maleek yelled, running through the thickening crowd. He still had his tech goggles on and wore and belt strewn with hanging tools that swayed along his narrow waist.

"Get back to work, mister!" Kim giggled.

"Has Fenner moved your bed onboard the ship now?" Brian asked.

"It would make things easer," Maleek sighed. "My mom suggested the same thing, but of course, she was being sarcastic."

"Well, don't let Fenner hear that idea, he'll probably go through with it," Kim teased. Maleek nodded wearily in agreement.

"So, do you know what Fenner's going to tell us?" Brian asked. "Hudson said he didn't know anything about it."

"Yeah, Fenner's been real secretive about our findings. I don't think Hudson's even been onboard in the last few days, just us tech-geeks."

"You're not going to tell us anything, are you," Kim asked knowingly.

"Not supposed to," Maleek said. Brian expected him to give in and indulge them in a full preview, but instead his friend remained quiet while they walked. The silence frustrated Brian, who found it ridiculous that Maleek's loyalty to Fenner trumped his desire to tell his friends what they wanted to know. Kim, the diplomat that she was, turned the topic of discussion back to something trivial. It was evident that Maleek appreciated having the pressure taken off, at least for the moment.

As Brian, Kim and Maleek made their way into the brightly-lit town hall, they were bombarded by dozens of warm greetings and salutations. Months after the battle, most still considered them heroes of the colony, a label Brian was beginning to appreciate less and less as time went on. As they entered the cavernous main hall, he found an open spot on one of the bench rows closest to the elevated stage at the front of the room. It was a lucky find. Within ten minutes the entire place was packed with citizens, each wanting to get as close as possible to the stage. Hudson and a few others had to play ushers, as nearly 400 colonists packed themselves into a building made for little more than half that number. It was only the second public meeting since the invasion, and everyone seemed to want assurance that the worst was behind the colony. Brian stood up for a second and tried to spot some familiar faces. Although Jade had stayed home, her husband Matt was supposed to attend, as well as Derrick, Suna and a host of other friends whom Brian hoped to see. It was useless, though; the crowd obscured his view completely. The only direction he could see in was toward the stage.

Silence fell as the lights dimmed. Brian heard a groan from Kim that echoed his own. *Leave it to Fenner to fan the flames of drama.* Kim let out an even bigger groan, this one laced with disgust, when Fenner leapt on the stage and was greeted by a thunderous applause. The High Councilor soaked up the praise for a moment before raising a hand to hush the crowd. Brian saw the other Council members standing on the sides of the stage, including Kim's parents. They *did* look just as attentive as the other crowd members, as if the coming speech would bestow some magical answer to all their problems.

Despite the drama that accompanied the initial moments of the meeting, Fenner didn't hesitate to jump right into the technical details of his team's findings. "As many of you know, a small group of engineers has been studying the Adherent ship for the last few months, trying to gain every bit of information we can. Most of our focus has been on finding out where they came from and how far their technology has advanced. I'm pleased to report that we've made progress on both fronts, but I have some bad news to go along with the good."

The crowd waited.

"The good news is that we've deciphered their language and writing. Apparently, it's just an advanced form of the old communications code used by the military back in our time. Whether or not this is actually their official language is unclear, but it did allow us to access all of the ship's systems, including data and weapons. Once we accessed all the ship's systems, we were able to determine its origins and the extent of the Church's expansion. That's where the bad news begins."

Fenner paused for a moment to heighten the drama of his statement.

"It appears that our worst fears have come true. The Church's empire has thrived and grown considerably since our departure from Earth. Their star charts indicate that there is a new outpost only twenty light years from Elysium. Even worse, the command headquarters back on Earth has targeted this system for colonization."

A collective gasp let loose from the darkened audience.

Fenner continued: "I have little doubt that the small expedition force we encountered will be followed by another, larger invasion force once it is determined that this planet is inhabited. Even if the Adherents never managed to directly contact their base before we destroyed them, they surely sent out data regarding this star system before they even landed. After analyzing the ship's drive engine and propulsions systems, we have determined that a new strike force could arrive any day. It appears that the Adherents have somehow discovered how to travel faster than light, although the details of this technology are still a little unclear to us. At any rate, they can get here quickly if they want, which means we're in danger."

The audience's reaction went from one of concern to complete pandemonium, a reaction Fenner had obviously counted on. Brian admitted to himself that the news was disturbing, but in light of the recent attack, it came as no surprise. "Please, calm yourselves!" Fenner yelled over the chaos. "We have options, and hopefully, some time to consider them. A couple of weeks ago we managed to send out a distress signal that indicated the ship was lost in an ion storm as soon as it entered the system. The code we sent also reported that this system was barren, and unsuitable for colonization. I believe it will buy us some time, but sooner or later, we still face the inevitability that more ships will arrive to explore the area." Fenner cut his pause short, before his audience had a chance to respond. "There's one more important thing we discovered how to operate onboard the command ship: its weapons systems. For this portion of the meeting, I'll turn things over to one of our best engineers, Maleek Williams."

Brian reeled back in surprise as Maleek stood up and ascended to the stage. He hadn't said anything about speaking to half the colony, a detail Brian felt would have been good information to know beforehand. What was even more stunning was the fact that it was Maleek, and not one of the older, more experienced engineers, who was delivering the details. *Fenner must really be putting his faith in him*, Brian thought.

Regardless of Fenner's motivations, Maleek began speaking with a confidence Brian would have thought beyond his friend: "Apart from the smaller, particle and energy-based weapons, the ship carries several high-yield graviton bombs, each capable of decimating a planet's surface. We've figured out how to deploy these weapons from space," Maleek added. "At this point we understand the propulsion systems and the weapons systems enough to use the ship's capabilities like the Adherents intended."

"What's the purpose of that?" Raasch spoke up from the side of the stage. His question was directed toward Fenner, not Maleek, and seemed to echo everyone else's. The other Council members looked particularly concerned about this new emphasis on weapons and propulsion systems.

"Ah, I'm glad you asked, Councilor," Fenner leered as he stepped in front of Maleek. "You see, there's no way we can fight off another invasion. I think all of us agree on that. Most of our success a few months ago can be attributed to luck. But, if we take the fight to the Church, we stand a good chance of ending the threat forever."

Upon hearing Fenner's claim, the audience exploded once again into heated discussion. It took several minutes for Fenner to quiet everyone down. Brian and

Kim simply watched in silence. Kim seemed to be gathering strength for an upcoming battle.

"Please, hear me out," Fenner pleaded. "The base which launched the ship we have in our possession is apparently small, and the ship's databanks indicate that it still relies on Earth for supplies and troops. I propose that we fly the ship back to Earth, launch the graviton missiles located in the weapons bay, and get out of the system before the Adherents even know we're there. The plan is akin to killing the mythical Hydra; severe the main head and the others will die."

Before the audience had time to react to Fenner's proposal, Bill Collins suddenly appeared on stage. "There's no guarantee that plan will work, Fenner! What if you do manage to destroy Earth and the Church survives? Every ship in their fleet will come to destroy us!"

Fenner's expression morphed from one of calm determination to fiery passion. "That's a possibility no matter what, Collins. At least with my plans we have a chance!"

"It's reckless! We have to explore other options," Bill argued, turning out toward the crowd. Nobody spoke as the two men stood and looked outward imploringly.

Fenner, recognizing his competition, took Bill's lead, and directed his next comments out toward the audience. "We can't sit by helplessly and be slaughtered like lambs! We have the power to end this threat within a matter of weeks. Remember what the old proverb states: God helps those who help themselves!"

The High Councilor's invocation of religious speech now caused Kim to bolt out of her seat and jump up on the stage to join her father. Everyone, including Fenner, was shocked by her presence. A low hum erupted from the darkened room as the colonists beheld the growing conflict with awe. "Fenner, why don't you just admit that this mission is more about a personal vendetta than the safety of the colony? My father's right. Even if you do kill millions, it won't stop them from coming here to try and exterminate us."

Fenner quickly regained his composure, although he lost much of his stature in the face of such a powerful opponent. Bill Collins had the respect of his fellow colonists, but his daughter had their adoration. "With all due respect, Ms. Collins, you should leave the tactical decisions up to others," Fenner sneered with a condescending grin. "Please sit down and allow us to finish the presentation."

It was one of the only times Brian had seen Fenner miscalculate. His remarks were instantly met with hostility as the colonists cried for Kim's opinion to be heard. "Let her speak, Titus!" Brian heard over and over again. After a few moments, Brian found himself yelling the same thing. Fenner's face hardened under the assault, yet he stepped back slightly and gestured with his hand for Kim to speak.

"As many of you know, the Adherent soldiers were defeated so easily because they were infected by microbes from this planet. A few more days and they probably would have died outright, even without our help," she began. Kim paused briefly, and Brian noticed a cautious hesitation in her eyes. She was obviously choosing her words carefully for this argument. "What I'm trying to say," she continued, "is that this planet protected us when we needed it. I know it sounds strange, but I'm confident that we'll be safe as long as we stay here."

"What will the *planet* do when an Adherent fleet arrives in orbit and blasts us into pieces?" Fenner asked sarcastically. "If they suspect the possibility of infection again, they won't even bother landing on the surface."

Kim looked frustrated. Brian could tell she wanted to say more, although didn't trust the crowd's reaction. For their part, the audience looked torn. On the one hand, they loved Kim and wanted to believe her, but Fenner's arguments were just too logical to dismiss. Even Brian felt conflicted. He wanted to believe Kim, but agreed with Fenner's assessment of the situation. The colonists simply didn't have many practical options, and once again, Fenner's plan seemed to be their best chance at success. And besides, blowing up the home planet of the Adherents, even if it was Earth, seemed a fitting punishment for centuries of terror and oppression.

"I can see that nothing I say will persuade you otherwise, so I can think of only one solution," Kim said, her voice carrying the tone of defeat. "I'll come with you, Fenner."

Fenner stepped forward and surveyed his audience, sensing doubt and confusion. Brian saw him thinking, formulating some sort of a response to Kim's proposal. He obviously hadn't expected this kind of opposition at a meeting he had gone to such lengths to orchestrate. Finally he managed to contort his taut face into a fake smile and came up with the response his audience wanted to hear. "That would be an excellent idea, my young Minister. Your faith will give us strength on the journey."

At first, Brian felt the urge to leap from his seat and pull Kim off the stage, but he stopped himself, reasoning that Bill or Minister Chang, or somebody else in the audience would do the deed for him. To his horror, though, he saw Bill's head lower as the audience applauded Fenner's plan and Kim's proposal to partake in it. Brian then remembered that Chang was at home, sick in bed. There was nobody left to step in and fix the situation. From the moment Fenner had proposed the mission, Brian had wanted to come along. Now, he had to come along, to protect Kim if nothing else. Although it would break his mother's and sister's hearts, he simply didn't have a choice.

Brian waited near the back door of the hall for over an hour after the meeting, waiting to catch the Council members as they left the building. Kim, who had stayed up on stage during the intense discussion following Fenner's proposal, had managed to get everyone to agree to a colony-wide vote on the matter. The vote would be held within a week. Brian was already sure of the outcome, yet still hoped to dissuade Kim from going with Fenner. *Maybe Bill will stop her,* he thought, reasoning that Kim's father had just been waiting until after the meeting to talk some sense into her. But as Bill exited the building, Brian saw the same long face he had seen up on stage. Apparently, Kim was still stubbornly devoted to her plan. Rachel was right behind Bill, looking even more downtrodden than her husband. Brian approached them. Just as he reached Bill, however, he stopped himself. Although he had known Bill all his life and considered him family, the look of frustration and anger in the man's eyes was frightening.

"No use, Brian," Bill said, having anticipated the question. "I can't get her to listen. Maybe in a couple of days, when things calm down a little. Even if the vote goes through and we take the ship back to Earth, she may think twice about coming along. Then again, I have a hard time figuring out what that girl is thinking anymore."

Brian turned his gaze from Bill to Rachel, wondering if she had some input on the matter. She met Brian's eyes through a veil of glassy tears. "Maybe you should talk to her, Bri," she suggested.

"I will," Brian promised, although he knew it would be difficult. Even if Kim had doubts about her decision, she wouldn't let Fenner have his victory, not completely. By coming along in the ship she obviously felt she could somehow restrain him and perhaps even prevent the attack.

"She's still inside talking to some of the others," Bill said, placing a firm hand on Brian's shoulder. "I know you think Fenner's plan is a good idea, and in some ways, I do too, but Kim doesn't need to come along. If you stay here on Elysium then maybe she will too."

Brian shifted slightly. It was more than just the weight of Bill's hand. No matter what, Brian felt like he was letting somebody down. By staying, Brian knew like he was decreasing the colony's chances of survival. By leaving with Fenner, however, he was letting Bill down. "I'll talk to her," Brian finally responded, not agreeing to anything specific. Bill was apparently satisfied with that response because he quickly patted Brian on the shoulder and headed off into the darkness with Rachel. Neither said anything about getting Kim home. Perhaps they antic-ipated a long, drawn out battle to be waged over the issue.

As Brian stood and contemplated his next move, Kim emerged from the building. "I know what you're going to say," she muttered angrily, brushing past him. "I just spent over an hour trying to sell this whole thing to everybody. I cer-tainly don't need you giving me a lecture!"

"I didn't say a word!" Brian said, shocked at her fury.

"But I know what you're going to say!"

"Do you?"

"Yes. You're going to say the same thing my dad said, even though you agree with Fenner."

"Well ..."

"He's going to get everyone killed, not to mention blow up our former home!" she almost yelled. Kim seemed to suddenly realize that she could be heard by some of the nearby colonists. Embarrassment washed over her face as she bit her lip. "He's going to murder millions," she hissed, leaning within a centimeter of Brian's face. "And it will accomplish nothing!"

Brian looked around and saw that there were several people around the out-side of the building who were pretending not to listen to their conversation. "Can we just go somewhere and talk?" he asked.

Kim took a deep breath and closed her eyes for a minute. "I'm sorry, Bri. I'm, I'm just upset about the whole thing." She seemed to relax for a moment and laughed at her outburst. It wasn't funny, but Brian laughed too. He suggested that they head back toward Independence since it was getting quite late. Although Rachel and Bill hadn't mentioned a curfew, he felt a need to get Kim home. Maybe just spending time with their daughter would relieve some of the night's stress.

Upon reaching the outskirts of Independence, though, they began to argue again, this time at full volume. Soon, going home was the last thing on Brian's mind. As he and Kim circled around their home village and into the woods north of the valley, the wilds around them seemed to intensify their impassioned argu-ments.

"Damn it, Kim, we don't have any other options! Even your parents agree with Fenner's plan, at least on some level."

"That's because they're scared, Brian. Everyone's letting their fear dominate them. Fenner recognizes that and feeds on it."

"He's doing this because he thinks it's right, Kim. Say what you want about him, but Fenner looks out for this colony. The fact that he's willing to go on a suicide mission proves that."

"And you want to go with him!"

"Well, you're going with him," he pointed out. This statement seemed to get to Kim, but she maintained her composure.

"My reason's different. I'm going so that Fenner doesn't needlessly kill innocent people."

"And what if you can't stop him?"

"I'll try. At least it's better than giving into him, like everyone else has."

"That's a terrible reason."

"Well, it's not my only reason."

"What?"

"I said it's not my only reason."

"What other reason is there?" Brian asked as he grabbed her arm and brought her to a halt. The sounds of the night engulfed them now that they had stopped yelling, and thin rays of pinkish-red moonlight filtered down through the tree branches onto Kim's serious face. She looked at the ground, as if physically hiding from Brian's question.

"Kim, what other reasons are there?" he asked again, this time deliberately.

She looked him in the eyes and gave in. "Because I knew that as soon as Fenner announced his plan, you'd want to go along. There, that's the other reason. I knew you'd follow him to the ends of space if you thought the plan had a chance of keeping this colony safe."

"Is that a bad thing?" Brain asked, feeling a little guilty, and very defensive.

"No. It's just, I don't want you to go," she admitted, tearing up. Brian leaned forward to hug her, but she grabbed him first, tightly around the mid section. Neither of them said a word for several minutes.

Finally, Brian relented. "I won't go then. Fenner and whoever he picks to go with him can handle themselves."

"What about the colony?" she asked in a worried voice. "I told everyone that I was going. What are they going to think about me if I back out now?"

"Who cares," Brian said, shaking her a little. "Kim, you need to start thinking about your own happiness for a change. Forget what everyone else thinks. They'll love you regardless."

"I don't know, Bri."

"You do, Kim. You know you have some sort of power. It may be charisma, or something more. I'll admit I don't understand it. But, I do know it grabs people and draws them to you. Let Fenner have his glory—screw him. People don't respect him like they respect you."

"What about the Church?"

"You said it yourself, Kim. The planet will protect us. As long as we're here, we'll be safe. I believe you." Brian wasn't sure if he believed everything he was saying about the planet, but he knew it was his only chance at pacifying Kim.

She looked deep into his eyes, even deeper than that. Brian felt like she was rummaging through his thoughts, his soul, looking for the true motivations for his argument. Although she wouldn't find an undying faith in the supernatural like her own, she would find a reason that was good enough. "Fine," she said, almost in a whisper. "We'll stay."

Brian was surprised at his success. *Maybe she's tired, just like I am*, he thought.

Despite their physical and mental fatigue, Brian and Kim decided to walk through the woods away from their village. It was a silent decision, one that didn't require any sort of deliberation, a sort of therapy to wash away the tumultuous emotions that had dominated the night so far. It was a simple treatment: they just held hands and walked. It had been months since they had ventured away form the colony, through the wilds that had matured and nurtured them as adolescents. A warm breeze had kicked up, rustling the thick foliage encroaching on the rough path. As they reached a small stream that filtered down through a series of rocks into a pool below, Kim took her jacket off and tied it around her waist. Brian tugged at her hand and led her off the trail. Kim didn't resist. She knew where they were headed.

Few people in the colony knew about the sheltered pool that carved its way through this particularly thick part of the forest. Even fewer had ever bothered to climb down the sheer granite walls framing the water on three sides. In years past, Brian and Kim had made a point to visit the isolated pool during the early summer months, when thousands of firefly-like insects peppered the air like stars in a globular cluster. The creatures cast a calm, bluish light, which combined with the red glow of Ares to create a luminescent display of stunning contrast. The warm, clear water seemed to sparkle from an internal source as it reflected the surreal mosaic above.

"There they are," Brian said triumphantly as he jumped the final meter down to the grassy carpet surrounding the water.

"They're beautiful," Kim said, as she joined him at the water's edge. The tiny glowing creatures made their way skyward from the surface of the water. It looked as if they were headed off into space to join the sea of stars.

"I don't remember them being this thick," Brian noted.

"It's been a while since we've been here, but I think you're right." Kim stopped once her feet hit the soft, tissue-like grass and sat down, pulling Brian with her. As they sat and watched the beautiful scene in front of them, she laid her head on his shoulder. Brian felt that she was sweating slightly. It was hotter out than it had been earlier in the night. He felt physically drained from the drama of the meeting and fight, a feeling that was exacerbated by the hike to the small pool. Mentally, however, he felt alive, but calm, a combination he rarely experienced. The soft, gentle rhythm of the waterfall feeding the pool further added to this serene feeling.

"We should go for a swim," Kim said, suddenly perking up. "Remember the first time we came here?"

"Yeah, you pushed me in!"

Kim laughed as she stood up. "It wasn't my fault you were wearing all of your clothes. I told you that I wanted to jump in before we even got near the water."

Brian remembered walking home soaking wet while Kim had poked fun at him the whole way. That had been in the early days on the planet, back when he was still learning to appreciate the whole experience of being outside. Brian looked down at the pants and shirt he was currently wearing and realized that he had once again overdressed.

"We should just come back tomorrow night. I had no idea we were going to come here when we left earlier."

"That's an easy problem to fix," Kim said playfully. Quickly shedding her thin cargo pants and stepping into the water.

Brian tensed as he saw her smooth, slender thighs rising naked from the water. He hadn't expected this, certainly not tonight. But as he realized that she was waiting for him to come along, he quickly got over his shock and clumsily took off his own pants. *The underwear too?* He thought, not quite sure about Kim's intentions. *Better leave them on.*

The water felt extremely warm, almost like bath water. There was no need to even cringe as it submerged his naked skin. Brian found that the water, which came up to Kim's waist where she was standing, failed to rise above his mid thighs. He was terribly exposed, and painfully aware that his excitement was clearly visible through the insufficient guise of his underwear. His fears were quickly alleviated, however, as she moved in and pressed herself against his body. Kim felt warm and safe, although Brian could clearly feel her heart pounding beneath her chest. He looked down at the partially exposed scar on her shoulder and ran his fingers over it gently. Then he kissed her hard, and ran his hands up her sides. She shuddered and responded with an even stronger kiss. They stayed like this for a while, Brian couldn't tell exactly how long, but Kim eventually pulled herself away slightly and looked into his eyes. The smile she gave him wasn't really playful; it wasn't anything Brian had seen before, but he knew what it meant. He slowly removed her form-fitting shirt and pulled it over her head. She sighed slightly, raising her arms in compliance with the act. Brain tossed her shirt over to the bank, happy that it cleared the water. Kim giggled at him, and he smiled back, embracing her again and kissing the length of her bare neck. He barely noticed his own shirt being pulled off, but the feeling of Kim's soft breasts pressing against his chest added to his excitement. He was in another world, one completely removed from the anger and frustration of the night's meeting and the trauma of battles past. Brian lifted her up slightly and floated her back to the shoreline. He laid her body down on the soft bed of grass, removed her under-wear, and made love to her.

Kim remained tied to Brian as she struggled to catch her breath, keeping her legs wrapped tightly around his own. He wanted to tell her that he loved her, but decided against it. The word *contrived* came to mind. And besides, she knew how he felt. Finally it was Kim who whispered the words into his ear, amid soft kisses that she bestowed upon his hairline. Brian turned his head and looked into her dark eyes. "I love you too."

Kim smiled, kissed him once more on the lips, and shifted slightly so she lay on her back, staring up at the moon. Brian did the same, admiring the unwaver-ing light cast forth from the familiar red guardian in the sky. He soon felt entranced by the sight, and his exhausted body began to let his conscious mind slip. Sleep was averted only by a cool breeze sweeping through the woods and over his naked body. He shivered a little, and sat up to look for his clothes. Kim lay still, continuing to gaze upward at Ares.

"Kim?" Brian said, concerned by the glassy look in her eyes.

It took a moment to respond, but when she did it was clear that she was lucid. "We have to go," she said in a calm voice that carried frightening conviction.

"Where?"

"With Fenner. Both of us."

Not this again! "Why? I thought you said Elysium would be safe!"

Another long silence passed before she answered him. "It's not Elysium that I'm worried about. It's Earth."

Kim's response frightened Brian. *What did she mean?* He didn't bother to voice his opinion, or ask any questions. Any potential argument was crushed by the underlying strength behind Kim's voice. They were going with Fenner, back to the home they had left twenty lifetimes before.

▼

THE MEEK SHALL INHERIT

Only one obstacle stood in Brian's way of going on the mission to Earth: Fenner. Brian knew that his friends and family would protest his decision, but he also knew that they wouldn't try and stop him. Furthermore, he didn't feel guilty, not even in front of Bill. After all, Kim had been the one who had made the decision; he was merely following along in order to protect her. Or maybe she was protecting him in some way; Brian wasn't quite sure. Either way he didn't have a choice. The morning following Kim's decision, Brian went to find the High Councilor.

It didn't take long to figure out where Fenner was located. He was onboard the Adherent command ship making last minute preparations for the trip. As Brian approached the ship, he was stopped by two younger colonist men standing guard at the bottom of the main loading ramp.

"Sorry, Bishop," one of them said. Brian wasn't sure what his last name was, but he did know him as "Tom."

"I need to talk to Fenner."

"Can't let you do that," the other one said. Brian couldn't remember his first name, but he was large, and looked somewhat dumb.

"Why not?"

"Fenner said that only authorized personal are allowed onboard the ship. They could compromise the mission."

"The colony hasn't even voted on whether or not there's going to be a mission," Brian argued. He knew that the vote would pass by a large margin, but hoped that he could disrupt the two men enough so that they'd let him pass. It didn't work.

"Unless Fenner says otherwise, you're not coming up."

Brian suddenly felt a wave of frustration pass through his body. He put his head down and attempted to brush past the men. The one named Tom grabbed his arm.

"Get the hell off me!" Brian spat, pulling his arm away. "Fen—"

"What's going on?" a voice yelled down from inside the ship. It was Bill.

The two men backed away from Brian a bit, obviously unsure as to who was in trouble.

"I need to talk to Fenner," Brian yelled up. Bill heard him and descended the ramp. "So what's the problem?" He looked at the faces of the two men.

"Fenner said to keep everyone out," whined the big one.

"Did he?" Bill asked, cocking his left eye slightly. "Well, despite what Fenner thinks, he's not the only one running this colony. Everyone's cleared for access, regardless of what he says."

The two men listened to Bill, but still looked unsure.

"Understand?" Bill said, reiterating his point with a harsh, commanding tone. Brian remembered Fenner's story about Bill's military service. It had been hard to believe before, but Brian could now detect the icy, authoritarian glare in Bill's eyes, a look that often characterized Adherent military officers.

The two men nodded hastily. They looked scared.

"Go find yourselves something productive to do," Bill suggested sternly. As the men took off toward the village, Bill sighed heavily. "Idiots. They're the kind of people Fenner knows how to manipulate."

Brian nodded his head in agreement.

"So, you're here to see him."

Brian nodded again. He began to feel self-conscious. Did Bill now consider him an idiot too?

"Come on," Bill said, in a more relaxed tone. He put his arm around Brian and led him up to ramp into the belly of the ship.

"Kim," Brian began, feeling a need to explain his actions.

"I know, Bri," Bill said. "Kim told us everything this morning. She said it was her destiny to return to Earth, or something like that. There's no stopping that girl when she sets her mind to something."

"I tried!"

"I know." Bill laughed a little. "It's scary as a parent when you realize your child has grown into a better person than yourself. I wish I had her convictions, even if I hate where those convictions are taking her."

"Do you think the vote will pass?"

"You know it will."

"Are you going too, Bill?"

"Even if Kim wasn't going, I would. Fenner can't be allowed to take control, especially not when he's got the kind of power this ship can afford. I agree that we have to investigate what the Church's plans are for Earth, but I'm not sure if attacking is the answer. Hopefully, I can just keep Kim safe on the trip."

"I know how you feel."

"And I know how you feel, Bri." Bill stopped in the middle of one of the ship's tight, outer corridors. "You don't have to come. In fact, I wish you wouldn't. The colony needs you, especially now that your father's gone. Your mother needs you too."

Brian looked at Bill like he was crazy for even suggesting that he stay behind.

"Hey, hey, enough with the eyes, Bri. Like I said, I know you feel the same way I do. I'm not telling you that you have to stay. But if you go, I just want you to go for the right reasons, not out of some false sense of duty. You've proved your bravery over and over again. You don't have to prove anything else; your father would be proud. He was proud."

"I'm not going with you guys because I want to prove anything," Brian said.

"Is it Kim then?"

"Yeah."

"I understand. I guess love's as good a reason as any, right?"

"Right."

Bill's comment made Brian feel strange. After all, Bill was Kim's father. The fact that Bill knew of their romantic relationship on such an intimate scale, especially the morning after such an eventful night, was a little unsettling. *It's a stupid thing to feel uncomfortable about*, Brian reasoned. Bill had always been supportive of their relationship, even after it had turned romantic. Whenever Brian and Kim had traipsed off into the woods, Bill and Rachel's only demand was that they stay safe. Perhaps it was because they felt guilty imposing new rules on children whose lives had always been dominated by the arbitrary life of the Church. Even more likely was the fact that Brian and Kim had always been together, a facet of existence as constant as the unwavering influence of gravity or time. Now, as Brian made his way to Fenner, alongside Bill, he realized that he was once again following this force, the unbreakable bond that had always seemed to exist between himself and Kim. To choose any other course of action would be unnatural.

Bill led Brian through the command ship to the room where they had killed the creature that had acted as the "brain." In the months since the colonists had begun working on the ship, they had experienced the most problems with getting the ship's systems to function using traditional computers alone. Despite the expertise of Maleek and the other technicians, frequent system-wide problems still seemed to crop-up on a daily basis. Most of the problems could be attributed to half the ship being wired with twenty-fourth century components brought down from the *Apostle 4*'s tech bay. The body, or "brain," as Maleek referred to it, had been removed from the ship following the attack and had totally been devoured by the infection within another day or two. In its place stood a new computer console, which looked strangely out of place amid the almost alien surroundings. As Brian entered the room, he noticed the tangled mass of cables and machines grafted onto the Adherent technology. It was a wonder anything worked at all.

"What are you doing here, Bishop?" Fenner asked as he bent over a dissected console. He didn't bother to look up.

Brian noticed that Bill had left his side and was talking to a colonist on the other side of the room. He felt abandoned.

"Well, what do you want?" Fenner said impatiently, rising from his work just long enough to shoot Brian a harsh glance.

"I want to come on the mission, Fenner."

"Ha!"

Brian paused for a second, not quite sure how to respond. *I should have expected this game.* "I said I'm coming on the mission."

"Too late, Bishop. You had your chance to participate."

"This is different."

"Is it?"

Brian struggled to find an argument Fenner couldn't twist around to work in his own favor. He decided bluntness was the best tactic to counter Fenner's subversive manipulation. "If you want me to beg, it's not going to happen, Titus."

The work going on in the room suddenly stopped as the others heard Brian call Fenner by his first name. It was a bold move, one meant to provoke rather than appease. To everyone's surprise, however, Fenner responded with a genuine chuckle. "No, I don't suppose you would."

The High Councilor stood up and walked past Brian out of the room. Brian followed, close behind.

"It's because of your little girlfriend, isn't it?"

"I'd go even if Kim wasn't," Brian answered coldly, having already anticipated the question.

"Then what is it?" Fenner asked, coming to a halt near the bridge and starring down at Brian. "You have nothing to offer me. I've got all the technical expertise I need, and there's already too much baggage going along as it is. I'll call you if I need bait."

"Just because I wouldn't serve on the Council, doesn't mean I don't care about what happens to this colony," Brian argued, trying to ignore Fenner's verbal jabs.

"There are almost a thousand others who would say the same thing, Bishop."

"But they don't have what I do, Fenner."

"And what is that?" The High Councilor leaned in closer to Brian's face, as if searching for traces of weakness.

"Courage. Leadership."

"Others who are coming along on this trip have those in abundance, namely me."

"But you can't do it alone Fenner, you told me yourself."

Fenner paused for a moment. Brian had him. "Are you offering some sort of alliance?"

Brian glanced to his left and right, making sure that nobody was around to here their exchange. "Whether you like it or not, we've been allies since the Adherents first found Elysium. Think about it; I've supported everything you've done as a leader, Fenner. You're right, I did act as the bait during the attack, but your plan wouldn't have succeeded if I hadn't put my ass on the line!" Brian found that he was pointing his finger at Fenner's chest, not to mention raising his voice.

Fenner leaned back, continuing to search Brian's face for weakness, or perhaps even an ulterior motive.

"Why else would I come to you, Fenner? It would be much easier just to ask Bill or one of the other Council members. The decision isn't yours alone to make."

"What do you want, my approval?"

"I want you to know that I'm interested in protecting the colony at all costs, just like you."

"What about Collins and his daughter?"

"If you're right about the Church, Fenner, then they'll support an attack. I'll help convince them if they're hesitant. Kim doesn't want violence, but she also wants Elysium to be safe."

"This isn't going to be a democracy when we reach Earth," Fenner noted. "If the mission is approved by the colony, and it will be, then I will be given primary command. The Collins' and everyone else who is coming along will be onboard this ship because I approved it."

"Sure."

"So, if anyone resists my decisions, especially at a critical moment, you'll–"

"I'll support you if it will keep the colony safe. That's all I'm promising at this point. In return for all of this support, Fenner, you should consider listening to the others if they have legitimate concerns or suggestions. I may not want Kim to go, but she'll have insight that you won't."

"I'm well aware of that girl's … capabilities. I'm just not sure about her motives."

"They're sincere, just like my own," Brian insisted.

"As are mine, Bishop." Fenner smiled broadly and placed a heavy hand on Brian's shoulder, just as he had a few months before. "You may come, but don't let me down, boy. The colony is counting on you."

Brian knew that both of those statements were true. And a week later, following the vote to proceed with the mission, he told his mother and sister the same thing: "The colony is counting on me. I have to go."

CHAPTER 30

▼

HOMECOMING

Eighteen colonists, Brian, Kim, Fenner, Bill, Maleek and Hudson included, constituted the new crew of the Adherent ship. As it blasted off from the soft, green floor of the valley, Brian gazed down at his home for what he worried may be the last time. Within seconds, the ship was too high for him to see any faces, but he knew they were down there: his mother, sister and friends, everyone and everything that mattered. Brian remembered that he had once prayed for an Adherent ship to come and whisk him back to Earth. How things had changed. Now he wished to stay on Elysium, his true home, forever. The black, dying world he had left as a child represented death rather than salvation. To return to Earth meant to leave the life he had been given. It meant forsaking his soul's second chance.

The powerful Adherent drive engines quickly shuttled the ship past Ares and the other two moons orbiting Elysium. Once it had cleared the gravity well surrounding the planet and its moons, the colonists engaged the subspace drive. Despite Maleek's insistence that the drive was safe for normal humans to operate, Brian felt a swift burst of fear as he heard the ship's engines powering up for the jump. Although others had obviously used this type of space travel before, Brian felt like a pioneer, the first to experience faster than light travel. As he stood on the bridge, the stars around the main viewport began to bend and contort under the exotic forces of time and space. Brian closed his eyes for a moment, fearful that the scene would overwhelm him. He opened them just in time to see the entire universe engulfed by a wave of fiery blue light as the ship entered subspace.

Kim's warm hand entered his own as their eyes attempted focus on something their physical senses quite simply had not been designed to process.

The computer calculations done prior to the jump indicated the trip back to Earth would take just over two weeks. Once the subspace drive had been activated, the ship would essentially run itself for most of the journey. Maleek and the others engineers had done a fantastic job of learning and adapting to the Adherents' technology. Still, they hovered around the computer consoles from the moment they left Elysium, keeping a constant vigil over the systems in case anything went wrong. Brian spent most of his time in one of the ship's cargo holds that had been converted into a makeshift sleeping area for the colonists. Fenner had been right: Brian did feel like spare baggage.

To pass the many hours of boredom, Brian let Kim teach him how to meditate. Despite her best tries, however, Brian couldn't seem to let his mind relax enough to enter the realm of consciousness that hers did. Even worse, the closer they got to Earth, and further away from Elysium, the less focused Kim herself seemed to become. It was as if she had lost touch with some of the strength that had infused so much of her personality over the last few years. None of the others could see the change; she hid it well, but Brian noticed. He considered asking her about it several times during the course of the trip, but decided not to draw attention to her obvious discomfort. Things were getting tense enough as it was. As the ship neared its destination, Fenner began to bounce from station to station, looking over everyone's shoulder as if they would somehow fail him. Brian doubted that the High Councilor even bothered to sleep the last week of the trip.

During the final days of the voyage, Brian resorted to childish games and jokes to keep Kim occupied. Many of the word games they played dated back to their earliest days as Chang's students, back when their world seemed so defined and promising. Although Kim obviously appreciated Brian's attempts to keep her occupied, he could tell his efforts did little to alleviate her suffering. The hours eventually stretched into days as Brian made a point to lose track of time. Only a growing sense of impending conflict signaled that any time had really passed at all.

Finally the moment came when Fenner announced they were to drop out of subspace in the Sol system. The crew went into well-coordinated action as the engines cut, checking the systems, and most importantly, the weapons stored in the belly of the ship. Although Brian still had no specific job on the ship, he instantly shed his cocoon of despondency, eager for the moment when he may be needed. The time had come to deliver the Church's present back to its doorstep. Even without a defined role, Brian knew that his survival and everyone else's would depend on the decisions made in the next few minutes, decisions that he may have to support, even if they threatened those he loved.

PART III

▼

CHAPTER 31

▼

IF I FORGET THEE, OH EARTH

The first thing Brian noticed was how close to Earth the ship had dropped them out of subspace: well within the orbit of the moon, from the looks of it. The colonists had used a preprogrammed destination embedded within the ship's navigational database to get them this close to the planet. Most likely, the coordinates were intended to be entered in the case of an emergency, so that the ship could return to its home base. As Brian looked out the main viewport, however, he could see no orbiting space stations; no ships, military or otherwise; no visible alarms greeting their arrival whatsoever. All was quiet.

They were on the dark side of the planet, although the shimmering border of day could be seen in the distance, steadily burning its way toward them. Directly below, the unbroken darkness of night stared back at Brian. *Where are the lights?* Brian thought to himself, noticing the utter lack of illumination. *Where are the cities?* The most obvious answer to his question was that the poisonous clouds, which had been so thick in his own time, were now solid and impenetrable. *It's time to put this place out of its misery*, he thought, looking to Fenner.

The High Councilor wasted no time implementing his plan. "Ready the missiles," he ordered coldly to the woman seated at the weapons command console. She was a middle-aged woman named Laura, a resident of Little Houston who had lost her family in an Adherent raid years before joining Fenner. She followed his commands without hesitation.

Bill shifted his weight nervously at Brian's side. His discomfort was obvious. "Run a deep level surface scan," he instructed Maleek, who manned the primary sensor console. Maleek glanced quickly at Fenner, as if to question Bill's order, but he complied before the High Counselor had a chance to give his approval.

Brian and Bill leaned over Maleek's shoulder, jockeying for the best view of the display. Kim hung back near the exit of the bridge, apparently analyzing her comrades more than the planet below. After a few seconds, the scan results registered on the display. Bill read them aloud. "Isolated power signatures, pretty small-scale. Evenly dispersed life-signs. Minimal cloud cover. Stable atmosphere—no excessive hydrocarbons."

The readings didn't seem to make any sense. It was almost as if the cities had simply disappeared. If Elysium had been scanned from space in the same way, its readings would have been very similar.

Upon hearing the report, Fenner pushed his way to the console. Brian could hear the High Counselor's heavy, perturbed breathing as he read the results for himself. "Scan again. Perhaps they've moved underground," Fenner growled. "Scan for radiation too, there's bound to be plenty."

"I already did. There's no abnormal radiation of any kind," Maleek said.

"Ah—there's got to be more down there. They've found some way of hiding themselves; a cloak maybe."

"What if there isn't anything down there?" Bill pointed out. "The sensors don't lie. We can't proceed until we know more about what's down there."

"This ship's logs indicate that Earth is still the primary base for the Adherents. As you pointed out, Collins, the computer doesn't lie."

"I read the same logs as you did, Fenner. They're vague. We don't know what's down there."

"The longer we stay here and deliberate, the more risk we're putting ourselves at," said Fenner. "Forget the readings. This is still the heart of the Church. Don't forget why we came here!"

Bill seemed to ignore Fenner's growing frustration. He walked over to the colonist man who was stationed at navigation. "Is it possible that we've arrived in the past or future?"

Brian hadn't thought about that possibility. Their knowledge of the subspace drive was extremely limited, despite their ability to use it. Perhaps they had somehow drifted through time, as well as space.

"No," the colonist at the navicomputer said. "The star charts indicate that we're right where we should be. No time dilation or acceleration occurred during the trip through subspace. We would have known right away."

"See, Collins, we're right where we should be," Fenner argued.

"I don't know, Fenner, something doesn't feel right. There are too many variables."

"Like?"

"Like the fact that there are no apparent signs of any major bases or installations. Maybe this ship's computers are wrong, out of date, or something. We can't just launch the missiles, not when there may be innocent people down there."

"Innocent? We are talking about the Church here, Collins!"

"I don't care, Fenner. It's a no-go until we can figure out what's going on." Bill walked back over to Maleek. "Can you pick up any radio or subspace chatter?"

Maleek didn't get a chance to comply with Bill's request. Brian watched as Fenner placed his face directly against Bill's.

"I see. You never had any intention of attacking Earth, did you Collins?"

It was more of an accusation than a question. Fenner was angry.

"I agreed to come along and assess the situation. If I see a threat, I'll be the first one to order the attack."

"You're forgetting the number one rule of a military engagement, Collins. The aggressor always has the advantage. You're also forgetting that I'm in command of this mission! The others have voted on it."

"First of all, Fenner, this isn't a military mission. Furthermore, nobody said you were in command of anything. The vote was just for whether or not we were coming here. It wasn't an open invitation for you to blow up half the planet."

Bill and Fenner stood face to face, both tense under the growing stress caused by their argument. Nobody else on the bridge moved. Suddenly, Fenner smiled and lowered his head so that he was gazing at the floor, or at Bill's feet. Brian couldn't tell.

"Rollins, Hernandez, Smith. Go to the weapons bay and make sure Hudson has the missiles prepped and ready. We'll need them soon," Fenner said in chilling voice.

The three colonists hesitated for a moment, not sure whose direction to follow. Bill, however, nodded in affirmation, and they quickly hustled off the bridge, the door closing behind them. That left Bill, Fenner, Brian, Kim and Maleek. Brian wondered for a moment why he and the others had not been asked to leave as well. Then he came to a conclusion: Kim wouldn't listen, and Fenner was looking for two allies in Brian and Maleek. It made sense: three against two. Brian had been so engrossed in the growing argument between Fenner and Bill that he hadn't taken the time to evaluate his own feelings on the situation. True, there were some questions that needed to be answered about Earth, but the longer they sat motionless in orbit, the more risk they were putting themselves in. At this point, Brian would have preferred to just launch the missiles and engage the subspace drive back toward Elysium.

A tense silence set back in once the door had shut behind the other colonists. Fenner raised his eyes to meet Bill's and abruptly ceased smiling. Brian was weighing the situation in his mind, trying to decide what he was going to do if the two men started fighting. Separating them seemed to be the best course of action, although it would take more force than was currently on the bridge to subdue both men. He then decided it would be best to stop the fight before it happened, if only he could think of something to say. It was Kim, though, who finally broke the deadlock. "Why don't you just tell them, Fenner?" she suggested in a knowing, slightly accusatory voice.

"Stay out of this," Fenner hissed.

"What's she talking about?" Bill asked, puzzled by his daughter's words.

"She's babbling," said Fenner.

Kim took a step closer to her father and Fenner. "Why don't you tell him what you know, Fenner? What you and I both know."

Fenner looked like he had been wounded, almost like an animal caught in a trap. Kim's words had somehow totally disarmed him.

"Fenner doesn't want us to investigate the planet because he already knows what it will confirm," Kim charged. "You can see the fear in his eyes."

"Watch what you say," Fenner warned in a low, menacing tone. His threatening demeanor only seemed to strengthen Kim as she stood in the middle of the bridge and addressed her small, yet attentive audience.

"He's lying. He's been lying for weeks."

"How do you know this?" Bill asked in an astonished voice.

"I just do. Like I said, it's in his eyes. The lie he conceals is eating away at him. I've noticed it since we left Elysium, but haven't understood the cause until now. He knows something he's not telling us. I think Maleek does too."

Brian, who couldn't believe what he was hearing, turned to look at his friend still seated at the sensor display at the front of the bridge. Maleek had his back turned to them, a nonverbal sign that Kim was onto something.

"Maleek," Bill said in a commanding tone. "What's she talking about?"

"This is ridiculous!" Fenner complained. "You can't take her seriously. Maleek, don't answer anything. It's a trick."

"Maleek?" Brian said, almost in a whisper.

His friend responded in a shaky voice, one which carried the shame of defeat. "She's right. Fenner and I falsified the ship's logs. This ship wasn't based anywhere near Elysium. It launched from Mu Arae, and was only part of a long-range survey project. According to the original log reports in the computer, there's not even an Adherent outpost within fifty light years of Elysium. They basically found us by accident."

"That's enough," Fenner said angrily.

Maleek continued anyway. "As far as we can tell, the Church doesn't know anything about the colony, or Elysium. The soldiers, or whatever they were, never sent a message back to their base. Within a few hours of landing, the ship's brain became too sick to function properly. We simply changed the logs to make it look like the Church had plans to colonize Elysium."

"So why are we here? What's the point of coming to Earth?" Bill asked. He was looking at Maleek, although his questions were clearly posed to Fenner.

Fenner remained silent.

"Revenge," Kim murmured. "He wanted revenge."

"That's ridiculous," Fenner said. "Do you honestly think that I'd risk the safety of the entire colony for such a shallow reason?"

"It's not shallow at all, really Fenner," Kim said in a murmur that would have sounded condescending coming from anyone else. From her lips, though, the statement contained true sympathy. "The sorrow felt for losing a loved one is intense enough, but when a man's pride is taken, the desire for revenge can become even more powerful, especially for someone like you."

"Shut up," Fenner whispered. Brian had never seen him so vulnerable.

"All of those people, the ones you led and who loved you in return; all dead, abandoned by their leader so that you could run away to a safe corner of the galaxy. You left them, Fenner. I wonder how long the ICLF lasted without their leader. A month? A year? Surely they met a horrible end, just like you knew they would. Regardless of what you think, though, killing millions of people on Earth won't make it better. It'll just damn your soul a little deeper into the personal hell you've created."

"Shut up!" Fenner screamed, suddenly lunging at Kim. She eluded the main trust of his blow although he managed to clip her shoulder with his fist just enough to send her whirling like a top against one of the computer consoles.

Bill was on Fenner in an instant, grabbing his outstretched arm and twisting it behind the High Councilor's back. Fenner responded immediately by throwing his weight back into Bill and sending them both flying into Brian. The impact with the two men felt like a shuttle wreck. Although they managed to keep their footing and continue the struggle, Brian was knocked to the ground near Maleek, temporarily dazed by the violent assault. As Brian lay on the ground, he watched Bill and Fenner fight like the two trained soldiers that they were, both throwing attacks that would instantly incapacitate normal combatants. Brian saw Kim prop herself on the opposite wall. She looked to be unhurt although the empty look she gave him indicated that she too was shaken by the assault.

The next thing Brian felt was Maleek's large, bony hands helping him to his feet. Once Brian had regained his senses, he analyzed the brutal melee. Even if he could jump in and land a blow or two on Fenner, he doubted it would do much. The High Councilor had already absorbed or deflected several of Bill's strikes. Brian frantically looked around for some sort of weapon. His eyes fell upon several metal rods that had been used to frame one of the colonist computer terminals connected to the ship's original computers. There were several extras stowed beneath the console, should the frame become unstable during the trip. The rods were hollow, but strong. He made his way toward the small cabinet where they were stored.

"What are you doing?" asked Maleek, who body-blocked Brian. "Just stay out of it." As Brian looked into his friend's face he could see that Maleek knew what he was planning.

"Get out of my way!" Brian yelled, hitting Maleek across the face with a closed fist. He lunged toward the rods and grabbed one from the pile. As he stood with the weapon in hand, he watched the fight for a few more seconds, thinking about the wisdom of such a brash maneuver. Bill had taken several shots to the face, and it looked like Fenner was gaining a clear advantage. Brian knew that once Bill went down, Fenner would probably kill him. Still, he hesitated. Fenner was almost like a god, a dark god who seemed impervious to pain. More importantly, Brian realized that part of him still agreed with Fenner about the Church. *Maybe Earth should be destroyed for the good of everyone; even if it does cost millions of lives.* Brian watched Fenner slam Bill's face into the main computer console and made his decision. As the High Councilor placed his boot on Bill's neck, he exposed his entire flank. Brian didn't need a second invitation. He wound up and swung the rod, striking Fenner squarely across his chiseled jaw. The rod made a hollow, plucking sound as it hit, signaling that a decent amount of force had been applied in the swing.

Fenner reeled back in pain and shock, leaving Bill free to slump down onto the floor. Brian hadn't been aware that Bill was injured so badly, and eyed Fenner nervously with the rod cocked back again. To his horror, Fenner quickly recovered. He shook his head, spit out a tooth, and gave Brian the most terrifying look he had ever seen. "You've made your decision, Bishop," he said coldly. "Pity you won't survive long enough to regret it."

Within a millisecond of speaking, Fenner leapt at Brian, so fast that the second swing with the rod barely had time to connect with his shoulder. Brian found himself on the ground, with two iron-fisted hands planted firmly around his neck. He couldn't breathe. It wouldn't be long before he lost consciousness. Time seemed to stop as Fenner's dark massive form hovered above, a look of perverse delight twinkling in his eyes. In slow motion, Brian's own foggy eyes detected two more black forms overhead, behind Fenner. Brian found that he could breathe again as Fenner removed his hands and violently shook off his two attackers. Kim and Maleek flew back like leaves blown by the wind. Fenner, in his rage, seemed to forget about Brian as he rose and went after Maleek.

"You stupid bastard!" Brian heard Fenner scream as he started hitting his one-time accomplice. Brian struggled to come to his senses, throwing his arms out in a blind search for the rod. He grasped it as it began to roll under one of the computer consoles and attempted to drag himself to his feet. Maleek wouldn't be able to hold out much longer.

A sudden bang on the door made Fenner pause for a moment. Behind the thick metal, Brian could just make out the sound of Hudson's voice. He was calling for somebody to open the door. Kim, who had now risen to her feet, made her way to the keypad next to the door. Brian hadn't realized that it had been locked. As Kim fumbled with the controls, Fenner shifted his attention to her.

"I don't think so, dear," he said, lunging toward her. Kim kicked at his groin, but the blow missed its mark and hit his solid thigh. As Fenner cocked his large fist back, Brian pulled himself up the rest of the way and wildly swung the rod at the lower portion of the High Councilor's body. The swing wasn't intended to connect with any particular body part although it struck the backside of Fenner's knee with a great deal of force. The High Councilor's leg buckled under the assault, and he seemed to forget about the punch he planned on delivering to Kim's face. Brian stared at Fenner for a moment, unsure as to how bad he had injured him. Hitting him again, especially in the head, just seemed so … brutal.

"Hit him again, Bri!" Kim screamed, sobering Brian up. It seemed like an odd suggestion, especially coming from someone who was normally so gentle. She was right, though. Fenner needed to be stopped.

Brian swung again, this time at the side of Fenner's face. He closed his eyes slightly as the rod hit, flinching at the pain he knew he was causing. Fenner fell on his knees and stayed there for a moment, dazed. Then he crumbled onto the floor in a large, dark heap. Brian worried that he had killed him even though Fenner had apparently been bent on doing the same to everyone else on the bridge.

Kim turned back around and unlocked the keypad to the door.

"What the hell is going on in here?" Hudson said, upon entering the room. He looked at Brian, who was still standing over Fenner with the bloody rod.

"Fenner went crazy and tried to kill us," Kim gasped.

Hudson looked at her, then Brian, then down at Fenner again. "Why?"

"He wanted us to launch the missiles," Kim said, running over to her father. Bill was regaining consciousness by the sounds of his groans, although it would probably be a while before he could stand.

"Isn't that why we're here?" Hudson said as he gently removed the rod from Brian's hand and threw it on the ground. Several other colonists squeezed in through the doorway to survey the grizzly scene.

"He lied to you," Kim said, cradling her father's head in her arms. One of the colonists trained as a medic walked over and began to examine him. The others inspected Fenner, who looked to be in worse shape.

"About what?" Hudson asked.

"He falsified this ship's logs to make it look like the Church knew about Elysium. Just ask Maleek."

Maleek simply nodded.

Kim continued. "It was a scout or survey ship that just found Elysium by chance. They had no idea we were on the planet until they came into the system. The Adherents never even sent out any transmissions before we killed them."

"Why didn't you say anything before?"

Brian thought Hudson had a good point. *Why didn't Kim say any of this before?*

"I wasn't sure until we came here," she answered. "It was clear as soon as we came out of subspace that something wasn't right. Earth looks like it's changed. It's possible that it doesn't have anything to do with the Church anymore."

"Where did the ship come from then?" one of the colonists asked.

"Mu Arae."

"So what's down there?" Hudson asked, motioning outward toward the planet below.

"I don't know," confessed Kim. "But we can't just fire the missiles. If there are people still down there, it'll be murder."

Hudson seemed to consider her words for a few moments. Brian worried that he too may side with Fenner and decide to launch the missiles anyway. Despite their rocky beginnings, Fenner and Hudson often agreed on tactical matters.

"Well, what do we do now?" Hudson asked, turning to Kim.

"We should leave," said Bill, who was coming around. "If we're not going to attack, then we should get out of here. Earth doesn't appear to be any sort of a threat."

"You're right, Dad. We should leave. I feel like we shouldn't even be here," she said.

"Alright let's move then," said Hudson in a commanding tone. He still looked conflicted, perhaps even a bit confused, but at least he seemed to agree. The other colonists took their places at the bridge consoles without hesitation. "We need to get the subspace drive prepped and ready for the jump home," Hudson added.

"Hurry," said Kim in a strange voice. Her demeanor had suddenly changed from one of confidence to fright.

"It'll take at least an hour or two," started Hudson, before he saw what she did and cut himself off.

Everyone on the bridge, Brian included, followed Kim's gaze toward a point on the edge of the planet's horizon around which space seemed to shimmer and distort.

"What the hell is that?" one of the colonists cried.

"Maleek, engage the sub-light engines. Turn the ship around," Hudson ordered.

Brian could feel the fear begin to grip his comrades as the section of distorted space began to approach the ship. It was clear that running would not be an option. As Brian watched his friends work manically, he felt a sense of intense helplessness, perhaps even uselessness. All he could do was stand and worry.

Within five minutes, the large section of distorted space became two distinct entities. Even before the Adherent ships seemed to materialize out of nowhere, every colonist onboard the ship knew the threat they posed.

"How are our tactical systems?" Hudson asked Maleek.

"Minimal. We didn't spend much time working on those systems. I'm not even sure how to target the main cannons properly."

"Well, you're going to have to figure it out fast," Bill groaned, rising painfully to his feet.

Brian could tell Bill's suggestion was borne out of frustration rather than any practical concern. If the two large Adherent ships, both of which were closing within weapons distance, wanted to fight, there was little the colonists could do but surrender. *We should have just launched the missiles,* a small voice said in the back of Brian's mind. *Fenner was right.*

A harsh, blaring sound burst forth from every corner of the ship. It was obviously a statement in the language spoken by the Adherent soldiers although the colonists had little clue as to what it meant. From the tone, it seemed like some sort of an order.

"Where the hell is that coming from?" Bill asked.

"I don't know. The com system's locked into some outside signal," one of the colonists answered.

"There's no way to shut it off without disabling the whole system," said Maleek.

"Well, whatever they're saying, they sound angry!" noted Bill. "What's their range?"

"1,000 kilometers and closing."

Well within weapons range, Brian knew. He looked at Kim, knowing that it may be the last time he did so. She looked sad, but not defeated. Brian could not detect the slightest sign of remorse in her face for ruining Fenner's plan. Despite the fact that she may have doomed them all with her compassion, Brian felt no anger toward her. Launching the missiles *had* felt wrong. He was glad he hadn't done it, even if his failure to do so had been a tactical error. As Bill staggered over to the weapons console, Kim came to Brian's side and took his hand.

"Do we have shields?" Bill asked.

"No. We're not sure how to activate them!" said Maleek.

"You really had this plan thought out, didn't you?" Bill scolded Hudson, and perhaps Fenner's unconscious body.

"Fenner said everything worked like it should."

"And you just blindly went along?"

"Dad!" Kim yelled, trying to lessen her father's assault on Hudson. "He didn't know."

"Well–"

"Power spike!" Maleek yelled.

Although nobody on the bridge was familiar with the systems aboard the closing ships, they knew what Maleek's declaration meant. The ships were charging their weapons. Before anyone had a chance to brace themselves for the impact, several green-colored bolts shot from the closest ship and collided with a terrible fury against the back section of their own ship's hull.

The explosion rocked the entire ship, sending everyone sprawling across the bridge. Brian landed face down on the cold, hard floor although he managed to catch Kim as she fell on top of him. The first explosion was followed by another, this one smaller, more localized. Brian felt Kim brace for another impact, as he did, but it never came. After a few moments of calm, Brian and the others stood up. It was only then that they saw the true danger of their situation.

Outside the main viewport, the looming planet below was getting closer. The ship was beginning to list slightly and seemed to be floating dead in space. Maleek's observation of the internal systems only confirmed their predicament: the ship *was* falling toward the planet. Brian could see the two other ships breaking off from their pursuit, allowing their wounded prey to meet its fate on the fiery outer edges of the atmosphere.

The last coherent thought entering Brian's mind as their ship descended into the atmosphere was that they were falling toward western Asia, the inhospitable wasteland where billions had once perished under the might of the Adherent war machine. If they somehow survived the crash, he was sure that the hellish world awaiting them would rival that of any in the Church scriptures.

Brian awoke with a start, confident only in the notion that time had passed since he had lost consciousness. He physically checked himself before his eyes even had a chance to focus and found that he hadn't been wounded seriously in the crash. Perhaps he was only dazed and couldn't remember the last few chaotic moments before impact. At any rate, his comrades on the bridge seemed to be in an equally incoherent state of shock. Thankfully, nobody on the bridge seemed to be seriously hurt, a fact that conjured up a brief memory of Maleek gaining partial control of the ship as it plunged into the pitch black landscape. The action would have made Maleek a bonafide hero once again if he hadn't been somewhat to blame for getting them into this mess in the first place.

"Is anyone hurt?" asked Bill as he once again pulled his beaten body from the floor.

A few moans and curse words were all the answers he received although they confirmed that everyone was well enough to complain.

"Where did we land?" Bill asked Maleek, who had somehow managed to remain seated at the ship's navigational controls during the crash.

"I can't tell. Somewhere in the old Quarantine Zone."

Brian helped Kim up and looked out the main viewport at the surroundings. Although it was morning, a thick blanket of fog obscured the scene. Despite the gloom, Brian could make out tall, dark objects looming just outside the ship in the ghostly shroud.

"We won't have much time," Bill said. "Hudson, we need to get as many supplies as we can gather from cargo and put some distance between us and this ship."

"Do you think they'll come looking for us?"

"I don't know who is even down here to look for us, but it's a safe bet that anyone within fifty kilometers saw this ship go down."

Bill's words made Brian shudder. The Adherent ships had let them crash on Earth rather than pursuing or boarding them. *Was there something down on the planet's surface that they feared?*

The crash had left the ship powerless, save for a few minor systems that ran on the backup bridge generator. Their first objective was to try and access the other areas of the ship. Nobody seemed content to be trapped on the bridge, especially when the fate of their comrades in the other parts of the ship was still unknown. There had been no communication between the bridge and the other sections since the attack.

Maleek and another colonist accessed the door's electronic locking system while Hudson, Bill and Brian wedged the two halves open with the same rod Brian had used to beat Fenner with. The High Councilor lay motionless on the floor while everyone struggled with the door. At Bill's request, he had been bound and sedated.

The opening of the bridge doors was met by a hiss of air as the electronic override broke under the force. To everyone's surprise, a solid, metal bulkhead greeted them as soon as the doors opened. Apparently, the bulkhead was designed to seal of the bridge from other areas of the ship in the event of a hull breach. After a few more minutes of frantic work, Maleek managed to short out the bulkhead controls so that the sheet of metal slid up into the ceiling. As soon as the door parted from the floor, the colonists were met with an open breeze from the outside. Nobody spoke, although Brian knew that everyone feared the same thing: the ship's back portions had depressurized under the assault while still in space.

Mercifully, the dozen bodies of the colonists in the back sections of the ship had been ejected during the violent tumble into the atmosphere. The only sign of their tragedy was a small trace of blood on the engine room wall next to where the hull had buckled. It was a miracle the ship hadn't broken apart completely during re-entry. The designers must have constructed the ship to withstand extreme damage while still maintaining structural integrity. Bill made sure that the others didn't dwell on the loss too long and shuffled the group onward toward an exit. Kim made a point, though, to utter a brief, yet heartfelt, prayer.

Brian hadn't known any of the dead colonists very well, but he still shuddered at the thought of them tumbling into space. Close acquaintances or not, they were still his comrades.

Following a quick survey of the areas not sealed off by bulkheads, Bill led the group back to the large hole in the engineering section of the ship. The bulkheads had prevented them from reaching the cargo section of the ship as well as the main exit. Getting out of the ship wasn't a problem, but traveling a great distance without supplies would be dangerous, especially in the Quarantine Zone. They didn't even have any weapons, save for a couple of spare pistols. As they climbed up and stood on the dorsal side of the black ship, the truly dire nature of their predicament became apparent.

They were in a swamp. The air was so dank and heavy that Brian initially found it difficult to breathe. The tall, dark forms which he had seen out the viewport now revealed themselves through the mist to be trees; large trees stretching up from the black waters to an unseen canopy above. From beyond the rear of the ship, Brian could detect rays of sunlight filtering down through the corridor of destruction the ship had carved during the crash. But even this direction seemed impassable. There simply wasn't enough dry land to walk on around the ship and judging by how far it had sunk down into the muck, trudging through the water wasn't an option. Even if they had ground to walk on, they had no bearings and little sense of where to go. They were on an alien world. The worst part was the extra weight. Brian remembered the tiny gravitational differences between Earth and Elysium, and wondered if he could run for more than thirty meters if he had to do so.

"What should we do with Fenner?" the colonist woman named Anne yelled up from below. She and Laura were attempting to prop Fenner's large body up against the wall. Brian didn't think that they could carry the High Councilor through the swamp.

Hudson looked at Bill. "It's your call, Bill," he said, shrugging his shoulders. "If Fenner attacked you, I don't have any problem leaving him behind."

Bill seemed to weigh his possibilities for a moment. "No, we can't leave him here. Believe me, though, part of me wants to. Besides, I don't think we can just leave that easily. This swamp could cover half the continent."

"So, now what?"

Brian heard Bill laugh under his breath. It was a beleaguered, desperate sound, a sound that screamed resignation. "Build a raft and try to float out of here."

"Are you serious?"

"No. We don't even know which direction to go."

"What about the computers?" Brian asked. "If we can get the mainframe running, can't we access some maps or something?"

"No," answered Maleek. "There's hardly any info about Earth in the databanks, besides its location. It's almost like whoever programmed the computer didn't want those things coming home."

"So, now what? Wait here to get picked up by someone?" Hudson was getting frustrated.

"What if nobody comes at all?" Brian asked. Looking around at the slimy creatures and God knows what else that lived in the marsh harshly demonstrated the difficulties of finding food. Within a couple of days the meager rations they could salvage from the ship would vanish.

"The only thing I can think of is to split up and send a couple of scouting parties off in different directions. We still have the radios in working condition," noted Bill. "I think there's enough exposed ground to the south to move a ways on foot."

The plan wasn't very promising, but it was better than sitting around, Brian figured. At least they would be moving.

"That'll have to do," said Hudson in a depressed voice.

"We'll send two groups of two. The others can wait at the ship until we find a way out of here."

Brian looked off the edge of the ship, down at the area Bill had referred to as "dry ground." It looked like mud, deep mud. For a moment, he considered staying on the ship.

"Brian," Bill said, looking him in the eye. "You and Hudson can take Anne and Ramirez. I'm too hurt to make it very far. I'll stay here with Kim and the others."

Bill's declaration met with silence. As the others pondered his words, a faint humming sound began to be audible somewhere off in the murky distance. At first, it sounded like one of the thousands of ambient noises springing forth from every living creature within earshot, but it soon became apparent that this new sound was artificial.

Hudson ran to the edge of the ship in the direction from which the sound seemed to come.

"What do we do?" asked Maleek, who couldn't seem to decide whether he wanted to jump back down into the ship or run off into the depths of the surrounding swamp. Nobody had an answer for him. All were frozen in indecision.

Then something peculiar happened. Without a word, everyone, including Bill, seemed to turn to Kim all at once, as if she were going to provide some ingenious tactical solution to avoid being captured or killed. Maybe it was simply because she had remained quiet so far, but Brian felt that it was for some other reason. Perhaps it was because she always seemed to know what to do when everyone else did not.

"There's nothing we can do," she said, in a calm soothing voice. "But if they were going to kill us, they would have done it already."

"You don't know that," said Hudson. "We could have just been lucky so far."

"No, she's right," said Bill. "They probably want to know why one of their ships suddenly showed up in orbit, unannounced."

Captured. The word repeated itself over and over in Brian's mind. The last thing he wanted was to be put in a holding pen or tortured for information. Death would be preferable. If he had a pulse rifle, he would have considered fighting to the death, even if it meant condemning his comrades, including Kim, to death as well. He thought back to the stories he had heard as a child of the Church's torture chambers. His imagination ran wild with the possibilities of what several hundred years of refinement probably brought to the process.

But Brian would never get the chance to fight back, even if he had something to fight with. Just seconds after hearing Kim's declaration of hopelessness, he and the others were knocked down by the massive wind caused by a descending ship. As Brian looked up and struggled to get to his feet, he saw the massive, hovering form break down through the mist and descend on their position. Several bodies jumped down out of the ship and landed on the hull next to him. To Brian's shock, they looked nothing like the black clad monstrosities he had encountered on Elysium. Instead, the figure that approached Brian looked totally human, aside from a large, protective helmet obscuring his eyes. The man stood over Brian and looked down. Brian noticed a rifle in his hand, although it wasn't pointed at anything in particular.

"Just stay still," the man ordered. "We'll take you out of here."

The man's benign words lessened Brian's fear a little. *Are they here to rescue us or something?* Brian hoped. But his hopes were stifled as his eyes settled on symbol adorning the front of the man's helmet. It was the familiar symbol of the Eye, staring right back into Brian's soul. Perhaps his feelings of hope had been premature.

CHAPTER 32

▼

THE MORE THINGS CHANGE ...

Sedatives. Tranquilizers. Brian couldn't remember being shot or stuck with anything, but the dazed, incoherent state he was currently in signaled that something had been done to keep him immobilized. Inside the shuttle, Brian tried to shake off the dream-like state as he struggled to absorb his surroundings. His head and neck were free to swivel as he lay on his back, but his vision was blurred. Even worse, the rest of his body seemed unresponsive. As hard as he tried, he couldn't get up or roll over. Strangely, the inability to move didn't frustrate or scare Brian. The only emotion he felt was an odd combination of calmness and curiosity. *I must be drugged*, he reasoned.

A few meters away, Brian could see someone lying on a cot similar to his own. He couldn't tell who it was, but it definitely was someone other than Kim. A woman, apparently a medic, bent over the motionless body as she ran a scanner-like device from waist to head. Brian suddenly became aware that he too had someone checking him over, and he attempted once again to raise his head to get a look at who it was. He was stuck. It was useless to try and fight whatever force was holding him down. Speech was impossible, as well. Whatever he had been given, it was doing the trick of keeping him compliant. He ceased straining his neck muscles and closed his eyes, intent on fighting off the sleep which was tugging at his conscious mind. *Where are the others?* Brian asked himself. Some inner sense seemed to tell him that they were far away, perhaps on a different ship. The memories of the seconds following the arrival of the hovering ships remained elusive as ever. He couldn't even remember being brought on board the ship or seeing what happened to the others. There was nothing Brian could do but lay back and enjoy the temporary peace the drugs allowed him.

Sleep came and went as the hours slipped by. In truth, Brian couldn't tell how long the trip was taking, or where they were going. Finally, his slowly clearing eyes settled on a small, lone viewport overheard. Outside, white, billowing clouds whisked past, breaking up an otherwise perfect, blue sky. Before long, the blue became tinged with a pinkish-magenta hue, before relenting to a deep purple and eventual black. Now Brian was sure he had fallen asleep or passed out. The grogginess he had felt since being taken into custody was gone, and his newly functional vision quickly adjusted to the low, calm lights of the cabin. His ears were working well too and picked up a multitude of ambient hums and chirps of the ship. There were several dark uniformed people milling around the cabin now, efficiently, yet quietly, doing their jobs. Their movements sped up slightly as Brian heard the hum of the engines whine louder than before, a sign that the ship was nearing its destination. Brian found that he could now sit up, and did so.

"Who are you?" he asked the short, dark haired man who was closest to him.

The man looked at Brian, then over to the woman who was packing up equipment next to the other bed. Brian still couldn't tell who was on the bed. The woman was blocking his view. She looked at Brian, then back at the man, giving a nod that carried some positive signal.

"We're the Civil Patrol," he answered plainly. "We're dropping you off at Central Processing in New Jerusalem."

Brian thought about it. *New Jerusalem.* He didn't remember any city with that name. "Where are they?" he asked, confident that the man knew *who* he was talking about.

"A few are on this ship in the other recovery cells, but the rest are on the other shuttle."

"Where are we going?"

The man seemed slightly annoyed. "I told you, Central Processing. You need to be examined and debriefed."

"What does that involve?"

The man appeared confused by Brian's questions. After a few awkward seconds of silence, the woman spoke up. "Where did you come from?" Her voice wasn't threatening although she was obviously seeking information for official purposes rather than merely satisfying her curiosity. She also had a strange accent, a trait that made her even less trustworthy. Brian didn't answer her.

"What colony are you from?" the man asked. His tone was slightly warmer and more genuine. "How did you end up on that ship?"

Brian still didn't answer. He leaned back against the wall and tucked up his legs under his arms.

"If you're afraid, you shouldn't be. We're just trying to figure out what's going on."

Brian's instincts told him that he should remain mute, at least until *he* figured out what was going on. Asking more questions would just expose him as an outsider. As far as these people were concerned, he was just a normal colonist who had returned to Earth under extraordinary circumstances. The unfamiliar people around him knew nothing of Elysium or the mutiny. The truth could get him killed, or worse.

The man and woman broke off their questioning and turned their attention to work as the ship began its final descent. Brian saw that it was Anne who was lying on the nearby bed although she seemed to still be under the sedation Brian had experienced during most of the trip. When the ship hit the ground, two more uniformed men helped her out of bed and led her toward where Brian assumed the exit was. He didn't follow, instead waiting for somebody to come and get him. Despite the relatively benign appearance of his captors, he still half expected to be dragged out of the ship and shot. After another minute or two, the man he had talked to came back and placed a firm hand on his arm. "Let's go," he said, gently, yet steadily, pulling Brian off the bed.

The first thing that hit Brian as he descended the shuttle's exit ramp was the warm, moist air. It was definitely tropical wherever they were, and he could detect the unmistakable smell of dense vegetation all around. He could see what looked to be trees, maybe palms of some sort, in the murky darkness. Ahead, looming above the flat, paved landing area, rose a large, cylindrical tower adorned with a multitude of flashing lights. Despite its large size, the building did not bear the hard, industrial lines of Adherent architecture from the twenty fourth century. Instead, the building looked more organic, as if its soft lines were meant to inspire a feeling of calm majesty in those who entered.

"Brian?" a familiar voice yelled from his right. It was Kim.

Brian came to a standstill despite the physical urgings of his escorts. Kim was exiting the shuttle that had landed behind the one Brian had arrived on. Hudson and Maleek followed, all looking as dazed as Anne had appeared. They were each being led by uniformed officers of some sort, Civil Patrol, if the woman Brian had talked to could be trusted. When Kim broke away, they looked slightly concerned although they allowed her to run over to Brian and join his entourage.

"Where is your dad?" Brian asked, worried because he hadn't seen Bill yet.

"He's fine. They're taking him off the ship now. They split us all up."

"I think they drugged us, too," Brian whispered.

"Where are they taking us?" she asked.

"Central Processing," said one of the officers in front of them.

Kim looked at Brian inquisitively. He simply shrugged his shoulders, not knowing what Central Processing was himself. It sounded like a typical Adherent name, though: cold and functional.

Brian wasn't sure if the tower-like building ahead was Central Processing, but it did appear to have some sort of importance. Following a brief security check by more uniformed officers, this group clad in gray, Brian and his comrades were crammed into small, wheeled service vehicles and chauffeured through a series of attractive, well-kept courtyards to a shorter, yet much larger, building.

Although he should have felt terrified, Brian wasn't. *Maybe it's because Kim's here*, he reasoned. It wasn't just because of her physical presence, either, although it certainly helped. More importantly was the fact that his captors, or rescuers, depending on the viewpoint, were allowing her to be with him. There seemed to be a chance that Brian and the others would be treated well, at least up until they were sentenced to death for hijacking another Adherent starship.

Their hasty, somewhat disorienting journey ended for the night in a small, yet neat, cell, which looked more like living quarters than a prison, apart from the relatively small size. There was even a small window in the room looking out over a central courtyard. Following a quick survey of the cell, Brian sat down on one of the two small beds that were positioned on opposite sides of the room. Kim walked over to his side, but stayed standing until the last of the officers left and shut the heavy, metal door. After a few moments, the door opened again, and Maleek was coaxed into the room. He stood at the door for at least a full minute before bowing his head and taking a seat on the other bed. Neither Brian nor Kim spoke a word to him.

Brian glared at his friend, at the darkened mark he had left on Maleek's face many hours before. He wanted to jump up and berate his once-trusted comrade for putting the colony in so much danger. Maleek had sided with Fenner, going so far as to lie to those who cared most for him. Coming to Earth had put them all in jeopardy. There may have been reasons for such a despicable and stupid act, but Brian would have to wait for any sort of interrogation. The room they were being held in was probably bugged. It was a good tactic: placing the younger members of the group alone so they could talk and inevitably betray vital information that the older adults wouldn't allow them to under normal circumstances. Luckily, Brian was quite familiar with this technique, having been such an adept student back in his Adherent days. He would divulge nothing. Instead he just stared at his friend, and let his frustration bore into Maleek's soul. To his credit, Maleek didn't hide from the visual scouring although he eventually bowed his head toward the floor and appeared to close his eyes.

"It's fine, Bri," Kim whispered, rubbing his hand gently. "Let it go."

Kim's words calmed Brian slightly, even though he still felt a little like punching Maleek. Still exhausted from the lingering effects of the sedatives, he lay back on the bed and tried to center himself. Kim got up a few minutes later and put her hand on Maleek's shoulder. Brian couldn't hear what she whispered, but Maleek immediately nodded his head and lay back on his bed. Kim returned to Brian and lay down as well, letting out a long, strained sigh, which signaled that even she was nervous about their fate.

As hard as Brian tried to sleep that night, a gnawing feeling of anxiety kept him awake. Kim was asleep, as evidenced by her steady breathing, but she shifted restlessly. *Was she having one of her dreams? Could she dream now that Elysium was so distant?* There was no way to tell, and Brian didn't want to ask. Instead, he held her for a while, then got up and paced around the room. His chief concern was how the others were faring. He had not seen Bill or anyone else since being off-loaded from the transports. If they were being questioned, or worse, Brian would have no way of knowing what information they were giving their captors. Brian hated it; not knowing. He had always preferred facing his problems in the most immediate and direct way possible. Relaxing in a cell didn't coincide with this life philosophy.

A pale, bluish light filtered in through the small window and cast ghostly shadows across the room. Brian stopped his aimless pacing and approached the source of light. The lone, circular disk bore down from the clear sky above. It was an alien moon, as Brian had never been accustomed to it as a child. He instantly thought of Phobos and Demos when he saw it, but in the absence of another companion, Earth's moon seemed cold and lonely. In the distance, his ears could detect the faint hum of a passing ship over the steady drone of insect noises intensified by the brick-laden courtyard below. There was a row of warm-colored lights bordering a path through the gardens that led to a large, rectangular building. On the path stood two men; guards perhaps, although Brian didn't see them carrying any weapons. Other than that, there were no signs of human activity. In the distance, above the buildings surrounding the courtyard, rose hills dotted with many lights, perhaps houses. These too looked static, like yellow brush strokes on a blue-black canvas. A faint breeze carried the now familiar scent of Earth to Brian's nose. It was a very organic smell although it lacked the sweetness of Elysian air. Brian thought back to the Earth he had left, and how such a radical transformation could have occurred. The portions he had seen so far looked nothing like the industrial wasteland he remembered from childhood. *What had changed it?*

After a few more minutes of scanning the area, Brian gave up trying to make sense of his surroundings and returned to bed. He pulled a blanket over his exhausted body and once again put his arm around Kim. She murmured slightly, but didn't wake. He pulled her warm body tightly against his and fell asleep.

To Brian's satisfaction, and initial surprise, he didn't have to wait long to discover their fate. In the morning, he, Kim and Maleek were woken abruptly by several men dressed like the ones the night before. As his eyes struggled to adjust to the almost blinding sunlight flooding into the room, he and his companions were herded out of bed and across the courtyard to the rectangular building. As they were being escorted to their destination, Brian became acutely aware of the many curious onlookers who stopped in their tracks and surveyed the strangely dressed teenagers in their midst. Brian noticed that these onlookers wore rather simple, white tunics, attire which identified them as possible civilians rather than public servants. It was difficult to determine just what social class these people belonged to, though. They all looked the same.

Brian, Kim and Maleek soon found themselves sitting in an ornately decorated room, an office of some sort, judging by the massive, official looking desk in front of them. Brian found it strange that the officers who had escorted them into the building left as soon as they were seated. Apparently, there was little fear of the three captives escaping.

"What is this place?" Kim murmured to nobody in particular. Her perplexed tone mirrored Brian's thoughts.

Neither Brian nor Maleek answered her. They were too busy examining the room. The chairs they sat in were wooden, like most of the furniture. Everything looked to be antique, perhaps centuries old. A warm breeze carrying the faint scent of the sea blew through an open set of doors on the other side of the room, fanning out a series of soft, waif-like curtains. Paintings covered the walls, religious ones, depicting scenes from the *Final Testament,* which Brian had once been intimately familiar with. The most curious decorations, by far, however, were the several clocks scattered throughout the room. These too were made out of wood and made the most distinct chirping sound as they ticked away. Brian remembered seeing one as a child and jumping back in terror as an artificial bird had suddenly popped out of the interior. Kim's eyes had obviously fallen on the clocks too, and she now got up to inspect the one closest to her seat.

"Kim, what are you doing?" Brian hissed, concerned that she may earn the wrath of some unseen guard. Despite their almost enchanting surroundings, Brian made sure not to forget that they were in a potentially hostile environment.

Kim didn't respond to Brian's urgings. She seemed too transfixed by the clock to care. Suddenly, the tall, wooden box signaled the passing of an hour, sending Kim reeling back against her chair. Brian and Maleek jumped too.

"Do you like my collection?" a voice asked, as a man emerged from behind them. The three of them jumped again. Kim sat abruptly back in her seat before quickly regaining her composure.

The balding, middle-aged man didn't seem to mind the lack of an answer. In fact, it looked as if he enjoyed gaining such undying attention from his new acquaintances. He brushed between Brian and Kim and stood next to the clock she had examined.

"This piece is over a thousand years old," he said proudly. "It was made in a place called Germany."

Still, the strange man received no response from his audience. Brian and the others were totally confused by his relaxed tone and irreverent speech. The man had the same strange accent as the officers onboard the transport although his mood seemed much more jovial and laid back.

The man looked at the clock for another moment before taking a seat behind the massive oak desk. "So, you must have had quite the adventure."

Maleek looked over nervously at Brian, not quite sure whether to respond. Brian tried to ignore his friend and looked the man in the eyes with the blankest expression possible.

"Ha! You kids are good. Your resolve is admirable, if a bit misguided," the man chuckled. "I'm the last person you need to be afraid of. This isn't some sort of interrogation."

"Then what is it?" Kim asked in a defiant tone.

"Call it … a conversation. I'm High Minister Andrews, the leader of New Jerusalem. I just want to find out about you kids."

Nobody reciprocated his introduction.

Rather than showing frustration, the Minister's smile only broadened. "I can see that you kids are definitely a product of your era."

"What do you mean?" Brian asked in an ignorant sounding voice. *What did this man know?*

"What I mean is that you act as though you're going to be tortured for information or something."

"Is that the case?" asked Kim dryly.

"No! No! Of course, not," Andrews said, waving his hand back and forth as if dismissing an absolutely ridiculous notion. "Even if I did want information, that's the last thing I would even consider doing! As you can see, things have changed much since your time. We've moved beyond such barbaric practices. That kind of behavior may have been necessary in harsher times, but we have little need of violence in our society. There simply isn't any place for it." Seeing that his audience was far from persuaded, Andrews continued. "This is an era of peace, the Golden Age which was prophesized in Scripture! You do remember, don't you? Or has it truly been that long?"

Your time? That long? At this point, it was clear to Brian that the man knew at least something of their origins. The hijacking, the colony, it was likely he knew it all. Where he had gotten the information was still a mystery.

"What about those things, those monsters that attacked us?" questioned an angry-looking Kim. "Are they products of this Golden Age as well?" Brian had rarely seen her act so aggressive. Underneath her composed exterior he could detect a smoldering frustration that threatened to burst into a conflagration. Andrews may have been eager to espouse the enlightened attitudes of Adherent culture, but to Kim and Brian he seemed like an unwelcome reminder of the zealotry that had defined their childhood.

"You must be referring to the Colonial Guard," Minister Andrews said knowingly. Brian didn't appreciate the pompous look on his face. The man had quite a bit to answer for.

"I apologize for any problems they caused your people."

"They killed dozens," Kim charged. "And it would have been worse if we hadn't stopped them."

"An unfortunate tragedy," Andrews noted, unconvincingly. "I promise that we'll investigate the matter once the ship is salvaged from the old Quarantine Zone."

"What's there to investigate?" Brian asked.

"You have to understand," Andrews said, "we've never had a problem with the Guard, at least, not like the one your comrades described."

So the others talked, Brian said to himself. He wondered why they had felt compelled to tell this man sitting in front of him anything. Perhaps they had been tortured after all.

Andrews continued: "Our soldiers are extremely well-adapted for the harsh environments in which they operate; a trait which sometimes makes them … efficient. Some may even describe them as aggressive. It's our policy not to allow them to enter Earth space except in the case of emergencies. There simply isn't any need for their talents here. They follow orders superbly, and we've never experienced a problem with them. But, from what some of your friends told me earlier, they acted without direction, without discipline when they found your colony. Perhaps they felt like your colony presented some sort of threat. Your people do have a violent history and they are, after all, allowed to operate with a great deal of autonomy. We've been analyzing the ship's computers since we found you yesterday. It appears that our soldiers were infected with some sort of pathogen, too. Normally, the ship's brain would be able to deal with such an infection, but it seems that it was incapable of ridding itself of this one. A curious problem, indeed. That must account for their inability to suppress your resistance."

Brian still didn't believe anything the man was saying. Andrews could have very well ordered the Adherent soldiers to wipe out everyone on the planet. Realizing that Andrews would continue to claim innocence in the matter, he shifted his line of questioning. "So, what are you going to do with us? Are we prisoners?"

"No, of course not. You may join your friends as soon as we finish this discussion. They're waiting in the building on the other side of the courtyard, except for one. Fenner, I believe his name is."

"What about him?"

"Due to his … uncooperative, and potentially violent, behavior, we have been forced to seclude him in a separate holding cell. Unfortunate, really."

"When can we go home, then?" asked Kim. This was a question Brian hadn't expected her to ask. It was almost too obvious.

"What?" asked Andrews. He looked puzzled, yet still managed to keep the same, unwavering smile on his face.

"If we aren't prisoners here, then when can we go home?" Kim asked again, this time very coldly and very directly.

For the first time Andrews looked like he had been taken off guard. "Home? Back to your colony? No, I'm sorry, that's not going to be an option."

"That's what I figured," said Kim.

"Don't worry, though. You'll see your families again; very shortly, I hope."

"What do you mean?" Brian asked worriedly.

"It'll take several weeks to organize and get ships there, but I'm confident that we can relocate your people within six months, five if things go as planned."

Brian sat stunned. Andrews made his statement with such nonchalance that his words sounded more like some sort of cruel joke.

"Relocate?"

"Yes, of course. We can't have a colony of Apostates living out beyond regulated space. It's been over 300 years since we've even uncovered a concentrated group of you people! It's amazing that you've survived all this time on your own, without the help of God, no less!"

"What happened to all of the other groups?" Kim asked in the same, jaded tone as before. "Did you kill them?"

"As far as I can remember, most of the Apostates from your century were successfully converted, eventually, that is. Those who resisted violently were not. But like I said before, it's been a long time since the Church has had to rely on such drastic measures. The last couple of groups that were uncovered converted without any resistance whatsoever."

"They won't go. They'll fight you," Kim said with icy conviction.

"Who? Your fellow colonists? They won't have a chance," Andrews said. "We should be able to collect them without any sort of problem. If we show up with enough force, I think we can avert any sort of hostilities. Like I said before, we're beyond the barbarity of past generations. This is God's work that's being carried out. Your friends and families will be reintegrated into our society, a very generous fate for those who have committed murder and blasphemy on such an abhorrent level. When they are returned to Earth, nobody will even remember the hijacking or the colony that existed on that God-forsaken planet. You and your people have been given a second chance at redemption, assuming God forgives your past sins."

It was like a bad dream. The difficult years of readjustment; the sense of peace and belonging that was finally achieved; the battles, the work, the sacrifices; all of it was going to be erased, as if it had never existed. It was almost too much to handle. Brain recognized Andrews; saw him for the public face the Church had always strived to achieve. It was a facade, a fallacy, and yet, it was a model that was stressed so zealously it was hard not to be fooled by it. Brian wanted nothing of the dream, this Golden Age that was being sold to him for the second time. He had seen what price such an Age came at and balked at the rewards. Besides, he had been exposed to an alternative, a way of life beyond the grasp of such narrow minds as the one sitting in front of him. To live without freedom; to breathe air that was not of Elysium seemed like Hell itself. *I'll die before I let them take it.*

The rage building in Brian's chest was tempered by a knock at one of the ornately carved doors to the side of the office.

"Come in!" chimed Andrews in an upbeat tone.

The person who entered the room from the side door defied every expectation of Brian's. Rather than another uniformed officer or faceless citizen clad in a white tunic, a young girl slid into the room and over to Andrews' desk. She was intensely pretty and graceful, although seemingly frail. Her skin was so fair that Brian could almost see the blue tint of veins running just beneath the surface. Still, this did not diminish her exotic beauty. Like Jade, this girl had shimmering blonde hair that ran down her back like a solid wave of gold. Her most striking feature, however, were her eyes; two pale blue orbs that bespoke of obvious spiritual purity. She was not attractive like Kim. The aesthetic qualities Brian immediately attached to this girl were more reminiscent of admiration, a feeling totally removed from sexuality. It was almost as if the girl was too perfect, angelic, and yet, she hadn't even opened her mouth.

"Was there something you wanted, father?" she asked in a light, airy voice. Brian found it tough to guess her age based on looks, but now estimated that she was in her mid-teens, slightly younger than he and his friends. She certainly did not look like she carried the same vitality as the rest of his peers back on Elysium. This girl epitomized the ideal Adherent female: physically dependent on the spiritual dogma of the Church.

"Yes, dear. These are the guests I was telling you about."

Guests? Brain found the word hard to accept. He and his comrades were anything but guests here on Earth. Just why Andrews was introducing them to his daughter was anyone's guess.

"Hello, my name is Grace," the girl said pleasantly, adding a shallow bow.

Brian, surprised by the whole situation, involuntarily stood up and returned the gesture. "Hi, I'm Brian."

Kim, whose facial expression had suddenly shifted from hardened resolve to warmness, also stood up. "Hello, Grace, I'm Kim." Brian saw her force a smile out of the corner of his eye and knew that Kim was putting on her most diplomatic guise.

Grace returned Kim's smile without question, before turning to Maleek.

"Hello," she said, giggling slightly under her breath. It was obvious that she was nervous, as was he.

"Hi," he said, failing to rise. Brian found the little wave he gave her ridiculous although Maleek's reaction wasn't surprising, especially under these awkward circumstances. Brian thought he saw something in the gaze between the new acquaintances, something beyond simple curiosity. The possibility that Maleek was somehow drawn to this girl made Brian even angrier at him. Despite Grace's apparent charm, she was the enemy. Andrews would not have brought her to this meeting if he didn't have something planned. Suddenly, Brian regretted bowing to her. Kim was better at playing the role of diplomat, anyway.

"Grace is one of the top students at the New Jerusalem Academy," Andrews proclaimed, as if his audience cared. "She'll be graduating a full year early."

"I'm sure that's quite an accomplishment, Grace," Kim said. The younger girl was apparently too naïve to pick up on the condescending tone of the compliment. Grace simply smiled and looked slightly embarrassed by the attention of strangers.

Andrews was slightly more perceptive. His tone darkened. "I have decided to ask Grace to act as your guide the next few weeks."

"Guide for what?" Brian asked, even though he had a good idea of what the position meant.

"For your education," Andrews said. "I've discussed it with the other High Ministers and we've agree that you are to be reintegrated into the Church as soon as possible. Now, you may be a little old for the Academy at this point, but then again, you three have missed out on a lot. I couldn't let you be re-educated in good conscience, that is, unless you had someone like my daughter to guide you."

"What do you mean?" Kim asked, her voice carrying trepidation.

"Surely you remember your education?"

Brian, Kim and Maleek each nodded wearily.

"Well, I've done some research and found that you were quite the scholars in your time."

"What?" Brian laughed. The idea that Andrews had access to such ancient knowledge was ridiculous.

Andrews was prepared for Brian's doubt. He read a series of facts from a small sheet of paper. "Brian Bishop. Son of High Counselor David Bishop of Chicago. Demonstrates high aptitude for rhetoric, leadership and tactics. Recommended for early entry into the Tau Ceti military academy." Andrews listed off the facts in rapid succession, his voice taking on a new, more menacing tone. He looked Brian right in the eyes as he spoke, as if to emphasize the power he now had over him.

Brian's only reaction was to sit in stunned silenced, his jaw wide open.

"Oh, yes, Brian. I know all about you."

"How?"

"Simple. Records. The Church database extends all the way back to the Unification Wars. I have access to everything. Once the analysis is complete on the ship you recklessly brought back to Earth, I'll know everything there is to know about the only two chapters in your life that matter: the ones lived under the loving embrace of the Church."

Loving embrace? More like iron fist. Regardless of how hard Andrews tried to smooth over the situation, Brian recognized the threat posed by the man. The High Minister obviously expected them to be assimilated back into Adherent society. If they resisted outwardly, perhaps violence would indeed be used as an eventual tool to get them to comply. They would have to find some way to resist, a means of escape that didn't bring them into direct conflict with Andrews. Despite Brian's growing disdain for the man, he recognized that the High Minister was attempting to be charitable, at least, in his own distorted way. Perhaps this was a weakness that could be exploited.

"That's really all I have for you right now," Andrews said. "The officers will escort you back to your room. Your friends will be waiting there; you may talk with them as you please. I'll arrange for each one of you to have personal quarters. It shouldn't take more than a day or so. Grace will come and get you tomorrow morning for school."

"Tomorrow?" Kim asked, unable to hide her reluctance.

"At daybreak. I suggest you get some rest. Like I said before, you have a lot to catch up on. Grace and some of her friends are close to attaining their rank as Citizens. If you work hard enough, you may even graduate with her next spring, but I don't expect that kind of progress. It's just a hope, really."

Andrews smiled and stood up. Grace, who had been patiently standing at his side, gave a nervous little wave like the one Maleek had upon meeting her.

"Oh, and just one more thing ..."

Brian braced himself, anticipating more questions.

"Why are you the only one who kept your Eye of God?"

The question was directed at Kim. Brian felt stupid for not remembering this very important physical difference between the colonists and people on Earth. Andrews, Grace, and everyone else they had met on Earth so far carried the Eye of God on their foreheads. These marks were much more elegant than those of Brian's time period. The new marks looked to be made from a delicate, gold-like substance that shimmered brilliantly in the light. Brian was so accustomed to Kim's mark that he rarely thought of it, but in comparison with these new marks, it stood out like a glaring blemish.

"I wear it to remind me of the past," she answered confidently.

Andrews looked to be puzzled once again. Grace seemed to be downright confused. "The past? But, God is eternal, Miss Collins."

Kim stood up at this point and looked him directly in the eye. "And don't forget Ever-Seeing, Minister," she added.

Andrews stood quietly for a few uncomfortable seconds before his smile returned. "You have a lot to learn, my new friend."

With this statement, he looked satisfied and turned to exit the room. Brian noticed the now horrified look on Grace's face before her father pulled her by the arm out of the room. Brian supposed it was the first time she ever witnessed someone counter her father's power.

As soon as Andrews and Grace left, Brian slumped down in his chair and gave Kim a look that partially vented his brewing hostility. He shook his head back and forth slowly to articulate his determination to resist this "re-education." He noticed Kim's eyes had softened and looked ready to give way to tears. It was disheartening to see her begin to lose control, but he didn't blame her. It was like a nightmare. After all they had suffered and fought to preserve, they found themselves back in the most familiar and unwelcome of environments. For all of its extraordinary changes on the exterior, the Church remained the same stifling poison it had always been. The worst part was that now Brian was smart enough to recognize it.

CHAPTER 33

▼

TENDING TO THE
WAYWARD OF THE FLOCK

"This is your fault, Maleek! I can't believe you made such a dumb choice!"

Brian didn't care about potential eavesdroppers anymore. It was clear that Andrews and the Church knew everything about them. The small, cell-like quarters magnified Brian's growing voice, and broadcast his frustration to the surrounding rooms.

"Bri, stop," Kim said, trying to calm him down.

Her pleas were useless, though. Brian continued to pace back and forth, angrily ignoring her. He stared at the ground for the most part, but looked up occasionally to blast Maleek with a scalding glare.

Maleek took the barrage without rebuttal. He merely sat on the bed with his head bowed, staring at the floor.

"Nobody would have believed Fenner if you hadn't backed his lie! The Adherents found us by accident, and never even gave away our location to Earth, or any other base. That's right, isn't it? That would have been the end of it, but you and Fenner just had to push our luck."

"You went along with it," Maleek said, finally mustering a defense. "You didn't seem to care too much about the credibility of the threat at the time. You saw your chance for revenge and took it, just like I did."

"Credibility? That's bullshit! They had just blown up half of the colony! Why wouldn't I expect them to be a threat? The bad part is that you knew otherwise, and still led us on some damned suicide mission! You've put the entire colony at risk now! How's that for a threat! You heard Andrews, it's over."

"Come on, Brian! They killed your dad. They killed mine too! Don't pretend like they don't deserve to be punished!"

Brian was almost taken off guard by the strength in Maleek's voice. Something, perhaps Fenner's influence, had changed him.

"I agree that the Church needs to be destroyed, but not like this," Brian reasoned. "What you had in mind was murder, just like Kim said. Most of these people here probably don't even know about what happened to the Apostates, to *us*, hundreds of years ago. Things aren't like they were when we lived on Earth. And besides, those things that attacked us aren't even based in this system. Andrews said they don't even come to Earth unless there's an emergency. You could kill everyone on Earth, and it wouldn't change anything. It just gives them a new reason to wipe us out. It's reckless."

"You're calling me reckless? You're the most reckless of all us, Brian, shooting first and thinking later. You're the one who's just like Fenner. Since when have you cared about thinking things through?"

"Since I grew up, Maleek."

"When? A month ago? Think about it, Brian. The Church will continue to grow as long as Earth exists. In any case, they would have found us again."

"You don't know that."

"I know that using the missiles was our best chance of survival."

"It was a reckless plan."

Brian was just about to add more to his argument when Bill entered the room. It looked as if he had come without an escort, and Brian wondered for a moment if Andrews had been sincere when he had insisted that they weren't prisoners. "That's enough, you two," Bill said commandingly. "It's a pointless debate. Nobody could have foreseen what we would encounter here. If we had found Earth in the same state we left it in, then I would have been the first to launch the warheads. Brian's right, though, things are different."

"Only on the outside," muttered Maleek.

"I take it you've met with Andrews?" Bill asked.

"We had the pleasure," sniped Kim.

"What did he talk to you about?"

"Just our education," she answered. "We've been assigned to the city's Senior Academy. His daughter is going to be personally tutoring us."

"Good," said Bill. His answer shocked Brian. It actually sounded like Bill meant it.

"What?"

"It's good that you're being accepted back so easily," Bill clarified. "I was worried there was going to be some sort of physical conditioning involved, but it looks like they feel schooling will be enough to convert you."

"What do you mean, Bill? How is any of this positive news?" Brian asked, somewhat astounded. "He did tell you about their plans for Elysium, didn't he? They're going to get the others and bring them back to Earth!"

Bill's next response astounded Brian even more. "At this point, Brian, I'm just glad you kids are going to be all right. I want all three of you to go along with what Andrews and the others tell you. Don't put up a fight. No attitudes and no schemes. Understand?"

Maleek was the only one who nodded. Brian and Kim just stared at Bill. At first, Brian thought that Bill was merely planning something and wanted them to play along for the time being, but as he looked into his eyes, eyes which had grown wise and cautious over the years, he realized that Bill was being serious. It was in this moment that Brian realized how much Bill had changed; how his priorities had shifted away from ideology and toward the safety of those he loved most. Bill was getting old.

"Kim, Brian. Listen to me. Regardless of what happens to me or anyone else on Elysium, you two can be happy here, as long as you have each other. We left Earth so that you kids could have a better life. Now you have a chance to have that life."

"But we already have found a life, Dad!" Kim argued. "The colony, Elysium is our life. It's our home. This place, even though it looks different, is still the Church! If these people are happy, then that's fine, but we can't live here."

"It will take time, honey, but you'll adjust, just like you did before. And besides, I don't want you to live out the rest of you lives as fugitives. That's not any sort of freedom, either."

Brian felt defeated when he heard Bill's words, but Kim seemed absolutely devastated. She, more than anyone else, seemed to have formed a connection with Elysium, a connection that went far beyond simple familiarity. Brian was convinced that separating Kim from her home would lead to her spiritual demise.

"What about you?" Brian asked, hoping to force Bill to examine his stance a little more.

"At this point, Bri, I'm prepared to accept my position. After the others are brought back from the colony, the adults will probably be given low-level service jobs, places without influence. Places we can live in peace."

"As faithful members of the Church," Brian pointed out. "Bearers of the Mark. Are you happy with that?"

"I can live with that," said Bill. "And so can you. Your father would have wanted you to live, Brian. It's no use fighting anymore. Whatever happens in the future, you and Kim have to take care of each other and live your lives."

Brian saw it; saw the defeat on Bill's face. And still, his words carried some glimmer of hope, buried deep beneath the resignation. Bill must have had a plan, but whatever that plan involved, it obviously didn't include Brian and Kim. Apparently Bill felt that the children had suffered enough. He may still be willing to risk his own life to fight for freedom, but the younger generation was no longer considered endangered enough to gamble with.

"We understand," said Brian, lowering his head toward the floor. He knew Kim wouldn't answer for herself, but was sure that his answer was good enough for them both. After all, Brian was the rash one. If he could be reasoned with, then she could too. Brian's agreement to do as Andrews commanded went against everything his conscience told him, but he could still see the reason in Bill's argument. He only hoped that Bill still carried some desire to try and save the colony.

The next morning, Grace came with a small entourage of attendants who took Brian and Kim several blocks away to their new living quarters near the main city Cathedral. The quarters were located in a squat, rectangular building bordering the Cathedral gardens, where future clergy members were housed during their schooling. The small, well-kept apartment Brain and Maleek were assigned to was boring, but comfortable. Its sterile, white interior was broken only by the multitude of religious symbols and propaganda art that adorned the walls. Much more aesthetically appealing were the two large windows that opened up and provided an excellent view of the gardens and surrounding city buildings. As much as he hated to admit it, Brian couldn't help but admire the shining white architecture and calm, well-ordered streets around him. Too bad the picturesque setting had been paid for by the blood of millions and built on a foundation of lies.

To Brian's dismay, the living quarters were segregated rather than co-ed, although Grace assured him that he would see Kim as often as he liked so long as it was before curfew. As with everything else that came out of Grace's mouth, her promise turned out to be true, although Brian bristled at the thought of seeing

Kim on such a confining schedule. They certainly wouldn't have any opportuni-
ties for the midnight walks they used to enjoy back on Elysium, not to mention
any romantic contact, which violated strict Adherent moral standards.

Of much more immediate concern, however, were the awful clothes Brian was
issued as part of his new wardrobe. The flowing white robes, although comfortable, made ambitious movement difficult, and Brian immediately missed the
tight practicality offered by a decent pair of cargo pants. Even worse, the robes
instantly robbed him of individuality, and perhaps even a bit of masculinity, as he
was sure was the intention. He was now a member of the Church, just another
sheep in the Lord's flock.

The first few days of school were rough for Brian and Kim. At first they
attempted to block out the voices of their instructors, but were soon called out
for their inattention. In response, both broke their promise to Bill and insisted on
arguing their case against Church theology. To Brian and Kim's frustration, however, the instructors and students greeted their resistance with apparent pity
rather than anger, a reaction that proved difficult to counter. Unlike the guarded
atmosphere of the twenty fourth century, those in the modern Church were so
assured of their spiritual superiority that they didn't feel threatened or persuaded
in the least. Resistance to the indoctrination merely brought about more concerned attention, as if Brian and Kim were sick patients who needed a spiritual
remedy. It *was* sickening. Brian would have almost preferred being tortured; it
would have saved him from the deluge of sympathy that seemed to pour forth
from the mouths of every individual they encountered both in the Church Academy and the city. There was little if any need for Brian and Kim to even be put
on house arrest. They were such public figures that after only a few days time
leaving the confines of the Cathedral grounds became an ordeal. Everywhere they
went Brian and Kim were greeted by curious citizens wearing concerned looks.
No wonder Andrews had been so confident about their prospects of rehabilita-
tion. Already, Brian felt like a black blight on an otherwise pristine, white canvas.
It became clear that the spiritual aspects of the struggle were only a small part of
it. Brian worried that sooner or later a hidden desire to fit in may emerge and
deaden his resolve. He realized that even Kim could eventually fall prey to this
passive-aggressive socialization process. For now, though, he would try to resist.

For his part, Maleek seemed to adapt much more readily to his new environment. Within a few days he was already taking his seat next to Grace in class and
picking out lines from the *Final Testament* during study sessions held in Brian's
living quarters. Maleek seemed content, almost happy in his new position. The
other Academy students, especially Grace, liked him, and there was talk that he

would be given an opportunity to attend a prestigious technical school once he completed his re-education.

Brian knew the reason for Maleek's rapid conversion; it was Grace. He was falling in love with her, and she, apparently, with him. Maleek, the once ardent supporter of the Apostate cause, a willing disciple of Fenner, now seemed to be abandoning his ideals and his people for a girl. Brian had been able to forgive Maleek for lying about the Church and helping Fenner, but converting for some petty infatuation was a far greater sin. Brian now hated his friend for being so weak. It made things easier, having a focal point to collect his feelings of frustration and anxiety. Andrews and the Church seemed untouchable, beyond attack, yet Maleek was just a few meters away at all times, slowly giving away his soul to the machine that had cost him so much.

As those first few days turned into several weeks, a feeling of hopelessness began to wash over Brian. Soon, Andrews said the Adherent ships would travel to Elysium and take the colony by force. Bill's lack of concern seemed to make the terrible event inevitable. Each time Brian saw Bill, he noticed that the socialization process had eroded his spirit just a little bit further. Hudson and the other four adults, Fenner excluded, also seemed to be resigned to their fate as new Citizens of the Church. Although Bill and the adults were still monitored closely by the city's security force, they would soon be given just as much freedom as Brain, Kim and Maleek. It would fall on them to ease the transition for the colonists once they were brought back to Earth.

Fenner was the only one who actively resisted his captors, or so Brian had heard. Since his arrival on Earth, Fenner had been placed in custody in the city's only block of holding cells. Neither Kim nor Brian had seen him since the day they had arrived. The rumor was that he had attempted to attack Andrews during their initial meeting. Hudson told Brian that Fenner had acted so volatile since that time that he had been branded a high-level security threat. The fact that he hadn't been executed yet signaled the Church hierarchy's newfound patience. Brian wondered often how long this patience would last. He also entertained the idea of visiting Fenner, despite the verbal abuse he would certainly endure. Still, despite the unpleasant nature of such a meeting, Brain felt compelled. As Bill and the others drifted further into apathy, Fenner once again emerged in Brian's mind as a magnetic fire marking the way to freedom. Although Fenner's path could just as easily lead to destruction, Brian reasoned that at least then the choice would be his.

CHAPTER 34

▼

AN ECHO FROM THE
GARDEN

The scene unfolding in Brian's living quarters was now a familiar one: seven Academy students of varying ages sat in a circle while Grace selected lines from the *Final Testament*. She would read a line, then pause, waiting for a response from the others. She never had to wait for long. Within seconds, one of the students, sometimes even Maleek, would raise his or her hand and initiate a discussion about the text that may last for several minutes. Brian found it difficult to believe anyone ever brought any new ideas to the discussions. He noted with disdain how robotically they spoke, as if reciting slogans and teachings from some master Church discussion guidebook. The discussions certainly lacked any of the critical thought that Chang's had back when Brian was in school. Rather than serve any thoughtful, or for that matter, spiritual purpose, these discussions seemed to be more about getting future Citizens accustomed to following a leader's cue, namely Grace's. Despite her normally quiet and reserved demeanor, Grace's personality transformed when she led these biblical discussions. It was only at these times that she betrayed herself to be the child of a High Minister. Brian realized that someday, Grace Andrews would wield a frightening level of power, just like her father.

Although the meetings were held in Brian and Maleek's apartment with the intent of exposing them further to the Adherent mindset, Brian rarely listened to the proceedings and never spoke. Whether or not this bothered Grace was unclear since she never chastised his obvious lack of attention. Brian didn't think she complained to her father about it, either. Minister Andrews would merely stop by one or two times a week and check on Brian like a worried foster parent of a spiritual orphan. During each of these meetings with Andrews, Brian remained polite, as did Kim, but he made it as clear as possible that he wouldn't give in to the socialization process as easily as Maleek seemed to be doing. Brian would simply nod his head as Andrews spoke and then inquire about the status of the colony. Always, the answer was the same: the time was approaching when the Church would collect the colonists and bring them back to Earth although Andrews never gave a firm date. Surely, it wouldn't be much longer until the Adherent gathered enough ships and made the trip to Elysium. Perhaps they were already on their way.

On this particular evening, the topic of Grace's discussion was the issue of Creation itself. According to Adherent theology, God created Earth to be mankind's kingdom. Since mankind was created in God's image, this somehow bestowed upon humanity, and Earth, for that matter, a divine position in the universe. It was a lesson Brian remembered from long ago; he had once been its most fanatical student.

"So, if this planet was meant to be our home, why is it so important that we expand God's influence among the stars?" Grace asked the group.

"Because we are His chosen creations," a younger male student responded.

"It's our job to spread His message," one of the girls added.

Kim, who was normally polite at these sessions, now shifted in her seat. Although she never contributed anything either, Brian liked having her around; the meetings were the only time females were allowed in male housing after curfew. Brian knew she couldn't resist saying something in response to Grace's question. It was too tempting, he realized, to share some of the information they had learned while living on Elysium, information that threatened to shatter the sheltered minds of the young Academy students.

"What about creatures that live on other worlds, maybe some you haven't even dreamed of?" Kim asked.

"Animals aren't in any sort of a position to be considered in God's plan," Grace insisted.

"I'm not talking about animals, Grace. I'm talking about other intelligent beings, like us."

"You're assuming that beings like these exist, Kim." Grace responded confidently. "It's merely speculation."

"Not true. We found evidence of an intelligent civilization on Elysium," Kim revealed.

Grace eyed her suspiciously, as if she suspected Kim of teasing her.

Brian watched the exchange between the two girls with growing interest. He could tell Kim was frustrated, sick of enduring Grace's endless quips about God and the Church. Although betraying the information about the alien ruins violated the secret they had all agreed to keep, there seemed to be no harm in divulging it now, especially if it flustered Grace in some way.

"If what you claim is true, then those beings would still fall into a different category than human beings," Grace reasoned. "Only we have a soul. Whatever the things are that you are referring to, they do not really know God."

Kim stood up, her stature morphing into something formidable. Now it was her turn to play Minister. The other students seemed to sink down into their chairs, fearful of the strange girl who so easily managed to eclipse Grace when she called upon her powers of persuasion. "You're wrong, Grace, once again. They had beliefs. They knew many things, despite their absence in the scriptures of the Church." Kim pointed an accusing finger at the book in Grace's hand. "Their absence just means that the people who wrote what you call the word of God didn't know something. They didn't know a lot of things. That's the fundamental flaw of the Adherents, though: the Church presumes to know it all."

Brian felt that it was a good time to jump in and back up the girl he loved. It was time for Grace to hear some truths, even if speaking those truths got Brian and Kim into serious trouble with their hosts. "That part of the *Final Testament* you asked the questions about, the one about spreading God's words among the stars?"

"What about it?" Grace asked. She was beginning to turn red, an obvious sign of being flustered. She was not used to facing such a hostile audience.

"It was written by the members of the Church Hierarchy who wanted to get people interested in colonizing nearby star systems. At the time, the cities were getting so crowded that the High Councils worried about starvation. Originally, those lines weren't even in the *Final Testament*; they were added later, when the Church leaders wanted something accomplished."

"That's ridiculous!" Grace cried, now rising to her feet. Brian and Kim had gotten to her. "Everyone knows the *Final Testament* has never been altered, not since the day it was written down by the Latter Prophets almost a thousand years ago!"

"How do you know that?" Kim asked. She looked around at the other young students seated around the circle. "How do any of you really know what the Ministers tell you is true?"

"That's enough!" Grace hissed, stomping her foot on the ground. Her left hand gripped her *Final Testament* so hard it looked as if her fingers would break the binding. "I've had enough of your Apostate poison tonight." She looked at the others, and they seemed to read her mind. Everyone got up quickly and quietly headed out of the apartment. Maleek, who had remained silent during the argument, left too, even though it was his apartment.

Grace glared at Brian and Kim for a few moments after the others left, then she regained some composure. "I'll see you in school tomorrow," she said curtly. "Good night."

As she turned and walked out, Brian thought Grace looked hurt, genuinely hurt. Perhaps she thought she had been reaching them the last few weeks. That may have accounted for much of her frustration.

Brian suddenly worried about what he and Kim had just done even though making Grace lose her composure did carry a childish sense of satisfaction. They had once again violated Bill's instructions not to cause any problems, this time in a very direct manner. Perhaps they had put themselves at risk by being so combative. High Minister Andrews may not tolerate such an open display of defiance. In the minutes following the barrage, Brian half-expected Andrews to barge in with a security contingent and haul them away to the holding cell where Fenner was being kept. But, after an hour passed, the apartment remained quiet. Nobody had come to punish them. Grace probably hadn't even told anyone about the exchange. She was loyal to her father but wasn't the kind of person who would tattle in such a petty, vindictive way.

"Do you feel bad about what we did to her?" Kim finally asked.

"Actually, I do," Brian admitted. "She doesn't know any better. It's like she believes that it's her mission to Save us."

"You're right," Kim sighed, standing up and pacing around the room thoughtfully. "I remember those days. Everything seemed simple, like it had a place."

"Were we ever that bad?" Brian asked, even though he already knew the answer to the question.

Kim gave a little laugh, eyeing him critically. "You were way worse, Brian. If anyone would have talked to you like we just talked to Grace, you would have reported them to Minister Petrov!"

"You're right," he admitted after a few moments, lowering his head. It was embarrassing, really; how completely he had devoted himself to the Church. They had owned every part of him, including his soul, if he did indeed have one.

"Dad was right about these people, though," Kim said. "They are different from our time. They're gentle, patient."

"I feel like we're ruining Paradise for them, or something. It's like we're the one dark spot on this perfect little spotless world."

"Don't forget how things got like this, though, Brian," Kim reminded him.

"True. I guess it's easy to be patient with us when we don't present a real threat."

"If they thought for one minute that we could influence anyone, I'm sure we'd be dead," Kim insisted. "Just look how they're going after the colony. Andrews said it himself: they won't tolerate a group of Apostates, even a small group like ours."

Brian found it almost sad that Kim so readily identified herself as an Apostate. Although in the eyes of the Church she may be one, she was also the most spiritual person he had ever known. Kim's belief ran even deeper than Grace's because unlike the High Minister's daughter, Kim had discovered her path on her own.

Confident that there would be no repercussions from their argument with Grace, Brian suggested that Kim head back to the female quarters on the other side of the gardens. Just as she was about to kiss him goodnight, however, the door slid open.

"Grace?"

"Yes," she responded. Her voice was tight with residual anger, but at least now it was controlled.

Kim took the lead. "Listen, Grace, Brian and I are sorry about attacking you like that, it's just—"

Grace held a hand up and stopped Kim in mid-sentence. She sat down on the couch in the center of the apartment and motioned for Kim and Brian to join her. Kim took a seat on the couch while Brian chose the closest chair in the sitting area. A few tense moments passed before Grace spoke.

"When you first arrived," Grace began, "I'll admit that I was pretty frightened of you. I know that sounds ridiculous, but you have to realize the kinds of stories we've been told since childhood."

"Stories?" Brian asked.

"Terrible ones, about the days before the Church took over," Grace clarified. "Of course, now I realize that these are probably embellished ... a lot, but it was difficult to look beyond them when you first joined us."

Brian wasn't familiar with the "stories" Grace was referring to, but judging from her tone, he imagined they were filled with acts of unspeakable barbarity and sickening depravity.

Grace continued. "When my father first told me about you, I expected savages, or something worse, people beyond all measure of restraint and intelligence." She paused, obviously thinking deeply about how to express her feelings. "I knew in the first moments that I met you, though, that my expectations were wrong, very wrong."

"That's good to hear," said Kim, her voice betraying her continued trepidation with the topic of conversation. Grace had a nasty, although unintentional, habit of saying insensitive things to Brian and Kim. It was really naivety more than anything.

Grace forced a weak smile, a gesture that perhaps signaled some embarrassment. Gone was the impenetrable facade of righteousness she normally erected around herself. As she sat in front of him, Brian realized it was the first time she actually seemed like a real person and not just a stilted caricature.

"I was especially nervous after learning that I was to be your guide during your first few months back on Earth. It wasn't because I thought you were savages, though; far from it. Instead I was afraid because it was immediately clear that you had seen and done things which I hadn't, things that I had never even dreamed of." She looked directly at Kim as she spoke. "Maleek's told me a lot about Elysium, of its beauty. It does seem like a gift from God, doesn't it?"

Kim nodded, squinting a little as she probed Grace's eyes.

"But it's not in the *Final Testament*. There's nothing in there, not one word about the planet," Grace said in a bewildered tone. It was like she was just realizing that fact, even though it seemed to Brian like an obvious conclusion.

"And what does that mean to you?" Kim asked her. She was clearly leading Grace toward a conclusion, but seemed careful to let the younger girl find the answer for herself.

Grace thought for a few moments. The room was silent again as Brian watched her intently. She looked to be struggling to find an answer. Finally, she found one: "It means that what I've suspected for a long time is true; the *Final Testament* is merely a path to finding God. It's not meant to be a master source of all knowledge. It's up to us, as Believers, to travel the rest of the way. With God's guidance, of course," she added quickly.

"Then you understand us?" Kim asked.

"I can understand why you have gone astray," she answered. "In your search for the answers, you've left The Path."

Now it was Kim's turn to feel frustrated. She stood up and began pacing around the sitting area.

"Kim, you can find your faith again. I'll help you," Grace insisted. "Then, someday we can return to that planet, together. I do want to see it."

"It won't be that way once the Church takes control of Elysium, Grace!" Kim leaned in to make her point more clear. "You don't realize why Earth is so idyllic. It's because all of the Church's resources come from other places, places far away that you'll never see. It may not matter if some dead moon gets chopped up for minerals, but Elysium will be destroyed. Even if it's not stripped for resources, things will never be the same for us."

"Things will change. They'll be better for you, Kim!"

"Not if your father forces us back to Earth, Grace. I appreciate you trying to understand, but I'm afraid you're never going to. There are things that have happened to us, things we've experienced, that have changed us forever. Your father knows that, and he fears it."

"My father's a good man." Once again, Grace was on the defensive.

"He is doing what he thinks is right," Kim conceded. "But what's right for him isn't right for everyone. It's the same problem we faced back in our time. Those who didn't want to be part of the Church or wanted to better their lives were persecuted. We thought those days were over after living on Elysium for a few years. We thought that distance and time would give us some freedom, but we were wrong. Just a few months ago we experienced the brutality of the Church again, as if we had never left Earth in the first place. We were hunted and people were killed." Kim looked at Brian. "People we loved died."

"My father's already apologized for that. It was an accident, remember?"

"It didn't look like an accident to me. Those soldiers, those things, may have gotten infected by some virus, but that doesn't change the fact that they wanted to remove us, maybe even kill us all. That seemed to be their mission, right from the start. Their getting sick just prevented them from completing it easily." Kim motioned with her hand back toward the wall and out toward the city beyond. "This is not God's work, Grace. None of it is. Your perfect world has come at a price. I'm sorry, but it's all just a mask."

Once again, Grace looked hurt although she didn't argue back. Kim did have a point, but Brian didn't think the High Minister's daughter would simply pull back the veil clouding her perception, intelligent as she was. Andrews and the Church had done their job too well. Grace was a child of the Church, a spiritual warrior for the Adherents. But Kim's words did widen the chink in her armor; an opening just broad enough to let some new ideas filter into her increasingly conflicted mind.

As Grace sat on the couch and attempted to absorb Kim's condemnation of her home, the doors to the living quarters slid open. Brian expected it to be Maleek, returned home after Grace had made her apology, but instead saw that it was Andrews and several security officers. Brian and Grace instantly stood up. Kim stared at Andrews, meeting his stern expression head-on.

"It's late, girls," he stated gruffly as he entered the room. "Well past curfew."

"We were just discussing the evening's Scripture reading," Grace insisted.

Brian supposed it was the first lie she had ever told her father. Maybe he and Kim were having an adverse effect on her behavior, after all.

Andrews seemed to sense lingering tension in the room. He eyed Brian and Kim suspiciously, no longer showing them the jovial face they were accustomed to seeing. "I just thought you two would like to know that I've sent word to our fleet stationed at Mu Arae. They'll be leaving for your colony in about two weeks."

Brian felt the thud in his stomach as an instant knot formed. Kim looked like the news had hit her even worse, as Andrews had no doubt intended.

"Don't look so depressed," the High Minister said, once again adopting his trademark smile. "In a few weeks you'll be seeing your loved ones again, assuming they don't resist our soldiers during the relocation effort."

"You said there wouldn't be violence!" Kim said angrily.

"Oh, I doubt there will be," he said, almost carelessly.

Kim and Brian looked at Grace, who suddenly seemed embarrassed of the man she had so adamantly praised only moments before.

"These two officers will help you back to your quarters, Kim," Andrews said, taking Grace by the arm and motioning for her to following him.

As Grace turned to go with her father, Kim called her name.

"Yes, Kim?"

Kim passed by the two men who now stood on her flanks and placed herself in front of Grace and Andrews. "There's just one more thing I want to tell you."

"It can wait for school, tomorrow," insisted Andrews, pulling on Grace's arm in an attempt to avoid Kim.

Grace didn't resist her father, but as she passed by, Brian noticed that Kim reached up and touched the young girl's face. He couldn't quite hear what she said, but it sounded like "You should see it."

Andrews apparently paid little attention to the exchange, and soon had Grace out in the hallway, away from Brian and Kim. Before she passed out of sight down the hallway, though, Brian saw the look on Grace's face. He recognized it as a look of sheer awe. She had seen it through the eyes of Kim. Somehow, she had visited Elysium in that moment Kim had touched her.

The two officers gently urged Kim toward the door once Grace had left. Kim didn't resist although she turned around one last time to give Brian a kiss. "Don't forget it," she whispered in his ear, before turning away, and at that moment, Brian saw the valley in her eyes.

When Maleek returned home a few minutes later, Brian told him about the High Minister's news, not quite sure how he was going to react. Maleek had managed to make himself into an enigma these past few weeks, impervious to Brian's normally adept perceptions. One minute he was Fenner's ally, intent on destroying the Church. Only days later, though, he had become Grace's disciple, a willing participant in the re-education process. Brian reasoned that it was because Maleek felt lost. This was a feeling Brian was accustomed to, although his lingering anger at Maleek's behavior still prevented him from truly empathizing.

Maleek sat down as he heard the news and stared blankly at the rest of the apartment beyond Brian. "It was only a matter of time before they went to get the others," he said in an emotionless voice.

Brian sat down on the couch and scanned Maleek's face, trying to find a clue that would explain his strange behavior. There was the possibility that the Adherents had done something to Maleek. Perhaps they had even manipulated his mind somehow. But as Brian scanned his face, he realized that such a process would leave few outward traces. It was pointless to even search.

"What are you staring at?" Maleek asked. He seemed annoyed by Brian's sudden attentiveness.

"Nothing. I'm just worried about you."

Maleek broke a smile and stood up. "I'm fine, Brian."

"Really?"

"More than you know."

Maleek's last response surprised Brian. *What didn't he know?* Apparently a lot, since the gleam in Maleek's eye that flashed as he turned to go to bed signaled to Brian a message words could not. Questioning Maleek more would be unwise for the moment, as Brian still suspected that their room was being monitored somehow. If Maleek was indeed concealing something, it was probably safest to keep it hidden for now.

CHAPTER 35

▼

THE CONVERT

Brian sat up violently as a piercing alarm woke him from sleep. His initial response was one of annoyance, although as he began to fully regain consciousness it shifted to concern. Someone was ringing the doorbell over and over again, a signal indicating a possible emergency. When Brian sat up and saw that it was in the middle of the night, his concern only grew.

As Brian rolled out of bed and shuffled through the darkness in a confused haze, he struggled to guess who it may be at the door. If it was Andrews, he probably would have simply let himself in. Kim was the more likely candidate since she couldn't access the door without a valid retinal scan after curfew. It must have been a serious situation for her to risk getting caught out of her quarters. Brian hastened his steps toward the door as the ringing intensified.

Almost a full week had passed since Andrews had told them about the fleet bound for Elysium. Without a realistic plan for doing anything about it, Brian and Kim had resigned themselves to the inevitable sequence of events that would uproot their friends and family. Maleek, for all his apparent secrecy, hadn't seemed overly concerned about things either, despite Brian's brief hope that he had thought up some sort of a plan. In the days following their brief conversation about Maleek's state of mind, nothing new had been revealed, much to Brian's dismay. Bill's lack of action was even more depressing. He had simply visited Brian and Kim after school the day following Andrew's revelation about the fleet. Rather than offering any valid support, he had merely reiterated his earlier directions to behave and do what the High Minister ordered. Everyone around Brian seemed to be set in a predictable sequence of events, which is why the identity of the person at the door surprised him so much.

"Grace?" he asked as he opened the door, not quite sure that his eyes had focused properly to the light of the hallway. He hadn't seen her outside of class during the previous week and assumed that Andrews had become nervous about his daughter getting negatively influenced by her new Apostate friends. The subtle changes Brian and Kim had begun to see in Grace's attitude toward them remained although it was difficult to observe her during class time and she always seemed to have somewhere to go immediately afterward. Maleek was the only one who had spent a substantial amount of time with her recently, but he was characteristically silent about the content of their interactions. Brian had meant to question him about his relationship with Grace, yet hadn't found the appropriate time. Besides, he was sure there wasn't much to tell, certainly not any information that would account for Grace's presence in front of him now.

Rather than answering Brian, Grace quickly brushed past him into the dark sanctuary of the apartment. She looked upset, so Brian left the main lights off.

"Are you here for Maleek?" he asked, still quite bewildered.

"I need to talk to you both," she finally gasped.

Brian looked at her suspiciously as she stood alone and scared in the middle of his quarters. Surely, Andrews would find out she was there, in his apartment.

Grace seemed to read his mind. "Don't worry, Brian. The surveillance system is off now. Maleek showed me how to do it."

So they have been watching us in here, Brian thought. "Won't they know the system is down and come here?"

"Not for a while, but we still need to hurry."

"Hurry?" Now Brian was really confused.

"Yes," Grace confirmed, looking around the apartment nervously. "I need to help you escape."

"What? No way, Grace. How do I know this isn't some kind of trick?"

"It's not," said Maleek, emerging from his room.

Brian looked at his friend, and then back at Grace, still not believing that she was in his apartment relaying such sensitive information. "Tell me what's going on!"

"Last night," Grace began. She seemed to have difficulty coming to grips with what she was saying. "Kim's father and that other man named Hudson were caught trying to steal one of the shuttles docked at the security tower."

"What?" Brian was stunned. He had heard nothing of the incident during the day. No rumors or anything at school, but Grace had seemed a bit on edge during their morning lesson together.

Grace continued, unhindered by Brian's disbelief.

"It's true. They injured two Civil Patrol officers before being apprehended. They're being kept in the holding facility in Central Processing."

"They must have been trying to get back to the colony," Brain said to Maleek in an excited voice. Even though the news of their capture was bad, Brian still felt a tinge of pride for Bill and Hudson. At least they hadn't given up. The only frustrating part was that the two men hadn't felt the need to seek Brian's help. Maybe if they had they wouldn't have been captured. Apparently, Bill had been quite serious when he had told Brian to take care of Kim. Embarking on such a daring task as stealing a shuttle from the Church seemed to carry a low probability of survival. Brian reasoned that Bill and Hudson had been lucky to be taken alive. In his time, they would have been shot on the spot.

"What's your father say about this?" Brian asked.

"That's the bad part," Grace added. She looked like she was on the verge of crying. Despite her normally frail physical appearance, Brian couldn't quite picture her doing so until he actually witnessed it. "He ordered for them to be executed," she said in a whisper.

This was news Brian had been expecting since they had first been captured in the Quarantine Zone several weeks before. Grace may have been shocked that her father was acting so brutally, but Brian understood Andrews. From the High Minister's point of view, he had been more than merciful with his Apostate guests. Bill's and Hudson's actions had merely confirmed that they could not be trusted, much less transformed into loyal Citizens. "Did he tell you this?"

"No, I was supposed to be in bed, but I heard him downstairs talking on his viewscreen. He sounded upset, so I went down to check on him. He's had a pretty quick temper since my mother died. I can usually calm him down, but this time he just seemed to get more upset."

"Is there any chance we can talk to him? Maybe we can convince your dad to spare them if you're on our side," suggested Maleek.

"I don't think that will work."

"Why not?"

"It gets worse," she insisted.

"How?"

"He told me to stay away from you outside of class, for good. He also said that letting you live with us was a mistake and that you're dangerous."

Brian exchanged a worried glance with Maleek. They were both thinking about the colony, about its likely fate. If the Church was no longer interested in converting the Apostates, then Andrews may decide to eliminate them. Brian looked back at Grace, whose expression was even more pained now than when she had initially entered the room. She was taking a huge risk in bringing this information to them, essentially betraying her father. Some of her motivation could probably be attributed to Grace's innate sense of compassion, but much of it hinged on her relationship with Maleek. Brian was sure that Maleek genuinely cared for the girl, but he had also wittingly pursued her as an ally since the day they had met, doing something Brian and Kim could not: influence her. It now appeared like it had been his plan all along.

"We need to get Kim."

"I've already called over to her dorm and told one of the younger students to bring her down to the east gardens. It's Alyssa; she'll do it without asking questions, as long as Kim follows along without asking too many, herself. She should be down there in a few minutes. If we go now, we can reach Central Processing during the fourth shift, when there are the fewest guards."

"Wait, what are you suggesting?" Brian asked.

"We need to get your friends out of the holding cells. They're going to be executed tomorrow night."

"Grace, you need to go back to you house," Maleek suggested. "You've done more than enough."

"That's true, Grace," Brian agreed, realizing that it was foolish for her to accompany them on such a ridiculously dangerous task.

"No, I'm coming. There's no way you can get into the building without my help, and if we do get caught, you'll need me to do the talking."

"And then what? Even if we do free Bill and Hudson, we still have to get a shuttle and somehow escape Earth. It's impossible, Grace."

Rather than argue with Brain, Grace merely pulled out a small datapad from her pocket and handed it to Maleek. He looked over the information, and his serious expression lightened. "It's a layout of the cellblock where they're being held. You stole this from your father's office, didn't you?"

Grace smiled shyly as Maleek bent over and kissed her on the check. She instantly blushed and looked happier than Brian had ever seen her. He felt terrible that she was being manipulated so easily, but reasoned that she was the best chance they had at success. If the colony was in danger, their only chance for saving it may be to rely on her help, naïve as it may be. There simply was no other choice.

"Executed?" Kim cried in a dangerously loud voice a few minutes later when she heard the news about her father. There were several guards who regularly patrolled the Cathedral grounds at night, and although none could currently be seen, Brian feared that every one of them heard her voice.

"Shhh!" He winced and quickly pulled her from the open courtyard under the protective ceiling of the terrace.

"We've gotta do something!" she cried again, this time at a more reasonable level.

"I realize this! Why do you think we're here?"

Kim looked at Grace. Her gaze seemed to deconstruct the young girl's face, looking for any trace of deceit. "What's your plan?"

"Easy," she answered. "We're going to walk right in through the front door."

CHAPTER 36

▼

PENANCE PAID

"I want these two thrown in the holding cells," Grace said commandingly to one of the guards at the front desk of Central Processing.

"What are you doing, Grace?" Kim cried in disbelief. "You said you'd help us!"

"Would you gag this one, Corporal?" asked Grace in an annoyed tone. "She has a tendency to run her mouth. And make sure the other one is secured well; he can be violent."

"What about that one?" the younger of the two guards asked.

Grace looked at Maleek for a moment and seemed to inspect him from head to toe. "He's with me."

The guard nodded and promptly bound Brian's and Kim's hands with restraints.

"I'll buzz Sergeant Gomez and tell him we've got two more prisoners," said the other guard cheerfully.

"Good," Grace said, smiling. "Can you believe these two actually wanted me to help them free the two Apostate prisoners?"

"Really?"

"Yes," Grace confirmed as she laughed at the idea. "As if I would actually betray the Church."

The guard's hand bore down in Brian's skin. Brian could feel the hate as the man spoke. "I was just saying yesterday how you couldn't trust this kind of scum. We should just get rid of the whole lot as soon as possible."

"That may happen sooner than you think," Grace said coldly. "But for now, I want to come down to the cell block with you and check on the other prisoners."

"Isn't it a little late?" the other guard asked.

"I want to ask them some questions about the attempted shuttle hijacking. My father feels that there may have been more to their plot."

"Does your father even know you're down here?"

"Not yet, but I'm sure he'll be happy to know I've uncovered this new plot and put these two in the cell block with the others. I'll also be sure to mention your name, Corporal, what was it?"

"Sanchez."

"Ah, yes, Sanchez. Please take us down to the cell block. It is getting late, after all."

Brian was sure at this point that Grace's plan was ridiculous. During their lengthy walk through the back alleys of the city, he had run over the possible sequence of events many times. Grace may have the ability to talk her way into the cell block area, but actually getting Bill and Hudson out was a different matter. No matter how smoothly the infiltration went, sooner or later, the effort would result in a chaotic fight with the guards, Brian was sure of it. Of course, he didn't have a plan for getting past the security system, or getting the cells open for that matter, but at least Grace had demonstrated her ability to get them into the building.

Brian tried to contain his nervousness as they made their way down the dull gray hall dotted with frequent security cameras and small nodes he suspected may conceal hidden weapon systems. They were taking a huge chance in trusting Grace. She could very well just ask the guard to throw them into the cell and leave them there, for real. She certainly seemed to have pulled off the lie flawlessly up until this point and gave absolutely no indication that she was faking anything. He pushed such possibilities out of his mind though as they walked, aware that there was little he could do about it if they were actually betrayed by the girl.

Grace and Maleek walked behind Brian, Kim and the guard. Grace had been right about the fourth shift; there weren't many people around. Brian remembered being led through the same area the night they had first arrived back on Earth and seeing the multitudes of workers and guards streaming through the corridors. If they were going to try and bypass security, now was the time to do it.

294 THE EYE OF GOD

The holding cells comprised only a small portion of Central Processing's lowest level and were located in the back section of the tower, nearest to the shuttle hangers on the east side of the city. Brian and Kim were escorted down a small set of stairs that led to the main cellblock door and were promptly buzzed in by the guards waiting on the opposite side. Brian instantly noticed the large plasma cannons located on either side of the door, unconcealed, and pointed toward any target the computer system deemed a threat. He tried not to shudder.

"Well, if it isn't Miss Andrews," the guard at the security booth said, obviously trying to gain the favor of the High Minister's daughter. "Welcome to cellblock 11A. The front desk called down and said you needed to see some of the prisoners."

"I do," confirmed Grace. "It will only take a couple of minutes. My father thought that it would be a good lesson for me. He says every Minister should know what the face of evil looks like."

"She also brought in these two," Sanchez added, referring to Brian and Kim.

"Put them in holding cell one," the guard at the security station said gruffly.

Just before Brian was roughly tossed along with Kim headfirst into the cell, he looked to his right and surveyed the long corridor housing the cell blocks. There were only three that had their bluish-colored shields up, although he couldn't actually see into them at this angle. The cells were probably those of Bill, Hudson and Fenner, as it didn't seem like the average Citizen in this day and age would cause enough of a problem to earn such lowly accommodations.

As the force field to their cell activated in front of them, Brian and Kim turned back to watch Grace and Maleek talk to the guard at the security station. Sanchez immediately left the scene for the front desk, leaving two guards: one at the station, and another patrolling further down the cellblock. From his vantage point, Brian could clearly see Maleek and Grace as they talked to the guard at the security station. It was agonizing to watch. He was helpless to do anything from this position. Neither Grace, nor Maleek for that matter, seemed capable of completing the next stage of the plan very easily, and Brian wondered for a moment if he should have been the one who was "with Grace."

"They're right down in those cells," the guard said, referring to Bill and Hudson. "Stay away from that far one, though. That guy's dangerous. He hasn't said too much the last few days though, just sits back and watches us with those eyes of his. Just tell Private LaLonde down there if he gives you any trouble."

"Thank you, Sergeant," Grace said politely. She began to descend the small set of stairs down from the security station, when she stopped. "Oh, Sergeant?"

"Yes, ma'am?"

"Could you do me a favor and enter my friend's bio signature into the security matrix? Those plasma cannons keep tracking him, and it's making me kind of nervous."

The guard thought about Grace's request for a moment. "I'm not really authorized ..." he began awkwardly.

"Please? My father's already given Maleek security clearance to pretty much every sector in the city. It's amazing how far he's come in just a few weeks." Grace put her arm on Maleek's back and patted it several times. "He's going to make quite the useful Citizen, especially considering his skills with computers. Quite the genius. We're blessed to have him with us now despite his former taste in friends."

The guard still seemed torn, but after a few more moments he relented and began punching in the needed sequence to add Maleek into the system. "This will only take a few seconds," the man insisted, hovering over the controls to the scanner.

Brian and Kim watched nervously as Grace slid her way back up the steps and behind the guard's right shoulder. She visibly, yet quietly, fumbled around in her pockets for a few seconds before brandishing the small, metal rod that held a powerful medical sedative she had confiscated from the infirmary earlier in the afternoon.

"Stay still," the guard told Maleek.

Grace put the sedative behind her back as she and Maleek waited for the signal from the guard. It was almost too much for Brian to watch as the seconds passed by in silence.

"There we go, you're in there," the guard said, backing away from the console.

Grace hesitated a second too long and missed her chance. She now stood motionless in front of the guard with the metal rod extended in his direction.

"What are you doing?" asked the man in total surprise. He was so shocked that he didn't even reach for Grace's arm. He simply stared at her in disbelief.

Maleek was quick to improvise, however. He lunged at the guard from the side and smoothly removed the man's pistol from its holster. This time the guard did respond to his attacker, and flung himself at Maleek.

"Shoot him!" Brian and Kim found themselves yelling as Maleek jumped back against the wall. He did as they asked, although more out of instinct than anything else, shooting the man right in the chest.

Grace's piercing scream accompanied the holocaust. Brian realized later on that it was probably the first time she had ever seen someone die violently, much less killed by the boy she loved. "No, Maleek!" she finally articulated, as if he had a choice in his actions.

No sooner had Maleek pushed the guard's body off of him than the other one opened fire from the far end of the cell block. Brian and Kim saw the bolts of energy fly past their cell and transform the security station into a sea of fire and flying sparks. Above all of the chaos, Grace could still be heard screaming until Maleek grabbed her and threw her down behind the relative safety of the computer console at the front of the circular security station.

The guard shot several more times, but immediately stopped his advance as Maleek fired back over the top of the console. As a stalemate ensued, Brian heard the guard call for backup on his com-link.

"Seal the security doors, Maleek!" Kim yelled, trying to make herself heard over the gunfire.

Maleek was one step ahead of her though, and several seconds later, the automated plasma guns came alive and decimated the helpless guard at the other end of the cellblock. Unfortunately, there was little time for congratulations.

"Now, open the cell blocks!" Kim ordered again, frantically pushing herself against the security shield.

"I can't get into that end of the system," Maleek yelled down a few seconds later. "It's stuck on the turret menu. I can't get it off without an access code!"

"Come down and see if you can hack the shield," Brian suggested.

Maleek vaulted over the console and began to inspect the cell's force field. Grace remained at the security station, however, obviously in shock over what she had just witnessed. As Brian saw her, he knew that she was having second thoughts about helping them out. Whatever strain of teenage rebelliousness she had been attempting to work out was now being overtaken by a tremendous deluge of regret. Breaking her friends out of captivity was bad enough, but now she had become an accessory to murder. Brian reasoned that she must be feeling similar to the way he had on the bridge of the *Apostle 4* six years earlier.

"The controls aren't responding down here, either," Maleek said in a frustrated tone.

"Forget it, just blast it!" Kim yelled, backing away from the shield.

Maleek turned his face away and followed her uncharacteristically forceful suggestion, shooting the control panel with the pistol. The panel exploded in a shower of sparks, and the shield flickered momentarily before dropping.

"Is that an alarm?" Brian asked Grace, referring to the faint droning sound that now seemed to be coming from outside the building.

Grace didn't respond. She merely stared at the body of the dead guard and sobbed.

"Grace!" Kim yelled, which seemed to grab the girl's attention. "Is that an alarm we hear?"

"Y-yes," Grace confirmed. "They know what we've done."

"Why don't you come down here with us," Kim suggested. "I don't want you near that door if they try to come through."

"Can you reprogram those guns to shoot at anything that comes through the doors?" Brian asked Maleek.

"I can try."

"Do it. It may buy us a couple of minutes."

As Maleek ran back up into the security booth, Grace backed away from him. He didn't try to approach her any closer although his eyes seemed to ask for her forgiveness.

"Grace!" Kim yelled again, as she made her way down to the other cells. Grace listened to her commanding tone, apparently more comfortable with following somebody who was upfront about her intentions.

The heavy forcefields over Bill's and Hudson's cells dampened their voices so much that Kim had to almost press her face against them to make her directions clear. They got the message, though, and immediately backed away from the shields as Brian retrieved the other guard's pistol and blasted the control panels. It was a crude, yet effective, solution to the problem of breaking them out, just as Brian had figured. He remembered an old lesson from Chang, the one that taught that the simplest solution is usually the best. If only getting out of the building was as simple as lowering the force fields had been.

"You two shouldn't have done this!" Bill scolded as soon as he was free. Kim ignored his condemnation and quickly threw her arms around her father. Despite the angry tone, Brian could tell Bill was glad to see her.

"How did you get in here?" Hudson asked.

"Grace helped us," Brian answered, nodding at the girl.

"Thank you," Bill said, bowing his head to Grace.

"You're welcome," Grace said. Her voice sounded a bit stronger now. Brian hoped that seeing Kim and Bill reunited may persuade Grace that she had done the right thing, at least for long enough to help them get out of there.

"They're outside the door!" Maleek yelled, once again jumping down from the security station and joining them.

"Is there a way out?" Kim asked.

"I saw a small maintenance shaft near Fenner's cell when we came in," noted Hudson. "It might go all the way out toward the hanger."

The mention of Fenner's name hushed everyone for a moment as they seemed to ponder whether or not to free the High Councilor from his cell. Fenner could, after all, be a great ally to have in a firefight. The only question was whether or not he would act like an ally if they let him out.

A loud thud on the cell block door made everyone forget about Fenner as they struggled to find the hatch Hudson was talking about.

"Got it," Bill said, calling everyone's attention to a waist-high metal grate that covered a shaft in the wall.

The piecing sound of drills could now be heard outside the door as an army of guards prepared to breach the cell block. Just as Bill pulled the grating away, the doors opened and the twin plasma cannons came alive. From where he was standing, Brian couldn't see the guards who had broken through the door, but he could hear the seemingly endless barrage let loose from the cannons and imagined the carnage that was unfolding. He doubted any of them had expected to be greeted by such a deadly surprise and almost felt guilty about being involved in such a brutal slaughter.

A few random shots made their way through the breech before the plasma cannons fell silent. For the moment, there were no targets left alive to shoot at.

"We need to move," Bill said, peeking his head into the darkened shaft leading away from the cell blocks. "Everyone inside the hole."

Maleek pulled out a small light from his pocket and went in head first, with Grace not far behind. It may have been safer for her to stay behind and wait to be apprehended, but there was the chance that the troops who finally got into the cell block would shoot anything that moved, regardless of who it was. Kim got into the shaft behind Grace.

"Should we get Fenner?" Brian asked Bill as he bent down.

Bill looked at him, then at Hudson.

"It's a risk, but ..."

Hudson was cut off by the sudden and total darkness that enveloped the room. It took a moment to get over the surprise, but everyone soon realized what had been done.

"They cut the power!"

"Maleek, toss back that other pistol!" Brian yelled into the shaft.

There was virtually no place to hide in the relatively narrow corridor between the two rows of facing cells, although several large support columns stuck out from the walls just enough to provide a minimal amount of cover from whatever came through the now defenseless door. Brian took the pistol from Maleek and quickly felt his way through the dark to the opposite wall.

"Brian, give Hudson that pistol and get into the shaft," Bill commanded through the blackness.

Brian could just see the outline of Bill's body thanks to an extremely dim red light filtering down from an emergency sign at the other end of the cellblock, but he couldn't quite see Hudson, who had taken cover behind the next closest support column to the door. He stepped out from the wall slightly and tried to make his eyes focus as quickly as possible.

"Can you see me?" Brian asked Hudson in a barely audible whisper.

"Yes, throw me the pistol, Brian."

No sooner had Brian let the weapon fly than an intense barrage of blue bolts shot through the air and almost ripped his hand off. Bill returned fire, with Hudson joining in a couple of seconds later.

"Go, Brian!" Bill yelled.

Brian took the cue and held his breath as he vaulted across the death-filled space between him and the maintenance shaft opening. Kim was right there to greet him.

"Let's go," said Brian. "They'll be right behind us, but we've got to get moving!"

Kim still seemed reluctant to leave her father fighting in the cellblock, but she moved as Brian asked. The shaft was too short for them to fully stand up in, so they settled on a crouching run. The sound of gunfire lessened more and more as they made their way toward the hanger area a few hundred meters away, and Brian soon began to fear that Bill and Hudson were going to hold their ground until they died rather than climb into the maintenance shaft.

"How much further do we have to go, Maleek?" Brian asked, knowing that there was no way his friend knew the answer with any certainty. Rather than receiving an answer, Brian was greeted by the blunt force of one of Kim's bony shoulders square in his face as the three people in front of him came to an abrupt halt. "What's wrong?"

"It stops. Shit, it doesn't go all the way through!" Maleek yelled, slamming his fist on the web of piping that blocked their way to the outside. Brian felt a sudden case of claustrophobia set in as his mind processed what a small, cramped space they had wedged themselves into while moving so quickly in the darkness. Whereas the shaft was large enough to permit easy travel in the beginning, in the last several meters it had shrank down to about half its original size.

"Back up!" Maleek ordered, sounding as if he felt the same sense of panic that Brian did. Now that they had been stopped for a few seconds, the space they were in felt like a hot, sweaty coffin.

Brian realized that Bill and Hudson still weren't behind them although the sound of gunfire was still raging back in the cellblock. He turned and scrambled back the way they had come, unsure as to what he was going to do now that their only obvious route of escape was blocked. As Brian neared the mouth of the shaft, however, he began to slow. His eyes were starting to adjust well to the darkness and he could make out almost every grisly detail in the scene. Through the metallic frame of the opening, he could see Hudson firing at the oncoming guards, illuminated by an almost constant barrage of gunfire. At his feet was Bill, laying horizontally and lifeless.

"Dad!" Kim screamed, clawing past Brian toward the opening. He caught her just before she exited the shaft and pressed her down on the floor to prevent her from going any further. Brian found it almost impossible to keep her immobile, especially since he felt sick to his stomach at seeing Bill laying there on the floor.

The fighting died down again as the guards apparently pulled back from the doorway and security station. "Stay down," Brian yelled in Kim's ears as he finally let her up to check on her father.

Bill was still alive but it looked like he would draw his last breath at any moment. Hudson took advantage of the brief lull in the attack and pulled Kim closely to the wall as she cradled her father's head in her lap. Brian exited the shaft and stood up to his full height, careful not to look directly at the scene in front of him. Seeing Bill dying was bad enough, but knowing that his father had probably died in the same way made the situation unbearable. Brian struggled to keep himself from breaking down as he searched the ground for the pistol Bill must have dropped when he had been hit.

"What do we do now?" Maleek asked. His voice was scared as he stood in front of the shaft where Grace still hid, shaking and terrified.

"I don't know. I don't know, damn it!" Hudson yelled. "There's nowhere to go!"

Brian knew at that point that he had to find the pistol and attempt to surrender along with Hudson. They would surely be killed for their crimes, along with Maleek, but perhaps he or Grace could persuade Andrews to let Kim live, if that's what she even wanted. Looking at her now crying over her dying father, with all hope slipping away, Brian thought she may invite a swift death along with those she loved.

But death didn't come through the doors to the cellblock. Instead, Brian and his comrades were blinded as the main lights were turned back on to their highest level. A booming voice accompanied the lights over an intercom system; it was Andrews.

"Please put down your weapons," he said in a calm yet strained voice. "You won't be harmed."

"We know about your plan, Andrews. Why don't you just kill us and get it over with!" Brian yelled into the air, not quite sure where to direct his defiance.

There was a long silence. Then, as if called down from the heavens themselves, Andrews emerged from the doorway, clad in white robes with his hands out-stretched.

"Please, I don't want my daughter to get hurt," he said in the most sincere voice Brian had ever heard from his lips. "I'm willing to make a deal at this point."

Brian was just about to ask him about the terms of this deal when Grace jumped out from the shaft and ran toward her father. Even if Brian had wanted to stop her, which he didn't, she was too fast. She had suffered enough for helping them and deserved to get out of the cellblock before things got any worse. Just as she was about to reach her father, however, a black shadow darted out from one of the cells and enveloped the girl. It was Fenner.

"No!" Andrews screamed, running toward the High Councilor.

"Not so fast," Fenner said slowly, his voice oozing with its characteristic menace. "One more step and I'll empty this little darling's skull of all its contents."

Brian could see that Fenner had the other pistol, and it was pointed right at Grace's head. Even though Brian had seen a multitude of terrible things in his life, this scene, perhaps, was the most grotesque. Once again Fenner had come to the rescue; he now held the most valuable asset in any sort of deal that was going to be struck with Andrews, and yet, he had somehow managed to cheapen their lives by resorting to such a despicable tactic. Grace had risked everything to help them escape, even if that escape had failed, but now she would play another role, that of an unwilling hostage.

Andrews' knees visibly weakened as he took an involuntary step toward his captive daughter.

"Not another step, I said," Fenner reiterated, tightening his grip on Grace.

"P-Please, let her go," Andrews sputtered. "I'll do anything you want."

Brain saw the High Minister throw up a shaking hand and wave the guards off who had begun to filter in quietly through the door.

"I'm glad to hear that," Fenner said as he closed the gap between himself and Andrews. "Positively delighted."

CHAPTER 37

▼

SACRIFICIAL LAMBS

The second worst thing Brian ever had to do was forcibly tear Kim away from her dead father. There was no other choice, though; they couldn't keep up with Fenner while dragging Bill's body along. Whether or not Fenner was crazy at this point was unclear, but Brian believed they were lucky that the High Councilor wasn't holding a grudge. Maybe it was because Fenner still believed that like Grace and Andrews, Brian, Kim and Maleek had a use, even if this use wasn't yet clear to them. Perhaps he even felt some sick sense of paternalism now that Bill was dead. Regardless of his reasons, though, Fenner had taken them along with his hostages to a ship sitting in Central Processing's main hanger. The ship was part of the deal he had made for the High Minister's life. Fenner promised that he would release Grace and her father if he was provided with a military-grade ship equipped with a subspace drive. In the world that Brian had once lived in, the Church never would have bargained, not even for a High Minister; but in this era, the leadership didn't seem very accustomed to dealing with terrorist demands. Fenner had gotten his ship almost as soon as he had asked for it but gave no timetable for the release of his two prisoners.

As they entered space, Brian expected to be attacked at any moment by cloaked fighters or attack ships. Apart from a worried transmission from the commander of the New Jerusalem Civil Patrol, however, there was no welcoming committee besides an endless sea of stars. Fenner insisted that he would let his hostages go in an escape pod before engaging the subspace drive, but Brian knew he was lying as soon as he made the promise. Once they made it back to Elysium, they would need something to bargain with since they stood little chance of fending off an attack. Grace and Andrews would serve their purpose again when the time came. Kim, the only person onboard the ship who would have openly condemned Fenner's actions, remained relatively quiet in the days following their harrowing departure from Earth, a predictable behavior considering the loss of her father. Brian tried to comfort her although it was clear that there were other pressing concerns weighing on her mind, like what to do once they arrived back at Elysium and found it under siege by more of those terrible killing machines called Adherent soldiers.

Brian worried too. He worried for the three colonists they had been forced to leave back on Earth and whether they would be punished for the actions of others. He worried for the safety of his friends and family on Elysium. He even worried for Grace and her father. But, most of all Brian worried about Kim. She had always been the one who had been able to maintain her balance, even under the worst circumstances. Now, though, she seemed distant, just like she had prior to the initial Adherent attack many months before. Brian feared that if she gave up and surrendered herself to apathy, then he too would lose his will to keep going. Fenner may be ruthless, but at least he had given them a second chance to see their home again. Even if they died defending Elysium, Brian could see himself happy if the end came while he stood on its heavenly surface.

Fenner had chosen his escape ship well; it was a fast prototype model, the best Andrews could get him. With the right subspace coordinates entered, the trip back home would take just over a week according to the ship's computer. Hopefully they would arrive at least a day or two prior to the taskforce, even though there was no way to be for sure. Andrews himself only had a rough idea of when his orders would be carried out and insisted that the cyborg-like soldiers that patrolled the outreaches of Adherent space acted with a great deal of autonomy, thanks to the sentient "brain" controlling each ship. Although the High Minister visibly chaffed at Fenner's bullying, he obviously still felt that assisting the High Councilor with minor things, like the basic operation of the ship, would keep him in favor and his daughter safe. Fenner didn't show much thanks for the help, though. At all moments he seemed to be there, hovering over his two hostages with a pistol. Brian wondered if he even slept during the first few days of the trip home. Hudson offered many times to take over guard duty, but every time Brian witnessed him asking, Fenner dismissed the idea and seemed to become agitated. It was clear he still didn't trust his fellow colonists completely; or maybe it was just because Fenner knew they didn't have the stomach to point a gun in some-one's face for hours on end.

The ship itself was much friendlier to normal humans than the one they had taken from Elysium to Earth, and required only a minimal amount of crew work. This was a good thing considering the tiny size of the crew. Brian filled his time by either talking to Kim or waiting on Fenner, who had become even more demanding now that those around him needed his help. Brian and the High Councilor never discussed the fight or the injury Brian had bestowed upon him, but the looks Fenner sometimes gave indicated that he strangely approved of the decisive behavior Brian had shown in the altercation. Fenner respected traits like power and decisiveness; perhaps he saw a place for Brian at his side someday after all.

On the fifth day of the trip Fenner finally decided to rest. Without a word, he forced Grace and her father into the common area where Brian and Kim were sit-ting and walked away toward the small sleeping area near engineering. Apart from a few words of encouragement, neither Brian nor Kim had said much to the hostages since leaving Earth space. There was an intense feeling of embarrassment present any time they saw Grace and Andrews, especially since Brian knew that the hostage situation was necessary, albeit distasteful. Maleek had been the only one who had openly tried to talk to Grace at length, although she had made it quite clear that his presence was not wanted in any form. Regardless, Maleek had catered to their every need, as if keeping them comfortable would magically atone for the turmoil they were being put through. Fenner didn't seem to mind Maleek's favorable treatment of the hostages too much even though he readily mocked the effort.

A long bout of silence passed once Grace and her father entered the room and sat down in the middle of the floor. The High Minister looked tired, but confi-dent, while Grace looked like a wounded animal hiding behind a stronger mem-ber of the herd. Maleek would have tried to spark a conversation, even if it was of the mundane variety, but he was currently on the bridge, checking the ship's power regulation. The swirling blue storm of subspace dominated the rather large viewport adorning the common area and lit the otherwise dark space with an ethereal light. Brian focused on the beautiful sight outside, trying to forget that he and Kim had been joined by two unwanted guests. She looked to be doing the same, sitting in a chair nearby with her legs gathered up tightly beneath her arms.

"Beautiful, isn't it?" Andrews suddenly asked.

"What?" Brian responded, surprised at the question.

"Subspace. You're watching it."

"Yeah, I guess," Brian answered nervously, partly confused by Andrews' laid back tone.

"You know, less than a hundred years ago many of our greatest scientists said that faster than light travel was impossible. When the breakthrough was finally made, though, we greeted the discovery like the gift from God that it was."

Brian looked at the High Minister, and his body stiffened. Andrews was getting at something, perhaps trying to influence him.

"The discovery finally allowed us to begin exploring the stars in a practical way, in order to find planets like the one you call home," Andrews continued. "Now it's just a matter of knowing where to look first. It takes time to expand, decades, even centuries, but sooner or later we will fan out through the galaxy to every habitable system. Like the Scriptures say, it's inevitable."

Brian looked over at Kim and saw that she was listening as well, suspiciously. "Get to it, Andrews," she said flatly, "I know you're trying to make a point."

Andrews gave his characteristic laugh, the one Brian hadn't seen since he and his daughter had been taken hostage by Fenner. "I'm just pointing out that you gain nothing by trying to fight us. We want peace, just like you do. Your colony, Elysium, will only prosper as part of the Church. It will grow and develop as other colonists start to arrive. Someday it may even become as beautiful as Earth. That's my hope for all the new planets we come across."

"But what if we don't want the Church? What if there are others out there who want you even less? Are you going to conquer them too?" Brian asked.

Andrews dropped his cool demeanor slightly as his attempt at persuasion bounced ineffectively off his target audience. "Conquer? That's hardly the word I would use. You were treated very well when you arrived back on Earth even though you were captured while trying attack us."

"That's not true!" Kim spat. "Fenner wanted to attack, but we stopped him."

"She's right," seconded Brian. "We stopped him from launching the missiles."

"Why? If you didn't intend to attack Earth, then why were you with him in the first place?"

Brian thought about Andrews' question for a moment, but Kim beat him to the answer. "We expected Earth to be something different than it was."

"What do you mean?"

Kim seemed to think for a bit before answering. "We expected something like the world we left, only worse."

"And what did you find?" Andrews asked, obviously leading her.

"Something different."

"Proving that your perception was flawed. If you just listened to our message—" Andrews began before Kim cut him off. At this point she had left her chair and was now standing over Andrews and Grace.

"Flawed? Are you kidding? Our fears turned out to be true. You are a threat. Those ... those things that attacked our home may not actually have come from Earth, but you are responsible for their actions. If they're your emissaries to the stars, then you can expect whomever or whatever you come across to fight your message like we did."

Andrews seemed disarmed by having his argument backfire so explosively. He shrank slightly as Kim continued her verbal assault. "If you think that we're going to stand by and watch you turn Elysium into a new base for your troops, you're wrong. I promise that not one of them will step foot on that planet!"

"Even now you're hatred blinds you to God's plan," Andrews said, trying another tactic. "Your choice to fight is ignorant of what we've been trying to accomplish for centuries. When your people are gone, humanity will once again experience the harmony it deserves."

"If fighting is the only alternative to the Church's plan, then I happily make that choice. And if you think getting rid of us will make things perfect, then you're wrong again."

"And why is that?"

"Because people need a choice; otherwise their faith, their entire existence, is meaningless. Just look at your daughter."

Andrews looked confused as he turned his gaze from Kim to the girl behind him. Kim was more than willing to elaborate. "Grace has always been the ideal student of your religion. She's intelligent, thoughtful and totally obedient, that is, until the minute she is given a choice, an alternative to what you've raised her with. It may seem pointless now that she's here against her will, but we never would have been able to escape if it hadn't been for her help."

Andrews looked angered by Kim's suggestion. "She was confused by your lies. You tricked her."

"We just helped her to see the truth. You have done an excellent job of raising her as a child of God, maybe too well. Because buried beneath all of the dogma and extremism, there is still a message of compassion waiting to be embraced by those who are looking for it. Grace minded her studies well and found that message. She also saw that you were violating it by trying to exterminate us."

Andrews suddenly stood up, and for a moment Brian thought that he might try to strike Kim in anger even though doing so may get him killed. "You Apostates are a poison," he hissed, echoing his daughter's words from a week before.

Rather than back down from his rage, Kim stepped forward and closed the remaining meter of space. "I'll make sure that you and Grace remain safe from Fenner," she said quietly, yet firmly. "But just remember that there are other forces in this universe, ones that can't be controlled. Now get out of here and go to your quarters. I'm tired of talking to you."

Brian, like Andrews, was shocked to hear Kim speak in such a cold, threatening way. It felt good, though. To show his support, he got out of his chair and stood next to her, but reasoned that nothing he could say would add to the power of her demand.

"Grace may stay if she likes," Kim added as Andrews took his daughter by the hand and left the room. It was a ridiculous statement; Grace would never defy her father while he was standing there, but Kim's gesture of kindness did earn one last look from the girl as she followed her father out of the room.

Once Andrews and Grace had been gone for a few seconds, Kim walked over to the viewport and stared outward. Brian thought she looked drained, as if the power she had summoned during the argument was leaving her.

"Are you okay?" he asked.

There was another long silence.

Kim finally answered him with a question. "Do you believe in God, Brian?"

He didn't know how to answer her. Surprisingly, she had never asked him.

Kim clearly sensed his turmoil and turned around. The warmness had returned to her face, and she smiled as she spoke: "It's fine if you don't; I still love you."

"No, no, that's not it," Brian stammered, trying to put emotions into words. "Back a few months ago, when I took Maleek and the others out to find Luke ..."

"At Lake Clarity?"

"Yeah. Well, when I thought we were going to die I wished there was one. I mean, I hope there is one."

"But, you're not sure," Kim finished for him.

"I don't know what to believe anymore," Brian confessed. "We've been lied to so much over the years, it's hard to believe anything I don't see."

"I understand," Kim said, walking up and hugging him around the mid section.

"But I feel, I *know* that we're doing the right thing," Brian added. "I know that Elysium is worth protecting. Maybe my conscience is God, or something. Do you think that's crazy?"

"No."

"Good."

Brian stood there holding Kim in the shimmering darkness of the ship, thinking about God, about life, and everything else they faced at the end of their journey. He still felt somewhat inadequate for not being able to formulate a concrete response to Kim's question, but this feeling began to ease the longer her arms stayed around him. If death awaited them on the other side of subspace, he may have to once again confront his feelings about God, but for now Kim's faith was enough for the both of them.

CHAPTER 38

▼

THE PROMISED LAND

"We're too late!" Brian exclaimed as they exited subspace and saw the long black shapes set against the backdrop of Elysium. He felt a terrible surge of grief rise up and force out any ember of hope still flickering in his body. They had failed; the Adherents had already taken the planet and would soon capture them as well.

"No, wait a second," Maleek said in a voice that buoyed Brian's spirits. "Those aren't Adherent ships; they're the colony transports!"

"What?" asked Fenner as he pushed his way up past Andrews and Grace.

Brian fought back his disbelief as his eyes tried to focus on the ships. Maleek was right; the colony transports were orbiting the planet. The strange thing about the scene was that Ares, too, looked like it was closer to the planet, as if it were following the transports that had broken free of its grip. It didn't make sense, and Brian wondered for a moment is his eyes were deceiving him.

"Contact the colony," Fenner ordered.

"New Haven, this is Maleek Williams. New Haven, come in," Maleek repeated over the com system as they entered orbit around Elysium. The static greeting his response was normal considering the fact that nobody in the colony was expecting a communication, but it heightened the atmosphere of tension smothering the bridge of the Adherent ship. The blue-green gem below looked to be untouched although there was no way to tell if the Adherent task force had already come and gone.

"Keep trying," Hudson suggested. "It may take a few minutes for anyone to pick up the message."

As he looked around the bridge, Brian wondered how they would be greeted upon arriving home. Rachel would be devastated over the loss of her husband, as would the other families whose loved ones died on the mission to Earth. Of course, his mother and sister would be relieved at seeing him under any circumstances, but the colony as a whole would soon receive the news that they were in even greater danger than before. Fenner had left with the promise of ending the Adherent threat forever and now returned with bad news: only two hostages, and less than a quarter of his initial crew. Where the blame would fall for such a mess was still unclear, but it was likely that Fenner would argue that others were involved in subverting the original plans, namely, Brian and Kim.

"You better pray that nothing's happened," Fenner muttered under his breath to Grace and Andrews, who stood in front of him nervously. Both looked concerned although Brian thought that underneath her fear, Grace was marveling at the exotic world sprawled out in front of her. He wondered if it lived up to the images Maleek, and especially Kim, had conveyed.

"Maleek, this is New Haven, we've got you on our sensors. Good to have you home," a steady, male voice suddenly came through on the com. "You're here just in time."

"Why is that?" Maleek asked.

There was another short pause. "Hold your current position. We'll send a shuttle up to meet you."

"New Haven, be advised: we are piloting a different Adherent ship than before," Maleek added.

"Understood," the voice said before abruptly being cut off.

Everyone on the bridge seemed confused, especially Fenner. The man on the radio sounded preoccupied, as if he had other concerns that were somehow more important than their return home. As Brian looked out again at the ships and the red moon beyond, he knew that something was wrong, something other than the Adherents.

Less than an hour later a shuttle arrived and docked with their ship. When the airlock doors opened, Brian was greeted by his smiling mother, Minister Chang, Councilor Raasch and Dr. Liniel, a planetary scientist who now served on the Colonial Council. Brian felt overjoyed as he embraced his mother, but the feeling quickly diminished as Jill Bishop made eye contact with Kim and realized that something had happened. "Where's your father, honey?" she asked in a shaky voice.

Kim didn't answer verbally but the tears in her eyes betrayed what had happened. Jill hugged her and fought back tears of her own. Chang, who looked much healthier than when Brian had left, placed a hand on Kim's shoulder and seemed to draw out some of the pain she was feeling, if that was even possible.

Never one to let human tragedy interfere with his schedule, Fenner took it upon himself to quickly break up the reunion and herd the new arrivals into the ship's common area. Before they even had a chance to sit down and hear the story behind the trip to Earth, the High Councilor began to interrogate them. "What's going on here? Why are you prepping colony ships for launch?"

Jill and the others looked at each other as if they were unsure as to how to answer Fenner's question.

"Because we may have to leave this planet very soon," answered Liniel. "At least for a time."

"What?"

"It's Ares," said Jill, still trying to comfort Kim by rubbing her back. "It's stopped in orbit over the colony.

"What?" Fenner asked in a skeptical tone.

"This kind of behavior is unprecedented," explained Liniel. "I've never seen anything like it. If the moon emitted a normal gravitational field for its size it would be ripping apart the planet as we speak."

"How is this possible?" asked Maleek.

"We don't know," confessed Liniel. "After six years we still haven't been able to determine the complete physical structure of the moon. It's possible there's some sort of exotic material on or under the surface that's causing this behavior."

"What's the worst case scenario?" Hudson asked.

"Worst case? It smashes into Elysium, and destroys the entire planet, although I find that scenario highly unlikely. For all we know, the moon does this periodically for whatever reason. Some more realistic short term consequences, however, are severe weather patterns and flooding. We've already seen some massive tide surges along the coast in recent days, indicating that the moon's gravitational forces seem to be growing."

"And you're willing to evacuate the entire colony based on this phenomenon?" Fenner asked.

"It's just a precaution, should the need arise," noted Raasch. "We need to be prepared."

"Well, I hate to ruin your plans, but we've got much larger problems than gravitational fluctuations," Fenner said sarcastically. "An Adherent fleet's going to arrive soon to attack the colony."

"What?" Jill said, rising to her feet. "What did you do, Fenner! Tell us what happened when you got to Earth!"

Fenner just smiled and sat back in his chair. "Don't look at me, Jill. Ask your son what happened since he's the one who has gotten to know our Adherent friends so well."

Brian took a deep breath and proceeded to tell his mother, Chang and Raasch the story of what happened once they reached Earth. He told them about the fight in orbit, the crash, Andrews, Grace, re-education, the escape, everything. Maleek added his own input several times, but for the most part, Brian took the responsibility for relaying what had happened.

"So you ordered the fleet to come here," Jill said to Andrews once Brian had finished telling the story. "To destroy the colony."

"I did," Andrews said calmly as he stood next to Fenner and Grace. "You don't really think I had a choice, do you?"

"I don't know, did you?" Jill asked in an annoyed tone. "Do you receive orders or simply make them?"

"I'm a Minister. I do what's best for the Church," he answered.

"Is there any way we can bargain with those who are commanding the fleet?" asked Chang.

"I don't know, but you'd be best served by surrendering quickly and being rewarded by a swift, painless death."

Fenner laughed at Andrews' comment as he viciously pushed the man to the floor from behind. "You should be so lucky, Andrews," he sneered.

"Fenner!" Jill scolded, taking Andrews by the arm and helping his to his feet. "Regardless of what Fenner says, you'll be safe while you're here. So will your daughter. Even if we wanted to kill you, which we don't, you're only useful to us alive."

"That's comforting," Andrews said smugly.

"I don't know who or what you think we represent, Minister, but we just want to live in peace," insisted Jill.

"You had your chance hundreds of years ago, when you were still Citizens," said Andrews. "Just accept that the only way to gain peace is to surrender."

"And die?"

Andrews simply nodded in affirmation. "You can't hope to win. I've been assured that there are almost a dozen attack ships in the taskforce coming to this planet and several other smaller vessels. Once our troops arrive, they won't hesitate to track you down and kill you all. I can do little to stop them. The assault will most likely occur from orbit, where you'll be unable to resist."

"Then you'll continue to be a hostage," Jill said in a tone that only partially masked her anger. "Fenner, we'll take the Minister and Grace down to the planet until the Adherents arrive. I don't want our most valuable assets to be on this ship. It'll be the first thing they attack."

"Ha! Nice try, doctor, but I think they're perfectly safe here. You just don't want them to be under my watch, do you?" Fenner observed slyly. "What's the matter, think I'll kill them just for fun?"

"Perhaps."

"That's a chance you'll just have to take because I'm not leaving this ship, and they're not leaving my sight."

"That's not your decision to make," Chang said angrily, pointing a shaky finger at Fenner. Brian had never seen the old man so upset.

Fenner looked unphased, as always. His smile merely broadened. "And who is going to stop me? You? I'm sick of having my actions monitored by idiots and weaklings. We don't have the luxury of playing nice any longer. I'm going to do what I think is right!" At this point, Brian noticed that Fenner was waving his pistol around carelessly, as if flaunting his leverage. His mother seemed to be watching the weapon as well, no doubt wondering how stable Fenner really was at this point.

"I see that you're unwilling to compromise, as always," she finally relented. "You may stay here on the ship for now, but we'll be back soon with a proper crew."

"You do that, Doctor, and feel free to take the others with you. I don't need them anymore."

Brian wasn't hurt by Fenner's words, but they did make him angry. The High Councilor may have gotten them off of Earth in one piece, but he still bore the blame for getting them into trouble with the Church in the first place. Brian reminded himself that it was Fenner who insisted that they attack Earth, even when he knew that such an act would serve no purpose other than petty revenge. *Damn him*, Brian thought, taking his place by his mother's side with Kim and Maleek.

Following Fenner's arrogant dismissal, Jill and the others quickly returned to the airlock leading to the shuttle. As Brian, his mother and Kim proceeded to board behind the others, however, Kim stopped.

"What is it, Kim?" asked Brian's mother. "Did you forget something?"

"I'm staying. I can't leave Grace here, not alone with Fenner," she said in a voice that was already gaining strength despite recent tears.

Brian had expected this reaction from Kim and had already made the decision to stay with her if she refused to leave. "She's right," he said, looking into his mother's pained eyes.

"You don't have to do this. Hudson and Maleek have agreed to stay here and watch Fenner, and there will be others coming up soon. You've done enough. And besides, I don't think Fenner will let you stay," Jill pleaded.

"He will," answered Kim quickly. "We've been on this ship for a week and know the layout and the primary systems. Fenner knows we're still the best help he can get, even if he doesn't trust us. He'll complain, but he'll let us stay if we insist."

"But I don't want you to stay, and neither will your mother, Kim."

Kim's resolve visibly weakened at the mention of her mother; Brian realized that Rachel still hadn't learned anything about what had happened on Earth, other than the fact that her daughter had survived. She would need Kim's support when she heard the news about Bill. "Tell her I'll be down as soon as things are prepared up here on the ship," Kim said, trying to sound positive. "I can return on the next shuttle that comes up from the colony."

Brian saw that his mother didn't fully accept Kim's promise, knowing that there may not be a chance to send a second shuttle up if the Adherent ships suddenly arrived. It was hard watching her come to the conclusion that there was little she could do to convince Kim, or Brian for that matter, to come with her.

"Mom, we'll be fine," Brian said, hoping to comfort her just enough to get her to leave.

"Just be ready to go when the next shuttle arrives," his mother said, hugging them both. "Even if the Adherent ships don't come, we still may need to evacuate if the situation with the moon becomes critical."

"I don't think you have to worry about the moon," Kim said. "It's been watching over this planet for a lot longer than we've been here."

Jill Bishop's expression lightened slightly as she heard Kim's reassurance. "That's true, but there was an old saying that both of your fathers used to use; I think it goes something like 'it's better to be safe, than sorry'."

As the airlock doors shut and Brian waved goodbye to his mother, he remembered hearing his father recite those very same words on several occasions. It had always been during mundane situations, none of which carried the importance of life and death; and now, as the forces of the universe seemed to be collapsing in on his world, playing things safe seemed like a one-way trip to sorrow for Brian. He now felt as if he would never walk on the soft grass of Elysium again, yet he also knew that it was a sacrifice that had to be made. He owed it to those he loved to try and disrupt the Adherent attack, and he also owed it to Grace to protect her from Fenner's potential wrath.

CHAPTER 39

▼

THE EYE OF GOD

The grainy transmission emanating from New Haven several hours after Brian's mother left came as no surprise to anyone onboard the Adherent ship: no shuttles could be launched for the rest of the day due to the severe gravitational forces now spewing from the core of Ares. The red moon hung large outside of the Adherent ship's main viewscreen, bathing everything in its angry crimson shroud.

"Shouldn't we keep a further distance than this?" Fenner asked nervously to Maleek, who was monitoring the ship's sensors.

"We should be fine," Maleek answered. "I don't want to use up too much energy unless we need to. Besides, the moon is moving into position directly above the colony now, right where we should be."

The bridge rattled slightly a few seconds later, shaking even Maleek's confidence in the accuracy of the ship's sensors. Fenner ordered for the ship to be pulled back further, despite the precious use of energy such a maneuver would require. Brian watched the moon closely as they pulled away, noticing how fluidic and threatening the once familiar red aura surrounding it had become. He focused his eyes closer, trying to cut through the spatial disturbances that deformed the image and obscured what strange processes were transpiring down on the surface. Of particular interest were several long, dark blotches that had only recently appeared near the moon's equator, strange apparitions that seemed to serve no purpose other than to tantalize his imagination.

"What are those things? They look like tears in the moon," Brian noted curiously.

The others paused a moment as they tried to spot what he was referring to, everyone that is, except for Kim. She already knew what the distortions were.

"The Adherents are here," she said in a dire, yet calm tone. "Those are ships that just dropped out of subspace."

Nobody doubted her claim, but Maleek frantically began checking the ship's sensors, as if trying to prove her wrong. "Shit, she's right. There are seven, no, nine of them, all moving into orbit between our position and the colony."

Upon hearing this confirmation, Fenner flew into action issuing orders at the speed of thought. "Bishop, go get Andrews and the girl. Maleek, contact the colony and tell them the situation, see if they can get a lock on the ships. Hudson, get the weapon systems ready and raise the shields," he barked.

Brian quickly did as he was told, acting just as much out of shock as conscious decision. He honestly felt like he would have more time to prepare for this moment, and now that it was here, he didn't know what to do. Even after all he had been through, watching his adopted home, the only home he had ever truly loved, be destroyed was unbearable.

Grace and Andrews were waiting patiently in the common area when Brian flew into the room and snatched them from their solitude. Neither of them fought back against being escorted although the High Minister's arm went tense in Brian's hand. Perhaps he knew what was happening, even before Brian had a chance to explain.

When Brian returned to the bridge with Andrews and Grace, he found that Maleek had already repositioned the ship closer to the Adherent taskforce. Ares was so close that it engulfed the entire viewscreen. The Adherent ships, although large, almost became lost against the overwhelming crimson backdrop. "Well, if they're not worried about it, then I'm not," Brian heard his friend say under his breath as he guided the ship even closer to the moon.

"Open channels on all frequencies and direct our com array toward the closest ship," Fenner ordered, the barely restrained excitement clearly audible in his voice. "Now hear this," he declared in a loud, deliberate voice. "High Minister Andrews and his daughter are onboard this ship. They will only be returned unharmed if the taskforce powers down its weapons and leaves this system immediately."

Brian realized how ridiculous and desperate those words sounded once they left Fenner's mouth. The idea that the ships would travel a hundred light years only to turn back simply because of two hostages seemed absurd. The silence greeting Fenner's transmission only enhanced this feeling of futility.

"That ship in the rear of the formation is breaking off," Kim noted, pointing at the viewscreen toward one of the black lines. Her eyes were open wide, as if she was attempting to absorb every detail of the scene, the moon included. Even as the ship rapidly moved on their position, Kim seemed unafraid. Brian once again noticed the calm determination in her voice, and hoped that she had a tangible reason to feel confident, since he surely didn't.

"Lock weapons and stand by," Fenner said through gritted teeth.

Brian drifted over to Kim and braced her for the coming impact of battle. The oncoming Adherent warship inched closer and closer on the main viewscreen, slowing down as it readied to make an attack run.

But the attack didn't come. Instead, the screen in the center of the bridge flickered for a moment as a cold, white face materialized. The figure was human, much more so than the now familiar Adherent soldiers walking around the background of the image, but the man had a mechanical harshness about him that Andrews and the other inhabitants from Earth lacked. The black, metallic clothing he wore, coupled with his pasty skin and sickly appearance fit in quite well with the cyborg crew members. "The Church wishes to see that Minister Andrews is still alive," the man said without emotion.

Fenner smiled and quickly grabbed Andrews by the collar and dragged him in front of the screen. "Here he is, intact for now! Who am I talking to?"

Brian thought he saw the traces of a smile touch the lips of the strange man on the viewscreen as he seemed to consider just how serious Fenner was about injuring Andrews. "I am Minister Volor, Church Regent of the Ceti Alpha sector. I have some news for you, Minister, that you should find very comforting," the man began, addressing Andrews directly.

Rather than look relieved by the promise, Andrews' expression darkened markedly upon hearing the man's words. The reaction scared Brian. After all, they were counting on Andrews being a valued asset, someone who could provide leverage under the right circumstances. Judging by the other Minister's demeanor, though, it certainly didn't seem to be the right circumstances for any sort of a bargain.

"What is the wish of the Church?" Andrews asked tentatively.

"You'll be happy to know that the Council of Ministers has found a capable replacement for you in New Jerusalem," the man revealed. "The honor has been given to Minister Vale."

Brian saw the blood rush to Andrews' face as he heard the news.

"On behalf of the Church," the Regent continued, "I would like to thank you for your sacrifice. Remember, God rewards the faithful."

Andrews could only muster one question at this point. "What about my daughter?" he asked weakly. "Are you willing to bargain for her life?"

Once again, the man on the viewscreen appeared to flash a sterile half-smile. "If she is pure you will see her soon in the afterlife."

With that simple statement, the transmission abruptly ended and the ship continued on its attack run. Brian, despite his own fears, couldn't help but notice the look of total devastation on Andrews' face. The man had just received a death sentence, both for himself and his daughter. He had outlived his usefulness to the God of the Adherent Church.

As bad as Andrews looked, however, Fenner looked worse. His last-ditch plan had just fallen apart in a matter of seconds, and now he faced a clearly impossible situation. "As soon as it gets in range, fire all forward weapons," he ordered.

Brian pulled himself away from Kim and took a position on the secondary weapons console between Maleek and Hudson. Two days before they had figured out how to operate the ship's weapon systems entirely from the bridge although by making such a modification they had lost the ability to fire on the Adherent ship once it passed around to the rear. As the ship closed in, Brian could see the rest of the taskforce moving toward Elysium, unconcerned with the two orbiting colony transports drifting defenseless in space. Brian hoped that his family and friends had already taken cover in the caves up in the hills and that they would somehow survive the coming orbital bombardment.

"Fire!" Fenner yelled as the ship's sensors indicated that they were within range. The shout jostled Brian out of his state of worry, and he promptly did as Fenner ordered.

A blaze of plasma and missile trails lit the space between the two ships and slammed into the forward shields of the Adherent vessel. Brian felt a powerful combination of excitement and disbelief as he realized they had hit their target. The Adherent ship had brazenly charged them, most likely because the Regent had underestimated their ability to operate the ship's systems. Now, as his own ship was bathed in deadly fire, he would pay the price for such overconfidence.

Brian almost stood up and yelled with joy, but he kept his composure and readied the targeting system to fire a second volley. His body went rigid as the power meters quickly filled back up on the console. Just as he was about to fire, the initial explosion cleared, and revealed the terrible lack of damage they had inflicted on the Regent's ship. Within less than a second Brian realized that their small ship stood almost no chance of damaging such a large and powerful warship and knew that *he* was the one who would pay for his overconfidence.

"Again!" Fenner yelled. But it was far too late for another attack. The oncoming Adherent ship fired its main guns and decimated their shields and much of the outer hull. Brian and the others were thrown around the bridge as their ship reeled backward from the force of the blast. Everything exploded into smoke and confusion as Brian struggled to get to his feet. Before he could succeed, however, a second blast knocked him down to the floor again.

After a minute or so went by without another attack, Brian was finally able to raise himself up behind one of the damaged bridge consoles and survey the scene. The first thing he noticed was that the Adherent ship had turned away and was moving to rejoin its formation. Brian looked to his left for Kim and found that Andrews was standing next to him, looking at the same thing. Grace stood by his side, her arms around his waist for balance.

"When they're done with the colony they'll come back to reclaim this ship," he said wearily. "You're adrift. There's nothing you can do but watch what's going to happen."

Brian tried to ignore the High Minister's words and turned to check on his friends. Nobody was mortally wounded, but Hudson was bleeding from his head. Kim looked to be unhurt and was helping Maleek out from under one of the computer consoles that had collapsed. A look of relief crossed her face when she saw that Brian too was relatively unscathed. Fenner, although physically fine, seemed to be the worst off. He stood a few meters away from Brian, his head lowered and his hands clutching the sides of the navigation console Maleek had been sitting at prior to the attack. Fenner seemed to sense that he was being watched.

"Damn you!" he screamed at the viewscreen, taking his pistol out and shattering the glass with a single shot. Everyone, Brian included, braced themselves as Fenner leaped up on the console and tore the remaining shards of the viewscreen off with his bare hands, revealing the clear, duraglass window behind it. He raised his pistol at the line of Adherent ships, as if he could actually hit them.

"Fenner! What are you doing?" Kim yelled from behind, just before Brian did.

He stopped from pulling the trigger, and seemed to respond to her voice for a moment, but as soon as his wild eyes fixed themselves on Andrews, he once again entered a rage. Brian saw what was going to happen and slapped the pistol away from the side, just before it went off in Andrew's face. Fenner, undaunted, blindly pushed Brian to the ground and lunged over the pile of debris separating him from Andrews. The High Minister pushed Grace away just before Fenner fell upon him, but could do little to stop the attack.

"Fenner!" Hudson yelled, struggling to get through the tangled wires and sharp glass that littered his section of the bridge. Brian watched him as he got up and assessed that Hudson, injured as he was, stood little chance against an enraged Fenner. Brian thought about looking for the pistol he had swatted away, but gave up searching after only a few seconds when he saw Kim jump into the fray.

"This isn't going to change anything!" she yelled, throwing herself between Fenner and his victim. At this point, Brian was sure that Andrews was unconscious, and that Fenner would beat him to death.

"Shut up!" Fenner yelled, throwing her down just as fast as she had grabbed him. "I've had enough of you, you self-righteous bitch!"

With that condemnation, Fenner suddenly shifted his attention away from Andrews and onto Kim. He quickly tore one of the monitors from the closest shattered console and prepared to smash it on Kim's head as she lay helpless at his feet.

Brian decided to simply jump onto Kim and absorb the blow since he could do little to stop Fenner directly, but Hudson was faster on the move.

"Stop right there, Fenner. Put it down!" he yelled, pointing one of the spare plasma rifles from the weapons locker at Fenner's chest.

Fenner laughed at the idea as if it were truly the funniest thing he had ever heard. "What are you going to do, shoot me?

"If I have to."

As Hudson spoke, Kim quietly moved out from under Fenner and slid back near the opposite wall.

The High Councilor's lips morphed from a sickening grin to a threatening snarl. "I should have pushed you out of that airlock when I had the chance, Corporal. You're too—"

Fenner's expression suddenly changed. Slowly, as everyone struggled to figure out what had happened, he looked down at his chest, at the small white hole now spewing soft white smoke. Upon seeing the wound, he staggered backward several paces and dropped the monitor on the floor. As he fell to his knees, Brian traced the line from Fenner to the blaster that had shot him directly to Grace, who still pointed the shaking weapon in her outstretched hand. She looked to be in even more shock than Fenner, but unlike the High Councilor, she would live through the ordeal.

With a pained groan, Fenner slumped forward onto the deck and let out his last breath. It seemed impossible that such a simplistic act had killed a man who had created and lived through so much conflict. Despite the precious seconds that were passing by, everyone on the bridge stared in stunned silence at Fenner's body. Fenner had been a willing bully and murderer during his life, actively eliminating everyone and everything standing in the way of his goals. Despite these traits, he had also been an ally, the one person who had seemed willing to fight the Church regardless of the cost. As Fenner's body heaved for the last time on its own, Brian felt that the hopes of the colony were somehow dying with him. Fenner had ultimately received a gift; he would never witness the fall of the colony or the ultimate failure of his work. He would also escape the punishment he so deserved for treating those around him so carelessly. Brian realized that Fenner had gotten off easy.

While the others watched Fenner's body in a continued state of awe, Kim shifted her attention. "Grace, put the gun down," she urged, slowly getting to her feet and approaching the frightened girl.

Grace's shaking became worse as she realized what she had done although she did as Kim asked. She lowered the pistol all the way and let it fall to the floor. The metallic sound made from the gun hitting the metal was muffled by the intense sobs she let loose as she held her hands out and ran into the embrace of her wounded father. Kim was quick to recover the fallen pistol, careful not to let Andrews capitalize on the situation. He was, after all, still their prisoner, and he certainly couldn't be trusted.

"Brian," Kim called out, placing a hand on his shoulder. The action snapped Brian out of his fixation on Fenner, and he forced himself to focus on what had to be done.

"Maleek, can you get the ship moving again?" Brian asked.

Maleek didn't answer right away. Instead, he quickly reclaimed his seat in front of the shattered navigation console and proceeded to access the few systems that hadn't been obliterated in the attack. "The auxiliary thrusters are still functional," he noted. "But those will only move us at an eighth of our normal speed. There's no way we can make an effective attack run, even if we could get the weapons working. We can't even ram them."

Brian saw Kim weigh Maleek's analysis in her mind for a moment as she gazed out toward the attack fleet and the glowing red mass of Ares. She seemed to become lost in the scene as if hypnotized by the hopelessness of the situation. Now it was Brian's turn to bring her back to reality. "Kim? What is it?"

"Engage the boosters, Maleek. Move us toward the fleet," she answered in a frighteningly cool voice.

Nobody argued with her suggestion, not even the normally pragmatic Hudson. If the colony was to be destroyed, then they should die with it, preferably before the bombardment began. Sitting by helplessly was worse than death.

The Adherent taskforce now loomed menacingly in orbit over the colony like a mechanical legion of archangels poised ready to inflict divine wrath upon the wicked. The ships were arrayed in a distinct pattern, a design that would, no doubt, inflict the most damage upon the planet's surface. At a distance of 20,000 kilometers, a faint spark of energy could be seen starting to emanate from each ship. As Brian's eyes focused on the ships, he saw blue pulses of energy converge at a point in front of the fleet as the ships prepared to fire on the colony.

As Brian watched, he realized why Fenner had lost control just a few minutes before. The feeling of helplessness that washed over the bridge was worse than any weapon the Church had in its arsenal. It was like a knife that cut away at the heart that had grown in the years since leaving Earth and coming to Elysium. Love, hate, anger, remorse and fear converged as the memories of his parents and of his home emerged for what may be the last time. Brian heard Maleek moan under the same revelation. *At least we're together*, Brian thought. *At the end.* He suddenly felt the need to hold Kim once more, to shield her from the terrible scene unfolding before them. More importantly, he needed her strength, to look into her eyes and know things were good at the end.

Another powerful explosion rocked the ship only seconds after Maleek engaged the engines, once again causing the bridge to erupt in a sea of sparks and debris. Several of the gas conduits running across the ceiling came loose and spewed cold, compressed air into the already smoky atmosphere. At first Brian thought they had been attacked again, but as he came to his senses on the now-shifting floor, he realized that the ship had finally begun to give into the severe damage it had received only minutes before. Even if they did survive this catastrophe, there was no chance they would be able to pilot the ship. The gravitational stabilizers were damaged, as evidenced by the erratic motion of objects and people on the bridge. Brian had the distinct feeling that they were drifting dead in space.

Over the chaotic sounds of breaking metal, hissing pipes and Hudson yelling suggestions to Maleek, Brian called Kim's name. It was useless, though. The only way he would be able to talk to her would be to physically claw his way through the bridge to her as the ship rolled uncontrollably in space. Brian looked to his right and saw Andrews trying to shelter Grace from the danger. He locked eyes with the man for a moment, and saw him as the scared, powerless father he now was. Brian quickly tried to stand and make his way toward the portion of the room where Kim was, but a firm hand grabbed his arm as soon as he reached his feet. It was Hudson.

"Help Maleek get life support back online!" he yelled at Brian.

Even though getting to Kim was his goal, Brian realized that they would die before he even had a chance to say anything to her if he didn't help get the ship stabilized. He immediately did as Hudson asked and worked frantically to minimize the damage caused by the explosion. Brian understood that saving themselves was quite pointless, considering the murderous intent of the Adherent ships, but the direct actions he was taking to help Hudson and Maleek gave him enough purpose to keep from losing all hope.

As Brian helped Maleek force a power conduit back into place, he noticed Kim kneeling at the viewport in front of the bridge. She was praying. From behind, she looked like a marble statue from one of the Cathedrals, unmoved by the passage of time or events. Brian almost yelled at her to come over and assist, but he quickly reasoned that she was trying to help in her own way. Realistically, there was little she could do to assist them anyway, and it would be best if she had something to keep her mind occupied. The damaged power conduit slid back into place under Brian and Maleek's weight, restoring the life support systems in the forward sections of the ship. Although Maleek moved on to yet another damaged system, Brian took a moment to examine Kim's posture from his vantage point on the far side of the bridge.

Her body, one of the most comforting sights for Brian since childhood, now seemed threatening and alien as she kneeled motionless with her back to him. Brian involuntarily began to approach her, but stopped abruptly as he saw her reflection in the glass. Kim's eyes, her normally beautiful, brown, soulful eyes, had turned the deep red of Ares. It was just like his dream from months before. Brian looked around and saw that Grace and Andrews were watching the transformation too, with frightened expressions on their faces.

"Come on!" Maleek yelled from under the main engineering console." We need your help, you two!" Neither he nor Hudson were watching Kim, however, and failed to see the miraculous event occurring outside of the ship. Brian saw it, though, and resumed his journey to the front of the bridge to be at Kim's side.

Ares now bathed the Adherent ships in its fiery light as the red moon bore down on them like an angry eye. Brian could see that the ships had broken their attack formation and were now frantically attempting to pull away from the moon, which was somehow growing in size and brightness. Soon, the shimmering energy pouring forth from its surface was so intense that even Maleek stopped what he was doing and turned to face the front of the bridge, still ignorant to the abnormalities being exhibited by Kim. The ship itself began to shake as the massive energy wave continued to expand.

"It's a gravitational spike!" Maleek yelled over the growing vibrations of the ship. He was referring to the anomalies Dr. Liniel had described during his visit, but Brian doubted that the current behavior of the moon could be attributed to such a simple explanation. Whatever was happening to Ares, whatever had been happening over the last few days, went beyond anything that had ever been witnessed by human beings. Brian was sure of it. As the brightness reached a painful level of intensity, he closed his eyes and knelt down to shield Kim. Perhaps she didn't need any assistance, but Brian certainly felt like he did.

"We're too close!" he heard Maleek say in a voice that way barely audible over the terrible roar of the ship's hull beginning to buckle under the stress of the energy, or gravity, or whatever it was that was coming from the moon. The only thing Brian could hear clearly was Kim's voice, even though it was coming through at only a whisper. None of the words were familiar, but the confident tone she delivered them in gave hope that they would survive whatever was happening.

Just as the blinding light began to burn through his closed eyelids, all of the chaotic noise and violent shuttering abruptly ceased. The red radiance diminished to a warm, calm glow, and Brian tentatively opened his eyes. The bridge was gone, or perhaps obscured by the light pouring in through the main viewport. Brian couldn't tell. All of his senses, including those governing time and space, felt like they had been suspended. The massive disk of Ares had dissolved into a red aura that seemed to encapsulate him. For a moment, Brian thought he had died. But as his eyes adjusted to the alien luminosity, Kim's form materialized in front of him. She was standing with her back to him, facing the same direction where the moon had existed only moments before. Her hair whipped back as if driven by a ghostly wind blowing from the most intense point of light ahead, where space should have been.

"K-Kim?" Brain stammered, still frightened by her transformation. His feelings of apprehension grew as her body seemed to tense in response to his words. She turned. Brian stepped back without thinking, but stopped his retreat when he saw the warm smile on her face.

"It worked, Bri," she murmured with satisfaction, her head facing downward and her eyes closed thoughtfully.

"What did?"

Kim looked up and opened her eyes, which were brown again and brimming with affection. "The colony. It's safe."

"How?"

"I told you we'd be safe."

Brian fought back feelings of frustration. Perhaps she really didn't know how they were saved. Right now, he didn't care. He just wanted the ordeal to be over. But as he looked into Kim's face, he realized things would never be the same.

She stepped toward him, taking his hands and kissing him tenderly on the lips. Her skin felt impossibly soft, and as she pulled back, Brian noticed the radiant transformation. The Eye of God on her forehead was gone, replaced by a transcendent look of sagaciousness eclipsing that of the oldest and wisest humans he had ever known. Kim had experienced something incomprehensible, something new, but the power gained from such an experience came at a price. Brian somehow understood the implications, despite his inability to fathom the power that now embraced his lover in its all-encompassing grasp.

"I-I have to go, Bri," she said, taking a step back toward the light.

The crushing blow of her revelation made Brian feel sick. He his mind flashed back to the fight in the tent at Lake Clarity, back to Kim's insistence that there was something she had to accomplish.

There was nothing he could do to stifle her destiny, but perhaps he could come with her. He opened his mouth to suggest the possibility, yet found himself muted by an unseen force. Kim seemed to hear the suggestion anyway, as evidenced by the pained expression that washed over her face. Her ethereal façade seemed to waver slightly as tears streamed down her face.

"I'm sorry, Brian. They still need you." Kim said, forcing a weak smile as she took yet another step back. "I love you. I always will."

The invisible hold on Brian suddenly began to crumble as anxiety gripped his body. He attempted to close the gap, but found Kim even further away than before. "No! Kim, no!" Brian yelled holding out his arms into the sea of brilliant light enveloping her body.

He took another step forward and fell against the hard, metal floor of the bridge. Brian opened his eyes and found that Ares once again sat calmly in its place in orbit around Elysium. What had taken less than a minute or two to occur had seemed like hours, but the nearby presence of Grace, Andrews, Maleek and Hudson confirmed that little time had actually passed. In that short span, however, much had happened. The Adherent taskforce, every single warship, was gone. Not even a trace of debris could be seen floating in orbit. The ships had simply been devoured by the moon's violent outburst, erased from existence along with the Church's plans to remove the Apostate colonists. Kim was gone, too, having been sacrificed to the unstoppable power that had saved the colonists.

Nobody apart from Brain had witnessed Kim's departure, and in the wake of the attack he offered little explanation to his stunned comrades. Only a faint, redeeming whisper of hope kept his shattered heart from consuming him in the days and months following her disappearance, a wordless promise that she was alive somewhere, waiting for him to join her.

EPILOGUE

▼

There were few things in the world High Minister Vale hated more than commotion, and that's just what he faced as he was so rudely interrupted from his sleep. Since being named the leader of New Jerusalem just a few weeks before, he had done everything in his power to ensure that things remained orderly and controlled in the city, especially after he received the news that the Adherent task force sent to destroy the Apostates had gone missing. Although he had taken every precaution to keep the information from the public, he suddenly feared that perhaps someone had talked and managed to create a minor level of hysteria. If that was the case, the culprit would be discovered and punished severely. After all, nothing escaped the gaze of God.

As he rolled over to grab his robes from the side of his bed, Vale noticed that it was quite literally the middle of the night. It was nearing autumn, and all of the shutters adorning the windows around his bedroom had been closed at dusk to shut out the cold. Nevertheless, he could hear the yelling down in the city streets as clear as if it were happening in his room. Something was wrong, something much worse than the news about the taskforce. Vale hurried in getting ready and attempted to contact his chief aide, Minister Ruiz.

"This is High Minister Vale; what in Creation is going on out there?" he asked over the small intercom situated next to his bed.

A weak voice came through in response on the intercom, but it was quickly drowned out by a sea of noise from the crowd out in the streets.

"Say again?" Vale yelled, as he repeated pressed the button on the receiver. In frustration, he wheeled around and charged directly toward the closest window, the one overlooking the courtyard next to the Cathedral. As he neared the closed shutter, however, his steps slowed until he stopped entirely less than a meter away from the window.

"What?" Vale heard himself whisper as his ears shut out the surrounding noise and his eyes focused on a point near his feet. Below the window sill, on the smooth, polished surface of the wooden floor, shone a long, bright strip of reddish light. He followed the thin ray up to the window and saw that the light was coming from some exterior source, perhaps out in the courtyard or one of the surrounding buildings. Concerned that it may be fire, Vale quickly stepped forward and threw the shudders back.

Vale winced in pain as his eyes struggled to adjust to the intense red light. His city was on fire, or so it looked at first. As he shielded his eyes and attempted to confront the light, he saw the massive crowd congregating in the city streets. Vale called out to them in a vain attempt to corral their fear, but his voice was quickly drowned out by the cries and excited voices below. Aware that such an appeal for calm was futile, Vale instead traced their gaze far up into the night sky above the city.

To his horror, the Minister found that the source of the light came not from the city, but from the sky itself. High above, among the backdrop of now-faded stars, loomed the once familiar moon, now red as the deepest color of blood. The brilliant orb didn't flicker or wane in the slightest; its intensity was unimpeded by distance or atmosphere. Even more alarming was how the light seemingly penetrated through to the core of Vale's soul, shattering any barriers that had been erected by pride or prestige. At that moment he was just another human being, living on a planet that now sat helplessly in the wake of undiminished power.

Vale quickly jumped back from the window, yet he remained fixated on the sight above. Although he knew nothing of the light or the nature of the universe, he understood the terrible implications of what he was witnessing. Even more terrifying was the revelation that he, the High Minister, along with his predecessors, had been wrong. The Day of Judgment had finally arrived, only it was in the form of something inhuman and wholly unfamiliar. For the first time in untold millennia, Earth and its inhabitants were bathed in a light mankind had known only in its infancy. Now, the Eye was upon them.

978-0-595-44339-0
0-595-44339-7

Printed in the United States
80809LV00003B/232-246